Oates, Joyce Carol
OATES, JOYCE CAROL
COLLECTOR OF HEARTS : NEW
TALES OF T

11-98)

P9-DNO-085

The

Collector

of

Hearts

OTHER BOOKS BY JOYCE CAROL OATES

My Heart Laid Bare
Man Crazy
We Were the Mulvaneys
Will You Always Love Me?
Zombie
What I Lived For
Haunted: Tales of the Grotesque
Foxfire
I Lock My Door Upon Myself
Heat and Other Stories
Black Water
Because It Is Bitter, and Because It Is My Heart
American Appetites
You Must Remember This
Marya: A Life
Solstice
Mysteries of Winterthurn
A Bloodsmoor Romance
Angel of Light
Bellefleur
Unholy Loves
Cybele
Son of the Morning
Childwold
The Assassins
Do With Me What You Will
Wonderland
them
Expensive People
A Garden of Earthly Delights
With Shuddering Fall

The Collector *of* Hearts

New Tales of the Grotesque

Joyce Carol Oates

A WILLIAM ABRAHAMS BOOK

DUTTON

DUTTON
Published by the Penguin Group
Penguin Putnam Inc., 375 Hudson Street, New York, New York 10014, U.S.A.
Penguin Books Ltd, 27 Wrights Lane, London W8 5TZ, England
Penguin Books Australia Ltd, Ringwood, Victoria, Australia
Penguin Books Canada Ltd, 10 Alcorn Avenue, Toronto, Ontario, Canada M4V 3B2
Penguin Books (N.Z.) Ltd, 182–190 Wairau Road, Auckland 10, New Zealand

Penguin Books Ltd, Registered Offices: Harmondsworth, Middlesex, England

First published by Dutton, an imprint of Dutton NAL,
a member of Penguin Putnam Inc.

First Printing, November, 1998
10   9   8   7   6   5   4   3   2   1

Copyright © The Ontario Review, Inc., 1998
All rights reserved.
Page 322 constitutes an extension of this copyright page.

REGISTERED TRADEMARK—MARCA REGISTRADA

LIBRARY OF CONGRESS CATALOGING-IN-PUBLICATION DATA:

Oates, Joyce Carol.
    The collector of hearts : new tales of the grotesque / Joyce Carol Oates.
        p.   cm.
    "A William Abrahams book."
    ISBN 0-525-94445-1
    I. Title.
PS3565.A8C6   1998
813'.54--dc21   98-17508
                                                                          CIP

Printed in the United States of America
Set in Century Expanded
Designed by Eve L. Kirch

PUBLISHER'S NOTE
These are works of fiction. Names, characters, places, and incidents either are the
product of the author's imagination or are used fictitiously, and any resemblance to
actual persons, living or dead, events, or locales is entirely coincidental.

Without limiting the rights under copyright reserved above, no part of this publica-
tion may be reproduced, stored in or introduced into a retrieval system, or transmit-
ted, in any form, or by any means (electronic, mechanical, photocopying, recording, or
otherwise), without the prior written permission of both the copyright owner and the
above publisher of this book.

This book is printed on acid-free paper. ∞

for Jane Shapiro, and for Brad Morrow

Some are Born to sweet delight
Some are Born to sweet delight
Some are Born to Endless Night

—William Blake, *Auguries of Innocence*

Contents

I.

The Sky Blue Ball	3
Death Mother	8
The Hand-puppet	35
Schroeder's Stepfather	49
The Sepulchre	70
The Hands	86

II.

██████████	91
Labor Day	107
The Collector of Hearts	113
Demon	122
Elvis Is Dead: Why are *You* Alive?	126
Posthumous	139

III.

The Omen	145
The Sons of Angus MacElster	150
The Affliction	155
Scars	166

An Urban Paradox   182
Unprintable   189
Intensive   204

IV.

Valentine   211
Death Astride Bicycle   228
The Dream-Catcher   232
Fever Blisters   249
The Crossing   260
Shadows of the Evening   280
The Temple   313

V.

The Journey   319

Acknowledgments   322

I

The Sky Blue Ball

In a long-ago time when I didn't know *Yes I was happy, I was myself and I was happy*. In a long-ago time when I wasn't a child any longer yet wasn't entirely not-a-child. In a long-ago time when I seemed often to be alone, and imagined myself lonely. *Yet this is your truest self: alone, lonely.*

One day I found myself walking beside a high brick wall the color of dried blood, the aged bricks loose and moldering, and over the wall came flying a spherical object so brightly blue I thought it was a bird!—until it dropped a few yards in front of me, bouncing at a crooked angle off the broken sidewalk, and I saw that it was a rubber ball. A child had thrown a rubber ball over the wall, and I was expected to throw it back.

Hurriedly I let my things fall into the weeds, ran to snatch up the ball, which looked new, smelled new, spongy and resilient in my hand like a rubber ball I'd played with years before as a little girl; a ball I'd loved and had long ago misplaced; a ball I'd loved and had forgotten. "Here it comes!" I called, and tossed the ball back over the wall; I would have walked on except, a few seconds later, there came the ball again, flying back.

A game, I thought. *You can't quit a game.*

So I ran after the ball as it rolled in the road, in the gravelly dirt, and again snatched it up, squeezing it with pleasure, how spongy how resilient a rubber ball, and again I tossed it over the wall; feeling happiness in swinging my arm as I hadn't done for years since I'd lost interest in such childish games. And this time I waited expectantly, and again it came!—the most beautiful sky blue rubber ball rising high, high into the air above my head and pausing for a heartbeat before it began to fall, to sink, like an object possessed of its own willful volition; so there was plenty of time for me to position myself beneath it and catch it firmly with both hands.

"Got it!"

I was fourteen years old and did not live in this neighborhood, nor anywhere in the town of Strykersville, New York (population 5,600). I lived on a small farm eleven miles to the north and I was brought to Strykersville by school bus, and consequently I was often alone; for this year, ninth grade, was my first at the school and I hadn't made many friends. And though I had relatives in Strykersville these were not relatives close to my family; they were not relatives eager to acknowledge me; for we who still lived in the country, hadn't yet made the inevitable move into town, were perceived inferior to those who lived in town. And, in fact, my family was poorer than our relatives who lived in Strykersville.

At our school teachers referred to the nine farm children bussed there as "North Country children." We were allowed to understand that "North Country children" differed significantly from Strykersville children.

I was not thinking of such things now, I was smiling thinking it must be a particularly playful child on the other side of the wall, a little girl like me; like the little girl I'd been; though the wall was ugly and forbidding with rusted signs EMPIRE MACHINE PARTS and PRIVATE PROPERTY NO TRESPASSING. On the other side of the Chautauqua & Buffalo railroad yard was a street of small woodframe houses; it must have been in one of these that the little girl, my invisible playmate, lived. She must be much younger than I was; for fourteen-year-old girls didn't play such heedless games with strangers, we grew up swiftly if our families were not well-to-do.

I threw the ball back over the wall, calling, "Hi! Hi, there!" But there was no reply. I waited; I was standing in broken concrete, amid a scrubby patch of weeds. Insects buzzed and droned around me as if in curiosity, yellow butterflies no larger than my smallest fingernail fluttered and caught in my hair, tickling me. The sun was bright as a nova in a pebbled-white soiled sky that was like a thin chamois cloth about to be lifted away and I thought, This is the surprise I've been waiting for. For somehow I had acquired the belief that a surprise, a nice surprise, was waiting for me. I had only to merit it, and it would happen. (And if I did not merit it, it would not happen.) Such a surprise could not come from God but only from strangers, by chance.

Another time the sky blue ball sailed over the wall, after a longer interval of perhaps thirty seconds; and at an unexpected angle, as if it had been thrown away from me, from my voice, purposefully. Yet there it came, as if it could not not come: my invisible playmate was obliged to continue the game. I had no hope of catching it but ran blindly into the road (which was partly asphalt and partly gravel and not much traveled except by trucks) and there came a dump truck headed at me, I heard the ugly shriek of brakes and a deafening angry horn and I'd fallen onto my knees, I'd cut my knees that were bare, probably I'd torn my skirt, scrambling quickly to my feet, my cheeks smarting with shame, for wasn't I too grown a girl for such behavior? "Get the hell out of the road!" a man's voice was furious in rectitude, the voice of so many adult men of my acquaintance, you did not question such voices, you did not doubt them, you ran quickly to get out of their way, already I'd snatched up the ball, panting like a dog, trying to hide the ball in my skirt as I turned, shrinking and ducking so the truck driver couldn't see my face, for what if he was someone who knew my father, what if he recognized me, knew my name. But already the truck was thundering past, already I'd been forgotten.

Back then I ran to the wall, though both my knees throbbed with pain, and I was shaking as if shivering, the air had grown cold, a shaft of cloud had pierced the sun. I threw the ball back over the wall again, underhand, so that it rose high, high—so that my invisible playmate would have plenty of time to run and catch it. And so it disappeared behind the wall and I waited, I was breathing hard and did not investigate my bleeding knees, my torn skirt. More clouds pierced the sun and shadows moved swift and certain across the earth like predator fish. After a while I called out hesitantly, "Hi? Hello?" It was like a ringing telephone you answer but no one is there. You wait, you inquire again, shyly, "Hello?" A vein throbbed in my forehead, a tinge of pain glimmered behind my eyes, that warning of pain, of punishment, following excitement. The child had drifted away, I supposed; she'd lost interest in our game, if it was a game. And suddenly it seemed silly and contemptible to me, and sad: there I stood, fourteen years old, a long-limbed weed of a girl, no longer a child yet panting and bleeding from the knees, the palms of my hands, too, chafed and scraped and dirty; there I stood alone in front of a moldering brick wall waiting for—what?

It was my school notebook, my several textbooks I'd let fall into the grass and I would afterward discover that my math textbook was muddy, many pages damp and torn; my spiral notebook in which I kept careful notes of the intransigent rules of English grammar and sample sentences diagrammed was soaked in a virulent-smelling chemical and my teacher's laudatory comments in red and my grades of A (for all my grades at Strykersville Junior High were A, of that I was obsessively proud) had become illegible as if they were grades of C, D, F. I should have taken up my books and walked hurriedly away and put the sky blue ball out of my mind entirely but I was not so free, through my life I've been made to realize that I am not free, as others appear to be free, at all. For the "nice" surprise carries with it the "bad" surprise and the two are so intricately entwined they cannot be separated, nor even defined as separate. So though my head pounded I felt obliged to look for a way over the wall. Though my knees were scraped and bleeding I located a filthy oil drum and shoved it against the wall and climbed shakily up on it, dirtying my hands and arms, my legs, my clothes, even more. And I hauled myself over the wall, and jumped down, a drop of about ten feet, the breath knocked out of me as I landed, the shock of the impact reverberating through me, along my spine, as if I'd been struck a sledgehammer blow to the soles of my feet. At once I saw that there could be no little girl here, the factory yard was surely deserted, about the size of a baseball diamond totally walled in and overgrown with weeds pushing through cracked asphalt, thistles, stunted trees, and clouds of tiny yellow butterflies clustered here in such profusion I was made to see that they were not beautiful creatures, but mere insects, horrible. And rushing at me as if my very breath sucked them at me, sticking against my sweaty face, and in my snarled hair.

Yet stubbornly I searched for the ball. I would not leave without the ball. I seemed to know that the ball must be there, somewhere on the other side of the wall, though the wall would have been insurmountable for a little girl. And at last, after long minutes of searching, in a heat of indignation I discovered the ball in a patch of chicory. It was no longer sky blue but faded and cracked; its dun-colored rubber showed through the venous-cracked surface, like my own ball, years ago. Yet I snatched it up in triumph, and squeezed it, and smelled it—it smelled of nothing: of the earth: of the sweating palm of my own hand.

Death Mother

Driving the car fast, then faster. Then braking. Then releasing the brake. And again her foot hard on the gas pedal and the car leapt forward and I wasn't crying, the side of my head striking the door handle but I wasn't crying. It's right for you to die with your mother *she was saying.* I'm your mother, I'm your mother, I'm your mother. *Drinking from the thermos clasped tight between her knees. Radio turned up high. So she'd sing. Talk to herself, and to me, break off singing and begin to laugh, and to sob.* You love me don't you, you're my baby girl, they can't take you from me. I'm your mother *and the car began to shudder, the gas pedal pressed to the floor and my head struck the window and everything went flamey-bright and went out. I was nine years old, it was November 1949.*

———

She saw, on the opposite bank, across the gorge, perhaps fifty feet away, an absolutely still, unmoving figure—a woman? in white?—and came to a halt, staring. Her mind was struck blank. She had no thoughts, at all. Someone brushed past her pushing a bicycle, a young man who seemed to know her name, addressed her familiarly, but she didn't hear him, didn't reply. It was all happening swiftly yet with dreamlike slowness yet still she couldn't quite comprehend except to think *But I would sense it: I would know. If she comes back. If that's possible.*

It was 6:50 A.M. The thermometer on the front porch of Jeannette's residence had read −5 degrees Fahrenheit but here on the open pedestrian bridge, in knifelike gusts of wind, it was even colder. Vapor rose in patches out of the gorge where thirty feet below water spilled noisily from conduits, flowing and steaming in a saw-toothed passage through ice. So Jeannette's view of the figure on the other side of the gorge was obscured.

She was in motion again, crossing the bridge, at about the halfway point now, *no turning back*. It was a familiar route, she took it every day, twice a day, over the deep gorge that wound through the wooded campus, the trick she'd learned at the very start was not to look down, still less to stare down, to slow to a dreamy halt and lean against the railing, stare down at rocks, trickling water. It was hypnotic but not if you didn't look. The footbridge sometimes swayed in the wind, and sometimes it swayed in no discernible wind at all. There were tales of student suicides from this bridge, rumors of other, not quite successful attempts, before Jeannette's time she believed, the tragedies of strangers. She was not thinking of that now, nor of the eerie-humming vibration of the bridge. She was all right. And not alone, she was just one of a number of students on the footbridge, not likely to be singled out. Others passed her with quick fearless strides, making the bridge sway even harder. The delicious manic-energy of dawn: you woke abruptly from sleep already excited, breath shortened, eager for—what? *Not possible. Don't be ridiculous. You know better.* Yet there the woman stood, unmistakably.

In one stiffening arm Jeannette carried her canvas satchel crammed with books and purse, with her free hand she groped for the railing, to steady herself. Below, where she dared not look, were jagged hunks of ice, icicles six feet long, gigantic glittering teeth, thin rapid hissing trickle of water, stunted shrubs growing weirdly sideways, even downward out of rock. Winter had been long, the gorge was filled with snow, unevenly, a look of caprice, the consequence of sudden small avalanches. Above, a gunmetal sky, lightening by slow degrees without warming. *You know better.*

She knew. She'd left home, she'd come to Nautauga College, she was a striking and lively and much-admired young woman here, she was not a person readily identified by those she'd left behind. If the woman on the opposite bank was in fact watching Jeannette she'd be confused, thrown off the scent, seeing how in a clumsy down khaki parka with a hood, in dark wool slacks tucked neatly into boots to conserve body warmth, hauling her satchel, she resembled any student at the college, or nearly.

Somehow, how?—this person I've become.

It was March 1959. She was on her way to Reed Hall, where she worked in the cafeteria. It was an ordinary morning. It would be an ordinary day. If she could force herself to cross the footbridge: to ignore the woman waiting for her. *Not for me. Impossible.*

Yet now—now she'd lost her nerve, that happened sometimes. It was something physical, you felt it in the pit of the belly. Anxiously recalling she'd left her desk lamp on, had she?—in her room. Had she left it on? Getting up so early, before dawn, winter mornings pitch-black as night, yet her pulse already racing, all sleep banished with icy water splashed on her face, in her eyes. Though she'd be late at the cafeteria she couldn't bear the possibility of her lamp burning for hours in the empty room. And maybe she hadn't made up her bed, she couldn't remember. It tore at her nerves like ripped silk to think of such small imperfections. So there was no choice but for her to head back. Already turning, hurrying. Against the flow of others, thickly bundled in winter clothes, breaths steaming, all of them known to Jeannette as she was known to them, their eyes caught curiously at her, they were mildly surprised at the look on her face, but she had no time for them, scarcely heard them, desperate to get off the footbridge, her head lowered, tears on her cheeks like flame swiftly turning to rivulets of frost she brushed at irritably, blindly with her mittened hand.

The last time, seven years ago?—when I was twelve. In the locked ward of the State Psychiatric Hospital at Port Oriskany. A three-year sentence to the women's prison at Red Bank ran concurrently with psychiatric treatment, so-called. Mother?—it's Jeannette. Don't you know me? Mother? *She'd been so drugged, her eyes so puffy, the pupils retracted to pinpricks, I couldn't tell whether she recognized me, or even saw me.*

But then it hadn't ever been clear—whether she'd known me, or my sister Mary. Loving, hugging, kissing us. Pummeling, punching, kicking, yanking at our hair that was wheat-colored, fine, a wan curl in it like hers. Trying to set me afire—an "accident" with a space heater. Trying to kill us all in the car. And Mary, what she'd done to Mary. Never clear whether she saw us, recognized us, at all: her daughters. Not herself.

The second time, no mistaking her.

Late morning, descending the steep granite steps of the Hall of Languages, Jeannette was talking animatedly with friends, talking and laughing when suddenly she saw the figure, the woman: *her.* Not twenty feet away. So calmly, obviously waiting for Jeannette, her daughter. Fixed and unmoving as a stone figure amid a diverging stream of students who scarcely glanced at her, and of whom she was oblivious. An eccentrically dressed woman of no immediately evident age except not young.

One of Jeannette's friends was asking was something wrong, Jeannette who was Jeannie to them, pretty Jeannie Harth, so suddenly still, frightened, staring. But recovering enough to assure them no nothing, nothing wrong, please go on without her.

Moving quickly away before anyone could question her. And calmly too making her way to the woman, the woman who waited for her. Thinking *She was never so tall before!*

"Mother?—is it you?"

Of course, Mrs. Harth—simply standing there, waiting. How like her if you knew her, or if you didn't. The pale pebble-colored lips drawn back from stained, uneven teeth, a sudden fierce smile— and her eyes deep-set and shadowed and the eyelids puffy, red-rimmed, faded brown eyes how like Jeannette's own, and Mary's. *We don't laugh, and we don't cry. Nobody knows our secrets.* Jeannette was clutching her mother's hand, Mrs. Harth was clutching Jeannette's, not taking her eyes from Jeannette's face.

For a long moment neither spoke. Then, awkwardly, both at

once—"My God, Mother—it *is* you!" and "I—was afraid you wouldn't know me, Jeannette."

So strange, amid the boisterous commotion of young people, in the bright-dazzling sun of noon; on this ordinary weekday, with no warning. Always, Jeannette had thought she'd be notified beforehand, her father at least would have called her, some warning if only a dream, a nightmare of her own. She was saying, trying to speak evenly, "Where have you come from, Mother? Are you—?"

Mrs. Harth continued to stare at her, hungrily. "Am I 'out'? Yes, Jeannette. I'm 'out.'"

She spoke with that air of almost girlish, flirtatious irony, an irony that invited you to laugh though of course you must not laugh, that Jeannette remembered with sudden, sick clarity.

Now we should hug one another, should kiss but Jeannette stood awkward and unmoving, still clutching her mother's hand; as her mother clutched hers, her fingers surprisingly strong. But then she'd always been a strong woman, don't be deceived.

How odd, how eccentric, Mrs. Harth's appearance: on this freezing winter day in upstate New York she wore a cream-colored, somewhat soiled and wrinkled cloth coat in a bygone feminine style, a sash tied and drooping at her waist, like a negligee; her gloves were beige lace; about her head, only partly covering her thin, graying-yellow hair, was a gauzy pink-translucent scarf of the kind a romantic-minded woman might wear on a cool summer evening. An odor of dried leaves, like camphor, lifted from her. Mrs. Harth's eyes were slyly quick-darting and alert as if she was aware of others watching yet would not acknowledge these others. Her papery-pale, puckered skin was tightly creased across her forehead, a maze of wrinkles, though she was only—how old?—not old!—forty-two, forty-three? And that face once so beautiful, was it possible?

Jeannette said quickly, fighting the urge to cry, "Let's go somewhere warm, Mother—you must be freezing."

"Me? *I* don't mind the cold, I'm used to it."

A quick comeback reply, like TV. And the ironic smile, the anxious eyes.

And there suddenly Jeannette was leading her mother, arm linked firmly through her mother's arm, in the direction of Nautauga's Main Street, away from the college. She knew of a tearoom patronized by local women shoppers, where students rarely went. Friends called out to her, *Hi Jeannie!* like chattering birds she did not hear. A young man, a tenor in the college choir, who'd taken Jeannette out several times, passed within inches speaking to her and Jeannette may have murmured a response but did not look up, staring in confusion at the trampled snow underfoot. Mrs. Harth said brightly, "There's a friend of yours," as if she expected to be introduced, or was teasing Jeannette with this possibility, and quickly Jeannette murmured, "I don't know him well, really," and Mrs. Harth said, "But you have many friends here, Jeannette? Don't you?" her voice low and even and not at all accusing, and Jeannette said, laughing nervously, "Not many! A few," and Mrs. Harth said, emphatically, "You were always selective about your friends. Like me."

They walked on. It could not be happening yet, how simply, it was. Mother and daughter, daughter and mother. Jeannette Harth's mother Mrs. Harth, come to visit. Why was it so unusual, why should it seem to upset Jeannette quite so much? Mrs. Harth was saying, giving Jeannette's arm a little tug, "No one can betray you like a friend—or a 'loved one.' You know the expression 'loved one'? Eh?"

"I . . . don't know."

"It isn't strangers who break our hearts!"

This was uttered with such smiling vehemence, such a steaming breath and a coquettish toss of the pink-gauzy head, Jeannette stared at her mother, uncomprehending.

Why. Why here. Why now. What do you want of me.

Making their way across the icy quadrangle, through a gauntlet of sorts, Jeannette hearing, not-hearing her name called out—that pretty lyric-melodic name that so suited her, in this place: *Jeannie! Jeannie Harth!* Girls from her cottage, girls from the dining hall, a young man from her philosophy class. Jeannette dared not look at them, with Mrs. Harth gripping her arm. Dared not reply beyond a vague mumble of recognition, acknowledgment. For of course Mrs. Harth was staring at them critically. For of course she would judge them, her daughter's friends, what few friends she had. *Eh! God! Is that the best you can do! I call that pitiful.*

Yet how fair-minded, how pleasant saying, "It seems very nice here. 'Nautauga College.' Not like Port Oriskany, not like Erie Street, at all. Or your old school, eh? You fit right in here, Jeannette, I can see!" Clearing her throat, a gravelly-grating sound, and Jeannette flinched thinking *she will spit, she will spit it out* but no she did not, must have swallowed it, all the while smiling and glancing about lurching a little, slipping on the sidewalk so that Jeannette had to steady her, practically support her. What ridiculous shoes Mrs. Harth was wearing, Jeannette stared in disbelief: cheaply shiny black patent-leather pumps with painfully pinched toes and a thin, near-stiletto heel. A ladder-run in one of her beige nylon stockings.

They were standing on the curb waiting for the light to change. Flashing red, warning DONT WALK DONT WALK. Jeannette was saying what a surprise, how wonderful to see her mother, hesitantly asking how long would she be visiting, did she think? and Mrs. Harth said "That depends."

"Depends—?"

The light changed to green WALK WALK WALK. Hand in hand, Jeannette and Mrs. Harth crossed Main Street. "Upon circumstances," Mrs. Harth said, clearing her throat. "Upon *you.*"

Jeannette's breath was gone, she could not reply. Mrs. Harth squeezed her hand in girlish excitement, like one sharing a secret just a bit prematurely. She said, "I have all my earthly possessions with me in my car. Did you know I have a car? Did you know I have my license? I'm parked there." Pointing beyond Main Street, matter-of-factly. "There is nowhere else I have to be now that I'm *here*, Jeannette. With you."

———

She was driving the car fast, then faster. Then she braked. Then released the brake. And again her foot hard on the gas pedal and the car leapt forward and I wasn't crying, the side of my head hit against the door handle but I wasn't crying. I couldn't see where we were going only the tops of trees rushing past. It's right for you to die with your mother *she was saying.* I'm your mother, I'm your mother, I'm your mother. *That smell of her when she hadn't bathed, hadn't washed her hair. The animal-smell. Her hair snarled and matted. But she was pretty—Mother. Even with the smeared Noxzema on her face, where she'd been picking at herself. Sometimes a trickle of bright blood through the greasy white face cream. From a scab on her face she'd picked. And her fingers, her nails, the nails bright red. The cuticles bloody.* Just you and me, nobody will know where we are, it's right for us to be together. I'm your mother forever and always. Forever and always! *Drinking from the thermos held tight between her knees. Drinking then wiping her mouth on the back of her hand. The radio turned up high. So she'd sing. She'd talk to herself, and to me, and she'd sing, and she'd break off singing and begin to laugh, and to sob. Speeding through a red light pressing the palm of her hand against the car horn. The sound of it filled the car, so loud. And her laughing, angry sobbing.* You love me don't you, you're my baby girl, they can't take you away from me. I'm your mother, I'm your mother *as she hit the brakes and the car jumped and skidded and swerved and there was the sound of another car's horn and Mother yelled out the window sobbing and jammed her foot on the gas pedal again and the car leapt forward throwing up gravel where we'd drifted onto the gravel shoulder of the highway. I wasn't crying, my face was wet and my breath coming choked but I wasn't crying, I knew there was no way out, Mother was saying* You love me, I'm your mother and I love you, you're my little girl, it's right for us to die together *and there was a siren coming up fast behind us and the car swerved and shuddered, the red speedometer needle at eighty-five miles an hour, the car wouldn't go any faster and Mother was sobbing and I was thrown against the door, my head hit the window and everything went flamey-bright and then out. I was nine years old. That was November 1949. I hadn't known about Mary. What had happened to Mary. Where Mother had taken her, and left her.*

———

"I don't know what your father has told you about me, Jeannette. Or any of them. It's in their interests to lie about me."

In the cozy interior of The Village Tea Room, amid a clatter of dishware, cutlery, women's raised voices, amid lavender-floral wallpaper and hanging pots of ivy, Mrs. Harth had reluctantly removed her gauzy scarf, her soiled cream-colored coat, which was draped over the back of her chair. Yet she'd kept her beige lace gloves on. Her hands shook just slightly as she poured tea for Jeannette and for herself. Her eyes were sunken but bright, alert. Watchful. Her mouth twitched and smiled. *You love me, I'm your mother. I'm mother, mother.* As Mrs. Harth spoke in her low, intense, earnest voice she repeatedly touched Jeannette's arm; and Jeannette shivered at the strangeness of it, the wonder, not simply that after seven years her mother had returned to her, in fact it had been much longer, many times Mrs. Harth had disappeared from the house and returned and disappeared and returned again, the times confused, bleeding into one another like loose snapshots in an album, and the child Jeannette had once been was not a child she knew or could recall or wished to recall. Not simply that strangeness, but the strangeness too of touch: another living being touching you: flesh and bone, another's secret heartbeat, warm-coursing blood, another's vision of you, knowledge of you, desire. For there were men who had touched Jeannette too, or had wanted to touch her, in desire. And always that immediate response, that panicked shuddering sensation *Don't touch me! Don't hurt me!* yet again *Please touch me, please hold me, I'm so lonely, I love you.*

"Jeannette?" Mrs. Harth's lips pursed, hurt. Creases like bloodless knife cuts bracketed her mouth. "Aren't you listening?"

Jeannette said quickly, "Yes. But I don't remember."

"What don't you remember?"

Jeannette ducked her head, smiled. For the question was really a riddle, wasn't it. *What don't you remember?*

Jeannette said, childlike in earnest, staring at her mother's hand gripping a delicate china cup, the tattered fingertips of the beige lace gloves, "—I don't remember very much about what Dad told me, it was a long time ago and we never talk about it any longer." She paused, still smiling. *We never talk about you any longer. I would not ask, and he would not tell if I did ask.* "And I don't remember much about—what happened."

Mrs. Harth's lips twitched in a smile. Her eyes were steely, resolute. "What happened—when?"

When Mary died. When they took you away.

Carefully, Jeannette said, "When Mary died."

There was a silence. Mrs. Harth touched her hair with beige-lace fingers; her hair that was stiff-looking, thin, the hue of stained ivory. Groped for her teacup. At the sound of Mary's name, so soft as to be almost inaudible, Mrs. Harth's subtly ravaged face became impassive, almost peaceful.

Beneath her coat, Jeannette saw, her mother was wearing an oyster-white dress, or was it layers of filmy pale cloth like curtains?—there seemed to be no collar to the costume, no visible buttons. The gauzy material was draped loose across Mrs. Harth's bosom in rumpled layers. Since they'd been seated in the tearoom, a sharp, acrid smell as of something brackish wafted against Jeannette's nostrils amid the warm yeasty smell of baked goods. Her mother's body. Her mother's hair, clothes. Recalling the odor of her mother's body in the days of her mother's sickness which she had believed, as a young child, to be the odor of the very air, very life itself. The rank tallowlike smell of the hair that was so fascinating, the briny stench of the champagne-colored negligee Mrs. Harth wore inside the house, and wore, and wore as if it were a loose second skin. The soiled undergarments on the bathroom floor, kicked about, bloodstained panties, Jeannette and Mary crouched staring in fascinated horror, reaching out daringly to touch. *Dirty girls! Both of you! Aren't you ashamed!*

What is there to do with *shame*, where exactly do you hide *shame*, you pretty girl, and "popular," too!

Every morning no matter how freezing the fourth-floor bathroom of the residence, showering, shampooing her hair, vigorously, harshly. The body can't distinguish between *cleansing* and *punishing* for the body is ignorant, and mute besides.

In high school, back in Port Oriskany: she'd been a different girl, then. Where they know you, you're known. Where you're known, you're *you*. Shrinking in the rest rooms dreading what she might overhear, you don't want to eavesdrop, not ever. And after gym class having to strip naked amid the squealing giggles of the other girls so easily naked, pale and slippery as fish, darting through the stinging needles of water, the hot shower first, then warm then cold then the foot-rinse, in a paroxysm of shame so her body prickled and her eyes rolled in their sockets. *Don't look! don't look! I'm a freak, I'm not one of you!*

Mrs. Harth was watching her closely, it was possible that Mrs. Harth knew exactly what she was thinking. Saying, "So! You're happy here, Jeannette? So far from home?" Inside the woman's level, uninflected voice, doubt sounded sly as a hinge that needs oiling.

Jeannette said quickly, "I—love it here."

"Eh?"—Mrs. Harth cupped a hand to her ear.

"I love it here."

There was a pause: a moment for contemplating such a claim.

Mrs. Harth sipped her tea in thin, savorless swallows, like a duty. She did not mean to sound suspicious of course, but—"How did you happen to come *here*, Jeannette? Of all places?"

"I have a scholarship. A work-scholarship. It pays my full tuition and—"

Mrs. Harth interrupted, *"Only* here? You didn't win any other scholarships, anywhere in the state?"

Jeannette's gaze plummeted to the tabletop. Lavender table-cloth, so attractive, feminine. Just-visible stains, rings from the teapot. Scattered crumbs from the cinnamon toast Mrs. Harth had broken into small pieces, most of which lay on her plate uneaten. *Don't you know I can read your mind. Don't you know I'm your mother, your mother, your mother.*

Jeannette said quietly, stubbornly, "I did. But I wanted to come here, to study music."

"Music! That's new."

"Music education. So that I can teach."

"Teach."

Mrs. Harth took a small sip of tea, swallowed with an expression of disdain. After a pause she said, as if they'd been speaking of this all along, "Your father is a bitter man—I don't wonder, Jeannette, you've come so far to escape him. And *her*."

Jeannette protested weakly, "But it wasn't for that reason at all, Mother. Really—"

"Yes," said Mrs. Harth, grimly, laying a beige-gloved hand on Jeannette's arm, both to comfort and to silence, "—I don't wonder."

It was past one o'clock when Jeannette and Mrs. Harth emerged from The Village Tea Room into the bright, cold, gusty March air, Jeannette had missed her one o'clock lecture not having wanted to hurry her mother, not wanting to be rude. The question in her mind was where would her mother spend the night.

Mr. Harth had remarried, soon after the divorce. The end of that, the beginning of something new. There was a second *Mrs. Harth* in Port Oriskany but the woman was not quite real to Jeannette, a nice woman, a kindly woman, generous and, yes, motherly. So many women of a certain age were motherly.

Never had Jeannette told her father's wife *Don't imagine that I need, or want, another mother: I don't*. But the woman seemed to know, just the same.

Jeannette had a class, her three o'clock music lecture, and somehow it happened that Mrs. Harth was coming with her. "Where else would I go, dear?" she said, smiling, sliding an arm through Jeannette's. "I'm all alone here except for *you*."

"You might not like the class, Mother. It's—"

"Oh, I'm sure I will! You know I like music."

"But this is—"

"—*love* music. You know I used to sing in the church choir when I was a girl."

No choice, then. Jeannette led the way.

"Introduction to Twentieth-Century Music" was held in the amphitheater of the Music School, on the far edge of the quad. The

lecturer was Professor Hans Reiter, a popular campus figure, burly
and good-natured and explosive in his enthusiasms, a bearish dark-
bearded man with a boiled-looking skin, thick glinting glasses. He
played records and tapes for the class at a deafening volume sometimes, and lectured over the music. Often, in the right mood, he
played piano from a standing position as he spoke—rough, impassioned playing, the inner soul of music Jeannette supposed. She
loved Professor Reiter and was shy of him. Usually she sat with
her friends near the front of the room but this afternoon, Mrs.
Harth's arm tight through hers, she avoided even glancing in that
direction (were her friends looking for her? looking at her? at her
and this woman so obviously her mother?) but sat with her mother
at the very rear. The subject of today's lecture was Stravinsky and
The Rite of Spring. Incantatory chords, breathless leaps of sound,
that strident-erotic *beat beat beat* Jeannette tried to hear purely as
music, not as pulsations in the blood. She hunched over her notebook taking notes rapidly, eyes downcast. Beside her Mrs. Harth
sat stiff, arms folded across her chest. Now, in the amphitheater,
she was cold. Would not remove her coat. Not at all charmed by the
professor's lecture style, his bouncing-about at the front of the
room, witty exegesis of the composer's "revolutionary genius"
amid the "dense philistine ignorance" of the era. How forced, self-
dramatizing, braying Reiter sounded, to Jeannette's ear! She was
deeply embarrassed, after the class murmuring an apology to Mrs.
Harth as they left the building, quickly as Jeannette could manage;
Mrs. Harth laughed a dry mirthless laugh, arm tight through
Jeannette's, saying, "So that's what a 'college lecture' is. A fat,
loudmouth fool like that—'professor.' And that ugly beard. And
such silly music, like you'd hear on the radio. Imagine, a man gets
paid for such nonsense!"

It was the very voice of Jeannette's childhood, raw envious
spiteful Port Oriskany, glowering with satisfaction. Jeannette cast
her eyes down to the trampled snow, and said nothing.

But Mrs. Harth, stimulated, was speaking animatedly. She was
incensed, outraged, yet amused—you just had to laugh, didn't you?
What a fancy college education is worth. So much fuss, people

putting on airs, and what is it? *She'd* had to quit high school at the age of sixteen to work, to help support her family; oh yes, *she'd* hoped to be a teacher, too. "But nobody ever handed me a 'scholarship' on a silver platter." This was the first Jeannette had ever heard of any of this, but she did not question it; only murmuring she was sorry, and Mrs. Harth added, with bitter satisfaction, "*I* had to drop out of school to work, then to marry. Too young for any of it—but it had to be. And babies, too—had to be."

Had to be. Had to be. The words hung in the air like steaming exhaled breaths.

Jeannette heard herself asking, "Where—would you like to go now, Mother? I'm afraid I have library assignments, and I have to work the dinner shift at the cafeteria, and tonight I have a choir rehearsal. . . ." Her voice trailed off weakly. *All I wanted was a life, a new life for myself that has nothing to do with who I am, or was. All I wanted was to be free.* Her body was chill and clammy inside her clothes and her heart beat so quickly, Mrs. Harth must sense it.

Mrs. Harth was squinting at her. That dry ironic smile playing about her lips. With the air of speaking to a small or dull child she said, "Jeannette, I'm all alone here in—'Nautauga.' And anywhere in the world. Except for *you*, dear. How long I visit, where I go depends on *you*."

Laughing, that delicious cascading sound. And her eyes bright, her long nails fluttering the air like shiny crimson butterflies. Get in! Hurry get in, girls! Before it's too late! *That humid-hot August day, early evening; Mother had left us to live somewhere else and Dad would never speak of her but suddenly there Mother was— come to pick Mary and me up at Grandma's in this car that was silver on top and aqua on the bottom—so pretty!—so shiny!— Grandma was inside so didn't see, we were playing in the front yard and Mother came laughing to pull us away, her finger to her lips meaning* Quiet! quiet! *laughing driving us all the way to the beach to Lake Oriskany and she wasn't the way we remembered her but so pretty now, so happy! a sharp lemony smell in her hair, her hair not greasy but shiny, whipping in the wind like laughing*

and her mouth bright red like Ava Gardner's on a movie poster.
Hey: You know I love you, your mother's crazy about you, you're
my baby girls aren't you!—*at a stoplight hugging and kissing us
till it hurt, and another time pulling over at the side of the road so
cars honked passing us, then at the beach Mother ran up and
down the boardwalk pulling us by the hands buying us fizzing
Cokes and orangesicles which were her favorite too, sharp-tasting
orange ice and vanilla ice cream at the center so delicious!—and
Mother's legs were pale and covered in pale brown hairs in the sun
where she drew her dress up, past her knees, she was barefoot her
toenails bright crimson and there was a man up on the boardwalk
leaning on the railing watching us, watching her and he came
down to the beach and he and Mother began talking, laughing,
Mother said,* These are my little girls Jeannette and Mary, *saying,*
Aren't they beautiful! *and the man squatted in the sand beside
Mary and me smiling at us, said,* They sure are, yeah they're
beautiful *smiling up at Mother*—just like you.

*Mother and the man went away only for a few minutes Mother
said kissing us* I'll be right back: don't go away! don't go away or
the police will come and arrest you! *but they didn't come back and
didn't come back and we were crying and a woman asked us who
we were, were we alone, two little girls like us?—she took us to the
ladies' rest room up on the boardwalk and bought us Cokes and we
took them back to the beach because Mother would be so angry if
we were gone and after a while a policeman did come by, asked us
where we lived and we were crying hard by now, we were afraid to
tell him because if he took us away when Mother came back she
would be so surprised so hurt so angry she would never take us
away in her car again, she would never love us again so it was a
long time before we told him, I think it must have been me who
told, I was the older of the sisters, I was always the older I was
Jeannette.*

That was why she never wanted to be alone with another girl.
Especially a girl she liked, trusted. One of the girls in Briarly Cottage where she roomed. You had to be careful. Might start talking,

telling too much. Might start crying. Lose control, say too much, once it's out it can never be retracted. *The worst thing: to give yourself away in exchange for not enough love.*

"Tell me which way to turn, Jeannette!—I've never driven in this city before."

Mrs. Harth spoke gaily and coquettishly yet at the same time in reproach. Jeannette gave directions: left onto Main Street, three blocks to the bridge, left again on Portsmouth to South Street . . . Strange how, through the filmy windows of Mrs. Harth's lead-colored Dodge, the familiar streets, the redbrick "historic" buildings of Nautauga College, even the long sloping campus lawn were altered; how childish, self-absorbed, unattractive Jeannette's fellow students appeared, on the sidewalks, crossing against traffic. The car's windshield was coated with a fine grit that reflected sunshine in a way that made everything bleakly, flatly sepia-stained, as in a fading photograph.

Mrs. Harth's car was one Jeannette had never seen before, of course. A 1954 model Dodge, lead-colored, with rust-stippled fenders and bumpers; riding oddly high off the ground, so you had to step up to climb inside. The smell was brackish-sour. In the back, what appeared at first glance to be random debris was in fact Mrs. Harth's personal possessions: untidy piles of clothes, shoes, a pillow with a stained embroidered pillowcase, cardboard boxes, grocery bags stuffed with items. A soiled gray blanket, taped to the left rear window, had slipped partway. The car windows were rolled up tight and Jeannette's nostrils pinched against the smell her mother seemed not to notice.

Jeannette didn't want to think what such evidence suggested.

Crossing a two-lane bridge over the Nautauga River, which was a narrow but swift-flowing river, now covered in ice, Mrs. Harth overreacted at the approach of a truck, pressed down hard on the gas pedal and swerved toward the railing; Jeannette felt a moment's sick panic—*She will drive us off the bridge, that's her plan!* But Mrs. Harth regained control of the car, driving on.

Jeannette remembered those wild, wild rides, her mother at the

wheel. To Lake Oriskany. But the return—back to Erie Street—
was vague, undefined; like a dream of profound intensity that
nonetheless fades immediately upon waking.

And now they were at Jeannette's residence, the quaintly called
"Briarly Cottage" which was an ordinary woodframe dwelling of
four floors with a shingled dormer roof like a heavy brow, on a half-
block of similar drab houses, once private and now partitioned into
rooms for students who couldn't afford better housing, nearer campus. Mrs. Harth stared with a look of personal hurt, incredulity.
"*This* is it?—your 'residence'?"

Jeannette murmured it was fine, fine for her, she'd made good
friends here. There were eighteen girls, scholarship students—

"And you so proud of that, your 'scholarship,' eh!" Mrs. Harth
said, removing the key from the ignition and throwing it, with an
emphatic gesture, into her bag. "*I* wouldn't wonder this fancy college put you here on purpose, to insult you."

"Insult me?—why?"

The question hung in the air, unanswered.

With mincing steps, for of course the sidewalk hadn't been shov-
elled, Jeannette helped her mother ascend the walk to the house.
The older woman's arm was tight through hers; their breaths
steamed faintly, as if in anticipation. Beneath the dry camphor
smell of Mrs. Harth's hair and clothes was a sharper lemony smell,
all but indistinguishable. Her skin, maybe. That heat that used to
rise from her skin. As Jeannette was about to open the front door, a
Negro girl came out, one of Jeannette's friends, big smile, big eyes,
a friendly and popular girl named Kitty, and in an instant Kitty
glanced from Jeannette to Mrs. Harth to Jeannette again, seeing
whatever it was in Mrs. Harth's face, maybe noting how, with an in-
voluntary intake of breath, Mrs. Harth's arm tightened on Jeannette's, and her smile dimmed discreetly, and she only murmured,
"H'lo, Jeannie," in that way that signals no reply of any animation
is expected.

Inside, Mrs. Harth said in a lowered voice, with grim satisfaction, "*What* did I tell you?—there it is! Putting you in a place with
one of *them*, that's the insult."

Jeannette protested, "But, Mother—"

"They give you tuition money, oh yes, but they make you beg—*crawl*—for it. *I* would never."

"Mother, that's ridiculous. Nautauga College is—"

" 'Ridiculous,' am I? Oh? For speaking the truth, miss? Which your father would never, eh? Which you're ashamed to hear." Mrs. Harth sighed, drawing her filmy glamor-scarf off her head, as if reluctantly; glancing about, her forehead creasing, nostrils pinching, into the cramped parlor off the front hall. Fortunately, none of Jeannette's housemates was in there. "*I* call this pitiful," Mrs. Harth said. "A daughter of *mine*."

"I'm happy here," Jeannette said, with childlike stubbornness. "This is my second year and I'm *happy here*."

"Of course, you'd tell yourself that," Mrs. Harth said simply. "That's what people do."

And there were the steep stairs, three flights to Jeannette's fourth-floor room. And there was the antiquated bathroom with its ineradicable odors, door ajar. When Jeannette opened the door to her room she winced at the sight, seeing it through Mrs. Harth's eyes: the ceiling that slanted beneath the eaves, the narrow cotlike bed covered with a cheap chenille spread, a college-issue pinewood chest of drawers, aluminum desk, ugly crook-necked lamp and shabby swivel chair. On the bare floorboards, a thin machine-woven rug Jeannette had bought for $9.98 at a local discount store, liking its rust-orange gaiety; on the walls cheap glossy prints of nature photographs and works of art—van Gogh's "Starry Night," for one. Jeannette's hope had been to make the small room seem spacious by suggesting, as of windows opening out, other dimensions, other worlds. Instead, the reproductions, all of them slightly curling from the radiator heat, gave the room a cluttered tacky look.

The single window in the room looked out over an expanse of weatherworn roof and snow-smutty yards; in the distance, across the gorge, drained oddly of color and flattened like paper cutouts, the handsome spires and towers of the college.

Mrs. Harth was breathless from the stairs. But entered the room tall, incensed. "So!—*this*."

Jeannette closed the door behind them, trembling with dread.

"These hundreds of miles you've come—such pride in your 'scholarship'—imagining yourself so superior to your mother, eh? For *this*."

Jeannette protested, "Mother, I've never imagined myself—"

"Oh no? Don't lie: not to Mother. *I* can see into your heart."

Mrs. Harth paced about, untying the sash of her flared coat, sniffing and squinting and peering into corners. Here was her old energy, liquid-bright eyes and sharp elbows, that girlish air of conspiracy, angry elation. "It's good I came here! I knew I was wanted! To rescue you! Take you away, eh? I *knew*."

"Take me away, Mother? Where?"

Mrs. Harth put a forefinger to her lips, slyly. Then placed that same forefinger to Jeannette's lips, to seal them.

Yes it was an accident. I always believed so. She loved us, she held us and kissed us and slept sometimes in our bed with us or she would take us into her bed, hers and Dad's, during the day, for a nap. And she would bathe us. There was no difference between her and us. I always believed so. The accident was with Drano. You know what Drano is—liquid Drano. The sharp terrible fumes stinging your eyes, burning your nostrils. Sit! Damn you, sit! *she was screaming. Because we didn't want to, we were trying to get away. Because the enema bag, the tube, was known to us, and we hated it.* Sit! In this tub! You bad girls, you dirty girls, obey your mother! *But I squirmed out of the tub, out of her hands, naked and slippery as a fish.*

"*Christus, der ist mein Leben, Sterben ist mein Gewinn . . . dem tu ich mich ergeben . . .*"

Jeannette was singing as she'd never sung before, an edge of anxiety to her voice, eyes fixed urgently on the young choirmaster's face. Her soprano voice rising, pleading as if it were an impersonal cry through her throat, "*. . . mit Freud fahr ich dahin.*" Bach's exquisite cantata, the music that coursed through her blood, filling her with an almost unbearable yearning; the tension of the long day, dread rising to panic yet to a strange sort of elation, now her mother had returned to her, now the waiting was over. She hadn't realized how long she'd been waiting.

There was a stop, phrases repeated. The choirmaster's name was McBride and he was demanding, sometimes impatient. Short-tempered. Jeannette imagined herself in love with him, he was so distant from her. Yet he'd chosen her to sing one of the solos in the upcoming Easter concert. Again, now, to the top of the page, and again: Jeannette sang until her lungs ached, her eyes welled with tears. Even if Mrs. Harth would be taking her from Nautauga, even if there would be no Easter concert. Did it matter what the German words meant? *Since Christ is all my Being, Dying is all my gain. To Him my soul is fleeing, nought can her joy regain.*

Jeannette had left her mother back in her room, in her bed, sleeping. Mrs. Harth had been too exhausted even to have dinner. In the morning, she said, they would decide what course of action to take. What was best for Jeannette. What must be done, where they would go. She'd spoken softly, framing Jeannette's face with her cool dry hands. Jeannette had cried a little but Mrs. Harth had not cried, for there was no need.

We don't laugh, and we don't cry. Nobody knows our secrets.

Mrs. Harth was not in the amphitheater yet midway in an ascending phrase *Mit Fried und Freud ich fahr dahin* Jeannette saw her figure there at the very rear, stiff with disapproval, arms folded across her chest, as she'd sat in that identical seat for Professor Reiter's lecture. Seeing, Jeannette lost the words of the cantata, faltered and broke. The other singers continued. Sopranos, altos, tenors, basses. It was as if a deer had fallen dead, shot by a hunter, as the herd ran on, oblivious. Jeannette hid her eyes and when she lowered her hands she saw at the shadowy rear of the banked rows of seats nothing more than carelessly slung-down coats, parkas.

Of course, Mrs. Harth wasn't there. What need, to follow Jeannette to choir rehearsal?

At this moment sleeping in Jeannette's bed in one of Jeannette's flannel nightgowns.

Later, McBride led Jeannette exactingly through her first recitative which at the start of rehearsals she'd delivered self-consciously, as if distrusting her merely spoken voice; tonight, the words seemed to burst from her throat. "Nun, falsche Welt! Nun hab ich weiter nichts mit dir zu tun . . ." McBride nodded: O.K. Then to Jeannette's chorale part, the rapturous evocation of a savior raised miraculously from the dead: "Valet will ich dir geben, du arge falsche Welt . . . Da wird Gott ewig lohnen dem, der ihm dient allhier." It was a spirited, demanding passage, and Jeannette was equal to it. Though her throat was beginning to ache and her eyes felt seared, burnt in their sockets from exhaustion.

McBride was smiling, he *was* impressed.

Rehearsal ended at 10:30 P.M. Jeannette edged away, grabbed her parka, hurried up the aisle to leave before anyone could speak to her; her problem was, at Nautauga, she had too many friends. Too many people who were attracted to her, or believed they were. *They don't know me but what they know, they like.* She was hurrying out of the semidarkened building except at one of the front doors she paused leaning her forehead against the door, she felt her heart beating quickly yet calmly, what premeditation! what cunning! *It's a fantasy, you're being ridiculous. You know better.*

Still, she'd seen him looking at her, she'd been seeing, and not-seeing, for weeks. Since the start of rehearsals, though he'd never seemed explicitly to be favoring her.

Waiting for McBride, who, a few minutes later, as she'd known he would, came whistling by; McBride in his sheepskin jacket and fur hat, a swagger to him, the kind of man who controls by withholding praise until you're weak and ravenous with hunger. Others were with him but he waved them on, he was looking at Jeannette, who'd turned her face toward him, baring it like a flame, mute and exposed.

McBride politely asked would Jeannette like a ride home and Jeannette said yes thank you, calling him, as all the undergraduates did, *Dr. McBride.*

They walked to McBride's Volkswagen parked in a nearby lot, their booted feet breaking icy crusts of snow. It was very cold now— -10 degrees Fahrenheit. But no wind, only a dry crackling air that burnt the nostrils and made the eyes well with tears of hurt and protest. Their breaths steamed like little private pockets of thought, or desire. When Jeannette slipped on a patch of ice, McBride murmured, "Hey!" and deftly caught her elbow, just enough to reposition her; his touch, his gloved fingers against the bulky fabric of the parka, made her feel giddy, faint. He was talking in his brisk animated way about the evening's rehearsal that had gone fairly well, considering the enormous difficulty of Bach's music and the choir's relatively untrained voices. There was a phrase of his he used often, wryly, yet with a kind of brotherly affection for his singers: "We're getting there, eh?"

A windless still night, palely illuminated by a three-quarters moon, a mad-eye moon, high overhead. Jeannette's eyes ached from just this moonlight as if she'd been crying, for hours, without knowing it.

Wait for you. Don't stay away long. Jeannette?

No, Mother. Where would I go?

This, then: they climbed into McBride's car laughing at their mutual awkwardness, their long legs, and McBride asked Jeannette where she lived for of course he had no idea and Jeannette told him and he asked was that the far side of the gorge and she said yes. He said she would have to direct him, then—he wasn't familiar with that side of campus. He lived on the east side, himself.

Driving then out of the lot and onto a side street and a few blocks to the very bridge, nearly deserted now, which eight hours before Mrs. Harth had driven them across in the lead-colored Dodge. Where they might have had an accident, swerving into the railing and through into the frozen river, but by chance had not. Jeannette's pulse raced now as then and she knew McBride sensed it.

Here too, as out of the gorge, thin drifting columns of mist rose dreamlike from the river; the effect was of something delicate as lace, or very breath itself, fading as you stared. McBride said casually, driving the Volkswagen as if it were a clever toy, "Jesus, it's beautiful here, isn't it? Upstate New York. It feels like the Arctic to me. I'm from Brooklyn, you know—this is all new to me."

It was the most Jeannette had ever heard the man utter, and the only personal revelation.

McBride followed Jeannette's soft-murmured directions, turning left, and again left, approaching hilly rutted South Street. At first he wasn't going to take note of Jeannette crying. For she cried that softly, unobtrusively; you could ignore it if you wished. For she was a well-mannered girl, discreet. She'd had no lovers, nor had she ever been close to loving. This, McBride seemed to know, or to sense; he was eleven years her senior, a lifetime.

Finally he said, "Look, Jeannette, what's wrong?—has something happened to you?" and it was that plunge, a blind plunge like stepping through cracking ice, the irremediable shattering. It may happen but once in a lifetime, and that once will be enough. For Jeannette heard herself cry, "I can't go back there! My room! Not yet! I can't—" Already McBride had braked the car, jammed the brake down with the heel of his boot; the car spun on the salt-strewn ice, but held. They sat, side by side, at first motionless and not looking at each other as Jeannette wept now freely, helplessly. "All right," McBride said. "You don't have to. You can do something else."

McBride brought Jeannette Harth back to his apartment, where they would spend the night.

And all this unpremeditated, the sheerest chance.

McBride who'd been married unwisely young, and divorced; who knew better than to involve himself, or even to appear to involve himself, with undergraduate women, many of whom openly adored him—there he was, leading a terrified trembling girl into his darkened apartment, quiet as stealth; himself terrified as if he'd been handed a musical composition he'd never before seen nor even heard played and shoved out on stage before a vast audience and made to perform, playing a musical instrument clumsy in his hands, exposed to public ridicule. Yet: how excited, how happy he was, and how Jeannette laughed, breathless, giddy, as he poured them each a glass of red wine and his hand was perceived as shaking as much as hers, or nearly. Jeannette meant to say, "I've never drunk this before!" but the words came out, "I've never done this before!" Swallowing, she tasted tartness as of overripe fruit; an inky pool spread immediately in her panicked-parched mouth, warming her throat, her chest, even, uncomfortably, her belly. She could not have said if it was delicious, or bitter, or both.

Bravely then Jeannette began to speak, as in a recitative. She was in love with him—Dr. McBride. She'd been in love with him for—a long time. Her voice was so faint, McBride came to sit clumsily beside her, stroking her hands, which were chill and inert. "I know I should be ashamed," Jeannette said miserably, "—I know I shouldn't be telling you this." McBride laughed, saying, "Who should you tell, then?"

Eventually they were in McBride's bedroom, and lying in an anguished-delicious tangle on his bed. McBride may have sensed that Jeannette was not telling him *why* exactly she was here, *why* tonight, that there was something withheld; it was all happening too fast for him. Though he was older, should have known better. But there was Jeannette saying, "Please make love to me? You don't have to love me." So childlike in pleading, her voice slurred by wine. McBride kissed her eyelids and told her she was beautiful but did not make love to her precisely, nor would he. Jeannette said, "It's enough for me to love you, you don't have to love me, I promise!" McBride said, "Well, maybe." They were lying together perspiring and short of breath partly undressed on McBride's bed. How dizzy, and how happy! How strange to Jeannette that she should feel, in a stranger's arms, such extraordinary happiness, such buoyant happiness, she took to be love. And she might utter his full, remarkable name now: *Michael McBride*.

In this place unknown to her, a room darkened except where moonlight slyly entered an unshaded window.

———

When Jeannette awoke, wine-groggy, it was much later, yet still dark; by the faintly glimmering undersea-green numerals of a bed-side clock she saw it was 6:15 A.M. Where was she, and what had she done! She eased herself from the part-undressed heavily sleeping man; crept silently into another room, where a single light still burned—there was her parka, there her mittens, her boots. On a coffee table cluttered with newspapers, magazines, books—two bottles of wine, one empty and one part-filled. *What have I done, what will happen now!*

In a bathroom mirror she examined her flushed, slightly swollen face, her vein-reddened eyes. She filled a basin and lowered her burning face to it, water cold as she could bear.

Leaving his apartment, by stealth leaving the redbrick apartment complex she'd known, in fact, was his, though she had never before approached. How had she been so reckless! so shameless! *Weil du vom Tod erstanden bist, werd ich im Grab nicht bleiben* she was singing under her breath, there was McBride's habit of singing, whistling to himself, even if she never saw him again, never would she forget him, his kindness to her, and the intimacy between them—*Dein letztes Wort mein Auffahrt ist!*

And now she was approaching the gorge. Out of which vertical vapor-clouds were lifting, of the shape of icicles, dreamlike and silent. No one was in sight, it was just dawn. A somber dawn that more resembled dusk. Jeannette paused before stepping onto the footbridge—was there anyone on the other side, waiting? Through her life after this morning she would recall how, returning to the residence, to her mother, she had no idea of what she would say to the woman, nor even of how she would present herself: a daughter who had committed an unspeakable betrayal against her mother, a daughter who had simply done as she'd pleased, and not an ounce of guilt? She crossed the footbridge without daring to look down, and on the other side began to run, all the way up the hill to South Street and to the gray-shingled woodframe house that was Briarly Cottage, where, with dream-logic, there stood Mrs. Harth in the street by the lead-colored Dodge, seemingly waiting for her. The car's motor was running, poisonous pale smoke billowed from the exhaust. And there, Mrs. Harth in her creamy flared cloth coat with the hastily tied sash, the gauzy scarf tied tight about her head. Waiting for Jeannette, for how long? She must have been sitting in the car, the motor running, and seeing Jeannette approach she'd climbed out, calling to her before she was well within earshot, "Get here! Get in this car! At once! We're leaving!"

Jeannette balked, stopping dead on the walk.

It was now dawn, faint bruised-red cloud strata in the eastern sky, by quick degrees lightening, though very cold. Jeannette saw her mother's mouth working angrily and her breath in steamy puffs that looked angry, too. "Jeannette, come here! Get in this car! How could you! Dirty, filthy girl! Get here, get *in*. I'm taking you *away*."

Jeannette shook her head. "Mother, no."

Mrs. Harth said contemptuously, " 'No'?—how dare you! *I'm* your mother, I say get *in*."

Jeannette had approached, like a cautious child, or a dog, to about ten feet of the Dodge, whose chassis vibrated and shuddered as if in disbelief; she would come no closer, in terror that her mother might rush at her, grab her. How weakly she might yield, as she'd done long ago, if those talon-fingers seized her! Mrs. Harth's sunken eyes glared, her mouth worked. "Get *in*! I'm telling you— get *in*! I'm taking you away!"

Jeannette hid her eyes, banishing the sight. Yet: *I will see her, I will hear her, all my life.*

Had anyone heard her mother's cries, was anyone watching from the windows of the cottage, or from other houses on the block?—would word of this, however *this* might be interpreted, be passed on, among Jeannette Harth's friends, and those who hardly knew her at all? Would *he* hear, eventually?—or would she tell him herself, eventually? Jeannette stood mute and stubborn, shaking her head *no, no, no*, until finally, Mrs. Harth climbed into the car and slammed the door behind her and in a paroxysm of fury, tires spinning and sliding on the icy street, drove off: downhill on South Street, spewing exhaust, a right turn at the bottom of the hill, past a row of parked cars, within the space of twenty seconds, so quickly!—out of sight.

———

It was Friday morning she left. Sunday, my father called to tell me that Mother was dead. She'd driven her car off a bridge in the city of Derby, sixty miles east of Port Oriskany, into the Cassadaga River; the car had broken through ice, Mother had drowned. There were no witnesses to the "accident" and she'd left no message behind.

The Hand-puppet

How strangeness enters our lives. The mother had known that her eleven-year-old daughter Tippi had had an interest in puppets, and in ventriloquism, since fourth grade, but she'd had no idea that Tippi had been working in secret, upstairs in her room, on a hand-puppet of her own invention; nor that the child, by nature a shy, somewhat withdrawn child, planned to surprise her with it in quite so dramatic a way—thrusting the ugly thing into her face when she stepped into the kitchen one Monday morning to prepare breakfast, and wriggling it as frantically as if it were alive.

"H'LO MISSUS! G'MORNIN' MISSUS! WHAT'S TO EAT MISSUS!"—the voice was a low guttural mocking drawl, the mother would have sworn a stranger's voice.

The mother was of course taken totally by surprise. She'd had no idea that her daughter had come downstairs before her, and so stealthily! It was all so premeditated, seemingly rehearsed, like theater.

"Oh God!"—the mother responded in the way the daughter must have wished, giving a little shriek and pressing her hand against her heart; staring, for an instant uncomprehending, at the big-headed baby-faced puppet cavorting a few inches from her face. Afterward she would recall that, in that first startled instant, the puppet had seemed somehow familiar, the close-set black-button eyes, the leering red-satin mouth, but in fact she'd never seen anything like it before. It had a misshapen body made of stiff felt that was mainly shoulders and arms; the head was bald and domed, like an embryo's; the nose was a snubbed little piece of cotton made prehensile by a strip of wire. How obscene, the mother thought.

"Tippi, how—clever!" the mother said, seeing that the child was hiding clumsily behind a part-opened closet door, her arm, in the flannel sleeve of her pajama top, tremblingly extended. "But you shouldn't scare the life out of your poor mother, that isn't very nice."

"SORRY MISSUS! SORRY MISSUS!" The puppet squirmed in exaggerated delight, stretching its red mouth, making a series of mock bows.

The mother tried to interrupt but the low guttural drawl continued—"MISSUS I BEEN HERE BEFORE YA! AN' I GONNA BE HERE WHENYA GONE!" There came then a crackling lunatic laugh the mother would have sworn issued, not from her daughter's mouth, but from the puppet's.

"Tippi, really!"—the mother, now annoyed, but smiling to conceal her annoyance, pushed the closet door open, to reveal the daughter there, mere inches away, breathing quickly, eyes shining, flush-faced with excitement as a small child caught in mischief. "Isn't it a little early in the morning for this sort of thing?"

Boldly, Tippi kept the puppet between her mother and herself, the big domed head and antic face still cavorting—"DID I SCARED YOU MISSUS! SOOO SOORRY MISSUS!"

"Tippi, please. That's enough."

"TIPPI AIN HERE MISSUS TOO BAD! BYEBYE!"

"Tippi, damn—!"

Exasperated, beginning to be a little frightened, the mother took hold of the puppet, grasping her daughter's antic fingers inside the cloth torso. For a moment the fingers resisted—and surprisingly strong they were. Then, abruptly, Tippi gave in, ducking her head. Rarely disobedient or rebellious, even as a toddler, she seemed embarrassed by this display; her sallow skin blotched red and her pale myopic eyes, framed by milky-blue plastic frames, seemed to dim in retreat. She mumbled, "Sorry Mom," adding in an undertone, "It's just some silly thing I made."

"Tippi, it *is* amazing. It's . . . ingenious."

Now she'd regained some measure of control, the mother complimented the daughter on the hand-puppet. What was surprising, unexpected, was that the daughter had been so creative— fashioning a professional-looking puppet out of household odds and ends, pieces of felt, strips of satin, ribbons, buttons, thumbtacks— she who seemed so frequently overwhelmed by school, and whose grades were only average; she whose creative efforts, guided by one or another teacher, and always on assignment, had seemed in the past touchingly derivative and conventional. The mother warmly noted the clever floppy rabbit ears, the drollery of five prehensile fingers and a lumpy thumb on each hand. The slightly asymmetrical domed head with a prominent crooked seam like a cracked egg. "When on earth did you make this, Tippi? And your voice—how on earth did you do *that*?"

The daughter shrugged, not meeting the mother's eye. Mumbled again a vague apology, disparaging words about the puppet— "silly, dumb, didn't turn out right"—then she was hurrying out of the kitchen, the puppet carelessly crumpled in her hand. She ran upstairs to get ready for school, a soft-bodied child in flannel pajamas, barefoot, her heels coming down hard on the stairs. The mother, hand still pressed against her heart, stared after her in perplexed silence.

How strangeness enters our lives.

It was in fact, it would remain in memory, an ordinary schoolday morning. The Monday following the weeklong Easter recess in the public schools. Lorraine Lake, Tippi's mother, usually came downstairs at about 7:30 A.M. weekdays to prepare breakfast for her husband and daughter, but on this morning, the morning of the hand-puppet, Mr. Lake, sales manager for a local electronics company, was in Dallas at a convention. So there was just Lorraine and Tippi, whose school bus would arrive at about 8:10 A.M., stopping at a corner up the road. Mr. Lake traveled frequently, so his absence on this morning would not be disturbing; in fact, such mornings, mother and daughter at the breakfast table, mother and daughter exchanging casual remarks as the radio on the windowsill played cheery-bright morning music and chickadees fluttered about the bird feeder outside the window, were routinely pleasant, companionable. It might be said that Lorraine Lake looked forward to them. And now, her nerves jangling from the surprise, the oddity, of the hand-puppet, felt subtly betrayed by her daughter.

It was deliberate, she thought. Premeditated. Because I'm alone. She would never have done that to her father.

Staring out the window above the sink, as into a void. The Lakes lived in a rural-suburban landscape where, in summer, the foliage of crowded trees created a dark screen, like a perpetual cloud ceiling; in winter and early spring, before the trees budded, the sky was predominant, pressing. Yet it seemed always the same sky— opaque, dully white, layers of stained cumulus clouds like ill-fitting flagstones.

Lorraine Lake stared, and, by degrees, into focus came the needle-thin red column of mercury in the thermometer outside the window: 41 degrees Fahrenheit. This too was a familiar fact.

Briskly then Lorraine Lake prepared breakfast. Hot oatmeal with raisins and sliced bananas for Tippi, toast and black coffee for herself. A ritual, and pleasure in it. I am the mother, Lorraine Lake was thinking. I am not *"Missus"*! She was a fully mature woman of forty-two and she was not a woman who believed she might have cultivated another, more worthy, more mysterious and sublime life elsewhere, a life without husband, child; a "true" life without the trappings of the identity that accrued to her in this shining kitchen, this rural-suburban brick-and-stucco colonial house on a curving cul-de-sac lane. If Lorraine Lake had had a life preceding this April morning, this nerve-jangled moment, she did not recall it with any sense of loss, nor any particular sentiment.

I do these things because I am the mother.

Because I am the mother, I do these things.

Remembering how, the previous week, Tippi had stayed home, most of the time upstairs in her room. A quiet child. A shy child. A good child who seemed, at a casual glance, younger than eleven—lacking a certain exuberance, a spark, an air of resistance. MISSUS I BEEN HERE BEFORE YA! AN' I GONNA BE HERE WHENYA GONE! Tippi seemed to have few friends at school, or, in any case, rarely spoke of them; but there was a girl named Sonia, also a sixth grader, who lived in the neighborhood, who'd sometimes invited Tippi over . . . but had not, recently; nor had Tippi asked if she might invite Sonia over. The realization was alarming. I don't want my daughter to be left behind, Lorraine Lake thought. I don't want my daughter to be unhappy.

Recalling how, as a small child, Tippi had chattered incessantly to herself, sometimes, it had seemed, preferring her own solitary company to that of her loving, doting parents'. Thank God she'd grown out of that stage! In later years too the child talked to herself, but usually in private; in her room, or in the bathroom; which isn't uncommon, after all. Now, Lorraine Lake recalled with dismay having heard, just last week, a low guttural voice in the house, a radio or TV voice she'd assumed it must be . . . she'd been on the telephone the other day when she'd heard it, at a distance, and had thought nothing of it. She realized now with a sick sensation that this had been the puppet-voice, the "thrown" voice of Tippi's ventriloquism.

How had the child, practicing in secret, grown so adept? So quickly?

Could one be born with a natural gift for—such a thing?

When Tippi came back downstairs, her face washed, her limp fawn-colored hair combed, she carried herself stiffly, as if she'd been wounded. Her appetite for the oatmeal, and her usual glass of fruit juice, was conspicuously restrained. She wants praise for that ugly thing, Lorraine Lake thought, incensed. Well, she's getting none from me. It was almost 8 A.M. Except for the cheery-bright radio music and the excited tittering of chickadees outside the window, there was a strained silence. Finally Lorraine said, with a sudden smile, "Your puppet is very . . . clever, Tippi. And the *voice*, how on earth did you do that?" Tippi seemed scarcely to hear, spooning oatmeal slowly, chewing with apparent distaste. She was a child who loved sweets and often over-ate, even at breakfast, but this morning her very mouth was sullen. "I had no idea you were making anything like that," Lorraine persisted, enthusiastically. "Was it a secret? A project for school?"

Tippi shrugged her shoulders. Her milky-blue glasses were sliding down her nose and Lorraine had to resist the impulse to push them back up.

Tippi mumbled something not quite audible. The puppet was "silly." Hadn't "turned out right."

Like all the other girls at her school, Tippi wore jeans, sneakers, a cotton-knit sweater over a shirt; Tippi's sweater was so baggy as to resemble a maternity smock. Such clothes should have disguised the child's plumpness, but did not. Tippi's plain prim moon-shaped face seemed to Lorraine to be stiffened in opposition, and in the newly tasted strength of opposition. Lorraine asked, with her bright, eager smile, "But is it a project? Are you taking it to school?"

Tippi sighed, messing with her oatmeal; her pale eyes, lifting reluctantly to Lorraine's, were obdurate, opaque. "No, Mom. It isn't a *project*." Her lips twisted scornfully. "And I'm not taking it to dumb old school, don't worry."

Lorraine protested, "Tippi, I wasn't worried. I was just—" She hesitated over the word "concerned." Saying instead, "—curious."

"No, Mom. I'm not taking it to dumb old school, don't worry."

"I said, Tippi, I *wasn't worried.*"

Which was not the truth, but Tippi could not know. So much of what a mother must say in a household is not true, yet it is always in the interests of other members of the household not to know.

On these mornings, the arrival of the yellow school bus with its invasive sound of brakes was always imminent, awaited. If a child, of the six who boarded the bus at the corner, was late, the driver sounded the horn, once, twice, a third time; waited a beat or two; then drove off, with an invasive shifting of gears. Lorraine Lake had not realized how she'd come to hate the yellow school bus until a dream she'd had one night of its careening off a bridge?—sinking into a river?—a confused, muddled dream, a nightmare best unexamined. When Tippi had been younger, Lorraine had taken her hand in hand out to the corner to catch the bus; Tippi was one of those tearful-sullen children reluctant to go to school, and many mornings a good deal of cajoling, coaxing, kissing, admonishing was required. Now, Tippi was older; Tippi could get to the bus by herself, however reluctantly, and however inclined she was to dawdle. But by custom in the Lake household it fell to Lorraine, the mother, to take note of the time when the time moved dangerously beyond 8 A.M.; it fell to Lorraine to urge Tippi to finish her breakfast, brush her teeth, get on her outdoor clothes and get outside before the bus moved on. Weeks ago, in the dead of February, in an uncharacteristic mood of maternal impatience, Lorraine had purposefully remained silent as if unaware of the time, and of course Mr. Lake, skimming computer printouts at the breakfast table while Tippi ate her cereal, took not the slightest notice, and Tippi had in fact missed the bus that morning. But the upset to the household, the flurry of accusations and refutations and hurt feelings, the unleashed anger, had hardly been worth it; and the result had been that Lorraine had had to drive Tippi four miles into town, to school—as she might have predicted.

This morning, however, solemn-faced, pouty-mouthed, in her bulky quilted jacket looking like a mobile fire hydrant, Tippi Lake left the house in time to catch the bus. Lorraine called goodbye after her as always but Tippi scarcely glanced back, and her voice was flat, almost inaudible—"Bye, Mom."

"TIPPI AIN HERE MISSUS TOO BAD! BYEBYE!"

The ugly jeering words echoing in Lorraine Lake's head.

And what else had the hand-puppet said, his stunted arms flailing and his mouth working lewdly—"MISSUS I BEEN HERE BEFORE YA! AN' I GONNA BE HERE WHENYA GONE!"

It was not possible to believe that Tippi had said such things. That she'd been able to disguise her thin, childish voice so effectively, and "throw" it into the puppet. That she'd had the manual skills to create the puppet, let alone the concept. No, it just wasn't possible. Someone else, an older student, perhaps a teacher, had put her up to it.

I know my daughter, Lorraine thought. And that isn't *her*.

After Tippi left on the school bus, the house was so unnaturally empty. There was the relief of the sullen child's departure, but there was the strained absence as well. The radio wasn't enough to fill the void, so the mother switched it off. "I know my own daughter," she said aloud, with an angry laugh.

The urge to search Tippi's room was very strong. Yet she resisted. If Tippi said she wasn't bringing the hand-puppet to school, then that was so. Lorraine would not violate her daughter's trust by seeming to doubt her, even if she doubted her. And if she found the obscene little puppet in Tippi's room, what then? "DID I SCARED YOU MISSUS! SOOO SOORRY MISSUS!" Lorraine had a vision of tearing it to bits. "BYEBYE!"

Later that morning, Lorraine drove to town. She had an appointment with a gynecologist which she'd several times postponed since an examination of a year ago had gone badly. This morning's appointment was a secret from Mr. Lake and Tippi. (Not that Tippi would have been much concerned: when health or medical matters were mentioned, Tippi seemed simply not to hear. Her eyes glazed, her pert little mouth remained shut. This is a trait fairly common in children of her age and younger, Lorraine had been told. A form of denial.) Lorraine Lake was not a superstitious person but she had a dislike of sharing with others private matters that might turn out happily after all.

As she drove the several miles to town, her eyes moved over the eroding countryside without recognition. More woodland being razed for a new shopping mall, another housing subdivision, Sylvan Acres, rising out of a swamp of frozen mud. Mustard-yellow excavating vehicles were everywhere. Grinding, beeping. Flutter of wind-whipped banners advertising a new condominium complex. When Lorraine and her husband had first moved to their home, ten years before, most of this area had been farmland. Now, even the memory of that farmland was confused, eroded. A trust had been betrayed. This is America, the mother thought. Her mouth twisting. Don't tell me what I already know.

Dr. Fehr's waiting room was companionably crowded as usual. Several of the women were hugely pregnant. Lorraine began to feel stabs of panic like early contractions. But when her name was called—"Lorraine Lake?"—she rose obediently, with a small eager smile.

Undressing as she was bidden in an examination room, clumsy in her nakedness, a woman no longer young, embarrassed by flesh. Rolls of it, raddled and pinched. Drooping breasts oddly yellow-tinged as if with jaundice; the nipples raw-looking, scaly. As if something had been suckling her without her knowledge. How strangeness enters our lives.

A cheerful blond nurse, very young, weighed Lorraine Lake as she stood barefoot, rigid on an old-fashioned scale, weight one hundred twenty-two, then took her blood pressure as she sat, self-conscious in her flimsy paper smock, on the edge of the examining table. Something was wrong with the instrument, or with Lorraine Lake, so the nurse took another reading and entered the data on a sheet of paper attached to a clipboard. Lorraine said with a nervous laugh that she was always a little nervous at such times, so perhaps her blood pressure was a little high, and the nurse said yes, that happens sometimes, we can wait awhile and take another reading later. There was a gentle rap of knuckles on the door and Dr. Fehr entered brisk ruddy-faced and smiling as Lorraine recalled him, a man of vigorous youngish middle age, glittering round glasses and goatish ears in which graying-red hairs sprouted. Asking his frightened patient in the paper smock how she was, nodding and murmuring, "Good, good!" at whatever the answer, looming over her beneficent as a midday sun. Forcing rubber gloves onto his capable hands he said, just slightly reproachfully, "You've been postponing this awhile, Mrs. Lake"—a question posed as a statement.

The examination, familiar as a recurring nightmare, was conducted through a confused roaring in Lorraine Lake's ears. The curious localized pain in the uterus, the physician's invasion to be endured stoically, like a rape by Zeus. The patient was lying rigid on the examining table, head back, jaws clenched, eyes shut; fingers gripping the underside of the table so desperately she would discover afterward that several of her nails had cracked. The Pap smear swab, the chilly speculum, the deep probing of Dr. Fehr's strong fingers . . . seeking the spongy tumor, grown to the size of, what?—a nectarine, perhaps. After all these months.

Whatever words Dr. Fehr was saying, kindly or chiding or merely factual, Lorraine Lake did not hear. Blood roared in her ears like a crashing surf. She was blinking enormous hot tears from her eyes, that rolled down her cheeks onto the tissue paper that covered the examining table. She was thinking of the pregnancy that had inhabited her body nearly twelve years ago. The enormous swelling weight of the baby. The pressure, the billowing radiant pain. They praised her, who had not after all been a young mother, not *young* as such things are measured. They insisted she'd been brave, tireless, pushing! pushing! pushing! for more than eighteen hours. Giving birth. As if birth were something given, and given freely. In truth, Lorraine Lake had wanted to say that the birth had been taken from her. The baby forced itself from her. A vessel of violence, of hot unspeakable rage. And the terror of such knowledge, which she could share with no other person, certainly not the man who was her husband, the baby's "father." And the forgetfulness afterward, black wash of oblivion. *God never sends us more than He knows we can bear* one of Lorraine's older female relatives assured her. Lorraine laughed, remembering.

Dr. Fehr, vigorously palpating uterine tissue, seeking the perimeters of the spongy tumor, must have been surprised. The laugh became a cough, the cough a fit of sobbing, unless it was laughing, a gut-wrenching laughter, for in addition to experiencing pain the patient was being roughly tickled, too.

Through a teary haze the alarmed faces of doctor and nurse stared. Then, ordered to lie flat, the weeping patient was quieted; no longer hyperventilating; the mad pulse in her left wrist deftly taken by a man's forceful thumb. "It's just that my body isn't my own," Lorraine Lake was explaining, now calmly. "I'm in it, I'm trapped in it, but it isn't my own. Someone makes me speak, too—not these words, but the others. But I'm terrified to leave my body, because where would I go?" This question so earnest, Lorraine began to laugh again, and the laughter became helpless hiccuping that lasted for several minutes.

It was decided, then, when Lorraine Lake was herself again, and upright, able to look Dr. Fehr unflinchingly in the eye, that, yes, of course, she would have the operation she'd been postponing—a hysterectomy. The fibroid tumor was nonmalignant, but steadily growing; it was in fact the size of a nectarine, soon to be a grapefruit; not dangerous at the present time, but of course it must come out. Lorraine Lake was a reasonable woman, wasn't she. She had no phobias about hospitals, surgery, did she. "A hysterectomy is a common medical procedure," Dr. Fehr said gently.

"Common as death?" his patient inquired.

Frowning as he scribbled something onto the sheet attached to the clipboard, Dr. Fehr seemed not to have heard.

"No. I guess nothing is as common as death," his patient said, with an awkward laugh. She may have believed herself a person with a reputation for drollery and wit, in some other lifetime.

In any case, the examination was over. Dr. Fehr in his white physician's costume, his round eyeglasses glittering, got to his feet. The patient would call his office, make arrangements with his nurse, for the next step preparatory to surgery. "Thank you, Doctor," Lorraine said, stammering, "—I—I'm just so sorry that I broke down—" Dr. Fehr waved away her apology as if it were of no more significance than the female hysteria that had preceded it, and was gone. Left by herself, Lorraine wiped her eyes on a tissue, wiped her entire face which stung as if sunburnt. She whispered, "I *am* sorry, and it won't happen again." She crumpled the tissue, along with the ridiculous baby-doll paper smock, and dropped both into a gleaming metallic wastebasket.

"A common medical procedure."

Driving then, not home, for she could not bear the prospect of *home*, but in the direction of Tippi's school. The midday sky had lightened somewhat but was still stippled with clouds, a pale luminous sun like a worn-out penny.

It was noon recess. Boys and girls everywhere in the vicinity of John F. Kennedy Elementary School—in the playground, on the school's steps, milling about on the sidewalks. Traffic moved slowly here, monitored by crossing guards. Lorraine looked quickly for Tippi, but did not see her; no doubt, Tippi was inside the school building, in the cafeteria or in her homeroom. How gregarious these children were! Lorraine braked her car, moving slowly along the curb, avidly watching the children, strangers to her, who were her daughter's classmates. Were any of those girls Tippi's friends?—did any of them even know Tippi Lake?—or care about her? Lorraine felt a mother's dismay, seeing how pretty, how assured, how like young teenagers many of the girls seemed, hardly Tippi's age at all. Some of the girls appeared to be wearing makeup—was that possible? At the age of eleven? Poor Tippi! No wonder she disliked school, and was reluctant to discuss it, if these girls were her sixth-grade classmates.

It was as she passed the playground that she saw Tippi.

There was the quilted jacket, there the familiar fawn-colored hair and short plump shape, at the edge of the playground not more than ten yards away. At first, it looked as if Tippi was in a group of children; then it became clear that Tippi was by herself, though advancing aggressively toward the children, who were younger than she; she was unaware of her mother, of course, or of anyone watching. The several children, all girls, shrank from Tippi as she thrust something toward them—*was it the hand-puppet?* Lorraine stared in disbelief. Tippi's face was fierce and contorted as Lorraine had never seen it, and her body was oddly hunched, tremulous with concentration, appalling to witness. The younger children moved away from Tippi, not amused by the puppet, but staring at it, the object animated on Tippi's right hand, with looks of alarm and confusion. *What was the puppet saying? What foul threatening words issued from its lewd red-satin mouth?* Two older girls, witnessing Tippi's behavior, approached her and seemed to be challenging her, and Tippi whirled upon them savagely, wielding the puppet like a weapon. Lorraine could see the very cords in her daughter's throat work convulsively as Tippi "threw" her voice into the big-headed baby-faced bald creature on her hand.

"Tippi!—my God."

Lorraine would have shouted out the window of her car, but by this time she'd driven by; traffic bore her along the narrow street, and there was nowhere to park. Her heart was beating so rapidly she was terrified she might faint. The panic of the physical examination washed back over her. That child is mad. That is the face of madness.

No, it's harmless, just a game. Tippi gets carried away by games.

Lorraine drove through an intersection—blindly through a red light—a car horn sounded in annoyance—she was trying to think what she should do. Drive around the block, approach Tippi a second time, call out her name and break up the incident—my God, it was unthinkable, her own shy, sensitive daughter bullying and frightening smaller children! But at once Lorraine changed her mind, no of course not, no she could not, dared not confront Tippi in the playground of her school, in such a way, so public—Tippi would be humiliated, and Tippi might be furious. Tippi would think Lorraine was spying on her—she would never trust Lorraine again.

The profound shock was: Tippi had taken the hand-puppet with her to school, after all.

Tippi had lied to her. Deliberately, shamelessly, looking her mother in the eye.

Still, Lorraine could not confront her daughter, not now. Better to think of it later. Another, calmer time. She decided to continue with her errands in town, as if nothing out of the ordinary had occurred, for perhaps nothing had. In any case she was damned if she was going to cry again, become hysterical a second time within an hour—no thank you, not Lorraine Lake.

That afternoon, waiting for Tippi to come home from school, she prowled the house, restless, agitated. A cigarette burned in her fingers. Several times she believed she heard, in the distance, the sound of the school bus grinding its ugly brakes—then nothing.

She steeled herself against the intrusion. Her aloneness would soon be violated by the child's noisy entry.

She was smoking again—the first time in twelve years. Her husband and her daughter would be shocked, disapproving; as she herself would have been, in different circumstances. The sharp nicotine charge in her lungs was like a thrust of love, imperfectly but passionately recalled. Why not?—we don't live forever, the mother thought. Except, mouthing the words to herself, what she actually said was, "We don't love forever." She heard this, and laughed.

She was passing by Tippi's closed door. She had not entered before, and she would not, now.

Instead, she climbed to the third floor, to the attic. Where rarely she went and then only on an errand of strict necessity; never for such a purpose—simply to stand, heart beating quickly, before a grimy window. Not knowing where she was exactly except it was a place of sanctuary, solitude. The sky was closer here, drawing the eye upward. She smoked her cigarette with a lover's abandon, coughing a little, wiping at her eyes. She was free here, she was safe here, wasn't she!—when Tippi came home, Tippi would not know where she was. Tippi would want to hurry to her room to hide the hand-puppet and she, the mother, would not be a witness to the child's stealth; each would be spared. But really she did not care. She was not thinking of Tippi, or of the loathsome hand-puppet, at all.

How beautiful! The gray impacted clouds had begun to separate, like gigantic boulders, shot fiercely with flame. There was to have been an afternoon thunderstorm, but the northeast wind out of Canada had blown it past. The mother stared, in a trance. She knew there was something behind her, below her; something imminent, threatening; a grinding of brakes, a jeering nasal child-voice . . . But, no: she was alone here, and she was safe. She leaned forward breathlessly: she saw herself climbing into the sky of boulders. As a girl, so long ago, she'd been wonderfully physical—athletic, self-assured. What buoyancy to her step, what jubilation, like that of a soul coming home! Her tall erect figure receded into the distance, and never a backward glance.

Schroeder's Stepfather

1.

How swift, and how irrevocable.

And how ironic: for by then the hurricane had blown out harmlessly into the Atlantic. No one in the entire state of New Jersey would die of it except, in a manner of speaking, as his stepson John interpreted it, poor Jack.

2.

Eighteen hours of pelting rains, gale-force winds, flooding in north central New Jersey where the elder Schroeders lived but at dawn of September 23 the air was sunny and unexpectedly steamy, there were glittering pools of water everywhere, smells of broken things, mangled green.

It was the first time in many years that John Schroeder and his wife Laurel were visiting his mother Miriam and his stepfather Jack Schroeder in Clifton, New Jersey, relations between John and the elder Schroeders had always been somewhat strained, but John's mother had written to invite them, she'd seemed to be appealing to them to please come visit, so John had decided they would make the drive down from Boston, why not?—a visit to his mother and his stepfather now he was safely married, fully and happily adult, could do no harm.

The first night, when they were undressing for bed, Laurel told John emphatically, as if it were a fact they'd been contesting, "Your mother is a very sweet woman, John, so kind, generous . . ." and John smiled, saying, "But she didn't protect me from him."

3.

How it happened: late Saturday morning they'd driven out together, John Schroeder and his stepfather Jack Schroeder, to investigate storm damage at Lake Chinquapin, where Jack Schroeder owned lakefront property, when the sight of his badly battered shingleboard cottage and dock so upset the elder Schroeder that he died on the debris-strewn bench: collapsed, fell, died within minutes: of what would be diagnosed by the emergency-room staff at Mount Royal General Hospital as cardiac failure.

Jack Schroeder had been a barrel-bodied man in the long years of John Schroeder's boyhood, mildly asthmatic, a hard drinker, fifty pounds overweight, now in his late sixties he'd seemed to have shrunk in both height and girth, and he'd had to quit drinking entirely, but it was plain that his health was dubious: his face slack and flushed as if newly sunburnt, his eyes small, rheumy, pinched at the corners, and his breath hoarse, often harsh, nearly always audible. Where at one time the man's bristling hair had seemed to lift from his forehead and even his shaggy eyebrows had seemed charged with static electricity, now what remained of his yellowish-white hair was a few lank strands combed ineffectually over his shiny bald crown; his hands trembled when he grew excited; his mood might swing within minutes from cheeriness and loquaciousness to worry, suspicion, distraction, dread. So John Schroeder had not been truly surprised, though of course he'd been badly shocked, by the fact of his stepfather's sudden death.

My God: one minute the old man was stalking about on the beach above his devastated dock, puffy-faced, flailing his arms, cursing out the insurance company for what he was certain they'd do, or would refuse to do, to compensate him for damages, the next minute he was tearing at his shirt collar, whimpering, "Oh, oh—*oh*" like a frightened child. Then he fell to his knees, and then clumsily forward onto his stomach and face before John could catch him, and suddenly he lay writhing in the wet sand amid the storm-litter of broken tree limbs, curling leaves, shattered glass. John supposed his stepfather was having a seizure of some kind, a stroke, an asthmatic attack or heart attack, he knew from his mother that Jack's health was poor, and he tried to remain calm thinking what to do, crouched over the stricken man and holding his shoulders, finally turning him onto his back so that he could give him mouth-to-mouth resuscitation as he'd been instructed twenty years before as a lifeguard, but the old man fought him, struck him in the face with his flailing fists, and then suddenly he stopped moving entirely, his terrible rasping breath stopped, there he lay like a big-bellied beached fish, his pink mouth gaping slackly open and his small damp eyes rolled up into his head. John, who'd been taught by his stepfather to call him "Father," and, somewhat clumsily, just a day or two before, to call him "Jack," could summon no proper word to call him now, but rose swiftly, and ran back to his car cupping his hands to his mouth and shouting, "Help! Help! Is anyone here—" though knowing there was no one there, or at least no one within earshot or visibility, so he hadn't any choice but to leave the unconscious man lying there on his back and drive three miles to the village of Chinquapin to call for an ambulance.

By the time John Schroeder placed his call, his stepfather Jack Schroeder was dead.

By the time the rescue squad arrived, John Schroeder's stepfather was dead beyond resuscitation.

4.

It was true, John Schroeder was legally the adopted "son" of Jack Schroeder, who'd married John's mother when he was eight years old, and had been fatherless for six years, yet he remained the man's "stepson" as Jack Schroeder remained John's "stepfather" after thirty years, and nothing would ever change that fact, not the physical diminution of the elder man, not his considerable loss of aggression and what John Schroeder's mother had nervously called his high spirits, not even his death out there at Lake Chinquapin in the very presence of the man who was his legally adopted "son" and had been so for nearly thirty-one years. John Schroeder could not recall his true father except to know that his name was not "Schroeder" and that he did not resemble his mother's second husband in any way.

Before marrying his wife Laurel, John Schroeder had been involved with several young women each of whom, in turn, had one day in a moment of unthinking intimacy dared to call him "Jack": and each time John Schroeder had had to explain quietly that he was not in fact "Jack"—his name was "John." If one or another of the young women forgot, or persisted, John would say, more forcefully, "I mean it: I'm not 'Jack.' There was room in my family for only one 'Jack' and that was the man who married my mother after my father died."

What John had told none of these women, not even his wife Laurel, was that there'd once been a child, a little boy, called "Jack," in fact often called "Jacky," but he'd lost his name at the age of eight when he and his mother went to live with a man named "Jack"— "Jack Schroeder"—the man who was his stepfather and who'd legally adopted him as his son. John told no one this because it was at once too obvious and too complex. And of no importance, he was sure, to anyone apart from himself.

5.

Had the old man, mortally stricken, sinking to his knees in the wet sand and then falling onto his soft slack bloated old-man's stomach and then onto his face cried out for help, for help from *him?*—his despised stepson? Had his terror-filled eyes risen to lock themselves to *his?*

And how had John Schroeder, now fully adult, now fully free, having long since forgiven his stepfather for the misery of his childhood, responded to this plea?

Says John, "I spat in the old bastard's face and watched him die."

6.

In his imagination, which had been, since earliest childhood, a fevered imagination, it had seemed that his mother remarried shortly after his father's death; so he was puzzled to discover, years later, that a decent interim had passed. You cannot blame a weak woman for marrying a man she doesn't love out of loneliness or financial desperation though of course he blamed her, he'd always hated her, never would he forgive her but he loved her in terror that she too would leave him, understanding even as a child of eight that you can only pity a woman for such craven relief and gratitude, you've heard her weeping and muttering to herself, the very worst times were when she hadn't been drinking but she *had* been praying, her hair disheveled and her face a powdery pasty color and the red lips smeared as if with kisses, the Bible fallen from her hands and too heavy to retrieve. Her name was Miriam, she worked as a receptionist-secretary for Rayburn & Schroeder Realtors Inc. in the little storefront corner office on Main Street, no she wasn't paid much but she was grateful for the job, any job, any kindness, and one of her employers, big good-natured yellow-eyed Jack Schroeder, sometimes drove her home from work, took her out for drinks, for dinner and more drinks, drove her home from work but failed to bring her home. . . and one day they were married: and one day Jack Schroeder who was forty years old, barrel-bodied, big-headed, with big slanted asymmetrical teeth and that wide wet sliding smile and those small bright eyes lit with merriment, or malice, or both, Jack Schroeder in a yellow polka-dot bridegroom's vest and a straw hat with a matching band squatted so he could look his new wife's little boy dead-level in the eyes and gripped the boy's thin shoulders so the boy wouldn't mistake his seriousness, or his strength, and said, "O.K., son, first thing we gotta get straight: *I'm* 'Jack' 'cause I been 'Jack' all my life, everybody knows I'm 'Jack,' so *you're* 'John.' You unnerstand? Eh?" And

he'd laughed happily, not at all unkindly, spraying the little boy
with a fine mist of saliva, enveloping him with a strong smell of
whiskey and cigar smoke and Jack Schroeder's unique and unmistakable aroma. "You unnerstand? Eh?"

7.

Later, he'd called the boy "Johnny," just to tease, "Johnny-on-
the-spot," he'd say, pinching the boy's cheek between his thumb
and forefinger so hard a red mark remained in the flesh for hours,
or giving him a cuff on the back of the head, "Johnny-on-the-*pot*,
eh?" roaring with laughter at the sight of the boy's perplexed or
frightened or terrified face, and as time passed and the boy
flinched and cringed before he was touched, often as soon as his
stepfather entered the room, or his heavy footstep was communi-
cated through the floorboards, he called the boy "Squinchy" which
was the most hilarious name of all.

Poised on the brink of sleep he hears it: a sly floating sound,
those derisive syllables—"Squinchy."

He feels the sudden grip of the fingers, steely-hard talons clos-
ing on his shoulders, his skinny upper arms, the delicate nape of his
neck. Knuckles rubbed hard against his scalp, a tattoo of punches
in his ribs. "What're ya scared of, Squinchy? Eh? 'Johnny-on-the-
pot'?" He hears the explosive wheezing laugh, feels the fine spray
of spittle. The smell of beer, whiskey, cigar smoke. The bovine heat
of the man. The broad chest that looked as if it were about to burst
out of its shirt, the high hard protruding stomach pushing against
a fine gleaming silver-buckled belt. "Hey Squinchy where ya
goin'?—what's the hurry? Eh Squinchy?" The bristling hair like
quills, the quivering jowls. The flashing wet of the big slanted teeth
and the eyes that were urine-colored, lightly threaded with broken
capillaries. "Squinchy—how's the boy? Got something in your
pants?" If John shrank from his stepfather it was an invitation for
the man to lunge at him, swooping in play, clapping his hands in
John's face as one might clap his hands at a cowering dog, several
times he clapped his hands hard against John's ears as if hoping to

burst his head as one might burst a balloon, in play, of course it was play, and when John whimpered or wept or screamed or reeled in shock, when he coughed, choked, stumbled and fell, a burning vile sludge bubbling through his teeth, Jack Schroeder would stare at him in disgust as if such contemptible behavior were done on purpose to vex *him*, disappoint *him* who had no son of his own of whom he might be proud.

Those years. A lifetime.

And repeatedly as in a dream John's mother said, those years, repeatedly, in reproach, pleading, "Jack is just teasing, honey—you know he's just teasing," or, "If you could learn not to *cry*, honey, that's what sets him off he just can't bear it," her own arms bruised sometimes as Jack Schroeder's drinking worsened, and that nervous spasm of her eyes as if perpetually in this house to which they'd been brought to live in she knew she must be on guard, never relax, speak softly, murmur, or mumble out of the side of her mouth as she had to watch doorways out of the side of her vision, for of course she and her son were living in Jack Schroeder's brick-and-stucco house on Elmhurst Avenue on sufferance and not because they deserved to live there, John was not "John Schroeder" because he'd been legally adopted by his stepfather because his stepfather was a damned generous man and not because he deserved to be adopted, a fact everyone knew, who in all of the world could not know, yes and the two of them cost Jack Schroeder money and Jack Schroeder was the kind of man who is most happy spending money in public even giving money away to local charities, master of ceremonies at local fund-raising events, president of the Clifton Chamber of Commerce and his photograph in the newspaper in attendance at the Boys' Club or the Consolidated New Jersey Scholarship Fund or the New Jersey Council of Community Services or the Clifton Volunteer Fireman's picnic or Parents Night at the junior high school, a deep sigh and a wide boyish grin and reaching into his pocket for wallet or checkbook, everyone in Clifton knew Jack Schroeder, everyone in the county knew Jack Schroeder he was damned generous and good-hearted thus well loved because that's the kind of man he was but he was the kind of man frequently upset and incredulous and crazed in private at the expenditure of money, his hard-earned money, where did it go, where in hell did it go, who were the leeches that were bleeding him white—"bleeding me white" was a favorite expression—and behind closed doors in the house on Elmhurst Avenue at any hour of the day including even the early morning before John could slip away trembling to school there might rise Jack Schroeder's indignant voice and of Miriam no sound except perhaps muffled sobs, the faintest and most futile of protests, the sound of shame, the sound of craven female pleading, the sound of the most ignominious and complete defeat: the very erasure of the human soul.

8.

There was Curly the golden-red cocker spaniel pup someone had given Jack Schroeder, Curly who was to be John's pet and John's responsibility, how he'd loved Curly poor doomed Curly who was his first pet and would be his last, the creature kept in the basement whimpering and whining all night long and why wasn't he housebroken after two weeks and Jack Schroeder took matters into his own hands since Johnny clearly couldn't, or wouldn't, the boy was eleven years old and in sixth grade and shy and silent and weak-eyed but there was a grain of stubbornness in him Jack Schroeder could detect since lately he'd learned not to cry unless severely frightened or made to endure true pain, nor did he visibly flinch when made to witness the puppy's "discipline": the measured blows with a rolled-up newspaper, in time the blows of balled-up fists, finally kicks so the small furry body flew about the basement like a football and even his screams were swallowed up in sheer animal horror. Naturally at such times Curly dribbled urine and feces onto the cement floor, panting Jack Schroeder observed in a voice heavy with sarcasm, "—You just look at the little bugger cross-eyed and he *shits*," and ordered Johnny to clean it up, and Johnny cleaned it up, and the blood too, and when he tried to comfort Curly, when he tried simply to touch him the puppy shrank from him convulsed in terror, his eyes the eyes of unseeing madness, the eyes of impending death, until finally in the puppy's fifth week in the Schroeder house Jack Schroeder initiated the strategy of punishing Curly for his misdeeds by rationing out food and water as meagerly as possible, his logic being, "If the little bugger doesn't take it in, he sure can't piss and shit it out," and this turned out to be true.

Long after the dog died John would hear him whimpering in the basement, lying tense and sweaty in his bed he could hear Curly two floors below as he'd heard him those nights, except now covering his head with a pillow didn't help and even today so many years later he can wake from a dream to hear the puppy whining, his claws on the cement floor clicking in desperation to escape but of course there was no escape: no escape from Jack Schroeder's wrath and the profound righteousness of that wrath.

And there came a day, an hour, weeks after John and his mother had buried Curly near the back fence of Jack Schroeder's property on Elmhurst Avenue, when Jack Schroeder cheerfully denied the puppy's existence: "Naw, nobody in *this* house ever had a dog—what kind of a dog? Too much yapping and fussing"—turning his cigar in his fingers, sucking at it unlit, one eyelid drooping in his familiar wink as he turned toward John's mother drawling, "Right, Mir'im? Eh? Never any dog around here, eh?" as John's mother stood smiling faintly, her powdered skin stretched in just-perceptible horizontal planes on her face, her eyes averted, so Jack Schroeder repeated his question as if making an effort to be patient with someone very stupid, "Right, Mir'im? Tell Johnny-boy what's the score," until at last, reluctantly, shamefully, John's mother shook her head, swallowed, murmuring, the very murmur of female submission and female defeat, "Oh I—I don't know."

The house on Elmhurst Avenue. Those years.

9.

They became lovers so naturally she asked him where was his home, who were his people, and he told her that his relatives, those still living, lived in Clifton, New Jersey, but that he saw them

rarely. Managing then to change the subject, to deflect her innocent line of questioning, so that Laurel was left with the vague impression that both John's parents were dead; and it wasn't until
two years later when they were making plans to marry that the
odd fact emerged, as if accidentally, that John's mother Miriam
was living after all: living less than three hundred miles away.

Laurel was perplexed, Laurel was disoriented, regarding John
with wondering eyes, and several times saying, to his annoyance,
"But—your mother *is* living? But—" so John felt obliged to say, as
tactfully as possible, "Yes. My mother is 'living.' But that hasn't
much to do with me, and nothing at all to do with you, has it?"

10.

He'd been drawn to her because, he saw, other men of whom
he'd heard impressive things had been drawn to her too.

The way she carried herself, and the way she spoke, and the way
light seemed to radiate from her skin. Her fair wavy hair, her intelligent eyes. He concluded that she was beautiful, and she was de-
sirable. He felt emotion in her presence but it was not a definable
emotion, thus not trustworthy, thus left to himself he would not
have been so certain that he wanted her and must have her to complete, not himself, but his idea of himself.

He recalled with some dreamy difficulty that his mother had
been an attractive woman once, a wan faltering watercolor-pretty
woman, otherwise lip-licking Jack Schroeder that fat tub of guts
Jack Schroeder would not have wanted her and would not have
elected to take on the burden, as he would subsequently, and
frequently, complain, of "another man's leavings": the widow, and
the brat.

11.

There was the basement stinking of a puppy's bowel-panic
but there was the basement of other days, and nights, as well: a

shadowy place: an almost sacred place: the place of "discipline": the place of which you did not think.

Jack Schroeder saying, not in his usual high-pitched or aggrieved voice, but calmly, "C'mere. Take down your pants."

12.

He was an architect with a small but elite firm in Cambridge, Massachusetts. He was an architect which meant that he was a master of space.

He'd left home permanently at the age of sixteen to live with a great-uncle in Newark, New Jersey, he'd worked after school and summers to pay room and board and then he'd gone to Rutgers University in New Brunswick on a scholarship and from there to Yale to study architecture, a life-summary he'd become glibly accustomed to reciting as if it were an account of someone else's life and not his. For what of it, of its exteriority, was in fact *his*?—in *his* head, most of the time, there were elegant spatial designs, ghost-structures, to be painstakingly translated into visual terms and set down on clean white paper.

His most recent project, the subject of a feature in a national newsmagazine, was an art museum in Tucson, Arizona. Tall tinted panels of glass and starkly white walls including adjustable interior walls and a roof designed like an immense venetian blind whose slats could be adjusted to modulate degrees of light: the beautiful airy structure had begun in John's imagination as a dream of light, a phenomenon of sheer light, and it was as this, wholly devoid of content or use, that John had willed it into being.

But it was a success in worldly, public terms, if just slightly controversial. By way of such terms the name "Schroeder" would be enhanced.

As soon as John and Laurel entered the elder Schroeders' living room on Thursday evening John spied, conspicuous on a coffee table, the weeks'-old issue of the glossy newsmagazine, and he felt his mouth twitch in a wry little grimace. And shortly afterward his mother Miriam alluded to the feature, opened the magazine to display it, as, no doubt, she'd opened the magazine to display the feature numerous times (had she friends? women friends? had she a life, now? in these "retirement" years?), murmuring, ". . . So proud of you, dear! And so surprised!" peering almost shyly at John through the subtly distorting lenses of her bifocal glasses, and there was John's stepfather Jack smiling too, nodding vehemently, old-mannish, his small watery eyes moving uneasily from John's face to Laurel's to John's as if he could not quite recall which of these two attractive and composed young people was *his*. But his very white dentures gleamed wetly and happily. He said, "Sure *are!*" tugging the magazine out of Miriam's fingers with childlike dispatch, scarcely noticing what he did, any more than Miriam seemed to notice it, and flapping the magazine down on his fattish thighs, boasting, "*I* was the one who spotted it here, not your mama, John, wasn't I, Mir'im? Eh?"

Miriam, making an effort to smile, smoothing her skirt across her lap with careful hands, alleged, yes, he was.

13.

How obscene, the word "mama" in that man's mouth.

How unreal this life of theirs, the two of them together in this semblance of domesticity, no longer in the house on Elmhurst Avenue which had been sold long ago but in a redwood ranch house on five acres of land outside Clifton—Jack Schroeder's retirement home. John knew from Miriam that, in the 1970's, the real estate company had nearly gone bankrupt, forced out of competition by younger, more vigorous, presumably more capable rivals; he knew that Jack Schroeder had had to sell off a good deal of the local property he'd acquired, and that he was no longer one of the prominent men in the area though he remained active, still, in local politics—since giving up real estate he'd become increasingly involved in the Republican party, in whatever local or county capacity they would have him. He no longer drank, nor did he smoke. It seemed clear to John that he was wary of *him*—blustery and bossy and sarcastic as ever when alone with Miriam, but immediately and innocently affable, even fawning, when John or Laurel appeared. He'd draw himself up to his fullest height—he was still a big man: no less than six feet tall, and massive in the chest and belly—and grin his boyish slanted grin, and say, "Y'know I was just telling Mir'im here—" cagily assessing John or blinking as if dazzled by Laurel, these strangers in his house who were in some vague way *his*: to deal with, to measure, perhaps even (who knows?) to exploit. Certainly he had numerous questions to ask of John about an architect's "millionaire clients."

And there was Miriam, John's mother, who'd written to him and Laurel to invite them to visit, performing the old housewifely duties like a smiling automaton, with oddly few questions of her own, content seemingly just to gaze upon her son and smile, and smile. As John stared at her thinking *Why? Why didn't you protect me from him? Why are you still with him? What is this life of yours, how can you endure it? Why didn't you take me away?—the two of us, away?—anywhere?—to save ourselves? Why?* Aging, Miriam had acquired a brittle look. As if her bones beneath the envelope of thin taut faintly shiny skin might easily break. She had a distracting habit of clearing her throat frequently, bringing her hand to her mouth, as if to hide her mouth. John wondered was she frightened of him: of her son suddenly taking her hands in his, forcing her to see him, to acknowledge their connection: *Why?*

But of course John would never do that. He would not want to upset his mother, he wasn't the kind of person to dramatize himself at another's expense. Oh never!

By his calculation he hadn't touched his mother in any urgent way in twenty-eight years.

Laurel, lovely shrewd Laurel, sensed these tensions but gave no sign, behaving, to John's amazement, in splendid daughterly fashion—doing most of the talking with Miriam, conspiring to be alone with Miriam, resisting Jack Schroeder's clumsy efforts at banter that excluded Miriam or seemed to have Miriam as its butt. She insisted that she was enjoying the visit. She insisted that she liked John's mother, what a sweet woman, rather effaced by her

husband, but intelligent really—"I can see so much of you in her,"
Laurel said several times.

Carefully John asked, "In our features, or in our personalities?"

Laurel said vaguely, "I'm not sure. Some amalgam, I suppose, of
both."

14.

The house in which his mother and stepfather now lived was a
cheaply flashy "ranch," but the other house was the true house, the
house of memory, pain, repetition. Vividly John could see the rooms
of that house; the staircase; the upstairs hall; the bathroom with its
old-fashioned fixtures; the tub that stained so easily, and so repeatedly, which poor Miriam had to scrub, scrub, scrub. . . . Vividly
he could see the kitchen of that old house. A wanly golden light of
late afternoon slanting through the windows. And downstairs in
the basement that same light eerily refracted or dimmed by the
scrim of dust on the windows. Such narrow windows they were,
dwarf windows measuring perhaps eighteen inches by ten, too
small for even a thin-boned child to climb through. Though more
than once, locked in for the night, having endured his "discipline,"
he'd dragged a rickety chair over to one of the windows to stand on,
to peer out.

Nothing to see even in daylight except grass, dirt, rubble. As if
in a grave. But still he'd stand there, peering out.

Always the command was, "Take down your pants, boy."

"Take" down and not "pull" down: why?

And next day when they were alone together in no immediate
danger of being caught his mother would whisper, half in reproach,
"If you could *cry*, John. Like you used to. He thinks you're taunt-
ing him, you never *cry*."

15.

Had John Schroeder planned to kill his stepfather Jack
Schroeder, or was it, the sudden expedient action at the lake,

wholly unpremeditated?—he would wonder, himself. Oh yes! He'd wonder.

Certainly he was, of all the men and women of his acquaintance, professional as well as social, the most premeditated of people; the most icy-calm; the most unsentimentally self-aware. He was certain there could be nothing about himself of which he was not aware—not because he'd had a few intermittent years of therapy in his late twenties but because it was his nature to be scrupulously self-analytic. Had he been a painter instead of an architect he would have painted self-portraits of the most exacting pitiless kind.

"How hard you are on yourself!" Laurel said.

"Not hard enough, surely," said John.

He knew for instance that there exists in the human psyche the temptation to forever cast one's life in the form of a narrative in which all others are supporting characters: there is the temptation to believe in the delusion of one's centrality: one's supreme importance.

He thought, bemused, Not me. That was beaten out of me long ago.

And so it was. Of that he was certain.

16.

Saturday morning and according to news bulletins the hurricane had blown out harmlessly to sea and Jack Schroeder was anxiously eager to inspect his lakeside property at Lake Chinquapin: for hours, the previous day, he'd talked of little else. "I think Jack is a bit obsessive about this, don't you," John asked Miriam, speaking as if sympathetic, but Miriam only said, circumspectly, "Well. It's what he has to think about."

So John naturally offered to drive out with him. To drive him, in fact. In John's new-model Toyota which Jack had made a show of admiring though he disapproved in general of "foreign" cars.

Thinking, as he drove, half-listening to his stepfather's rambling and not entirely coherent monologue, that there was no risk:

he'd never do what he most wanted to do simply because he
most wanted it and what we most want we must deny ourselves
forever.

17.

"Remember Squinchy?"

"Eh? What?"

"Squinchy. Remember?"

"Who? What's that?"

He'd heard, and he knew. John could tell by the way Jack stiffened in his seat and by the diminution of his voice.

"And Curly—d'you remember Curly?"

" 'Curly'?"

"The puppy. The cocker spaniel. You know."

Jack Schroeder worked his mouth, sucked at his dentures and
seemed to be considering how to reply, or whether to reply at all.
They were nearly at Lake Chinquapin and the storm damage was
considerable along the highway: fallen tree limbs, several abandoned cars, sections of the road swamped with muddy water to a
depth of about six inches.

"The puppy. Curly. Don't you remember?—I do." John paused,
looking straight ahead. He'd thought the wind had died down
but the tops of the trees were disturbed, quivering. "The puppy you
let die."

"I—don't remember."

"The puppy you killed."

"Eh? Puppy? I don't remember no puppy."

He'd heard and he knew but cagily he cupped a hand to his left ear
and leaned toward John, his gaze veiled.

John said casually, "Well. Never mind, Jack."

They drove on. Pale impacted sunshine seemed to glare from all
sides. A sign announced three miles to the Village of Lake Chinquapin, which, to get to John's stepfather's place, they would be
bypassing.

Jack Schroeder snuffled and cleared his throat and mumbled, in the awkward silence, "Never was any dog in our house I can remember, your mama said they made her nervous. She *is* highstrung y'know." And, when John still did not reply, nor even acknowledge having heard, he added, "*My* daddy hated 'em."

18.

John Schroeder had been trained as a lifeguard at the age of sixteen so naturally he would know the technique of mouth-to-mouth resuscitation and he'd have been certain to try it when his stepfather collapsed on the beach at Lake Chinquapin, if only for a few futile minutes.

Then he'd driven to the village and telephoned an ambulance and returned at once to the stricken man, which was where the ambulance crew found him: crouched over Jack Schroeder's body, which lay flat on its back on the debris-littered beach. John rose and said quietly, "My stepfather—I think he's dead."

19.

He will remember the flat slap of the waves, and the oily light gleaming on the waves, froth like human spittle or semen and a great bobbing net of seed-scum and storm-debris of all kinds, parts of boards, Styrofoam cups and containers, the carcass of a partly decomposed rat: and the vivid smells of these things: and the air warm and moist as breath: and he'll remember the lake's stillness and the expanse of water approximately a mile and a half wide looking out from the beach below Jack Schroeder's cottage but he won't clearly remember himself standing there for what must have been minutes and these minutes hardly placid, his right foot in its corrugated crepe-soled canvas shoe pressing down hard on a man's neck pressing a man's face hard into the sand until at last the man's heart bursts and the convulsive flailing of arms and legs and the muffled terrified cries end. He will try, but he can't quite remember.

In the end, he'll be forced to invent.

20.

He was shaking so badly he couldn't continue driving, falling behind the speeding ambulance until finally, chill with sweating inside his clothes, he turned off the road and stopped at a café. That was what the place called itself: Nickel's Café.

He drank two cups of coffee, bitter and black. And a glass of ice water. His nerves, severed, needed knitting-up again, coherence. A woman dressed as a waitress spoke to him patiently and repeated her question once or twice before he heard.

He stammered, "What? Yes? —I've just seen a man die."

Before leaving Nickel's Café he telephoned his mother. When she answered the phone, saying "Hello?" in a timid, hopeful voice, a voice he would not have recognized, he identified himself and asked to speak to Laurel, it was only to Laurel he could speak, his eyes shut, his heart painful in his chest, saying quickly, before Laurel could draw breath to ask if something was wrong, "My stepfather— I think he's dead."

There came a beat, a moment's silence. Laurel said faintly, "—Dead?"

"I think—I think he is. Yes I think he is. He collapsed at the lake, he was upset seeing the damage to the, the dock and the cottage, it must have been his heart, I couldn't do anything for him so I called an ambulance and they're taking him"—but by now they'd already taken him, surely—"to the hospital in Mount Royal. I— I couldn't— I tried but I couldn't . . ." And his voice trailed off in astonishment.

Laurel was saying, "Your stepfather—Jack—is dead? He's actually *dead*?"

"Bring my mother and I'll meet you at the hospital. You can drive their car, can't you? Jack's car? Prepare her for the shock but don't tell her, you know, don't tell her he's—dead—that is, I think he's dead, I think"—as the horror of it washed over him, that, in fact, the man might yet be resuscitated at the hospital, retrieved from Death, "—Just bring her, Laurel, and I'll meet you there." He paused, breathing quickly. A sensation as of neon light flooded his veins—brilliant and without warmth.

Laurel said tentatively, "John—? Are you all right?"

He said, "I don't know. I don't know yet."

There was silence. Then they spoke again, hurriedly, and made arrangements to meet at the Mount Royal hospital, and hung up.

In any case, Jack Schroeder was not resuscitated.

21.

There was a funeral, and there was a burial, and a surprising number of Clifton residents came to pay their last respects to Jack Schroeder, most of them older men, men of Jack Schroeder's generation. The younger Schroeders made most of the arrangements, or helped Miriam, who was bearing up under the shock with unexpected fortitude, for after all, as she said repeatedly, in a thin vague wondering voice, her husband had had warnings, their doctor had strongly advised him to lose weight, not to get overly excited or lose his temper yes and he'd strained his heart with so many years of drinking and smoking, poor Jack, poor stubborn Jack, you know how he is—how he *was*.

"Yes," said John. "I know."

Which may or may not have been the truth.

And after ten days the younger Schroeders drove back home to Massachusetts, having made plans for Miriam to come visit them at Christmas, and with relief John returned to work, he returned to work with a passion for wasn't his work his solace? his truest self? an "island" of sorts of which he was the sole inhabitant until such time as he relinquished it to other, subsequent inhabitants, who were, regardless of the prices they paid for the privilege, required to live within the restrictions he'd invented?

22.

Softly he'd said, "I'm going to kill you: wipe you out like wiping something foul off my shoes."

Softly he'd said, "No, Jack, of course I've forgiven you, isn't that what adults do, forgive one another for the crimes they've committed against children?"

His stepfather had not heard, or had heard. He'd gone red in the face, and his breath was coming in spasms, and when he sank to his knees stunned then fell heavily forward onto his stomach and onto his face it's possible that he was already dead or so bound for death that John's sudden foot on the nape of his beefy neck urging his face into the sand with the hope of smothering him (for is not smothering of all strategies of homicide the most difficult to detect? diagnosed usually as "cardiac failure"?) was unnecessary: except as a final gesture.

Revenge is secret justice yes but it *is* justice.

And if the dead man's face seemed to have been oddly mashed in the sand, if there were bruises and lacerations on the skin, even the back of the neck showing evidence of abrasion, that could be readily explained for he'd had convulsions, his death had not been an easy one, he'd fought it for minutes and fought even his stepson's attempt to save him. . . .

But no one at the hospital, nor, certainly, Miriam Schroeder, asked for a detailed explanation, only for an account: the death by "cardiac failure" of a man of nearly seventy with health problems, overweight by forty pounds, is hardly a medical mystery.

Softly he'd said, crouched over the man, pleading, begging, "God damn you, get up, do you think I believe this, do you think I believe you—*you*? Do you think you can make me believe you're dead?"

23.

It was winter, and very cold, and hand in hand like young or convalescent lovers they were walking somewhere, their booted feet sinking crisply into the snow, breaking the icy crust of snow, and

John seemed to be favoring his right foot, not limping but wincing when his weight came down on that foot, and sharp-eyed Laurel asked was something wrong? and John said no, not really, just pins and needles in his foot as if it's been asleep, a mild numbness, the sort of thing that comes and goes and if it's a circulation problem it's a very minor problem—"Nothing I'm going to worry about, right now."

The Sepulchre

This is the way it was, or will be.

An angry ringing telephone out of the impacted November sky and it's your mother's voice fading, accusing, crackling with distance and distress, Come home! Your father has hidden himself from me, I can't find him, I don't know what to do, I'm not a young woman any longer, I can't be expected to bear this alone!—and of course you obey. Immediately and unquestioningly and in a state of almost cerebral terror you obey.

That evening after two plane flights, a fifteen-mile taxi ride from the suburban airport north of the small upstate New York city in which your parents have lived their entire lives, a bumpy ride during which you've been hypnotized by the rosary of chunky shiny-black beads hanging swaying and clicking from the driver's rearview mirror, you hurry stumbling up the walk to the house seeing the porch light burning with its look of ferocity and vigilance, you haven't time to consider how many nights, how many years, that burning light awaited you, vigilant, welcoming, accusing, the eye of parental conscience whenever you were out past dusk, and all the hours between dusk and your return home. Your mother opens the door as you ascend the porch steps, you greet each other with an embrace, you hide your surprise at your mother's vehemence, passion—He's hiding from *me*! It's one of his cruel games! Oh, darling, we can't let anyone know!

And hiding too your dismay that for the first time in your mutual history you and your mother have changed places, she has become the daughter, the needy quivering child, and you, taller, stronger, fleshier, have become the comforting mother, the woman who will make things right.

Inside, the house feels tilted, about to swerve from its foundation, or you're breathless and dazed from the long suspension of terror you dare not even now relinquish. It seems that your father *is* gone—but where? Your mother insists he's in the house or on the property, it isn't the first time he's played this cruel trick on her, she's never told you or any of the relatives, she's never gone for help to the neighbors, nor has she called their doctor, or the police; she's always been able to find him in the past, or, if she hasn't, he's returned, always so innocent-seeming, so astonished at her distress. But this time, your mother says, I've looked and looked and I can't find him, I know he's here, he's here but he's gone, he's lost and can't find his way back, oh darling what can we *do*? You wipe your eyes and make an effort to clear your thoughts. From the taxi you'd seen that the house is glaring with lights, the big shadowed woodframe-Victorian house in which for the first eighteen years of your life you'd lived defined to yourself as to the world solely as the daughter of that house, virtually every light in every room burning, and the bright brittle November moon overhead a part of the vigilance, that look of a ferocious exposure, exclamation. This is an old once-grand residential neighborhood and the houses are in large wooded lots set back, and uphill, from the street; neighboring houses appeared so sparsely lit as to seem almost unoccupied, abandoned. And each house, in the wind-lashed night, behind its high hedge, or wrought-iron fence, or fieldstone wall, separate and prideful as a ship riding the ocean's waves, withdrawn from its neighbors.

Your mother's face is suffused with blood, her cheeks, her moist lips, she looks almost youthful speaking rapidly, accusingly, clutching at your wrist providing you with a cascade of facts, information. She is wearing a quilted floral robe, ankle-length, unevenly buttoned to the neck, that gives her the appearance of a doll upended;

her hair, usually so fastidiously arranged, is flatter on one side of
her head than the other, and is grayer, a brittle iron-gray, than you
remember. She is not an elderly woman but she has become an old
woman, the sight of her soft-creased flaccid flesh, the deep fissures
bracketing her mouth, pierces your heart. You recall your mother
saying, years ago, in pitying reference to an older relative, when
they're that age they can age, they can *go*, overnight. And the curious wan snap of her fingers.

Your eyes ache from the glaring of lights in the downstairs
rooms of the house, even the rarely used crystal chandelier in the
dining room, even the 60-watt bulb in the closet off the foyer. This
look of furniture that should be familiar to you made unfamiliar by
being out of place if only by inches, the living-room sofa yanked out
from the wall at an angle, the sideboard in the dining room dislodged from its place, everywhere you look doors flung open as if in
a sustained rage. You ask your mother how long your father has
been missing, and your mother says angrily he isn't missing, not to
himself he isn't he's in hiding, that's the kind of man he is. So carefully you ask when your mother saw your father last and she says,
drawing herself to her full height of indignation and wounded
pride, stiff as an upright doll, Yesterday morning, it was yesterday
morning after he was up so early prowling and bumping against
things in the dark, having to use the bathroom so many times a
night and scaring the life out of me and I told him, I told him please
stop, and we had words and he turned his back and walked away on
me and I didn't chase after him, since the stroke you know how he's
been, how selfish, how bad-tempered, sometimes we don't speak to
each other for days, I prepare the meals and we eat watching the
TV in the kitchen and we don't even acknowledge the other for how
long sometimes I don't know, it's like water seeping into water the
way time passes in this house, impossible to measure it. You're
young, you don't know. Someday, you'll know. So I haven't seen
your father in how long?—a day, a day and a half, the last time was
yesterday morning around seven I believe but it's the principle of
that man's behavior, Laurie, hiding from *me*, hiding from his own

wife, vexing me out of spite and cruelty and one time I found him in the basement behind the furnace and I almost had a heart attack and he laughed this mean way of his like coughing or clearing his throat and said, Isn't there any place I can have some privacy, do I have to crawl into my grave to have some privacy?—and this time I've called and called for him till my throat is raw and you can see how I'm shaking, he's hiding and listening and won't answer and now he knows you're here, I suppose it's some kind of victory for him.

Pausing, adding, with a swipe of her fingers against her eyes, *You* find him, then, he's *your* father!—you always loved him better than you did me!

Stung, you draw back staring at this distraught woman whose soft-creased face, bright-glittering eyes are suddenly foreign to you as a photographic negative of a familiar sight is foreign, the visual code reversed. You protest, Mother, what are you saying? Of course I never loved Dad more than you. Your mother says, turning away, You know what I'm saying. You and *him.*

And what if he has died, he has crawled away to die and it's Death she can't acknowledge.

You begin systematically to search the house. This ludicrous game of hide-and-seek. Your father is eighty-three years old and he's had a stroke characterized as mild a few years ago and several cardiac episodes characterized as minor and he walks stiffly, unsteadily, yet has been reluctant to use a cane, still less a walker. You know from your mother's reports that he has fallen several times and how serious these falls have been you don't know, though you do know that the elderly, falling, sometimes suffer concussions, lapses of consciousness so brief they don't know or remember afterward, nor can witnesses judge; these blows to the skull can cause pockets of blood to form in the brain. Forgetfulness, vertigo, amnesia, spells of irrationality and bad temper. Malaise, depression. Suicidal wishes. Then again, strange and alarming spells of childishness, giddiness, inappropriate playfulness. Your father, through his long life a man of a slightly sardonic, dry-edged dignity, a man of consummate intelligence, seems to be behaving, and to have behaved for some time, like no father you've known.

Your systematic search of the house room by room, absurd to begin with the downstairs rooms but your compulsion to be thorough is too ingrained to be overcome. Like father like daughter in this regard. Of course you're not thinking rationally.

Examining the living room, which is so much smaller, more modest in its dimensions than you recall, even the fieldstone fireplace and the beautiful gilt-framed Victorian mirror above the mantel; even the bay window so secretive, a place of refuge on rainy afternoons, hung with green velvet draw-drapes, now badly faded. Near the fireplace is your father's black leather lounge chair, there his table, lamp, stacks of *New England Journal of Medicine*, *Scientific American*, *National Geographic*, *The Guardian*, newspapers and paperback mystery books and crossword puzzles. The frayed leather hassock where after the initial stroke he'd carefully position his left leg, lifting it to set it in place, it had sensation he said but it seemed no longer his, like a stranger's leg grafted onto his body. And his foot bulky in double woolen socks ordered from L.L. Bean, for warmth. You stand staring at Dad's corner as if willing him to materialize, his wise pouched eyes, the shiny crown of his head, an eyelid drooping in a conspiratorial wink. Now you see me, now you don't!

Now through the dining room sadly pretentious as a room in a museum no one ever visits, still-gleaming silver candlestick holders though no candles in them, the massive cherrywood sideboard pushed out absurdly from the wall so you push it back, skidding along the hardwood floor. You switch off the chandelier and the room goes dark and through a window, beyond the opaque shadow of a wooded hill, the moon is so bright it hurts your eyes.

Madness. A whiff of it. Mixed with stale-lemony Old English furniture polish.

Your mother is in the kitchen, angry with you. Exactly why, you can't recall.

You avoid the kitchen, through the dining room and into the hall that runs the length of the house, the thought strikes you cold as a hand on the nape of your neck, *Of course he has died, that's why she is hiding, too.* You peer into the bathroom, where the light is on, steeling yourself to see your father, his body, his corpse, you note how, with what extravagance, the plastic shower curtain has been swept back as far as it will go on its runner, exposing the old, oversized tub with its old-fashioned shower nozzle and rusted drain: of course, the tub is empty. Bravely on then to the bedroom at the rear, you'd knock shyly at the door except the door is wide open and every light in the room is on, reflections vivid in every window. This is a spacious, handsomely decorated room, formerly a guest bedroom but for the past eight years your parents' bedroom, they'd moved down here after your father's first stroke; they've shared a bed for over fifty years. You, their only child, born late and now a woman of young middle age yourself, try to imagine such an abyss of time, such conjugal fidelity, and cannot; your mind dissolves in a vapor of unknowing. Fifty years!

Your mother has come up behind you, she's startled you, your nerves are bad. In an odd gesture, hurt, chagrined, tender yet emphatic, she smooths the crooked bedspread on the bed, adjusts a pillow, the pillow on *his* side of the bed. She says, He might just be watching us through the window there. Laughing at us both.

You glance around, the window is opaque with reflected light, you stoop to peer out the window seeing nothing except the hilly back yard. Your mother says, I meant this window here.

You see, above the bed, your parents' wedding picture. It's a photograph that has been softened, idealized with pastel crayon— your mother pertly pretty, with upswept pale hair, an unnatural glisten to her eyes effected by strategic dots of white; your father tall, grave and handsome, dark hair brushed in twin wings from his temples, his eyes, too, enhanced by white dots. A stiff, somewhat ludicrous formality, a wedding of mannequins. Now, no one gets married like that. No one marries for fifty years, the very prospect is absurd. From the perspective of your generation, it seems unnatural.

Even if he hates me, your mother is saying, now plumping up

both pillows, how could he do this to me? Humiliating me in front of my own daughter.

Mother, Dad doesn't hate you, Dad loves you, you know that. Don't be silly.

You aren't going to blame me for this, are you? It isn't fair to blame me.

Look, Dad is ill, obviously he isn't himself. When we find him we'll have to make an appointment for him to see the doctor. He—

He won't go, he won't even go for his regular checkup. I can't make him.

He will go. I'll see to it. He's ill, he isn't himself, he wouldn't do such a thing if he was himself.

Your mother laughs thinly, Oh wouldn't he!

He left no clue? No note?

If he did, Laurie, it wasn't for *me* to find.

Hardly conscious of what you're doing, where you're looking, you realize you're standing in front of the bedroom clothes closet whose door has been flung wide open. It's a large step-in closet smelling of mothballs. Even as an adult, a fully mature woman, you feel shy about seeing so bluntly your parents' things, disheveled clothes on hangers, a tumble of shoes on the floor, bedroom slippers. In the past, when you were a girl, no closet door would be open like this; indeed, you would not be in your parents' bedroom at such an hour of the day. It strikes you as a wild, horrific thought—obviously, your mother was looking for your father in that closet, switching on the overhead light and sweeping clothes aside as best she could, no doubt standing on tiptoe, panting with the effort. You have to resist the impulse to look inside the closet, too. Back in the shadows, out of sight. *How really clever of Dad it would be, how sly and cruel, to sneak back into a hiding place your mother had already searched.*

You adjust some of the clothes, pushing the hangers along the post, relieving the congestion, and your mother helps you, remarking that your father didn't take anything with him so far as she could discover, she'd gone through his things and she didn't think so which is why she believes he's in the house. Last she saw of him he was wearing his old brown wool bathrobe, not the nice navy-blue cashmere robe you gave him last Christmas, here's that robe hanging right here, over his flannel pajamas, wool socks on his feet and his old brown moccasins and he'd put on his overcoat to get the newspaper after they'd quarreled, she knew that without seeing him leave the house but he returned with the paper, read it in the kitchen and left the pages folded back the way he does, even with his eyesight so poor he has to have his precious newspapers, a waste of time your mother says, sniffing, I'd cancel them all if it was up to me.

Then what? you ask.

What? your mother says.

After Dad read the paper, then—?

How would *I* know? your mother says, blinking rapidly. I have my morning chores, I have calls to make, do you think I have nothing better to do than spy on some crazy old man?

All right, Mother, you say quietly. I understand.

Well—, she continues after a moment, his robe and pajamas are all he's wearing so if he's outside somewhere hiding he'll freeze to death and that will serve him right!—you know how fanatic he is about keeping his dentures clean, him worrying about germs like he does, well he didn't even take a toothbrush with him, wherever he went. And his pills, none of his pills, fourteen separate pills your father has to take every day of his life, well he left them all in the medicine cabinet, I've been checking. Not even his heart pills he *has* to take! Her voice trails off in disgust, dismay.

Maybe he took a handful with him, in his pocket, you suggest. How like a bright helpful child you are, providing a hypothesis to give your mother solace. And she almost smiles, considering.

Maybe! Wouldn't that be just like him!

You continue your methodical search of the house. It's ten o'clock, ten-thirty, eleven; your mother says she's going to bed, then changes her mind, she accompanies you for a while then turns back; you're dazed with exhaustion yet determined, if your father *is* here somewhere, to find him. Poking into closets, peering beneath stairs. *Is he watching through a window, is that his game?* You climb the stairs to the second floor, where your mother has left lights burning in the hall and in all the rooms. Dad? Daddy? you whisper. You imagine you hear low, throaty laughter—unless it's the wind. A distinct wind is beginning, out of the northeast; the temperature is dropping; there was a smell of snow in the air when you climbed out of the taxi and your quickened breath turned to steam and hastily you'd pressed bills into the driver's opened hand, Yes, here, please keep the change, thank you!—your gaze already captivated by the light, like a beacon, burning at the front door. *They have been waiting for me all these years. Mommy, Daddy, here I am!*

Here's your old room, your girlhood room, subtly altered. Your bed with its quilted floral coverlet, the gaily colored braided carpet, framed photographs of you on the walls—you as a baby, as a little girl, alone or with Mommy or Daddy, or other relatives; the touched-up studio portrait of you, a startlingly pretty if thin-faced girl of seventeen, in your white high school graduation gown. You don't remember that girl, quickly you look away from her, her eyes want to lock with yours but you resist. Your mother has been using this room as a sewing room, there's her old-fashioned Singer sewing machine with its foot treadle, boxes of needles, threads, buttons, a dressmaker's dummy. The door to the closet is open, your mother preceded you here, desperate in her search; you know no one is hiding inside but you can't stop yourself from peering in, holding your breath. Then you switch off the closet light, you switch off the lights in the room, shut the door and walk away.

All the rooms of the second floor, one by one examined, their lights extinguished. Then up the steep stairs to the unheated, drafty attic. The door stands open, lights are burning, bare overhead bulbs that make your eyes ache yet seem to give little illumination. Here, there's a smell that makes your nostrils pinch, it's dry, dusty, acrid, you walk cautiously through the attic keeping to the center where there's a wide prominent beam, as if you're fearful the floorboards elsewhere would collapse beneath your feet.

Stacks of your father's old medical journals, trunks unopened for decades, discarded items of furniture, and everywhere, scintillating in the light, cobwebs, some of them with living, fat spiders at their centers, exquisite filigree dotted with the carcasses of insects. How rapidly your heart is beating in this place, you must have expected to find your father here, collapsed on the floor, in a darkened corner where after a raging climb of two flights of stairs his heart gave out.

Dad?—Daddy? It's me.

Where are you hiding? Daddy?

When you return to the second floor, switching lights off behind you, shutting the attic up, you think you see, you're sure you've heard, your mother, waiting for you at the foot of the attic stairs murmuring something plaintive and querulous—but where is she? She isn't here. Mother? you say, raising your voice,—where are *you*? The absurdity of it, the fleeting possibility that you've lost your mother, too, in this cavernous house.

Mother? you call, not in apprehension but in mild vexation, and hurrying downstairs you turn your ankle on the bottom step and wince with pain. God *damn*.

Your mother is in the kitchen, she's put on a tea kettle. Her face is grim and sallow and lined but there's a glow of angry satisfaction in her eyes. You confess you've found nothing, no sign of him, she shrugs, You see? I told you so. You ask for a flashlight because next you're going into the basement and your mother indicates the drawer where such household paraphernalia are kept and bravely you take the flashlight into the basement, the door opens just off the kitchen and as you descend the shaky stairs you think *Here, he's got to be here,* you're excited for a moment, almost elated. *When he realizes who I am he will show himself. Of course!* Yet you're very frightened, too. Shivering and sweating. You think of Cleopatra, described by Plutarch, descending naked into a pit of adders to be killed.

The basement smells of damp concrete, something sweet-rancid, earthy. You shine the flashlight (its bulb is weak, like a single failing eye) behind the washer and dryer, you shine it behind the furnace recalling how your mother found your father there once, or claimed to have found him—of course, tonight, there's no one, nothing. With a trembling hand you shine the light into the farthest shadowed corners of the basement. Above you, around you, all is silent except for your quickened breathing.

The house will be sold, soon. This pretentious old house, its wide front veranda, its bay windows, turrets, Victorian fretwork, its excess of space. You'd never wondered, the child of the household, why your parents wanted so large a house, it had seemed quite natural to you until once you'd overheard your mother remarking to an aunt that she'd hoped to have a houseful of children but it had not worked out that way.

After the basement you put on your coat and step outside—the wind is cold, stinging your heated face—the moon still bright and mocking as a rounded, wondering eye—and cross to the garage, formerly a carriage house, enough space for three cars but your parents have only a single car, a decade-old Mercedes, parked there in the gloomy interior. Empty, of course. You shine the flashlight into the back seat. The thought occurs to you what if your father has locked himself into the trunk, is it possible he's that deranged, you don't have the car keys and so can't open the trunk but you press an ear against it murmuring Dad?—Daddy? You know that this is absurd, more than absurd it is futile. Toward the rear of the garage are stacks of lumber, sections of carpet, a six-foot roll of linoleum, shrewdly you shine the flashlight into these narrow spaces, tunnel-like spaces, reasoning that your mother would probably not have thought to look back here.

Outside, you walk about the back yard shining the flashlight at evergreens, leafless shrubs, trees, patches of grass shimmering with frost like powdered glass. They've let the rear of the property go, there are dead limbs that need to be pruned from these tall oaks, there's the weedy rectangle where your father used to have a vegetable garden, years ago. Another lifetime, really. Beyond the edge of the property, on the other side of a four-foot wall of fieldstone and stucco, is property owned by the township; a no-man's-

land of untended fields and woods; it's bordered by a county highway approximately a mile away where a few years ago a suburban
housing development sprang up. It's possible—you are beginning
to think it's probable—that your father climbed across this wall
where it's partly collapsed, fuming and hurt and determined to
punish your mother, and made his way into the woods; maybe he's
wandered off in the direction of the housing development. Who
would know, who would have seen him, who would find him if he
didn't want to be found? And if he's sick, if he's collapsed lying
helpless on the ground, how will he be found until daylight?

The moon is being eaten up by a bank of cloud filmy at first, then
solid, the light is rapidly waning and the first icy particles of snow
strike your face. Suppose your father has wandered off to die, is
that his prerogative?—or is he to be hunted down, captured, hauled
back home, saved?

You run back to the house, rush into the kitchen where your
mother has made tea—herbal tea, knowing you favor it—and seeing the look on your face she says quickly, While you were gone, I
think I heard him! and you say, You heard him? Dad? Where? and
your mother says, I heard him laughing, I think—somewhere close
by—maybe outside—outside the windows here. He knows you're
here, it's part of his game I guess, to get you here.

You heard Dad outside? Laughing?

Seeing your disbelieving eyes your mother says she's going to
bed. Let him stay outdoors all night and freeze if that's his game.

He couldn't have been back of the house, or looking in the windows here, you tell your mother carefully, because I would have
seen him.

He's anywhere he wants to be, *I* don't care. I'm exhausted and
I'm going to bed.

But, Mother, Dad isn't well—you must know that. Behaving like
this isn't like him—

Isn't it!

Mother, we're going to have to call the police.

Bitterly your mother says, It started with the police! He had
that blackout driving the car and they took his license away from

him and that was the beginning I think, he tried to get it rein-stated, he called a dozen people including our state congressman, he went to three or four doctors, they all told him it was too dan-gerous for him to drive anymore, at his age, with his medical prob-lems. So I have to drive us everywhere, unless I take a taxi. Three or four times a week I take the car out, I'm getting so I hate to drive, too, everybody drives so fast, especially at night. Sometimes Dad will ride with me when I go shopping but if he comes inside the store with me I'm a nervous wreck, he's so bossy and talks so loud and he's always ridiculing things or gets angry at the prices. Once in a while he'll come to church with me, and to the Senior Citizens' Center, but lately he hasn't, stays home and reads or pretends to be reading, sometimes he's out on the porch just staring at nothing and I have to touch his shoulder, give him a poke, before he even knows I'm there. The minister misses him at church, or says he does, you know how they are, always making the best of things, some of those people truly are Christians in their attitude, but Dad cuts himself off from such influences, wouldn't even come to church on Easter Sunday, it isn't worth the effort he said, let Jesus Christ come to *me*.

Your mother laughs, wipes at her eyes. Isn't that just like him—let Jesus Christ come to *me*.

Mother, you say gently, Dad might be stricken somewhere, he might need help. I'm going to call the police.

I told you, it's just one of his games!

Yes, it might have begun as a game, but something could have happened to him anyway. You haven't seen him in thirty-six hours—

Excitedly your mother takes hold of your wrist; squeezes it hard. Laurie, do you hear?

What?

That's him, laughing. Hear?

You stand very still, listening. Your heart is pounding and you hear blood pulsing in your ears and beyond that a faint whistling wail that's the wind, clearly the wind, an eerie high-pitched sound you remember from childhood when you'd wake at night feeling the house buffeted by wind like a ship at sea and you'd wonder if the walls, roofs, chimneys were built strong enough to withstand it, if your parents were strong enough to withstand it, and profound and alarming as this wonder must have been nonetheless you'd fall asleep in the midst of it and sink away, safe.

You try to hear laughter inside the wind. You want to hear laughter inside the wind. But there's nothing human in it.

Mother, I'm going to call the police. I'm sorry to upset you but this is an emergency.

Laurie, no! Not when he's hiding, watching us—gloating! I forbid you to go outside the family!

You stare at your mother, struck by this odd remark. *I forbid you to go outside the family.*

You say, reasonably, not wanting your mother to guess how upset you are, and impatient with her, But Dad has been missing for thirty-six hours, isn't that why you called me?

Not missing, I told you, he's *here*!

Mother, for God's sake—

Don't you dare raise your voice to me! I tell you he's *here* and we don't need the police or anybody else!

Your mother is so passionate, so convinced, to oppose her is tantamount to striking her. She's trembling so badly she has spilled tea onto her stiff quilted robe without noticing, and, biting your lower lip, repentant, you wipe at the wet spots, you apologize and tell her you'll look around outside a little more and if you can't find Dad there will be no choice about calling the police.

Tears shine on your mother's face. She sounds almost exuberant calling after you, I hope you'll be happy, then—you and *him*! I hope he's alive to bear the shame of it!

You return to the stone wall at the rear of the property. Wild gooseberry bushes have grown over everything, the tiny thorns catch in your clothes and pierce your bare skin. Icy-gritty particles of snow are being blown slantwise against your face. Something about the wall has snagged in your consciousness, you wonder if perhaps you've dreamt about this wall frequently over the years without ever clearly remembering. You shine the flashlight across the upright wall, the collapsed sections, the light lingers on what appears to be a groundhog's hole, then moves on. You're excited, it has something to do with the heightened wind and the laughter that's inaudible inside it and the snowfall, the first of the year. From this perspective, the old house is slightly downhill, not so large as it appears from the street; its steep roofs shine faintly with frost. The only lights now burning are in the kitchen and in the bedroom, where your mother has drawn the blind.

The four-foot fieldstone wall that once bounded all this property, even in the front along the sidewalk, is now badly dilapidated. Made of rock and stucco, built at the turn of the century when the house itself was built, it is, or was, an impressive wall; well maintained while you were growing up, then gradually neglected, and, here in the back, long since sunken in upon itself in sections as the earth froze and thawed, froze and thawed, dislodging the rocks, slowly pushing the wall from its foundation. Now the wall looks like a twisted outgrowth of the earth itself, much of it covered in briars and weeds. Some of the loose rocks, sunk in the earth, must weigh over one hundred pounds. Shining your flashlight from rock to rock, steeling yourself to see something you aren't prepared to see even as you prepare yourself to see it, a foot, a limp hand, the gleam of your father's scalp, you think of lunar rocks, rocks that have fallen from a great height, solitary and strange. What drew your eye previously is an opening of about a foot across, you search for a while before you locate it, your breath steaming as you stoop over it, considering. Here, the collapsed wall seems to have formed a kind of tunnel, a natural shelter; like an animal's burrow. To enter it an adult man would have to push, press, wriggle, squeeze like a snake. Yet it could be done. If passion, or desperation, were sufficient.

You draw your fingers across the jagged opening, you notice dried moss there, which looks scraped.

Dad? you whisper. Daddy? Please, Daddy?

Suddenly you lose control, you're convinced he's here, you kneel pulling frantic at the rocks that block your way, how heavy these rocks! how savage their resistance! stuck in the frozen soil, impacted in stucco, virtually immovable. Your fingernails break. Your fingers are scraped raw. Daddy, it's me! Daddy!—reaching now inside the opening as far as you can, groping blindly, eyes wild in your face, your fingertips brush against something not stone, not inanimate earth, you're certain, you're on hands and knees now pressing as close to the opening as you can, you've let the flashlight fall forgotten, no moon and almost total darkness and sobbing with the effort you reach inside feeling—what is it?—a hand, a foot— something swathed in thick wool—you hear nothing beyond your own hoarse, choking breath, Dad? Daddy? it's me, Laurie, you know who I am, don't you? you're leaning harder, and still harder, arm now sunken to its armpit, fingers blind and outstretched yearning for a touch, a grip, a handclasp.

The Hands

The telephone rang. It was 6 A.M. Windy dark outside. No one but the Old Man calling at such an hour.

In fact it's 5 A.M. where he is. Heart of the U.S. Static over the telephone line like the Plains wind that never ceases. But the Old Man's voice breaks through, for sure. Loud and aggrieved—accusing *I* never call *him*—but excited, too. Informing me of the new tenant in the apartment directly above his. Talk about coincidence!—this guy, total stranger, no name even on his mail-slot, looks enough like Eddy (my brother, older than me by six years, a loner in the family like the Old Man, last known address San Diego, CA) to be *his* brother. Boy, you better believe it! Coincidence.

Except: Mr. X is heavy-footed like he's taking out his vengeance on the floor (which happens to be the Old Man's ceiling, right?). Any God-damned hour of the day or night there's thumps—thuds—groans—shudders running down the walls like the beginning of an earthquake. Except nowhere else in the building (the Old Man makes inquiries) is affected. Worst of all, a true insult, is this Mr. X has some means of projecting himself so he is in my father's apartment. It's more than just "listening" like through a vent or a drainpipe, it's a means of projecting his thoughts so they are actually *in* my father's territory where they have no right to be.

At the present moment, which is why the Old Man is able to make this call a thousand miles away, the air is evidently free of the alien presence. The upstairs tenant is evidently *not home*.

If he was, says the Old Man in that way of his, angry, and self-pitying, I doubt I could pick up this receiver to dial!

But I'm really calling about the hands. *That's* the thing.

You know about the Ice Age?—in fact there were Ice *Ages*—plural!—two thousand feet of solid blue ice impacted in the very place (a valley carved out by a narrow river, northern Iowa) the Old Man is living. How and why the Ice Ages came to pass on earth there are the usual half-assed speculations. One guy says X, another guy says Y. For this they are made professors and get to yak on TV. Nor does the Bible touch it. The fact of mystery on earth. Whoever wrote the Bible, however many "scribes" were involved, never even caught on there was North America. They thought the earth was flat! So their opinions on anything including God are total bull. Anybody delves into the Holy Bible for reliable wisdom is a sap. Science is mankind's only hope. But it's a dying hope. You have to wonder. Fifty years ago there was a lot of squawk about controlling the weather, rainmaking to prevent droughts and famines. But now? Don't make me laugh. Hurricanes—tornados—earthquakes. Mississippi flooding. Drains backing up. Toilets. My plumbing in this dump, there's something clogging it so it backs up lately even after a shower. Some of this stuff, it looks like raw chicken parts, gristle and skin and broken bone, no blood, backed up in my toilet last week. Flushed and flushed the God-damned thing to no avail. Didn't call the landlord (that's another story!). Finally took the problem into my own hands fishing the revolting stuff out with a strip of wire mesh from the cellar. Almost gagged wrapping it in newspaper and disposed of it in the Dumpster behind the building and back upstairs there the God-damned toilet is backed up with more of the same!—so I fish it out again, big clumps of it, what I did was remove my glasses so I couldn't see this meat too clearly but I could still smell it, God damn. And the smell is still here, more or less.

Now it's my hands worrying me. They are "my" hands of course—I don't question that for a second—but there is a continual interference from a certain Mr. X. It registers itself as a numbness and/or tingling. For instance, if you're listening to a radio station especially in rural parts there may be a sudden weakness in the airwaves, after midnight I notice this a lot, and an alien radio station presses in. At first it's just a quick voice or a snatch of music or some asshole laughing. These fade, but you know it's the first sign. After that there's a steady deterioration. Until your original station is gone—kaput! And you're listening to teenage crap blaring your eardrums. The barbarian at the gate.

You kids today don't have a clue what that means. But my generation, *we* knew. Oh brother, did *we* know.

Anyway: the hands. I was telling you about the hands.

The coldness in them starting at the tips. Where the nails are purple like they're stained? God knows where it comes from. There's a numbness, all my fingers. While I was fishing the chicken scraps or whatever out of the toilet—it was real noticeable then. But then there's a thaw. I shut my eyes tight and count backward from one hundred and that seems to help. So when I return to myself it's like a long time has passed. And the hands have done something? Accomplished some task which makes them tired but leaves them excited, too. *They* know, but I don't. The hands, and this guy upstairs a dead ringer for Eddy.

The Old Man falls silent. Across the Plains there is a rampaging mindless wind. The tall grasses blown almost flat, undulating like waves.

Dad, why are you telling me these things? I have my own life now.

The Old Man takes this as an insult. Eh? he says. Why the hell did you call me, if you don't want the truth dangled before you?

But *you* called *me*, Dad.

Another pause. There's a sound of angry laughing, or the Old Man is clearing his sinuses. If I narrow my eyes I can almost see him, but I don't wish to do so. He's saying, on his way to slamming down the receiver in my ear, Jesus H. Christ! That's what I mean, then. You half-assed kids don't have a clue of the world. You don't have a clue, and you're too dumb to give a damn.

II

It was the most beautiful house I was ever to enter. Three storeys high, broad and gleaming pale-pink, made of sandstone, Uncle Rebhorn said, custom-designed and *his* design of course. They came to get me—Uncle Rebhorn, Aunt Elinor, my cousin Audrey who was my age and my cousin Darren who was three years older—one Sunday in July 1969. How excited I was, how special I felt, singled out for a visit to Uncle Rebhorn's house in Grosse Pointe Shores! I see the house shimmering before me and then I see emptiness, a strange rectangular blackness, and nothing.

For at the center of what happened on that Sunday many years ago is blackness.

I can remember what led to the blackness and what followed after it—not clearly, but to a degree, as, waking vague and stunned from a powerful dream, we retain shreds of the dream though we remain incapable of making them coalesce into a whole; nor can we "see" them as we'd seen them during the dream. So I can summon back a memory of the black rectangle and I can superimpose depth upon it—for it could not be flat, like a canvas—but I have to admit defeat, I can't "see" anything inside it. And this black rectangle is at the center of that Sunday in July 1969, and at the center of my girlhood.

Unless it was the end of my girlhood.

But how do I know, if I can't remember?

———

I was eleven years old. It was to be my first time ever—and it was to be the last time, too, though I didn't know it then—that I was brought by my father's older stepbrother Uncle Rebhorn to visit his new house and to go sailing on Lake St. Clair. Because of my cousin Audrey, who was like a sister of mine though I saw her rarely—I guessed this was why. Mommy told me, in a careful, neutral voice, that of course Audrey didn't have any friends, or Darren either. I asked why and Mommy said they just didn't, that's all. That's the price you pay for *moving up* too quickly in the world.

All our family lived in the Detroit suburb of Hamtramck and had lived there for a long time. Uncle Rebhorn too, until the age of eighteen when he left and now, how many years later, he was a rich man—president of Rebhorn Auto Supply, Inc., and he'd married a well-to-do Grosse Pointe woman—and built his big, beautiful new house on Lake St. Clair everybody in the family talked about but nobody had actually seen. (Unless they'd seen the house from the outside? Not my parents, who were too proud to stoop to such a maneuver, but other relatives were said to have driven all the way to Grosse Pointe Shores to gape at Uncle Rebhorn's pink mansion, as much as they could see of it from Buena Vista Drive. Uninvited, they dared not ring the buzzer at the wrought-iron gate shut and presumably locked at the foot of the drive.) Uncle Rebhorn whom I did not know at all had left Hamtramck far behind and was said to "scorn" his upbringing and his own family. There was a good deal of jealousy of course, and envy, but since everybody hoped secretly to be remembered by him sometime, and invited to share in his amazing good fortune—imagine, a millionaire in the family!—they were always sending cards, wedding invitations, announcements of birth and christenings and confirmations; sometimes even telegrams, since Uncle Rebhorn's telephone number was unlisted and even his brothers didn't know what it was. Daddy said, with that heavy, sullen droop to his voice we tried never to hear, if he wants to keep to himself that's fine, I can respect that. We'll keep to ourselves, too.

Then, out of nowhere, the invitation came to *me*. Just a telephone call from Aunt Elinor.

Mommy, who'd taken the call of course, and made the arrangements, didn't want me to stay overnight. Aunt Elinor had suggested this, for it was a long drive, between forty-five minutes and an hour, and she'd said that Audrey would be disappointed, but Mommy said no and that was that.

So, that Sunday, how vividly I can remember!—Uncle Rebhorn, Aunt Elinor, Audrey, and Darren came to get me in Uncle Rebhorn's shiny black Lincoln Continental, which rolled like a hearse up our street of woodframe asphalt-sided bungalows and drew stares from our neighbors. Daddy was gone—Daddy was not going to hang around, he said, on the chance of saying hello and maybe getting to shake hands with his stepbrother—but Mommy was with me, waiting at the front door when Uncle Rebhorn pulled up; but there were no words exchanged between Mommy and the Rebhorns, for Uncle Rebhorn merely tapped the car horn to signal their arrival, and Aunt Elinor, though she waved and smiled at Mommy, did not get out of the car, and made not the slightest gesture inviting Mommy to come out to speak with *her*. I ran breathless to the curb—I had a panicky vision of Uncle Rebhorn starting the big black car up and leaving me behind in Hamtramck—and climbed into the back seat, to sit beside Audrey. "Get in, hurry, we don't have all day," Uncle Rebhorn said in that gruff jovial cartoon voice some adults use with children, meant to be playful—or maybe not. Aunt Elinor cast me a frowning sort of smile over her shoulder and put her finger to her lips as if to indicate that I take Uncle Rebhorn's remark in silence, as naturally I would. My heart was hammering with excitement just to be in such a magnificent automobile!

How fascinating the drive from our familiar neighborhood into the city of Detroit where there were so many black people on the streets and many of them, glimpsing Uncle Rebhorn's Lincoln Continental, stared openly. We moved swiftly along Outer Drive and so to Eight Mile Road and east to Lake St. Clair where I had never been before, and I could not believe how beautiful everything

was once we turned onto Lakeshore Drive. Now it was my turn
to stare and stare. Such mansions on grassy hills facing the lake!
so many tall trees, so much leafy space! so much sky! (The sky
in Hamtramck was usually low and overcast and wrinkled like
soiled laundry.) And Lake St. Clair which was a deep rich aqua
like a painted lake! During most of the drive, Uncle Rebhorn was
talking, pointing out the mansions of wealthy, famous people—I
only remember "Ford"—"Dodge"—"Fisher"—"Wilson"—and Aunt
Elinor was nodding and murmuring inaudibly, and in the back seat,
silent and subdued, Audrey and Darren and I sat looking out the
tinted windows. I was a little hurt and disappointed that Audrey
seemed to be ignoring me, and sitting very stiffly beside me;
though I guessed that, with Uncle Rebhorn talking continuously,
and addressing his remarks to the entire car, Audrey did not want
to seem to interrupt him. Nor did Darren say a word to anyone.

At last, in Grosse Pointe Shores, we turned off Lakeshore Drive
onto a narrow, curving road called Buena Vista, where the mansions were smaller, though still mansions; Buena Vista led into a
cul-de-sac bordered by tall, massive oaks and elms. At the very
end, overlooking the lake, was Uncle Rebhorn's house—as I've
said, the most beautiful house I had ever seen up close, or would
ever enter. Made of that pale-pink glimmering sandstone, with a
graceful portico covered in English ivy, and four slender columns,
and dozens of latticed windows reflecting the sun like smiles, the
house looked like a storybook illustration. And beyond was the sky,
a pure cobalt blue except for thin wisps of cloud. Uncle Rebhorn
pressed a button in the dashboard of his car, and the wrought-iron
gate swung open—like nothing I'd ever seen before in real life. The
driveway too was like no driveway I knew, curving and dipping,
and made of rosy-pink gravel, exquisite as miniature seashells.
Tiny pebbles flew up beneath the car as Uncle Rebhorn drove in
and the gate swung miraculously shut behind us.

How lucky Audrey was to live here, I thought, gnawing at my
thumbnail as Mommy had told me a thousand times not to do. Oh I
would die to live in such a house, I thought.

Uncle Rebhorn seemed to have heard me. "*We* think so, yes

indeed," he said. To my embarrassment, he was watching me through the rearview mirror and seemed to be winking at me. His eyes glittered bright and teasing. Had I spoken out loud without meaning to?—I could feel my face burn.

Darren, squeezed against the farther armrest, made a sniggering, derisive noise. He had not so much as glanced at me when I climbed into the car and had been sulky during the drive so I felt that he did not like me. He was a fattish, flaccid-skinned boy who looked more like twelve than fourteen; he had Uncle Rebhorn's lard-colored complexion and full, drooping lips, but not Uncle Rebhorn's shrewd-glittering eyes, his were damp and close-set and mean. Whatever Darren meant by his snigger, Uncle Rebhorn heard it above the hum of the air conditioner—was there anything Uncle Rebhorn could not hear?—and said in a low, pleasant, warning voice, "Son, mind your manners! Or somebody else will mind them for you."

Darren protested, "I didn't say anything, sir. I—"

Quickly, Aunt Elinor intervened, "Darren."

"—I'm sorry, sir. I won't do it again."

Uncle Rebhorn chuckled as if he found this very funny and in some way preposterous. But by this time he had pulled the magnificent black car up in front of the portico of the house and switched off the ignition. "Here we are!"

But to enter Uncle Rebhorn's sandstone mansion, it was strange, and a little scary, how we had to crouch. And push and squeeze our shoulders through the doorway. Even Audrey and me, who were the smallest. As we approached the big front door which was made of carved wood, with a beautiful gleaming brass American eagle, its dimensions seemed to shrink; the closer we got, the smaller the door got, reversing the usual circumstances where of course as you approach an object it increases in size, or gives that illusion. "Girls, watch your head," Uncle Rebhorn cautioned, wagging his forefinger. He had a brusque laughing way of speaking as if most subjects were jokes or could be made to seem so by laughing. But his eyes bright as chips of glass were watchful and without humor.

How could this be?—Uncle Rebhorn's house that was so spacious-seeming on the outside was so cramped, and dark, and scary on the inside?

"Come on, come on! It's Sunday, it's the Sabbath, we haven't got all day!" Uncle Rebhorn cried, clapping his hands.

We were in a kind of tunnel, crowded together. There was a strong smell of something sharp and hurtful like ammonia; at first I couldn't breathe, and started to choke. Nobody paid any attention to me except Audrey who tugged at my wrist, whispering, "This way, June—don't make Daddy mad." Uncle Rebhorn led the way, followed by Darren, then Aunt Elinor, Audrey and me, walking on our haunches in a squatting position; the tunnel was too low for standing upright and you couldn't crawl on your hands and knees because the floor was littered with shards of glass. Why was it so dark? Where were the windows I'd seen from the outside? "Isn't this fun! We're so glad you could join us today, June!" Aunt Elinor murmured. How awkward it must have been for a woman like Aunt Elinor, so prettily dressed in a tulip-yellow summer knit suit, white high-heeled pumps and stockings, to make her way on her haunches in such a cramped space!—yet she did it uncomplaining, and with a smile.

Strands of cobweb brushed against my face. I was breathing so hard and in such a choppy way it sounded like sobbing which scared me because I knew Uncle Rebhorn would be offended. Several times Audrey squeezed my wrist so hard it hurt, cautioning me to be quiet; Aunt Elinor poked at me, too. Uncle Rebhorn was saying, cheerfully, "Who's hungry?—I'm starving," and again, in a louder voice, "Who's hungry?" and Darren echoed, "I'm starving!" and Uncle Rebhorn repeated bright and brassy as a TV commercial, "WHO'S HUNGRY?"and this time Aunt Elinor, Darren, Audrey, and I echoed in a chorus, "I'M STARVING!" Which was the correct reply, Uncle Rebhorn accepted it with a happy chuckle.

Now we were in a larger space, the tunnel had opened out onto a room crowded with cartons and barrels, stacks of lumber and tar pots, workmen's things scattered about. There were two windows in this room but they were small and square and crudely crisscrossed by strips of plywood; there were no windowpanes, only fluttering strips of cheap transparent plastic that blocked out most of the light. I could not stop shivering though Audrey pinched me hard, and cast me an anxious, angry look. Why, when it was a warm summer day outside, was it so cold inside Uncle Rebhorn's house? Needles of freezing air rose from the floorboards. The sharp ammonia odor was mixed with a smell of food cooking which made my stomach queasy. Uncle Rebhorn was criticizing Aunt Elinor in his joky angry way, saying she'd let things go a bit, hadn't she?—and Aunt Elinor was frightened, stammering and pressing her hand against her bosom, saying the interior decorator had promised everything would be in place by now. "Plenty of time for Christmas, eh?" Uncle Rebhorn said sarcastically. For some reason, both Darren and Audrey giggled.

Uncle Rebhorn had a thick, strong neck and his head swiveled alertly and his eyes swung onto you before you were prepared— those gleaming, glassy-glittering eyes. There was a glisten to the whites of Uncle Rebhorn's eyes I had never seen in anyone before and his pupils were dilated and black. He was a stocky man, he panted and made a snuffling noise, his wide nostrils flattened with deep, impatient inhalations. His pale skin was flushed, especially in the cheeks; there was a livid, feverish look to his face. He was dressed for Sunday in a red-plaid sport coat that fitted him tightly in the shoulders, and a white shirt with a necktie, and navy blue linen trousers that had picked up some cobwebs on our way in. Uncle Rebhorn had a glowing bald spot at the crown of his head over which he had carefully combed wetted strands of hair; his cheeks were bunched like muscles as he smiled. And smiled. How hard it was to look at Uncle Rebhorn, his eyes so glittering, and his *smile*—! When I try to remember him now miniature slices of blindness skid toward me ▇▇▇ in my vision, I have to blink carefully to regain my full sight. And why am I shivering, I must put an end to such neurotic behavior, what other purpose to this memoir?—what other purpose to any effort of the retrieval of memory that gives such pain?

Uncle Rebhorn chuckled deep in his throat and wagged a

forefinger at me, "Naughty girl, I know what *you're* thinking," he said, and at once my face burned, I could feel my freckles standing out like hot inflamed pimples, though I did not know what he meant. Audrey, beside me, giggled again nervously, and Uncle Rebhorn shook his forefinger at her, too, "And you, honeybunch—for sure, Daddy knows *you*." He made a sudden motion at us the way one might gesture at a cowering dog to further frighten it, or to mock its fear; when, clutching at each other, Audrey and I flinched away, Uncle Rebhorn roared with laughter, raising his bushy eyebrows as if he was puzzled, and hurt. "Mmmmm girls, you don't think I'm going to hit you, do you?"

Quickly Audrey stammered, "Oh no, Daddy—*no.*"

I was so frightened I could not speak at all. I tried to hide behind Audrey, who was shivering as badly as I was.

"You *don't* think I'm going to hit you, eh?" Uncle Rebhorn said, more menacingly; he swung his fist playfully in my direction and a strand of hair caught in his signet ring and I squealed with pain which made him laugh, and relent a little. Watching me, Darren and Audrey and even Aunt Elinor laughed. Aunt Elinor tidied my hair and again pressed a finger to her lips as if in warning.

I am not a naughty girl I wanted to protest and now too *I am not to blame.*

For Sunday dinner we sat on packing cases and ate from planks balanced across two sawhorses. A dwarfish olive-skinned woman with a single fierce eyebrow waited on us, wearing a white rayon uniform and a hairnet. She set plates down before us sulkily, though with Uncle Rebhorn, who kept up a steady teasing banter with her, calling her "honey" and "sweetheart," she did exchange a smile. Aunt Elinor pretended to notice nothing, encouraging Audrey and me to eat. The dwarf-woman glanced at me with a look of contempt, guessing I was a poor relation I suppose, her dark eyes raked me like a razor.

Uncle Rebhorn and Darren ate hungrily. Father and son hunched over the improvised table in the same posture, bringing their faces close to their plates and, chewing, turning their heads slightly

to the sides, eyes moist with pleasure. "Mmmmm!—good," Uncle
Rebhorn declared. And Darren echoed, "—*good.*" Aunt Elinor and
Audrey were picking at their food, managing to eat some of it, but I
was nauseated and terrified of being sick to my stomach. The food
was lukewarm, served in plastic containers. There were coarse
slabs of tough, bright pink meat curling at the edges and leaking
blood, and puddles of corn pudding, corn kernels and slices of
onion and green pepper in a runny pale sauce like pus. Uncle Rebhorn gazed up from his plate, his eyes soft at first, then regaining
some of their glassy glitter when he saw how little his wife and
daughter and niece had eaten. "Say, what's up? 'Waste not, want
not.' Remember"—he reached over and jabbed my shoulder with
his fork—"this is the Sabbath, and keep it holy. Eh?"

Aunt Elinor smiled encouragingly at me. Her lipstick was
crimson-pink and glossy, a permanent smile; her hair was a shining
pale blond like a helmet. She wore pretty pale-pink pearls in her
ears and a matching necklace around her neck. In the car, she had
seemed younger than my mother, but now, close up, I could see
hairline creases in her skin, or actual cracks, as in glazed pottery;
there was something out of focus in her eyes though she was looking directly at me. "June, dear, there is a hunger beyond hunger,"
she said softly, "—and this is the hunger that must be reached."

Uncle Rebhorn added, emphatically, "And we're Americans. Remember *that.*"

Somehow, I managed to eat what was on my plate. *I am not a
naughty girl but a good girl: see!*

For dessert, the dwarf-woman dropped bowls in front of us containing a quivering amber jelly. I thought it might be apple jelly,
apple jelly with cinnamon, and my mouth watered in anticipation,
we were to eat with spoons but my spoon wasn't sharp enough to
cut into the jelly; and the jelly quivered harder, and wriggled in my
bowl. Seeing the look on my face, Uncle Rebhorn asked pleasantly,
"What's wrong now, Junie?" and I mumbled, "—I don't know, sir,"
and Uncle Rebhorn chuckled, and said, "Hmmmm! You don't think
your dessert is a *jellyfish*, do you?"—roaring with delight, as the
others laughed, less forcefully, with him.

For that was exactly what it was: a jellyfish. Each of us had one, in our bowls. Warm and pulsing with life and fear radiating from it like raw nerves.

███████ ██████ flicking toward me, slivers of blindness. Unless fissures in the air itself?—fibrillations like those at the onset of sleep the way dreams begin to skid toward you—at you—into you—and there is no escape for the dream *is* you.

Yes I would like to cease my memoir here. I am not accustomed to writing, to selecting words with such care. When I speak, I often stammer but there is a comfort in that—nobody knows, what comfort!—for you hold back what you must say, hold it back until it is fully your own and cannot surprise you. *I am not to blame, I am not deserving of hurt neither then nor now* but do I believe this, even if I can succeed in making you believe it?

How can an experience belong to you if you cannot remember it? That is the extent of what I wish to know. If I cannot remember it, how then can I summon it back to comprehend it, still less to change it. *And why am I shivering, when the sun today is poison-hot burning through the foliage dry and crackling as papier-mâché yet I keep shivering shivering shivering if there is a God in heaven please forgive me.*

After Sunday dinner we were to go sailing. Uncle Rebhorn had a beautiful white sailboat bobbing at the end of a dock, out there in the lake which was a rich deep aqua-blue scintillating with light. On Lake St. Clair on this breezy summer afternoon there were many sailboats, speedboats, yachts. I had stared at them in wondering admiration as we'd driven along the Lakeshore Drive. What a dazzling sight like nothing in Hamtramck!

First, though, we had to change our clothes. All of us, said Uncle Rebhorn, have to change into bathing suits.

Audrey and I changed in a dark cubbyhole beneath a stairway. This was Audrey's room and nobody was supposed to come inside to disturb us but the door was pushing inward and Audrey whimpered, "No, no Daddy," laughing nervously and trying to hold the door shut with her arm. I was a shy child, when I had to change for gym class at school I turned my back to the other girls and changed as quickly as I could, even showing my panties to another girl was embarrassing to me, my face burned with a strange wild heat. Uncle Rebhorn was on the other side of the door, we could hear his harsh labored breathing. His voice was light, though, when he asked, "Hmmmm—d'you naughty little girls need any help getting your panties down? or your bathing suits on?" "No, Daddy, please," Audrey said. Her eyes were wide and stark in her face and she seemed not aware of me any longer but in a space of her own, trembling, hunched over. I was scared, too, but thinking why don't we joke with Uncle Rebhorn, he wants us to joke with him, that's the kind of man he is, what harm could he do us?—the most any adult had ever done to me by the age of eleven was Grandpa tickling me a little too hard so I'd screamed with laughter and kicked but that was years ago when I'd been a baby practically, and while I had not liked being tickled it was nothing truly painful or scary—was it? I tried to joke with my uncle through the door, I was giggling saying, "No no no, you stay out of here, Uncle Rebhorn! We don't need your help no we don't!" There was a moment's silence, then Uncle Rebhorn chuckled appreciatively, but there came then suddenly the sound of Aunt Elinor's raised voice, and we heard a sharp slap, and a cry, a female cry immediately cut off. And the door ceased its inward movement, and Audrey shoved me whispering, "Hurry up! You dumb dope, hurry up!" So quickly—safely—we changed into our bathing suits.

It was a surprise, how by chance Audrey's and my bathing suits looked alike, and us like twin sisters in them: both were pretty shades of pink, with elasticized tops that fitted tight over our tiny, flat breasts. Mine had emerald green sea horses sewn onto the bodice and Audrey's had little ruffles, the suggestion of a skirt.

Seeing my face, which must have shown hurt, Audrey hugged me with her thin, cold arms. I thought she would say how much she liked me, I was her favorite cousin, she was happy to see me—but she didn't say anything at all.

Beyond the door Uncle Rebhorn was shouting and clapping his hands.

"C'mon move your sweet little asses! Chop-chop! Time's a-wastin! There'll be hell to pay if we've lost the sun!"

Audrey and I crept out in our bathing suits and Aunt Elinor grabbed us by the hands making an annoyed "tsking" sound and pulling us hurriedly along. We had to push our way out of a small doorway—no more than an opening, a hole, in the wall—and then we were outside, on the back lawn of Uncle Rebhorn's property. What had seemed like lush green grass from a distance was synthetic grass, the kind you see laid out in flat strips on pavement. The hill was steep down to the dock, as if a giant hand was lifting it behind us, making us scramble. Uncle Rebhorn and Darren were trotting ahead, in matching swim trunks—gold trimmed in blue. Aunt Elinor had changed into a single-piece white satin bathing suit that exposed her bony shoulders and sunken chest, it was shocking to see her. She called out to Uncle Rebhorn that she wasn't feeling well—the sun had given her a migraine headache—sailing would make the headache worse—could she be excused?—but Uncle Rebhorn shouted over his shoulder, "You're coming with us, God damn you! Why did we buy this frigging sailboat except to enjoy it?" Aunt Elinor winced, and murmured, "Yes, dear," and Uncle Rebhorn said, snorting, with a wink at Audrey and me, "Hmmm! It better be 'yes, dear,' you stupid cow-cunt."

By the time we crawled out onto the deck of the sailboat a chill wind had come up, and in fact the sun was disappearing like something being sucked down a drain. It was more like November than July, the sky heavy with clouds like stained concrete. Uncle Rebhorn said sullenly, "—bought this frigging sailboat to enjoy it for God's sake—for the family and that means *all the family*." The sailboat was lurching in the choppy water like a living, frantic thing as Uncle Rebhorn loosed us from the dock and set sail. "First mate! Look sharp! Where the hell are you, boy? Move your ass!"—Uncle Rebhorn kept up a constant barrage of commands at poor Darren who scampered to obey them, yanking at ropes that slipped from his fingers, trying to swing the heavy, sodden mainsail around. The wind seemed to come from several directions at once and the sails flapped and whipped helplessly. Darren did his best but he was clumsy and ill-coordinated and terrified of his father. His pudgy face had turned ashen, and his eyes darted wildly about; his gold swim trunks, which were made of a shiny material like rayon, fitted him so tightly a loose belt of fat protruded over the waistband and jiggled comically as, desperate to follow Uncle Rebhorn's instructions, Darren fell to one knee, pushed himself up, slipped and fell again, this time onto his belly on the slippery deck. Uncle Rebhorn, naked but for his swimming trunks and a visored sailor's cap jammed onto his head, shouted mercilessly, "Son, get *up*. Get that frigging sail to the wind or it's *mutiny*!"

The sailboat was now about thirty feet from the safety of the dock, careening and lurching in the water, which was nothing like the painted-aqua water I had seen from shore; it was dark, metallic-gray and greasy, and very cold. Winds howled about us. There was no cabin in the sailboat, all was exposed, and Uncle Rebhorn had taken the only seat. I was terrified the sailboat would sink, or I would be swept off to drown in the water by wild, frothy waves washing across the deck. I had never been in any boat except rowboats with my parents in the Hamtramck Park lagoon. "Isn't this fun? Isn't it! Sailing is the most exciting—" Aunt Elinor shouted at me, with her wide fixed smile, but Uncle Rebhorn, seeing my white, pinched face, interrupted, "Nobody's going to drown today, least of all *you*. Ungrateful little brat!"

Aunt Elinor poked me, and smiled, pressing a finger to her lips. Of course, Uncle Rebhorn was just teasing.

For a few minutes it seemed as if the winds were filling our sails in the right way for the boat moved in a single unswerving direction. Darren was holding for dear life to a rope, to keep the mainsail steady. Then suddenly a dazzling white yacht sped by us, three times the size of Uncle Rebhorn's boat, dreamlike out of the flying spray, and in its wake Uncle Rebhorn's boat shuddered and lurched; there was a piercing, derisive sound of a horn—too late; the prow of the sailboat went under, freezing waves washed across the deck, the boat rocked crazily. I'd lost sight of Audrey and Aunt

Elinor and was clutching a length of frayed rope with both hands, to keep myself from being swept overboard. How I whimpered with fear and pain! *This is your punishment, now you know you must be bad.* Uncle Rebhorn crouched at the prow of the boat, his eyes glittering in his flushed face, screaming commands at Darren who couldn't move fast enough to prevent the mainsail from suddenly swinging around, skimming over my head and knocking Darren into the water.

Uncle Rebhorn yelled, "Son! Son!" With a hook at the end of a long wooden pole he fished about in the sudsy waves for my cousin, who sank like a bundle of sodden laundry; then surfaced again as a wave struck him from beneath and buoyed him upward; then sank again, this time beneath the lurching boat, his arms and legs flailing. I stared aghast, clutching at my rope. Audrey and Aunt Elinor were somewhere behind me, crying, "Help! help!" Uncle Rebhorn ignored them, cursing as he scrambled to the other side of the boat, and swiping the hook in the water until he snagged something and, blood vessels prominent as angry worms in his face, hauled Darren out of the water and onto the swaying deck. The hook had caught my cousin in the armpit, and streams of blood ran down his side. Was Darren alive?—I stared, I could not tell. Aunt Elinor was screaming hysterically. With deft, rough hands Uncle Rebhorn laid his son on his back, like a fat, pale fish, and stretched the boy's arms and legs out, and straddled Darren's hips and began to rock in a quickened rhythmic movement and to squeeze his rib cage, *squeeze and release! squeeze and release!* until driblets of foamy water and vomit began to be expelled from Darren's mouth, and, gasping and choking, the boy was breathing again. Tears of rage and sorrow streaked Uncle Rebhorn's flushed face. "You disappoint me, son! Son, you disappoint me! I, your dad who gave you life—you disappoint me!"

A sudden prankish gust of wind lifted Uncle Rebhorn's sailor cap off his head and sent it flying and spinning out into the misty depths of Lake St. Clair.

———

I have been counseled not to retrieve the past where it is ▮▮▮ blocked by ▮▮▮ like those frequent attacks of "visual impairment" (*not* blindness, the neurologist insists) but have I not a right to my own memories? to my own past? Why should that right be taken from me?

What are you frightened of, Mother, my children ask me, sometimes in merriment, what are *you* frightened of?—as if anything truly significant, truly frightening, could have happened, or could have been imagined to have happened, to me.

So I joke with them, I tease them saying, "Maybe—*you!*"

For in giving birth to them I suffered ▮▮▮ slivers of ▮▮▮ too, which for the most part I have forgotten ▮▮▮ as all wounds heal and pain is lost in time—isn't it?

What happened on that lost Sunday in July 1969 in Uncle Rebhorn's house in Grosse Pointe Shores is a true mystery never comprehended by the very person (myself) who experienced it. For at the center is an emptiness ▮▮▮ black rectangular emptiness ▮▮▮ skidding toward me like a fracturing of the air *and it is ticklish too, my shivering turns convulsive on the brink of wild leaping laughter.* I recall the relief that my cousin Darren did not drown and I recall the relief that we returned to the dock which was swaying and rotted but did not collapse, held firm as Uncle Rebhorn cast a rope noose to secure the boat. I know that we returned breathless and excited from our outing on Lake St. Clair and that Aunt Elinor said it was too bad no snapshots had been taken to commemorate my visit, and Uncle Rebhorn asked where the Polaroid camera was, why did Aunt Elinor never remember it for God's sake, their lives and happy times flying by and nobody recording them. I know that we entered the house and once again in the dark cubbyhole that was my cousin Audrey's room beneath the stairs we were changing frantically from our bathing suits which were soaking wet into our dry clothes and this time Aunt Elinor, still less Audrey, could not prevent the door from pushing open ▮▮▮ crying "Daddy, no!" and "No, please, Daddy!" until I was crying too and laughing screaming as a man's rough fingers ▮▮▮ ran over my bare ribs bruising ▮▮▮

the frizzy-wiry hairs of his chest and belly tickling my face until
what was beneath us which I had believed to be a floor fell away
suddenly ████████ dissolving like ███████ water *I was not crying, I
was not fighting I was a good girl: see?* ██████████████████████
██
████████████████████████████████████ waking then like floating
to the surface of a dream as again the tiny pink pebbles exquisite
as seashells were being thrown up beneath the chassis of the shiny
black car, and Uncle Rebhorn rosy-faced and fresh from his shower
in crisp sport shirt, Bermuda shorts and sandals drove me the long
long distance back to Hamtramck away from Lake St. Clair and
the mansions like castles on their grassy hills, on this return ride
nobody else was with us, not Audrey, not Aunt Elinor, not Darren,
only Uncle Rebhorn and me, his favorite niece he said, beside him
in the passenger's seat in the air-conditioned cool inside the tinted
windows through which, at the foot of the graveled drive, as the
wrought-iron gate swung open by magic, I squinted back with my
inflamed eyes at the luminous sandstone mansion with the latticed
windows, the portico covered in English ivy, the slender columns
like something in a children's storybook, it was the most beautiful
house I had ever seen up close, or was ever to enter in my life. And
nothing would change that.

Labor Day

At the very end of summer, our neighbors at the top of Colonel's Lane have lost one of their children.

A missing child! Seven-year-old Timmy Bonnard. He was last seen Saturday afternoon around three o'clock running along the beach headed for the steep twenty-foot wooden steps to the bluff and now it is a day and a half later and he has not returned. We have all studied the child's face in enlarged photocopies of family snapshots and we have answered questions put to us by Mahasset County Sheriff's deputies and we have even helped in the search, if not so extensively as some of the younger, more vigorous folks. Too restless and too nervous to stay close to home, or work in the garden, we've been tramping, like many others, along the shore and out into the dunes, peering anxiously at grasses and cattails whipping in the wind, skeletal scattering of newspaper and debris, crevices where a small body might be hidden. *Is that*—? the eye leaps to a frightened conclusion even as the mind realizes *But no.*

The Mahasset Peninsula is so narrow, and only eight miles long counting our bridges, it can only be a matter of time until the child is found. If the child is still in the area.

In their uniforms they came to search our property. All along Colonel's Lane they searched. Asking had we seen Timmy Bonnard, had we seen any strangers in the area, had we witnessed any suspicious behavior, had we heard anything, did we know anything. Frowning and methodical and polite enough, maybe a little brusque, holstered pistols on their hips and their two-way radios squawking and their squad cars blocking the lane. Poking around in garages, barns, decaying rabbit hutches, our toolshed and even the compost heap at the bottom of the garden! Don't know what you'd be finding there, I said, you can see nothing's been dug or stirred, and one of them half my age hardly bothering to look at me through his dark-tinted glasses, said, We'll be the judge of that, mister.

Always when we'd see the Bonnards, a family so large and so gregarious in their socializing we couldn't begin to count them, nor keep track of their children or their children's friends, we'd be struck by their good spirits. Most of them are blond, athletic-looking, darkly tanned by summer, smiling. Always smiling! Always shouting to one another in voices that break easily into laughter. They began summering here six or seven years ago, purchasing the ten-bedroom shingled saltbox the color of stained ivory on the highest point of the promontory above the beach. Colonel Judson's old house built in 1914 and one of the showplaces of the area, it's said. Though we've never been inside. All summer the lane is busy with the Bonnards' motor vehicles and those of their many guests—in August, when we went without rain for weeks, the dust would hardly settle from one of their hard-driven cars or station wagons or cycles before another, speeding back to the village, stirred it up again. *H'lo!* they're in the habit of calling, waving and grinning at us if we're outdoors, in the garden, even young people, complete strangers to us, call out *H'lo!* with happy familiar smiles. You'd think almost there was a taunt or a jeer in such familiarity from strangers, but that has never been the case I am sure.

Of course, even with it painted in careful black letters on our mailbox that's surrounded by marigolds, the Bonnards have no reason to know our name.

Starting around mid-June, the population on the peninsula swells to approximately nine hundred people; after Labor Day, it rapidly shrinks back to about four hundred. You get to think of it like the tide—high, low—in, out—except on a seasonal rhythm. At the top of Colonel's Lane well-to-do summer people from inland have bought up all the old houses fronting the ocean; at this end, near East Main Street, which is where we live, in a winterized Cape Cod, there are all year-round residents.

Natives, we hear ourselves called.

Like the Borneo Islanders? like the New Guinea headhunters and cannibals? I always ask. Tongue-in-cheek, only joking. But I make my point.

It was Saturday just past six, we'd only sat down to supper when the Bonnards came to our front door, the tall blond mother in white T-shirt and white shorts and the tall ashy-haired father in sailing clothes and one of the teenaged boys, *We're sorry to disturb you but have you seen our son? our son Timmy?* They must have been working their way along the lane, ocean-side down, beginning by this time to be worried, or more than worried, their strained smiles trying to be polite for these are well-bred moneyed people, no mistaking that, even in a time of stress, their eyes snatching at ours but of course we could not help them, we never notice children much, hadn't been on the beach in days, no, sorry, truly sorry, we wish we could help you but we can't.

Later, of course, we heard the news the little boy is *missing.* And others came by, police, a search party, there's an agitation of the air and a damp whining meanness to the wind off the Atlantic— you look up startled thinking you're hearing a siren but no, it's the wind.

Kidnapping? An abduction? A child molester, sexual deviant, "serial killer"—everywhere there are rumors, even over our local radio station there are rumors reported but no official news, no developments in the case or at least none that the general public has been allowed to know.

And in town, in the Village Food Mart, in Hamrack's Drugs, and yesterday at church—everybody is discussing *it.* This terrible thing. Have they found that poor child yet? Why can't the police do more? What a sweet darling boy, what a nightmare for the family, you see it on TV all the time and read about it, these kinds of sex perverts, these child-killers out on parole, and then they plead insanity and get acquitted, of course Timmy Bonnard might just be lost, maybe he wandered off and is lost and he'll be found, poor innocent child you just have to pray and pray it will turn out well.

But we wouldn't want to trade places with the Bonnards right now, would you?

This morning of Labor Day started off fine—sharp bright sunshine and temperature in the mid-sixties but then around noon the wind shifted, out of the northeast now and rain-laden. Too restless to stay inside so I tramped down to the beach. More people out than you'd imagine and it always surprises me, but of course these are summer people and some of them visiting just for the weekend so they have to get their money's worth. Staring at the white-capped frothy waves tall as human figures walking upright, then breaking, slapping the hard-packed sand with that sound of anger, outrage. And all along the beach especially toward the outer banks more of those damned jellyfish and some tentacled creatures stunned and motionless and the sandpipers hopping and pecking among them. And the wind taking your breath away.

Labor Day. September 6. Already it feels like autumn. Every year it happens so fast, you never get used to it, as soon as September comes on the calendar the weather will turn. A cold wet wind like it's blowing out of the future and the sun setting so much earlier day by day. How many hours the Bonnard boy has been missing, I figure about forty-eight. Not much chance of him being alive. Nobody wants to say so out loud but that's probably it. And probably the body is nowhere around here, it's hundreds of miles away buried in some shallow grave or dumped beside an interstate and maybe they will never find it.

No Labor Day beach parties today, with this weather. None of the blond Bonnards and their relatives and friends some of them near-naked in their skimpy suits running squealing into that water so cold only a damned fool would dip a toe into it.

No, my wife and I keep to ourselves. No, we have not. No, we wish we could but we cannot. Yesterday at the First Congregational we all prayed to God Timmy Bonnard will be found safe and sound but we keep to ourselves. Never so much as set a foot inside that grand house up there in the thirty-two years we've lived on Colonel's Lane, and never will. All these years and this is the first time in memory such a thing has happened around here, such a terrible thing, my wife's hands are shaking and up and down the lane there's too much traffic. If it isn't the Bonnards now it's the police. And sure to be somebody knocking at the door scaring the life out of us. None of these folks knowing our name until now the child is missing, taking the name off our mailbox like they had a right.

No, we keep to ourselves. We are sorry but we just can't help you. Lifting my hands which are trembling, palms up. Empty.

My wife has gone to bed taking her medication before the eleven o'clock news. The drizzle has turned to a hard pelting rain.

Flashlight in hand I descend into the cellar, cautious on the stairs which are starting to rot. It isn't a full cellar, just a space beneath the main part of the house. Our furnace and utilities are located upstairs at the rear though we're on high enough ground we don't get much flooding nor even seepage except if there's a serious storm. I shine the flashlight into the corners of the cellar, skimming the light along the ceiling beams where strands of cobweb are stirring like somebody has just passed through. The beams are low, and you can't stand up too well in here, or don't want to. It's drafty here, and smells of damp cement and earth and mouse droppings and God knows what all else, we never come down here. There's the old fruit cellar my wife used to stock, but no more. I tug at the door, it's hard to open it's so warped, and inside, the dusty shelves, a half dozen old canning jars and rusted cannisters and rubber rings it looks like the mice have chewed. The fruit cellar is only about the size of a step-in closet. All this should be cleaned out, I'm thinking. Maybe next spring. I squat, grunting at the pain in my knees, and peer beneath the shelves, shining the flashlight into the corners. Cobwebs here too, thick with insect carcasses, and live

spiders scurrying from the light. This would be a place, in the earth
here if you could dig it up then flatten it again with the back of a
shovel for instance leaving no trace.

No one here, nothing. But you never know.

The Collector of Hearts

Funny! You never met me, don't know my name but you're holding me in your hand. Turning me in your fingers, peering at what remains of me saying *This is—ivory? Carved? It's so beautiful.*

Old man must've been fifty, dyed muskrat-color mustache and a bald head clean and shiny as chrome, quiet-spoken but you know you wouldn't want to mess with him; that strong Daddy-type that's been my weakness. There he was showing me into his house. His family house he said. But his family was deceased. He was the only survivor—"Unmarried, and without heirs. A classic story." I wasn't listening, my eyes were darting every which way taking in this big old mildew-smelling house with high-ceiling rooms going off in all directions and a staircase off the front vestibule rising up to— what? I swear, there wasn't nothing beyond the landing but shadows. Like somebody'd been drawing it in, got impatient and erased it with a dirty eraser so it's all smudged.

I thought I'd better say something so I said, making a joke, "Well. There's a whole lot of kids, nobody needs more." I got this nervous habit giggling after practically every remark I make whether funny or otherwise and cracking my gum. Usually I get some response like "Cool" or if it's a guy, laughing loud and appreciative.

This old Judge Whosis made some mumble like he was trying
not to scold me for the gum. Touching my shoulder just with his fingertips like he was fearful of burning himself. Saying, "My collection of hearts." We were in a room of dark carved-wood walls, a
black marble fireplace taking up half of one wall, a stained old mirror above the fireplace where my head floated like that was all
it was—a head, no shoulders or body beneath. I liked my wet-
looking red lips and my hair was an Afro so pale and soft you
almost couldn't say what color it was, but I was surprised how
crisscrossed my forehead was from frowning (which I hadn't realized I'd been doing) and I couldn't seem to see my eyes, it was
weird.

"Wow." I giggled, and cracked my gum. "Wow. Cool."

It *was* cool: these glittery things, more than I could've counted,
on the fireplace mantel, on a long skinny table of some fine old
wood that's a little warped, on a round table where there's a fringe-
shaded lamp the old guy switches on, all over. Not like valentine
hearts—that kind of heart-shape, nor like the gold (maybe it's
fake-gold) locket I wear for good luck on a thin chain swinging between my bare breasts in my little zebra-stripe purple tank top,
but artistic-shaped hearts you could say, more like what you'd
imagine a real heart to look like. For isn't a heart an actual muscle?
There was a crystal heart on the fireplace mantel with facets
so gleaming-bright you almost couldn't figure out what it was.
There was a shiny grape-colored ceramic heart with a hint of actual
veins or arteries. Some baked clay earthy-colored hearts, beautiful shades of dark red, rust-brown, mahogany-brown streaked with
pale green. There was one spiky iron heart. There was one delicately engraved silver heart (but the engraved words were in some
language I didn't know, ODI ET AMO) and there was one heavy
gold heart gleaming like a little sun. On a table, eight same-sized
hearts carved of some cold-looking stony material I guess must've
been marble—cream-colored, powder-gray, dark-purple, midnight-
blue, white streaked with gray, pink like the inside of a wet mouth,
milky-black and pure pitch-black. There was a heart so beautiful,
dusty-rose-brown like my skin and glittering with mica like gold

dust or sparks, I drew in my breath and stood staring for the long-est time. All I could think to say was, "Wow. Cool." And cracked my gum real thoughtful.

Most of these hearts, as the old guy called them, you wouldn't probably identify as hearts if he hadn't said. They were about the size and shape of a man's clenched fist. I wondered where he got them, some special art store? antique store? I seemed to know you couldn't just walk into a department store like say Macy's and make such a purchase. Some of them must've been real expen-sive, too.

I'd been thinking (I mean, you always think in such ways, in-vited into a stranger's house) there might be something for me to pocket, the right-size item that can find its way into your pocket without you even knowing, exactly, but for sure these items of "the heart collection" were too heavy and clunky-size, but I didn't feel too disappointed, I was so curious and it's my natural nature to ask questions. "Does this open? Is that how it was made, in fit-together halves?" I lifted this coppery shining heart using both hands, it was heavier than you'd expect, and would've examined the underside where there was a fine seam, but Judge Whosis says real quick and kind of scared, "Please! Don't touch." And takes it from me with his trembly fingers and sets it back exactly on the spot it'd been on the table—in the very dust-outline where you could figure it'd been sitting for a long time.

But he was smiling.

We'd met in his courtroom just that morning. He was Judge ⸺ of the county criminal court. (I have to admit I'd forgot his name almost as soon as I heard it. Always I had this bad habit, names sailed past me if they were the names of somebody old, ugly, boring or what you'd call official like teachers, church people, social work-ers, public defenders, judges.) A straggly troop of us, six or seven females, the youngest being me, was brought over from the women's detention next door to the third floor of the moldy old county courthouse which was one of the places on this Earth I hated almost as bad as I hated the shitty detention house. But

Judge —— was a surprise. Not that he wasn't stern. He was. But
not mean and nasty like most. Not like a certain female judge where
if you're young, pretty and almost-white she'll fuck you over as best
she can. Judge —— was sort of scary-looking at first, wrinkled-
homely as a toad with that shiny bald head and dyed-brown
mustache like something painted on and he was wearing this
judge's robe that fitted him like a shower curtain would, but he was
alert and listening to the reports, asked serious questions about
those of us hauled before him so it wasn't like some assembly line
or something. He impressed me he was O.K. for an old guy so
weird-looking. He treated the older girls, hookers and crack ad-
dicts, O.K., though they all had to serve some time; and with me,
I'm next to last, brought up in front of his bench with the shakes,
not that I'm actually scared but I get the shakes easy, and I hadn't
had a smoke in eighteen hours so my voice is so low and trembling
he has to ask me to repeat what I said more than once. I'm here for
shoplifting and a bench warrant for some bad checks from last
Christmas; also I'd gotten in a scuffle with the security guard at
the Discount King where he'd insulted me with a racial epithet so I
went a little wild and bit the fucker in the hand and they're charg-
ing me for that, too—assault, for Christ's sake. The D.A.'s assis-
tant is laying it on like I'm a public menace and need to be
incarcerated for a long time, also she's pissed this is my third of-
fense as an adult, and my attorney's arguing some crap I'm not
much listening to. I see Judge —— regarding me in that frowning-
kindly way like I might've been his daughter or granddaughter almost. I had the hope he'd give me a suspended sentence so I told
my attorney I changed my plea to *guilty* and I got to say in this
breathy little voice, "Guilty, Your Honor," which gave me a shiver
and made the old guy's yellowish droopy eyes shine like somebody'd goosed him. So it was O.K. It was terrific. I wasn't bullshit-
ting for once, I was serious for I'd seen in the old man's eyes
something that had to do with *me*. Not some court number on a
piece of paper. And Judge —— says, "Eight months, suspended
sentence, counseling at County Health suggested." And that was

it! "Thank you, Your Honor," I said, wiping at my eyes, and this was no bullshit, either. "I'm r-real grateful."

I figured that was that, Jesus was I lucky. Then back at this place where I and a girlfriend (that I hadn't actually seen in over a week, I believe she'd gone off with some guy to Atlantic City) rented a room, there came a call for me at 6 P.M. I figured it was one of my boyfriends I wasn't in any hurry to hook up with—but it was this gravelly toad-voice I recognized right away. Judge —— saying he was concerned with my case, a young woman of my age, with my history of arrests, etc. He believed I was "clearly under a malevolent influence" and "malnourished both physically and spiritually." He said he would like to speak with me to discuss my case that evening. He was personally involved in sending certain deserving young people to training schools (business, barbering and hairdressing, restaurant work) and perhaps I would be eligible. I said O.K. it sounded good so he sent a car for me to bring me to his big old place on the River Road where there's mansions on a ridge overlooking the Delaware River, a section of the city remote to me as the far side of the moon though I knew of it, of course, and probably had had some dates from this neighborhood though for sure they'd never have identified themselves as such. The car pulled up this drive and I got out of breath just staring at the big old maroon-brick house with the pointy roof and half dozen chimneys. I laughed saying, "Hey. Wow," to myself, and cracked my gum. Have to admit I believed every word Judge —— told me and even some he'd only hinted at, like there was this special understanding between us *because I was special.* Which we all know or wish to believe in our hearts.

There was Judge —— at the side door of the big old house. He sent away the driver. He asked me please to come inside. He wasn't wearing his black judge's robe of course and looked more like an ordinary oldish man with a sizable gut riding his belt and a streak of something flushed and excited in his face. Right away he was saying he wanted to show me his "collection of hearts—which it requires a sensitive eye to appreciate." His own droopy-lidded eyes sort of eating me up like he wasn't aware, or couldn't help it, I'm wearing my zebra-stripe purple jersey tank top (just bare titties beneath) and my little gold-heart locket on a chain around my neck and a black vinyl miniskirt to practically just my crotch and I'd picked out my hair so it was fine and airy and exploded-looking as dandelion fluff. And platform shoes of spangle-blue plastic, with ankle straps. Inside, it smelled of mildew and maybe old newspapers and something sweetish-sharp like in a dentist's office (not my favorite smell in the world!) and sure not romantic (if that was what the old white guy was thinking) but I was smelling pretty good myself with this spray-on Chanel No. 5 I'd pocketed at Macy's a few weeks ago so it was O.K. I mean, no immediate danger I'd puke.

For I did have a kind of sensitive stomach. From a long time of stress where I'd forgot to eat regular, kept going on cigarettes, black coffee and what I could get on the street.

Judge Whosis saying, leading me along some hall, few people realize how lonely it is being a judge if you don't wish to belong to the "ruling elite" and I giggled and said, "Yeah, I bet. Must be weird," and cracked my gum. And Judge Whosis wiping at his damp lardy forehead with a pure-white cotton handkerchief somebody must've laundered and ironed for him, "It *is* . . . weird."

And he laughed too, and made a wet clicking sound with his tongue like that was his way, an old-daddy, grandpappy way you had to laugh fondly at, of cracking his gum.

The judge observed in silence as I blinked and grinned and marveled over the collection of hearts. Which was like no other display of anything I'd ever seen before, that I could recall. I said, "Your Honor, this is fan-tas-tic. Like a museum." I was maybe becoming a little uneasy, prickles on my bare arm and that side of my neck nearest the judge, for he was watching me all this while. But I believed (I don't know why!) the man could not be living alone in that house, not such a big old house where you'd need to have lots of servants; also I'd overheard him mumble something (I thought!) out in the hall on our way into the room with the hearts, such as you might say to a maid or somebody. So I was just a little uneasy, not panicked or anything, lighting up a cigarette without asking permission. But Judge Whosis said not a word of scolding, only frowned and said, "You'll anesthetize your taste buds, dear. And I have a little surprise for you."

To this I didn't know how to reply, except to giggle again, and shift my shoulders in that nervous habit I had, and exhale smoke as gracefully as I could through my nostrils.

By this time I'd seen about all there was to see of the heart collection at least in this room. I was hoping there wasn't any more. I was hoping there'd be something to eat, it was almost 9 P.M. and I hadn't eaten since breakfast at women's detention at 7 A.M. But the old guy had a few more hearts to show me, one of ruby-red glass he said was a "recent acquisition." And there was a fancy gentleman's cane, shiny black lacquer with a carved wooden heart-handle that was almost too big for me to wrap my fingers around though he was pushing it into my hand. "This is a new venture for me," he said, sort of puffing. "I intend to continue with the series. Next, an exquisitely carved ivory heart. On a cane exactly like this. What do you think? Do you approve of ivory?" Smiling at me with teeth like white enamel so I had to smile back, to be polite. "Yeah. It's O.K. Cool, I guess," I said. Ivory? What're we talking about? There was this old bald dyed-mustache white man, judge of the county criminal court, asking my advice about ivory? And puffing like he'd been climbing stairs. I said, "Where'd you get such a nice cane, your honor?" and Judge Whosis said, like he was proud, "I didn't. It's always been in my family. There are more in the attic. Originally, this came from India. My great-grandfather was a magistrate in India, under British rule." Lifting the cane like a sword the way a kid might, to scare you, and I gave a jump, guess I was more scared than I knew, but he seemed not to mean anything by it, just a clumsy way of moving. Again had me try to wrap my fingers around the handle of wood (fine-carved to resemble an actual heart with veins, etc.), and his fingers over mine, securing them on the handle, which made me uneasy, like I say the handle was too big and of an awkward shape. It was then I had a weird sensation almost like . . . God, I don't know! . . . inside the carved wood heart it was warm, and there was a weak pulsebeat. *A heart. An actual heart. There is an actual heart trapped inside here.* But this was crazy, I put such a notion out of my head the way you'd brush away a fly.

The judge led me at last into another room. Parlor? Old-fashioned velvet drapes, a velvet sofa to sit on. Bottles of champagne and sparkling water on a silver tray, shiny crystal glasses and some little sandwiches without crusts, chopped shrimp he said, turkey, ham, goat-cheese, a "miscellany" he'd ordered he said, also sticky walnut pastries. I was so hungry my mouth watered and I was trembling but made myself hold back for I'd always had good manners, I'd been ridiculed for my prissy-prissy ways by some companions, in fact. Judge Whosis made a fuss pouring champagne for me, but for himself he poured only the sparkling water, with a slice of lemon, saying he rarely drank even champagne, he had a "congenital condition." I drank down the champagne in about one swallow. He poured more, and I drank that down. My mouth was full with the little sandwiches. I was pretty happy now. I said, swallowing, "I'm sorry to hear that, Your Honor." Though I hadn't been listening all that closely. I bit into a walnut pastry, which was what the judge was eating, it was so sugary my mouth stung but, yes, it was delicious, so I ate it all. I drank down another glass of champagne. Wow! I was feeling fantastic. Like snorting coke. Nah, smoking crack. But this was legal, and this was good for me, this was "nutrition" which I had to accept I needed so my bones wouldn't hollow out and snap. The judge was asking me in a kindly voice like in the courtroom that morning about my background, my birth-mother and foster families, and I said real quick I didn't know, didn't believe in dwelling upon the past and he said, nodding, his second chin creasing against his chest, "That's wise, dear. That's wisdom. I, too, don't believe in dwelling upon the past. Except as the past is contained, preserved, in the present. As personal, private, prized history. For there you have the past in the present; but it's your selection of the past, it has become your work of art." I wasn't following this, but I nodded real vigorously. The judge was saying, smiling at me, crouched forward on the sofa with his big sticky-fingered hands clasped on his knees, "Not many times in my professional life has a young woman like yourself, or a young man, made a strong impression on me. I have wanted then to know her, or him, more intimately. To bring her, or him, into my life." I was eating, and I mumbled something with a full mouth. I was hoping he'd move on next to the subject of the training school, I intended to speak of the Trenton School of Beauty Culture where I'd started a nail-and-hair course just out of high school but never completed, maybe I could return to that, I had reason to believe I had a natural talent for such work, skillful hands and a winning personality and if my own God-damned nails keep breaking off I can wear fakes, nobody can tell the difference. But I was feeling kind of drowsy from the champagne I guess, which was a taste new to me, and that good food, peaceful like I wanted to curl up right there on the judge's sofa like a cat. Judge —— smiled kindly at me. He'd poured still another glass of champagne for me, more sparkling water for himself he'd been drinking down like a thirsty dog, and I reached for that final glass, already so sleepy I could hardly keep my eyes open. A thought came to me. I giggled, saying, "Hey, Your Honor? This isn't a love potion, is it?"

Says the old guy clicking his glass against mine, "I hope so, dear."

Demon

Demon-child. Kicked in the womb so his mother doubled over in pain. Nursing tugged and tore at her young breasts. Wailed through the night. Puked, shat. Refused to eat. *No he was loving, mad with love.* Of Mama. (Though fearful of Da.) Curling burrowing pushing his head into Mama's arms, against Mama's warm fleshy body. Starving for love, food. Starving for what he could not know yet to name: *God's grace, salvation.*

Sign of Satan: flamey-red ugly-pimply birthmark snake-shaped. On his underjaw, coiled below his ear. Almost you can't see it. A little boy he's teased by neighbor girls, hulking big girls with titties and laughing-wet eyes. *Demon! demon! Lookit, sign of the demon!*

Those years passing in a fever-dream. Or maybe never passed. Mama prayed over him, hugged and slapped. Shook his skinny shoulders so his head flew. The minister prayed over him *Deliver us from evil* and he was good, he *was* delivered from evil. Except at school his eyes misting over, couldn't see the blackboard. Sullen and nasty-mouthed the teacher called him. Not like the other children.

If not like *the other children*, then like *who? what?*

Those years. As in a stalled city bus, exhaust pouring out the rear. The stink of it everywhere. Your hair, eyes. Clothes. Same view through the same flyspecked windows. Year after year the battered-tin diner, the vacant lot high with weeds and rubble and the path worn through it slantwise where children ran shouting above the river. Broken pavement littered like confetti from a parade long past.

Or maybe it was the edge of something vast, infinite. You could never come to the end of. Wavering and blinding in blasts of light. *Desert*, maybe. *Red Desert* where demons dance, swirl in the hot winds. Never seen a *desert* except pictures, a name on a map. And in his head.

Demon-child they whispered of him. But no, he was loving, mad with love. Too small, too short. Stunted legs. His head too big for his spindly shoulders. His strange waxy-pale moon-shaped face, almond eyes beautiful in shadowed sockets, small wet mouth perpetually sucking inward. As if to keep the bad words, words of filth and damnation, safely inside.

The sign of Satan coiled on his underjaw began to fade. Like his adolescent skin eruptions. Blood drawn gradually back into tissue, capillaries.

Not a demon-child but a pure good anxious loving child someone betrayed by squeezing him from her womb before he was ready.

Not a demon-child but for years he rode wild thunderous razor-hooved black stallions by night and by day. Furious galloping on sidewalks, in asphalt playgrounds. Through the school corridors trampling all in his way. Furious tearing hooves, froth-flecked nostrils, bared teeth. God's wrath, the black stallion rearing, whinnying. *I destroy all in my path. Beware!*

Not a demon-child but he'd torched the school, rows of stores, woodframe houses in the neighborhood. How many times the smelly bed where Mama and Da hid from him. And no one knew.

This January morning bright and windy and he's staring at the face floating in a mirror. Dirty mirror in a public lavatory, Trailways bus station. Where at last the demon has been released. For it is the New Year. The shifting of the earth's axis. For to be away from what is familiar, like walking on a sharp-slanted floor, allows *something other* in. Or the *something other* has been inside you all along and until now you do not know.

In his right eyeball a speck of dirt? dust? blood?

Scared, he knows right away. Knows even before he sees: sign of Satan. In the yellowish-white of his eyeball. Not the coiled little snake but the five-sided star: *pentagram*.

He knows, he's been warned. Five-sided star: *pentagram*. It's there, in his eye. Tries to rub it out with his fist.

Backs away terrified and gagging and he's running out of the fluorescent-bright lavatory and through the bus station where eyes trail after him curious, bemused, pitying, annoyed. He's a familiar sight here though no one knows his name. Runs home, about three miles. His mother knows there's trouble, has he lied about taking his medicine? hiding the pill under his tongue? Yes but God knows you can't oversee every minute with one like him. Yes but your love wears thin like the lead backing of a cheap mirror corroding the glass. Yes but you have prayed, you have prayed and prayed and cursed the words echoing not upward to God but downward as in an empty well.

Twenty-six years old, shaved head glinting blue. Luminous shining eyes women in the street call beautiful. In the neighborhood he's known by his first name. Sweet guy but strange, excitable. A habit of twitching his shoulders like he's shrugging free of somebody's grip.

Fast as you run somebody runs faster!

In the house that's a semidetached row house on Mill Street he's not listening to his angry mother asking why is he home so early, has a job in a building supply yard so why isn't he there? Pushes past the old woman and into the bathroom, shuts the door and there in the mirror oh God it's there: the five-sided star, *pentagram*. Sign of Satan. Embedded deep in his right eyeball, just below the dilated iris.

No! no! God help!

Goes wild rubs with both fists, pokes with fingers. He's weeping, shouting. Beats at himself, fists and nails. His sister now pounding on the door what is it? what's wrong? and Mama's voice loud and frightened. *It's happened,* he thinks. His first clear thought. *Happened.* Like a stone sinking so calm. Because hasn't he always known the prayers did no good, on your knees bowing your head inviting Jesus into your heart does no good. The sign of the demon would return, absorbed into his blood but must one day re-emerge.

Pushes past the women and in the kitchen paws through the drawer scattering cutlery that falls to the floor, bounces and clatters and there's the big carving knife in his hand, his hand shuts about it like fate. Pushes past the women now in reverse where they've followed him into the kitchen knocks his one-hundred-eighty-pound older sister aside with his elbow as lightly as he lifts bags of gravel, armloads of bricks. Hasn't he prayed Our Father to be a machine many times. A machine does not feel, a machine does not think. A machine does not hurt. A machine does not starve for love. A machine does not starve for what it does not know to name: *salvation*.

Back then inside the bathroom, slamming the door against the screaming women, and locking it. Gibbering to himself *Away Satan! Away Satan! God help!* With a hand strangely steely as if practiced wielding the point of the knife, boldly inserting and twisting into the accursed eyeball. And no pain—only a burning cleansing roaring sensation as of a blast of fire. Out pops the eyeball, and out the sign of Satan. But connected by tissue, nerves. It's elastic so he's pulling, fingers now slippery-excited with blood. He's sawing with the sharp blade of the steak knife. Cuts the eyeball free, like Mama squeezing baby out of her belly into this pig trough of sin and filth, and no turning back till Jesus calls you home.

He drops the eyeball into the toilet, flushes the toilet fast.

Before Satan can intervene.

One of those antiquated toilets where water swirls about the stained bowl, wheezes and yammers to itself, sighs, grumbles, finally swallows like it's doing you a favor. And the sign of the demon is gone.

One eye socket empty and fresh-bleeding he's on his knees praying *Thank you God! thank you God!* weeping as angels in radiant garments with faces of blinding brightness reach down to embrace him not minding his red-slippery mask of a face. Now he's one of them himself, now he will float into the sky where, some wind-blustery January morning, you'll see him, or a face like his, in a furious cloud.

Elvis Is Dead: Why Are *You* Alive?

The first wrong thing about the funeral, which registered upon Meredith's consciousness as not simply wrong but disconcerting, frightening, was that the casket was on an elevated, spotlighted platform at the front of the church, nearly up on the altar; and that the casket was open, as at a ceremonial wake. But this *was* wrong, surely?—this should not have been? Meredith glanced about nervously, seeing that his fellow mourners—for it seemed that he was a mourner, stricken and angry with grief—took no notice of anything inappropriate or out of place. They were crying, sobbing, their faces shining with tears and distended with emotion, the grief of stunned children, but anger, even rage, too. Meredith felt a wave of dizziness rise in him—he was revulsed by these people, packed so solidly into the rows of pews, crowding him, who disliked crowds on principle, and often felt that he could not breathe even at a concert or a play in elegant surroundings, with cushioned seats and faultless ventilation, and had to excuse himself to hurry out into the lobby or outside into the night for fresh air. But *these* people!—coarse-faced, squat, many of the women conspicuously overweight, and many of the men bloated in the belly as if carrying a watermelon inside their ill-fitting suits!—who were they? And why was *he*, an executive at TransContinental Insurance, among them?

Mourning our dead King.

Our beloved Elvis who has passed over, God have mercy on his soul.

Yes but is The King really dead?—I can't believe he is really truly dead, God would not be so cruel would He?

But yes: the Lord thy God moves in ways that passeth mortal comprehension, praise to Him.

And Elvis our dead King is with Him, his soul in glory, and at peace, after the sorrows of this Vale of Tears, where so many jeered and mocked him, the King now in the bosom of The Lord in the rapture of glory, Alleluia!

Gathered in His bosom as His Only Begotten Son has been gathered in His bosom after the agony in the garden, the crown of thorns, the sorrow and the sacrifice and the outrage of Golgotha.

Alleluia!

All this Meredith knew, without needing to be told.

Knowing too, though, jammed into a pew of perspiring mourners at the rear of the church, he could not see the casket clearly, that it was Elvis himself who lay in state, beneath brilliant white lights like those of an operating room; propped at a slant before the altar amid hundreds of floral displays of all varieties (including giant gladioli in Day-Glo hues of orange and crimson, and immense sprays of purple bougainvillea, and those shiny-red plastic-looking phallic-shaped flowers found primarily in mobile home parks); and that the funeral was both immediately after Elvis's death and at the same time in the present—in 1993. So many years later!

Meredith was to recall afterward that he knew these things without knowing how he knew. Except: why was *he* here? And why alone, amid such inhospitable strangers?

And why afterward, waking, and through much of the day that followed, did he continue to feel choked with grief, and that deeper, inchoate anger?—staring at others, his colleagues at TransContinental and friendly acquaintances, even his wife, thinking *Elvis is dead: why are* you *alive?*

The next time, Meredith managed to crowd into a pew nearer the front of the little church, where, though his eyes misted over with tears, he could more clearly make out the black-leather-clad figure of the dead Elvis (a young Elvis, apparently?) lying in state in a splendid gleaming mother-of-pearl casket beneath the blazing-white lights and surrounded by the luridly bright flowers; he could hear the minister's impassioned eulogy, which went on for some time, delivered in a high-pitched, mournful, ranting-angry voice, though he could not distinguish most of the words, nor could he see the minister clearly—except to know that the man was big-bellied like so many of the congregation, with a flushed, contorted face, wide jaws, and gleaming white dentures that flashed with spittle as he spoke. And he was white, of course: all the men and women packed into the church appeared to be white.

Caucasian, the superior race. Master race?

Yes! But you must not say so.

Meredith had no idea if Elvis himself had been a believer, probably not, though certainly he must have been born of Protestant-Christian folks, possibly Baptists. The interior of this church was not familiar to Meredith, who knew little about religion, and who had been brought up in a freethinking, informally Unitarian household, but he understood from the minister's dress (a black mourner's suit with white shirt, black string necktie) and the absence of statues and stained-glass windows that it was a Protestant church; he seemed to know too that it was one of those cheaply "modern" churches that resemble discount stores from the outside, often built in starkly treeless lots adjacent to shopping malls or rural-suburban housing developments. Driving past, Meredith would scarcely glance at such a place, not out of a sense of class superiority (though of course he *did* feel, he *was*, superior to such Americans, wasn't he?) so much as indifference. He had his life, and it was not a life that touched upon such folk in the slightest. The odd, mildly comic names of such churches—Calvary Assembly of God, Friendship Baptist, Calvary Gospel, Bible Fellowship Evangelical Church—passed before his gaze without making the slightest impression upon him.

Except, perhaps, something about these churches *had* made an impression upon him?

Meredith found himself suddenly on his feet. He was weak-kneed, frightened. What was expected of him?—why was the air in the little church so heated, like the interior of a great mouth, and so highly charged? He wanted only to push his way out and escape (he seemed to know that his car was outside, but he could not recall which car it was, or whether it was any car he would recognize: nor did he know how far he'd driven to get to this place) but at the same time a terrible yearning, powerful as physical hunger or thirst, or sexual desire, was drawing him forward toward the front of the church and the mannequinlike figure of Elvis in the mother-of-pearl casket. *All rise! all pray! All come forward to honor The King!*

Clumsy on his feet, feeling like a stork towering half a head over the tallest of the other mourners, Meredith was being rather rudely jostled, nudged along. How impatient these men and women were! How fierce their grief, how they not only wept, but sweated with it! Meredith shrank from them, disdaining them, yet, unashamed and open as they were with their emotion, not seeming to know, nor certainly to care, how ugly, how red-faced and absurd they were, Meredith could not help but admire them. Yes and perhaps he wanted to be accepted as one of them. *Mourning our dead King. He who will never come again. He who is with the Lord Our God, sitting on His right hand, amid all His high host. Alleluia!*

Meredith wondered if the other mourners, or the minister at his pulpit, noticed him: his expensive charcoal-gray pinstripe suit, his off-white silk shirt, his striped silk necktie? his black leather Florsheim shoes? his hair which was silvery-blond, and cut in a way very different from their own? Did they notice his height? The expression of wonderment and revulsion in his face, as if he were a dreamer who had wandered into a dream of strangers, and could not comprehend where he was? *Are ye washed in the Blood of the Lamb? Do ye take upon yourself the holy wrath of The King?* Close behind Meredith, pressing against him with pendulous breasts, was an obese woman of young middle age, in a black polyester pants suit, with a wet, flushed, jowly face and small beady eyes all but lost in the fatty recesses of her cheeks—she did take notice of Meredith, when he glanced nervously back at her, and nodded, and smiled, a small tight reproachful grimace of a smile, *Elvis is dead: why are* you *alive?* It was a question so mysterious and so profound, so terrible, that it pierced Meredith's heart like a sliver of glass.

Meredith was being pushed along, Meredith had no choice but to go forward, filing up the aisle to the immense opalescent casket that, upended, looked like a candy box (cushioned in puckered white satin! gleaming with gold ornamentation!) about to spill its contents. And there was Elvis The King: dead, yet looking as if he were but playing at death, a sassy young Elvis with oily black pompadour rising like a rooster's comb over his forehead, and hooded, thick-lashed eyes that seemed about to spring open at any moment, and those full, sulky lips shaped to the faintest suggestion of a smile—or was it a sneer? Elvis still in his twenties, as his mourners wished to remember him, clad in his biker's regalia of black leather jacket with silver stud ornamentation and numerous zippers, tight-fitting black trousers and high-heeled leather boots. This was the Elvis Meredith remembered most distinctly, the Elvis of Meredith's young adolescence, how many years, in fact decades ago, a dizzying amount of time ago, could it be—nearly forty years? *Forty years since Meredith had been young? He who felt he'd never begun to live his life, or had, unaccountably, led the wrong life, the life of a stranger?* As Meredith approached the casket, hesitantly, his heart beating hard, he saw Elvis's long eyelashes quiver— it was obvious, the man was still alive. From the four corners of the church, out of speakers that amplified words, music, and thrusting percussive rhythm, there came, suddenly, the song of Elvis's Meredith had both loved and detested the summer of his fourteenth birthday, "Don't Be Cruel"—Meredith had been unable to get the infantile tune out of his head. And now it was being played, rippling and pulsing in the warm, close air surrounding him, unless it was sounding inside his very skull, *don't be cruel, don't be cruel, don't be cruel, a heart that's true, a heart that's true, a heart that's true,* unbearable drivel, brain-rot, nursery rhymes in the guise of pop trash. And yet, Meredith found himself weeping

like a child, bending over the opened casket and the living-dead figure of The King, a violent paroxysm of grief and desire overcoming
him as, nudged by the obese woman behind him, and urged, it
seemed, by the other mourners, his brothers and sisters in sorrow,
and in the singular exhilaration of such sorrow, Meredith bowed his
head, stooped, clumsily but warmly, and damply, and with some
pressure, kissed Elvis on the lips—those lips that had so long ago
fascinated him, fleshy and crude, mocking, unpredictable in what
they might part to utter, that he, Meredith, would never dare utter,
through a lifetime. *Mourning our dead King. Praise to The Lord.
Praise to The King. Alleluia!*

Meredith whispered, his lips puffy and cracked, *Alleluia.*

Meredith was weeping as if his heart was broken. For joy. Or
was it shame.

The obese perspiring woman in the black polyester pants suit
hugged him and patted his back and wept with him in sisterly com-
miseration, *I can't believe that he is really truly dead, oh but he is
with God in Heaven and will live forever, free of this Vale of Tears,*
and another mourner, a man, in fact it was the big-bellied minister
himself, a short, squat, but forceful man of vigorous middle age,
gripped Meredith by the upper arm and urged him back into the
aisle and on his way, *Walk tall, son! tall like a man! let the others
pay their final respects too, son!* clamping a hand on Meredith's
shoulder in parting: *The King is beyond mere mortal comprehension seated at the right hand of The Father gathered in His Bosom
as His Only Begotten Son has been gathered in His Bosom, it is
not for mere humankind to question such* and humbly Meredith
whispered, *Yes, yes I know. Amen.*

And then he was outside the church in the parking lot (which
was far larger than one would have expected, judging by the interior of the church: acres of shining American cars extending to
the hazy horizon) being issued a *scourge*, the fattish baby-faced
middle-aged man who pressed it into his hand spoke of it as a
scourge, and the word did not baffle Meredith but seemed entirely
appropriate: the thing was a weapon of a kind Meredith had never
seen before, let alone held in his hand, he who was the gentlest of

men and abhorred violence, a man of the highest integrity among his professional colleagues as among his family, friends, neighbors, still it was with a stab of excitement he gripped the *scourge*, examining it in wonder: a kind of machete, yet with numerous blades, and shaped like an old-fashioned wire rug beater, with a solid rubberized handle, *a scourge! a scourge! at last, a scourge!* which Meredith realized he had been missing these many years, all the years of his lost life.

With a pack of other mourners, all of them save Meredith short, stocky, squat, but surprisingly energetic, even agile, he found himself in a shopping mall, not one of the new, gigantic malls in the vicinity of his suburban home but an older, less luxurious mall, not one Meredith recognized, yet he seemed to know it was somewhere near his home, or where he'd once lived, and with the others he was accosting men and women to put to them the angry proclamation *Elvis is dead: why are* you *alive?* and as they stared in alarm, or shrank away, or tried to flee in terror, Meredith and the other mourners hacked away with their *scourges*, slicing their victims in the faces, in the necks, bringing the razor-sharp blades of the *scourge* down as solidly on a fleeing back as if indeed it were a rug beater, and the victim a rug so imbued with filth it required the most vigorous beating one could administer to be cleaned.

———

In his waking hours, in his daylight self, Meredith was a man of strong convictions, but rarely passions: he was not susceptible to swings of emotion, and did not value such behavior in others. If he were to contemplate his mind, his very brain, he would have envisioned it as a medical school model of some lightweight synthetic material, the brain tissue with a suggestion of veined and imbricated porousness yet smooth to the touch, and shadowless—a matter of anatomical surfaces. Mystery?—maybe. But so long as the mechanism functions, why ponder its depths?

Yet now that he was besieged almost nightly by this strange, ugly, obsessive dream, so unlike any dream he'd ever had before in his life, Meredith found himself lapsing into long minutes of contemplation, anxiety. He feared sleep, yet longed for sleep. He slept deeply, yet woke feeling exhausted, as if he'd scarcely slept at all. He was sickened with disgust but he was also curious. He felt repugnance, but also intrigue. How bizarre, yet how vividly real: the interior of the little church, the mother-of-pearl casket beneath the intense lights, Elvis who was dead yet not-dead, his amplified voice hammering from all sides *don't be cruel, cruel, cruel, a heart that's true, true, true,* until Meredith ground his teeth in misery, and laughed—"Christ, is it possible? But what *is* it?" With revulsion he recalled the pack of flush-faced, dwarfish mourners streaming out of the church as out of a hive, his fellow Americans, whom life since Elvis had cheated, furious and deadly as maddened bees. And the peculiar weapon each wielded, part machete and part rug beater!—comical in theory, but murderous in execution. Empowered with its latticework of razor-sharp blades to lacerate human flesh. To punish.

Elvis is dead: why are you *alive?*

Driving on the Turnpike twice daily, to and from TransContinental's corporate headquarters eleven miles from his home, seeing the faces of drivers in other vehicles, Meredith heard the percussive notes sounding in his head, the unanswerable riddle—*Elvis is dead: why are* you *alive?* He was increasingly susceptible, through much of the day, to lapsing into long minutes of abstraction, gazing at office workers, strangers on the street, or, in fact, and this was especially disturbing to him, his colleagues at TransContinental, his neighbors, friends, even his wife Sarah, unconsciously grinding his teeth, narrowing his eyes that were bright with baffled, resentful tears—*Elvis is dead: why are* you *alive?*

And why was he, Meredith, compelled to ask such a riddle?— why, virtually every night of his life now, was he compelled to punish, to kill, in the name of The King?

He did not want to know, for he understood it would be better for him not to know. *For then I would no longer be Meredith, but another.*

And the injustice of it! So many years of it!

———

Die! die! die! die! unbeliever! Meredith, panting and sobbing with emotion, was one of a furious group of Elvis's mourners who swarmed upon a man as he was unlocking his car in a suburban parking lot, the setting was nowhere Meredith knew, yet somehow familiar to him, the backs of commercial buildings, a stained-red translucent western sky of a kind depicted on scenic calendars, the mob was led by a frantic bullnecked little man who wore a tiny American flag in his lapel, all were wielding their *scourges*, hacking violently away until, bloodied, on his knees, trying vainly to shield his head, the victim looked up screaming in pain and terror—and Meredith saw, to his horror, that he was a business acquaintance of Meredith's, a corporate lawyer who did consulting work for TransContinental, and for an instant their eyes locked, even as, swept up by the passion of his brothers and sisters, Meredith raised his *scourge*, already glistening with blood, and brought it down again, and again.

Elvis is dead: why are you alive?

Cruelest, most unanswerable of riddles!

Meredith woke in his bed agitated, sweating—heart beating dangerously hard—nausea deep in his bowels—yet suffused, like that stained-red translucent sky, with the conviction that some secret, some revelation, was close at hand. So close! But someone was shaking his shoulder, Sarah was shaking his shoulder, asking what was wrong, was it another of his nightmares, begging him please, please wake up Meredith, at such times she was wary of him, and annoyed, for he might flail out and hit her like a terrified child, eyes rolling wildly in his head. Where was he?—who was this woman beside him?—what was this unfamiliar darkness? Meredith wrenched himself away from his wife swinging his legs around off the bed so that he could sit up, he could not bear the weight of her hand, he could not at such a time bear the weight of her hand, she whom he loved and had loved for thirty-three years *a lifetime! but not his,* wiping his heated face on a sheet, rubbing his eyes that were dazed and stunned as if they had beheld wonders, no not a nightmare he murmured, it had been a good dream actually—"A happy dream."

"A happy dream!" Sarah's voice was flat with disbelief. She must have stared at the back of his head in the dark, he could imagine her frowning, creased face, yet that look in her eyes of incredulity, bemusement, she knew him or believed she knew him, for thirty-three years is a long time, indeed a lifetime. "Well. You can tell me about it in the morning, Meredith."

Yes. Of course. Never.

The riddle was, by daylight, what *was* Elvis Presley to Meredith Bernhardt, and to this riddle too there was no answer, or none that Meredith Bernhardt could comprehend.

He'd been an adopted child. Or was he still an adopted child?— you did not lose such a designation, simply by growing into an adult.

Simply by becoming, as he had, in time, become, a father himself.

(In his dreams, he had no children, nor any memory of them, who were now grown and living elsewhere, fully autonomous and self-absorbed adults. Nor had he any wife, Sarah or otherwise. Nor any name, in fact: "Meredith" was unknown in that other, so rich and so intriguing world.)

Meredith had graduated from high school in Shaker Heights, Ohio, in 1958. He could recall those years only in patchy fragments, as if another person had experienced them: a tall, skinny, soft-spoken and obsessively hardworking boy with horn-rimmed glasses and a perpetually blemished skin and an air, secret beneath his congenial, low-keyed manner, of knowing himself superior to most of his classmates, for his grades bore this conviction out, and his teachers' praise for him, and his adoptive parents'—the Bernhardts were both professional people, educated people, Meredith's father a doctor and his mother a public health administrator for the state of Ohio. They were childless and liberal and cultivated and had an association with the Unitarian Church that was rather more

sociable than religious or indeed passionate and Meredith had no
vivid memories of attending that church or of any other church
through his childhood and adolescence. Nor had he any vivid
memories of Elvis Presley in that era, the only era in which Meredith might plausibly have been involved in rock and roll music, of
course his classmates were caught up in the Presley craze, and
there was the exasperating summer he'd been infected with one of
the ridiculous Presley songs, but, in truth, Meredith remembered
little of such things for he was, for some years, a serious music student, he took piano lessons each Saturday morning given by a lo-
cally renowned performing woman pianist, and his impression of
his high school years was, in retrospect, that of having walked
blindfolded through the 1950's as if quite literally blindfolded making his way through the corridors of the high school, past the rows
of green metal lockers stretching to the very horizon, dim as
dream-memory. He remembered little, and he regretted remembering little, he *was* superior, if sometimes a bit lonely.

As an adopted child, Meredith knew himself lucky, so lucky he
dared not think of what might have been, what his other life might
have been, what brothers and sisters he might have, living unknown to him, as he to them. His biological mother (which, even as
a boy, he knew not to call his "real" or "actual" mother—that would
have been stupidly cruel to his adoptive mother) had been only fifteen years old when she'd given birth to him and given him away,
first to relatives, then to an adoption agency, she'd allegedly "disappeared" with a man and there was no trace of her and Meredith
had never thought of her for there was no one of whom to think and
the mind cannot comprehend nothingness though he knew she'd
been very poor, her people very poor, West Virginia background,
they'd moved to Youngstown, Ohio, at the start of the war and
Meredith was born in 1941 and that was all he knew except to know
himself blessed for had his young mother been more loving and
true as a mother, had she loved him, and not given him away, how
different, how meager and impoverished his life would have been
and knowing this he shuddered and wept for very gratitude for
God's ways are not our ways, praise to Him.

———

"You sleep so well now, so deeply," Sarah observed, some weeks after the onset of the dreams, "—you look forward to sleep, I think, Meredith, don't you?" not precisely accusatory but probing, assessing him with her eyes, watchful eyes, for the Bernhardts lived alone now in the large handsome house of pale yellow stone, their children grown and gone and the house echoing with quiet, the peace of a prosperous middle age, a marriage of thirty-three years for which Meredith was grateful, such stability, such companionship, it was perhaps true that he might not have married Sarah had she not been the daughter of parents as prosperous as Meredith's own, not that he had not loved her for of course he had, we love those we love for all that is theirs, and why not a father's income as well as a pretty face, a winning smile, a pleasing voice, why not? Meredith reasoned that Sarah, for her part, would not have married *him* had he been, not Meredith Bernhardt, but someone else. Who?

Meredith laughed. Though it was not a laughing matter—this woman's probing interrogation.

Meredith laughed, and said, "I look forward to every hour of my life, waking and sleeping, Sarah, don't you?"

Sarah regarded him for a moment in silence. Her eyes, which were no longer young eyes, seemed to have grown doubtful, opaque. She was a handsome woman with an erect way of holding herself, a squarish set to the shoulders as to the jaws, and the unbidden thought flashed to Meredith in that instant *Elvis is dead, why are you alive?*

As if reading his mind, Sarah said, ironically, "Yes, of course, darling. Have we any choice?"

———

Late that evening, which was a blowy Sunday evening in November, Meredith found himself on the cellar steps, descending the steps into the earthy-smelling darkness. *Why? where? cruel? true?* The house was a century old, an expensive property, yes but the mortgage was completely paid off, Meredith had done well through his business career, he'd been an excellent provider, and had reason to take pride. Didn't he? Not like his biological father who did not in fact exist. Not like any of them who did not in fact exist.

Most of the cellar had long since been renovated and made comfortably modern, but there was, at the rear, beyond a door, an old unused fruit cellar, and an old coal bin unused for decades, and for some reason Meredith found himself there, groping in the semi-dark, on a top shelf of the fruit cellar, amid dust and the desiccated remains of insects, something with a rubberized handle, it *was* here!—Meredith's instinct had not failed him.

Metal, glittering blades, rubberized handle.

Yet, by day, how disappointing it was: smaller than the remarkable *scourge* of his dreams, measuring perhaps fifteen inches in diameter, sickle-sized, made of an actual rug beater, razor blades and shards of wicked-looking glass clamped onto the heavy metal in a bizarre fan-shaped display. Meredith gripped it, held it, weighed it in his trembling hand.

From the stairs, a very long distance away, so that her voice, though raised, sounded faint, Meredith's wife called, "Meredith? Where *are* you?"

Posthumous

This is the way it was, or will be.

In the distance as if emerging from the horizon as the earth rotates to dawn, a spiky-notched hammering, pounding. You imagine it in a building miles away, a building populated by strangers. But then it is closer. By leaps, by blocks, closer. And on the avenue twelve floors below your window there is an emergency siren. In fact two sirens, coils of sound like mad red ribbons, rushing and twining together from opposite directions: north, south. It's a familiar panic—*Is the alarm a fire? A fire in our building?*

The hammering noise, the pounding of men's fists, grows louder by quick degrees. There can be no mistaking it now: and the rude rattling of the doorknob: they are at the front door of your apartment. Voices, male voices. Heavy, booted steps. "Hello? Is anyone in there? This is the police, please open the door." A matter-of-fact declaration. Yet it fills you with terror. Lying in bed, you believe it is your bed, unless, so strangely, it is the floor, floorboards pressing through the carpet hard and solid seeming to push upward against your back, buttocks, tender naked heels. You are only partly clothed and very cold. Why are you so cold, you can't comprehend, the light woolen blanket wrapped tightly about you as in a child's urgent embrace but your legs are exposed, calves, ankles, feet. So exposed, the soles of your feet. *Why are you here? Go away! No one has called the police!* You try to sit up but can't, nor even push yourself up from your reclining position onto an elbow. Your legs seem twisted beneath you as if you've fallen from a great height. Your body is limp, paralyzed, as if every nerve, muscle, joint has been severed.

"Open this door, please!"—and another, deeper voice, "Police! Open up!" You hear the unmistakable sound of a door being forced, broken inward, *Go away! Leave me alone! You have no right!* Though your eyes are fixed stark and staring at the ceiling indistinct in shadows above you you can see the straining doorframe, the flying splinters. This is impossible, this cannot be happening, yet it is happening, and where can you hide? Crawl beneath the bed, when you can't move? Crawl into the bathroom, on the farther side of the room? The thin blanket is inadequate to protect you, there is something shameful in your near-nakedness, *Please leave me alone, please go away, we don't need you!*

Where is your husband, why hasn't he awakened?—or is he away, has he gone and left you alone and how long have you been alone waiting for his return? Married thirty years, and you can't recall his face! But no one will know.

The policemen pay not the slightest heed to your protests. There is a stamping and a crashing in the foyer of the apartment and the very floor shakes. A two-way radio emits a squawk like a parrot's, a blinding light is switched on overhead. You try to wrap yourself tighter in the blanket. *Leave me alone, how dare you,* you are sobbing, pleading, *don't look at me, go away!* In the bedroom doorway are strangers' faces, fleshy blurred faces and rude staring eyes. One of them is young, with glinting wire-rimmed spectacles that reflect the glaring overhead light. *No no no don't look at me!*

You are desperate to hide in the blanket and there is something congealed in it, sticking to your hair. And you are so cold you can't move: skin the sickly color of curdled milk, fingernails and toenails bruised from within as plums. So ashamed, so exposed, what right have these strangers in their uniforms to break into your apartment into your privacy into your thirty years' marriage into your soul now approaching you slowly, long trousered legs, gleaming leather belts, metallic studs, buckles, pistols drawn. Three uniformed men unknown to you staring down at you with expressions of a kind you have never seen before. "Je-sus God!" one of them says, whistling thinly. Another says, swallowing, "What *is* it? Is—?" The third says grimly, yet with an air of satisfaction, "Huh! You know what that is."

Through the rainspecked window a dark blue phosphorescent sky shot with veins of orange like something rotting.

Don't touch me, don't lift this blanket, go away, I am all right, I am myself, I will always be myself, I am only sleeping and you are my nightmare, apart from me you don't exist, don't touch me!

Two of them are squatting close by you, staring. A long moment of silence. One wipes his mouth on the edge of his hand, the other is speaking in that brusque matter-of-fact voice over the two-way radio. In the doorway of the white-tiled bathroom light bounces off the eyeglasses of the youngest policeman. It's a laugh, or a nervous clearing of his throat. Saying, If you think that's bad, take a look in here.

III

The Omen

A voice sounded close in my ear: *Here we are!*

It was early, before the sun had begun to burn off the coastal fog. The cries of gulls awakened me rudely. Why, louder than usual?—more penetrating, chilling? I lay in my bed and listened and decided that the cries were human cries, terrible to hear.

And yet—so early? When no one would surely be on the beach, still less swimming? In this secluded, windswept place, on a narrow spit of land three miles from the nearest village, and twenty miles from the nearest town. The great presence here was the Atlantic Ocean, and the sky.

How rapidly, when you have left your former life, the very landscape of that life becomes an abstraction, like a map.

A map you can fold up, and put away, and never trouble to look at again.

Yet the cries woke me. I had no choice. I dressed rapidly, with shaking fingers. Since coming to live in this remote place at the edge of the ocean I had become invisible, no longer required to see myself through others' eyes. I fumbled now with my clothing like a child not knowing how to push "buttons" through "buttonholes," tug up "zippers" against their natural resistance.

I had no time for shoes, but ran barefoot down to the beach.

We were in midsummer now, but the air was cold. Goose pimples formed on my arms. The damp salt air stung my eyes. Gulls *were* excitedly circling in the air—but, yes, there were children too, on the beach, by the water's edge, just below my cottage. They were crouched over something that lay in the surf. Sighting me, one of them waved, and called out words I couldn't hear; another poked him, as if in rebuke. These children ranged in age between approximately eleven and eight; I recognized two or three of them, among the group of six, but I did not know their names, nor did I know their parents. The cottages here are hidden from one another and from the sandy road that joins us with the mainland—that is the reason, after all, that we came here.

As I advanced upon them, the children fell silent, and began to retreat. The breakers were rough, windblown; the white froth riding the waves had an old man's look of incoherent rage. On the beach, the surf swept over, and washed back from, something that lay entangled with seaweed, motionless.

"What is it?"—I heard my voice, the voice of adult authority, cry out to the children.

But the children did not reply. Exchanging glances with one another—were they frightened? defiant? lewd? bemused?—they laughed and trotted away.

What a strangely shaped piece of driftwood, or debris, there on the beach. . . . Was it a human, naked body, a corpse? washed in by the tide? But it was too small to be a human corpse.

It *was* too small, about the size of one of the herring gulls so noisily circling overhead. At first I thought it might in fact be a fledgling gull, featherless, fatally out of its nest before it could fly: a limp, helpless creature about twenty inches long.

As I stooped over it, I heard myself whistle in astonishment—in shock.

The thing at my feet was not a bird, but, incredibly, a man—a fully mature man, the size of an infant. It was tangled in seaweed dark and shiny as eels, it was so pale as to seem, in the pallid dawn, faintly luminescent; it was naked, dead. *Not* a baby, nor a human fetus, but a man, of any age between thirty and fifty, with a large head hairless except for a fine, dark down, and smooth jaws, and thin bloodless lips drawn back tight in a grimace from small uneven pearly-gray teeth. The eyes were slightly protuberant, the bluish lids not quite shut over them. I saw the eyelashes quiver.

My God, how could it be!—*what* could it be!

I came closer, to squat over it. My heart was beating rapidly as if to warn me away.

The thing was dead, yet as the surf washed over it, rocking it gently, it gave an appearance of being alive.

It was lying on its left side, with a look of serenity after enormous effort and pain. The bony legs were bent at the knee, the gracefully curving back showed miniature knobs of bone along the spinal column. The head was disproportionately large for the body, I thought. Had it lived—had he lived—for this was, not *it*, but *he*— his neck would surely have been too frail to support his head. His shoulders too were abnormally narrow.

I was blinking, rubbing at my eyes. Had the mist affected my vision? Or was I still asleep, mired in a nightmare as in the soft, wet, shifting-sucking sand beneath my feet?

But this was no dream, the little man was real enough. I would have poked it with my foot except the gesture would have been too rude, I would have touched it—him—with my hand, but I could not bring myself to do so.

Him, not it. For clearly he was human, like me; and, like me, male.

The bluish eyelids quivered as if about to open. The little forehead was furrowed, as if stitched, somber, resigned, with thought.

A sensation of horror ran through me. Was it—he—alive?

Between the legs, in miniature, were perfectly proportioned male genitalia, pale like the rest of the body, flaccid and smooth as something skinned. The thighs were painfully thin, the bones at the hip joints prominent, as if about to poke through the skin. The belly, however, was round, and tight, a little potbelly, virtually. Which led me to think that the man was of young middle age, like me.

His navel was like a tiny gnarl or knot in the flesh. Like a tiny eye.

No sun had yet appeared, only a pale-glowering light devoid of warmth. Yet, by degrees, as it did most mornings, the fog began to fade. Objects defined themselves. The children had retreated nearly out of earshot but the gulls continued to circle the air not far away, vexed and impatient.

I became aware too of an unusual amount of debris on the beach this morning, as after a storm. (But had there been a storm? I did not think so.) Numerous sizable clumps of seaweed, driftwood, paper, shredded bits of Styrofoam, a briny smell as of dead fish. There were elongated pale figures here and there in the scattered debris but I didn't look too closely.

I was staring at the thing at my feet. The little man. The man.

In recounting this episode, I am conscious of arranging words with care; I am always conscious of arranging words with care. For misunderstanding frightens and angers me. Yet, my recounting of the episode with such care *is* a misunderstanding: for, at the time, I was weak with horror, a sense of helplessness, despair . . . certain repudiated emotions that, in fact, I had retreated to the edge of the continent, to escape. Seeing the little man made me realize that the physical world that gives birth to us, nurtures and contains and defines us, is not really *our* world. It is not the world we would have invented.

And yet—"Here we are!"

(Had I spoken? The words came back to me, borne by the wind, a sound of anguish, wonder.)

Did I imagine it, or did the little man's hollow chest rise, as if he'd inhaled a sudden deep breath . . . and did his lips move, just perceptibly, as if he were about to speak?

But I was standing, I stood at my full height, quick to cover sand and debris over his pathetic little corpse. I kicked with my bare feet, I dragged clumps of seaweed to bury him, quick! quick! to save him from the gulls.

I was shivering almost convulsively. That cold east wind, blowing relentless from the open sea. That glowering east sky, so grudging to turn transparent, to let the sun's light through. Icy-cold tendrils of water washed over my feet, mad-lapping froth-tongues tickled the soles of my feet. "It's better, this way! You'll see! It's the only way!"

Again, my words seemed to come at me from the outside, borne by the wind. My lips moved clumsily, as if far away, on the very outside of my being.

I buried the little man as best as could be expected of me. When I could do no more, I turned and walked swiftly away, not looking back.

Of course, it was impossible to return to sleep that morning.

And subsequent mornings . . . it seems I no sooner lay my head on my pillow in the dark when, abruptly, it's dawn, and I'm awakened by cries and shouts down on the beach. Why this has happened to me, if it is a curse against my person, or, as so much in the natural world, sheerly an accident, I don't know.

This morning, waking groggily, I staggered to the door against my better judgment, and looked out. Another time, the figures of children on the beach. Not directly below my cottage, thank God, but a few hundred yards to the north. There was quite a gang of them this time, as many as eight or ten, and they were circling something the tide had washed ashore, the boldest of them poking at it with their bare feet. I knew the place: it was where a crumbling concrete wall juts out purposelessly into the crashing waves, and where every kind of garbage seems to be funneled, seaweed, dead fish, jellyfish, God knows what all else. But what is that to me?

The Sons of Angus MacElster

A *true tale of Cape Breton Island, Nova Scotia, 1923.*
This insult not to be borne. Not by the MacElster sons who
were so proud. From New Glasgow to Port Hawkesbury to Glace
Bay at the wind-buffeted easternmost tip of Cape Breton Island,
where the accursed family lived, it was spoken of. All who knew of
the scandal laughed, marveled, shook their heads over it. The
MacElsters!—that wild crew! Six strapping sons and but a single
daughter no man dared approach for fear of old Angus and his
sons, heavy drinkers, tavern brawlers, what can you expect? Yet
what old Angus MacElster did, and to his own wife, you'd scarcely
believe: he'd been gone for three months on a coal-bearing merchant ship out of Halifax, returning home to Glace Bay on a
wet-dripping April midday, his handsome ruin of a face windburnt
and ruddy with drink, driving with two other merchant seamen
who lived in the Bay area, old friends of his, and at the tall weatherworn woodframe house on Mull Street overlooking the harbor he
dropped his soiled gear, freshened up and spent a brief half hour in
the company of Mrs. MacElster, and the nervous daughter Katy
now twenty years old and still living at home, Angus stood before
the icebox devouring cold meat loaf with his fingers, breaking off
morsels with his stubby gnarled fingers, and washing down his
lunch in haste with ale he'd brought with him in several clinking
bottles in the pockets of his sheepskin jacket, then it was off to the

Mare's Neck as usual, and drinking with his old companions, how like old times it was, and never any improvement in the man's treatment of his wife. Returned to Glace Bay for three weeks before he'd ship out again and already there was a hint of trouble, it was Katy put the call to Rob, the eldest son, and Rob drove over at once from Sydney in an automobile borrowed from his employer at the pulp mill under the pretext of a family emergency, and Cal in his delivery van drove over from Briton Cove, and there was Alistair hurrying from New Skye, and John Rory and John Allan and I, the youngest, live here in Glace Bay where we'd been born, freely we admit we'd been drinking too, you must drink to prepare yourself for the hurtful old man we loved with a fierce hateful love, the heated love of boys for their father, even a father who has long betrayed them with his absence, and the willful withholding of his love, yet we longed like craven dogs to receive our father's blessing, any careless touch of his gnarly hand, we longed to receive his rough wet despairing kisses on the lips of the kind he'd given us long ago when we were boys, before the age of ten, so the very memory of such kisses is uncertain to us, ever shifting and capricious as the fog in the harbor every morning of our waking lives. *Even at that late hour, our hearts might yet have been won.*

Except: unknown to us at the time our mother had gone in reckless despair to the Mare's Neck to seek our father, and the two quarreled in the street where idlers gathered to gawk, at the foot of New Harbor Street in a chill glistening wind, and we would be told that he'd raised a hand to her and she'd cried *Disgusting! How can you!—disgusting! God curse you!* tears shining on her cheeks, and her hair the color of tarnished silver loosened in the wind, and she'd pushed at the old man which you must never do, you must never touch the old man for it is like bringing a lighted match to straw, you can witness the wild blue flame leaping up his body, leaping in his eyes, his eyes bulging like a horse's and red-veined with drink, the flame in his graying red hair the color of fading sumac in autumn, and in a rage he seizes the collar of her old cardigan sweater she'd knitted years ago, seizes it and tears it, and as idlers from the several pubs of New Harbor Street stare in astonishment he tears her dress open, cursing her, *Cow! Sodden cow! Look at you, ugly sodden cow!* ripping her clothes from her, exposing our cringing mother in the halterlike white cotton brassiere she must wear to contain her enormous breasts, milk-pale flaccid breasts hanging nearly to her waist she tries to hide with her arms, our mother publicly shamed pleading with our father *Angus, no! Stop! I beg you, God help you—no!* Yet in his drunken rage Angus MacElster strips his wife of thirty-six years near-naked, as the poor woman shrieks and sobs at the foot of New Harbor Street, and a loose crowd of beyond twenty men has gathered to watch, some of them grinning and laughing but most of them plainly shocked, even the drunks are shocked by a man so publicly humiliating his wife, and his wife a stout middle-aged woman with graying hair, until at last Angus MacElster is persuaded to leave his wife alone, to back off and leave the poor hysterically weeping woman alone, one or two of the men wrap her in their jackets, hide her nakedness, even as old Angus turns aside with a wave of his hand in disgust and stumbles off to Mull Street three blocks away yet not to the tall weatherworn woodframe house, but instead to the old barn at the rear, muttering and cursing and laughing to himself Angus sinks insensible into the straw, like a horse in its stall in a luxuriance of sleep where, when we were small boys, he'd spent many a night even in winter, returning late to the house and not caring to blunder into our mother's domain not out of fear of her wrath nor even of his own wrath turned against her but simply because he was drawn to sleeping in the barn, in his clothes, in his boots, luxuriant in such deep dreamless animal sleep as we, his sons, waited inside the house shuddering and shivering in anticipation of his return, his heavy footsteps on the stairs, yet yearning for his return as a dog yearns for the return of the very master who will kick him, praying he would not cuff us, or beat us, or kick us, or yank at our coarse red curls so like his own in that teasing tenderness of our father's that seemed to us far crueller than actual cruelty for at such times you were meant to smile and not cringe, you were meant to love him and not fear him, you were meant to obey him and not turn mutinous, you were meant to

honor your father and not loathe him, still less were you meant to
pray for his death, steeped in sin as you were, even at a young age,
even in childhood touched by the curse of the MacElsters, emi-
grated from the wind-ravaged highlands north of Inverness to the
new world with blood, it was rumored, on their hands, and murder
in their hearts. And there at the house when we arrived was our
mother weeping deranged with shock and humiliation, her mouth
bloodied, and Katy tending to her white-faced and shaking as if she
too had been stripped naked in the street, and would be the scan-
dalized talk of all who knew the MacElsters and countless others
who did not, from Glace Bay to Port Hawkesbury to New Glasgow
and beyond, talk to endure for years, for decades, for generations
to this very day; and seeming to know this as a fact, Angus's six
sons wasted no time, we strode into the barn known to us as a
dream inhabited nightly, that place of boyhood chores, of boyhood
play, badly weatherworn, with missing boards and rotted shingles
loosened by wind, glaring-eyed Rob has taken up the doubled-
edged ax where it was leaning against the doorframe, and Cal the
resourceful one has brought from home a twelve-inch fish-gutting
knife, Alistair has a wicked pair of shears, John Rory and John Allan have their matching hunting knives of eight-inch stainless steel,
and I have a newly honed butcher knife from my own house, from
out of my own kitchen where my young wife will miss it, and the six
of us enter the barn to see the old man snoring in the twilight, in a
patch of damp straw, and panting we circle him, our eyes gleaming
like those of feral creatures glimpsed by lamplight in the dusk, and
Rob is the first to shout for him to *Wake! wake up, old man!*—for it
seems wrong to murder a sixty-one-year-old man snoring on his
back, fatty-muscled torso exposed, arms and legs sprawled in a
bliss of drunken oblivion, and at once old Angus opens his eyes, his
bulging red-veined horse's eyes, blinking up at us, knowing us,
naming us one by one his six MacElster sons as damned as he, and
yet *even at this late hour our hearts might yet be won.* Except, being the man he is, old Angus curses us, calls us young shits, spits at
us, tries to stumble to his feet to fight us, even as the first of our
blows strikes. Rob's double-edged ax like electricity leaping out of

the very air, and there's the flash of Cal's fish-gutting knife, and
Alistair's shears used for stabbing, and the fine-honed razor-
sharp blades of John Rory and John Allan's and mine, blades sharp
enough and strong enough to pierce the hide of the very devil himself, and in a fever of shouts and laughter we strike, and tear, and
lunge, and stab, and pierce, and gut, and make of the old man's
wind-roughened skin a lacy-bloody shroud and of his bones brittle
sticks as easily broken as dried twigs, and of his terrible eyes
cheap baubles to be gouged out and ground into the dirt beneath
our boots, and of his hard skull a mere clay pot to be smashed
into bits, and of his blood gushing hot and shamed onto the straw
and the dirt floor of the barn a glistening stream bearing bits of
cobweb, dust, and straw as if a sluice were opened, and we leap
about shouting with laughter for this is a game, is it?—will the
steaming poison-blood of Angus MacElster singe our boots?—sully
our boots?—will some of us be tainted by this blood and others, the
more agile, the more blessed, will not?

*This old family tale came to me from my father's father Charles
MacElster, the eldest son of Cal.*

(after Ovid)

The Affliction

Always they ask of him: When did you begin? Was it drawing at first, when you were a child, crayons, paints?—how soon did your talent emerge? And he's polite saying he doesn't remember exactly, probably he began at school, he hadn't much opportunity to draw or paint at home it wasn't that kind of household, working-class, parents weren't educated beyond ninth grade and had a difficult life, economically and in other ways he'd prefer not to discuss. Always polite, coolly formal and precise in his speech; an austere white-haired elder, a man of rumored (never substantiated!) secrets. He has the eyes of a *seer*, a *prophet* it's been written romantically of him, the eyes of one who has delved *deeply and unflinchingly into life*. Through his career of over fifty years he has avoided discussing his art professionally and now as one of the most respected artists of his generation he's become known and admired for what journalists call his *reclusiveness, his reticence, his Yankee integrity*. As sparing in his words as he has been prolific and extravagant in his art. Yet, the idiotic questions persist: when, how did you begin? how young? what is the source of your inspiration? of what substance is the remarkable material you work with? As if these are urgent questions multitudes of people are eager to know, multitudes eager to emulate *the artist*!

He's polite. Simply terminates the conversation, excuses himself saying he doesn't truly remember and doesn't wish to invent.

The *affliction*: the *things* never named. So long ago, before he was capable of speech, scarcely able to walk, approximately ten months old when the affliction first showed itself: a rash between his small fingers and toes, across his belly, in the region of his tiny genitals, an ordinary rash his mother supposed except it persisted, began to spread, striations in the smooth poreless flesh as if he'd been bitten by insects, raw, reddened, he whimpered and cried and picked at the afflicted areas of his skin with his nails though his mother bathed him frequently, in growing desperation rubbing salve on the rashes and taking him to the doctor who was puzzled by the affliction too, prescribing what medications he knew, which sometimes had an effect and sometimes had no discernible effect at all. Until at last when he was three years old and otherwise healthy a virulent eruption covered his torso and he was delirious with a fever of 102° F and an elder uncle of his father's was summoned, he who'd been mysteriously afflicted with a skin problem through his life, and this kindly man bathed the child in warm water and Epsom salts and showed the frightened parents how the welts, clots, boils—the *things* as he called them—might be safely extracted from the child's flesh, with an instrument no more exotic than a sterilized tweezers. For these *things* were not identical with the child's flesh but were excrescences of the flesh, toxins perhaps, infections or perhaps even parasites to be dealt with swiftly and practicably and flushed down the toilet. These were cobwebby strands of bloody mucus-matter, wormlike coils of puss, partly coagulated blood-clots. The child had to be held as, with a deft hand, the uncle extracted the *things*, some of them no larger than a kernel of corn, some as large as dimes, throbbing with heat and of an odor of rankness, like an overripe peach. The operation took about forty minutes. The child screamed in pain and terror, thrashing in the tub. But when the last of the *things* had been extirpated from his body, and damp, cold compresses placed on the afflicted areas, his fever began at once to subside; within a few days the wounds were healed, at least to the naked eye. "You see," the uncle said, "the affliction isn't fatal. It's something you can learn to live with, as I have. Until you scarcely think of it until it happens. And then, of course," he said, smiling, shrugging, "you have no choice."

Six weeks, three months, five months might pass between bouts of the mysterious eruption. There seemed no discernible pattern to it, nor any relationship to the child's general health, or behavior. If in the eyes of his anxious parents he was a *good boy*, or a *bad boy*, this had no bearing whatsoever upon the virulent *things* which seemed to possess a life, a purposeful will of their own, not in opposition to him but unrelated to him, wholly! Except of course the *things* were him, flesh of his flesh. Gradually he came to realize, with childish resentment, that other children were not afflicted as he was; no one even in his family except his great-uncle was subject to such *things* burrowing and churning in his flesh. So he knew he had to be secretive about it, for his malady was shameful, unspeakable—his parents chose not to speak of it, and never again took him to a doctor; if this was a sign of their blood's curse, they wanted no one to know. By the age of nine he was removing most of the *things* from his body unassisted; by the age of eleven, made precocious by his suffering, he'd developed ways of shielding his parents from knowing, or having to acknowledge, that he was having an attack; for, as he reasoned, they were not to blame for this curse he'd inherited, no more than he himself was to blame. Or, if somehow blamable, yet guiltless: helpless carriers of genes of an unfathomable code. At the age of twelve, sent home from school with suspicion of having chicken pox, in the early stage of the affliction he locked himself in the bathroom and with tweezers and a small scissors extracted the first wormlike excrescences as they showed themselves on his torso, determined to stop the *things* at their source, yet faster and faster they came, more rapid his pulse, he was weak and light-headed with fever, a voice seemed to taunt *What can you do! what can you do!* as he whimpered, wept as much in frustration as pain. His senses were heightened, his sense of smell particularly, the stench of overripe fruit, rank rotting flesh made him nauseated, yet he prevailed, he attacked the hellish coils, clots, sinewy threads with his instruments, ignoring his mother who rapped on the door begging him to open it, to let her help him.

But no: he would do it alone: he was not a child any longer, incapable of caring for himself. This marked the beginning of his new attitude toward his affliction, for he would master it, like his great-uncle; the *things* were shame, and pain, and disgusting to see, touch, smell, yet the *things* of which he could never speak to his classmates were precisely what made him different from his classmates, the carrier of a secret. In the hours preceding an attack, too, his thoughts seemed virtually to fly, he felt elation and terror as if the very sky were to crack open for his benefit and God to speak in thunder *What can you do! what can you do!—nothing.* Except, though he could not forestall an attack, he could confront it bravely, and briskly; as his great-uncle had shown him, with calmness, method. He would be a clinician of his own pathology. And how fascinating too the *things* were, once he forced himself to look at them and didn't quickly dispose of them averting his eyes: bits of tissue and nerve, blood-threaded, sometimes opaque but more often semi-translucent, of the fluid-slippery texture of a jellyfish. Some of the *things* were smaller than his smallest fingernail; others, tugged out of his flesh, pulled to their fullest, elastic length, measured as long as eight inches. Turning to contemplate his back in a mirror he sucked in his breath, astonished: there were swirls and arabesques in his flesh, bas-reliefs the size of half-dollars, constellations and peacocks' eyes, of every conceivable hue, though burnished gold as if a powerful light, or heat, emanated from the afflicted skin. Where he'd always felt shame now he began to feel pride. For the *things* were his, his alone.

It was then he acquired a microscope, to examine the *things* more closely. Discovering to his amazement tiny tendrils, or hooks, where to the naked eye there was only smoothness—which accounted for the pain of removing the *things*, embedded in his flesh. How complex their texture, wildly colored, and imbricated like a fish's scales! Amazing to him too, and only mildly repugnant, was the fact that the *things* when freshly taken from him appeared to be living organisms, that died and began rapidly to dry and calcify unprotected by his body heat.

Instead of flushing the *things* away down the toilet, shielding his eyes from them in disgust, he began to save them. For weren't they after all not symptoms of an affliction merely, but signs of something mysterious, not to be named? Placed on a flat surface, the *things* dried to shell-like shapes, of startling colors: bronze, blood-rust, tawny-golden, bruiselike hues of purple, orange-green, iridescent blue. How beautiful! His hands moved gropingly, arranging them into designs; while they were still moist, he could affix them, like putty, to a surface that might be upended. His first crude artworks, bas-reliefs, which he expanded by mixing in clay and acrylics, into strange, vivid, dreamlike designs, fascinating, mesmerizing. He made dozens of them, and hid them away. Someday he would show his shocked parents, someday even a trusted teacher at his school, but this would not be for years; until his secret places filled up with his artworks. Now, in the grip of the affliction, his fever and rapid pulse had much to do with his fervor for capturing the *things* in their moist, livid state, torn from his body and pressed directly onto the canvas; his blood too was often smeared on the canvas, bright red drying to an unmistakable red-black, one of his secret colors. He worked blindly, instinctively. Half-shutting his eyes, mixing the *things* in with other materials, modeling clay, acrylics, sometimes oils, strips of paper, cloth, dried thistles, flowers—he moved in a paroxysm of such intense excitement, he forgot himself for hours; there was no *self* where he stood; the pain of removing the *things* from his body was forgotten entirely in the ferocity of his concentration.

What a use to make of his affliction, he'd afterward think, exhausted, yet elated. His great-uncle, a man of limited imagination, like most men, would never have thought of such a thing.

So this is what I am, then: an artist. So that is my identity, my place in the world.

Things he would think of them, and of his artworks, too: *things*. Never to be explained, nor even hinted at, to any other person.

He became, surprisingly, a theoretician of his art: it intrigued him how, out of the chaotic mixture of his body's excrescences and what might be termed neutral materials, there could be fashioned a presence of a kind that, though inanimate, mimicked life: to glance at one of his artworks, however casually, was to feel a stab of—what?—an uncanny, panicked recognition?

Strange, too, how he came to know himself *healthy* as others could not know themselves, for he knew, intimately, what *unhealth* was; for him, in fact, a relatively small part of his actual life, over which he exerted, he believed, increasing control. When he was in the grip of the affliction, he gave himself over to it entirely—as his great-uncle had said, he hadn't much choice. But, the rest of the time, he was acutely conscious of being free of the affliction, and "well." What the world calls "well."

He laughed, thinking of it. His secret! Did others have such secrets, were other artists similarly cursed, and blessed? He did not know, and could not have risked trying to discover. *We can admire and respect one another but never know one another: so be it.*

Years, and decades. He left his home in a small New England city; he moved to New York; boldly, as if it were his fate, and no one dared impede him, he began to exhibit his art—collages, bas-reliefs, some of the works enormous, of the size of Picasso's "Guernica." His name became quickly known. His art became "controversial." As a young man in his twenties he accumulated awards, prizes, grants; he acquired a public, semipopular reputation; what was perceived as his *reclusiveness*, his *isolation*, his *uncooperativeness* with the media did not hurt him, at all. Unexpectedly, perhaps because he'd never sought it, he acquired, even, the respect of his fellow artists—some of them, at least. He was not a fashionable man, yet with disconcerting swiftness his work became fashionable; which is to say, it fetched high prices. It was described by critics with the artillery of words at their command—*powerful! haunting! disturbing! visceral!* Above all, *mysterious!* His exhibits seemed, to him, the work of another person; younger, more naive. Thus his reputation for aloofness, detachment. For being courteously indifferent to others' opinions, even when the opinions were generous, enthusiastic, seemingly informed.

Lavished with praise, he hid his uneasiness, or his mirth; he appeared to be listening thoughtfully. Saying, with downgazing gravity, stroking his jaw, Thank you. Thank you very much.

Make of it what you will: it's no more mine than yours.

The surprising fact of his life was that he was by no means always, and exclusively, the *artist*. He was a *man*, a *person*, even a *citizen*, with moderately strong political beliefs; even, again moderately, an *athlete* (tennis, long-distance running). In his twenties he loved a number of women and in his early thirties he dared to marry, and to become a *husband*, and a *father*. For the affliction was such a small part of his life, really. The affliction, the *things*— assimilated into his life as a cycle, a routine; though not precisely predictable, yet predictable as always, inevitably, *there*. Except for skin blemishes to be passed off as birthmarks or old acne scars, or a puffy redness about the face from time to time, and oscillations of mood and temper which seemed but part of his character, he could pass as "normal"; when an attack was imminent, he withdrew to his studio to deal with the *things* as he'd always done. No one dared interrupt him at such times, not even his wife. He'd told her at the start of their marriage *We love each other but we can't know each other. If you accept me, you must accept this.*

Of course, she'd accepted it. She would be an artist's wife, and not an artist.

Years, decades. Now in his seventies, a white-haired man bemused by his own physical presence: *This? me?—so be it.* Now at the Fifty-Year Retrospective of his work. Entering the museum anonymously, unrecognized in tinted glasses, a shapeless hat, rumpled workclothes, one weekday afternoon in winter. A senior citizen's ticket—of course! He was mildly anxious, his heartbeat quickened, though telling himself what did it matter?—he'd seen the exhibit as it was being hung, he knew the works, they'd passed through his hands and through his very body; his career was behind him, or nearly. The Retrospective, organized by this wellfunded museum in a northerly, seacoast city, consisted of over two hundred of his works, the strange collage/bas-reliefs for which he'd become internationally known; a half dozen galleries were given over to them, dramatically hung against stark white walls.

How is it possible, how do such things happen?—he'd long since ceased to inquire.

There was a larger, more heterogeneous crowd making their way through the exhibit than he would have expected—his first sensation was childish panic. Who were these people? City-dwellers, tourists? Why had they come, this windy weekday afternoon, to so peculiar an exhibit? He overheard snatches of foreign languages— German? Italian? Surprisingly shy, for he'd never been a shy man, of looking too openly at them, or inadvertently eavesdropping: he wasn't that kind of person, after all. He did not care in the slightest how these strangers reacted to his art, did he?—he'd never cared, and now he was an old man, hardly vulnerable.

In a short space of time, which, he knew, would pass swiftly, he would be eighty years old. The *things* still ravaged his body, but less frequently, and less virulently. He did not want to think that they were aging, too—wearing out. But it was true, of course. He might go as long as a full year between attacks; his art, correspondingly, was less plentiful.

Slowly, walking with a slight limp, which he'd only just recently noticed, he made his way into the first of the exhibit rooms. Early Work. How shaky he felt, how tense the atmosphere of the room, like the air before an electrical storm! He was certain he was not imagining it. The ventilation system left much to be desired. He peered through his glasses at the *things* in their transmogrified state and felt an instant's vertigo, that, exposing himself as he had, so shamelessly, he'd committed a transgression of a kind; a violation of human pride, propriety. Yet—if no one knew, could it be transgression? And who could judge *him*?

Moving through the rooms, and through his life. He was not certain that he felt anything at all. He did see, as critics had busied themselves pointing out, the evolution of the work of his youth, which was raw, crude, primitive—"powerful, visceral"—through stages of increasing complexity and strategic style; the phase of several years when he'd seemed to be emulating classic Persian designs, starkly geometric and severe in his colors; a reaction against this asceticism, a gradual loosening of shapes, a fluidity of color; a late return to the cruder and more savage designs, in which nameless life-forms seemed to bleed and ooze on the canvases, which had occupied the last several years of his life. He'd become, in his old age, obsessive in a different way—obsessed with perfection, with closure. With hiding himself even as, emotionally, he seemed to be exposing himself. But it was all a trompe l'oeil—wasn't it? Art's strategy, not art.

One thing, he had to admit, was clear: to the detached observer, it certainly did seem that the artist had been touched by some sort of inner vision, whether divine or demonic; this art, bizarre, enigmatic, so strangely, painstakingly detailed, seemed the very antithesis of the coolly contrived and arbitrary art of the contemporary American scene. And how gorgeous its colors, and textures!—a glittering winking galaxy of ancient shells, fossils, phosphorescent minerals; a richness that provoked the eye, but seemed to stir other senses as well. An art of the body, the body's inner being? Was that the secret here?

The artist made his way through the slow-moving, attentive crowd of viewers. A ringing began in his ears like the tolling of a distant bell. *What can you do! what can you do!*

In the last room, a gathering of viewers had accumulated before one of the largest canvases in the exhibit, "The Healing"; the artist had been told that this was the most popular of his works, if "popular" is the correct term. It was part of the mythology of this artist that certain of his works were so disturbing, yet so mysterious, that they struck viewers dumb and held them in rapt fascination, in the way of Titian's "Marsyas Flayed by Apollo," or Picasso's "Guernica," causing gallery rooms to become increasingly congested as more viewers entered, and others were slow to leave. The artist saw, with bemused irony, that this was so: a solemn, staring crowd of as many as thirty people stood before the painting. And more approaching!

"The Healing" was a creation of only a few years ago, so the artist should have remembered it vividly, yet he did not; not vividly; but in that way of a dream once overwhelming in its emotion, yet now long past. He had to grant, somewhat grudgingly, that it *was* . . . striking. It had become a controversial item, since a prominent critic had attacked it in print, and a second, equally prominent critic had vigorously defended it. And it had sold for an absurdly high price to one of the great museums of the world. "The Healing" contained certain of the qualities of the early art, a dramatic, eye-stopping array of colors and shapes, fluid-seeming, and moist; yet it was meticulously laid out, like a nineteenth-century engraving, suggesting, in the way of a fading dream, a subterranean city beneath a surface of dazzling motion. The artist stared at the work past the heads and shoulders of strangers, seeing not the bronze-lacquered sheen of the canvas, nor the rust-red grid beneath, the *things* in their crystalline, calcified state, nor any of the much-admired "painterly" features that must have captivated these credulous viewers; he saw instead, horribly, a white-haired man doubled over in agony, body covered in boil-like eruptions, who was coughing, choking, red-faced as with panicked fingers to save his life he reached far into his throat to tug out a shimmering-coagulated sticky ropy substance . . . hideous! unspeakable!

"That! What d'you suppose that *is*? 'The Healing'—eh!"

It was he who spoke, suddenly; derisively; shattering the quiet of the room, attracting glances. He was breathing hoarsely and his face was covered in beads of perspiration. He looked about, grinning; beside him stood a well-dressed middle-aged woman who'd annoyed him with her attentive face, her contemplation of the monstrous thing on the wall, and she took a step back, easing away from him, yet without so much as a glance at him. It was as if, in his place, there was no one—nothing at all.

To a young couple, who particularly irritated him with their intense, furrowed expressions, how like a pair of brain-damaged sheep, he said, laughing contemptuously, "It's fraudulent, phony—just something to make you *look*." He was speaking in a loud, wavering voice; his old-man's hands, the knobby knuckles, flailing about. But this couple, too, discreetly ignored him; whispered together and edged away. He was made to feel quite the fool.

He laughed, louder. Rubbing his eyes, that stung with moisture. "Sir? Is something wrong?"—a museum guard approached, frowning at him. So he *was* anonymous, he *was* invisible, after all: no one knew him. Laughing until his chest pinched with pain, his rib cage made of dried, brittle sticks collapsing in upon itself. Well, it *was* funny, hilariously funny—wasn't it?

Walking then blindly, pushing past these gaping fools, dazed and limping yet managing to retain his pride, his posture, through a confusion of rooms, airless claustrophobic galleries hung to the point of madness with others' *things*; then, suddenly, what relief!— he was in the open air, his heart pounding erratically and his breath short but he was in the open air, the perspiration on his face dried within seconds. He avoided the street, turned to walk through a sparsely wooded park, in the direction of a bay, drawn by the colder wind and by the smell of water, coming to a seawall, a place unknown to him, a part-crumbling stone foundation that nonetheless bore his weight as limping, wiping at his eyes he saw the choppy water, dark-sparkling phosphorescence of the undersea churned to the surface, waves of surpassing beauty. The sun shattered into a million fragments in the waves, one moment glittering like jewels and the next, as a cloud obscured the sun, opaque and flat; lead-colored; yet again, a minute later, as the sun reemerged striking the waves in scintillating nervelike patterns, hypnotic to the eye.

He stood there staring, he would stand there, buffeted by the wind, shivering, until, hours later, he was found, identified and helped away.

What can you do! what can you do!—nothing. Yet, he had to grant, he'd done well enough.

Scars

Strange to discover myself last week, in the midst of a protracted and exhausting siege of travel in the eastern United States, in K——, my former hometown! I had not returned to K—— in twenty-six years, I no longer had any close relatives living there, nor any sentimental reason for returning since I'd left to go to college at the age of eighteen. *And I was covered in scars, my face, my body, from those eighteen years.*

Yet suddenly, with no warning, there I was, as in a cruel dream—in K——.

(I must have signed a contract to bring me to K—— sometime in the spring. My contracts are elaborately drawn up by agents, I sign them without reading them, my head would ache to read them, I haven't time in my busy life to read them. Now I've become much in demand, I haven't time to consider exactly where, and when, I'm scheduled to appear. Yet it didn't escape me that for a visit to K——, in a dreary, economically depressed region of eastern Pennsylvania, far from any sizable city, my agents must have negotiated a shrewd fee.)

Talk to me of K——! My old, thrilling dreams of K——! To the neutral eye a small, typically American city of no special distinction, built up in the mid-nineteenth century on the eastern bank of the Susquehanna River; in the foothills of the Appalachian Mountains. Formerly coal-mining country, an iron-smelting region. In its prime in the 1950's, a moderately prosperous river city, K—— had about 45,000 inhabitants; now, since numerous factory closings, and a general decline in jobs, that number must have considerably dropped. In my memory K—— is a place of tall, gaunt, dying trees and perpetual wind bearing a distinct sulphurous odor; surrounded by stony soil, outcroppings of rock granite and limestone like scars in the earth. *Yes but I was so happy there. Such excruciating joy, I had to flee to save my life.*

There, to my surprise and embarrassment, at the cavernous old train depot—for K—— no longer supported an airport—was a small but enthusiastic throng of well-wishers to greet me. What enlivened faces, voices chanting in unison my name and "Welcome to K——! Welcome back to K——! K——'s most celebrated Citizen of the World—*welcome!*"

Here, their voices echoing in the high-domed, nearly deserted depot was a gathering of city officials, including the mayor and his aides, and K—— Arts Council people, who'd invited me; and a number of others, including, I gathered, former school classmates of mine, whose teasingly familiar faces loomed up at me out of the shadowy interior of the building like faces glimpsed in a fever dream. The mayor, solidly built as a fire hydrant, with a beaming face, a hearty handshake, identified himself as "Carly" Carlson—a 1967 graduate of K—— High School, from which I'd graduated in 1969; vaguely and uncomfortably I recalled "Carly"—a brash, popular athlete who'd never so much as glanced at me during the time we attended the same school, but who seemed to recall me now with much pleasure. As cameras flashed, "Carly" shook my hand several times, with such vigor that I had all I could do to resist wincing in pain. As a local television filmed us, "Carly" presented me with a bouquet of a dozen bloodred roses and proclaimed, "K——'s most acclaimed Citizen of the World—welcome back! Congratulations on your remarkable achievement!" He pronounced my name with sliding, melodic vowels as if it were, not a graceless ethnic-American name, but an elegant name. A gesture of his hand, and the K—— High School band, in formation at the rear of the gathering, struck up a spirited, brassy piece I recognized as the K—— school anthem; in an instant I felt dazed, dizzy with a stab of nostalgic emotion. I wanted to cry *Not again! Not again.*

Yet I gave no sign of my distress. Never, in K——, I vowed, would I show any true emotion.

Yet, the ride in the mayoral limousine through the old downtown to the newly refurbished Hotel K—— left me excited and shaken, for while the outskirts of the city were garishly built up, like the outskirts of most American cities, the city center had changed very little in twenty-six years. There were the old landmarks I recalled so distinctly, for how many times I'd walked, usually alone, on Main Street; the once-impressive and now weatherworn buildings—the First Bank of K——, the Savings & Loan of Susquehanna, the city's prestige department store Adams Brothers, the YW-YMCA on Elm Street and Trinity Church on Pine Street and on hilly Charity Street the small, expensive shops selling women's and girls' clothing I hadn't dared to enter, as a girl; except, I saw, most of these small shops were now vacant; one, the Tartan Shop, into whose window I would gaze yearningly, seemed to have become a video store. And there was the glamorous old Rialto Theatre—now a discount shoe store, its marquee glowering with fluorescent-bright advertising. Several of the dignified old buildings had been superficially renovated, with new, stylish, rather cheap-looking facades, a good deal of tinted plate glass, gleaming aluminum trim. Where South Main Street had been there was a pedestrian mall lined with spindly trees. Where derelict riverfront buildings had been there was a "civic center" of poured concrete and open, windswept terraces. As the limousine moved past, I found myself staring eagerly at the old Church Street Bridge, made of intricately structured wrought iron, with a narrow pedestrian walk where, as a girl coming home from junior high school, I lingered to lean against the railing and watch for long dreamy minutes the dark river passing swiftly beneath. "Susquehanna"—I whispered aloud. What mystery in that name! *But a river doesn't know its name* I would think shrewdly. *Nothing apart from human beings knows its name.* This simple realization filled me with gratitude, even rapture.

In my elegant suite on the sixth, top floor of the Hotel K——, overlooking the Susquehanna River that glittered in the pale light like a snake's scales, was a large floral display of several kinds of lilies, carnations, asters and rosebuds so intensely fragrant they seemed almost, as I approached, to take my breath away. On an ivory card in ornate black script was my name and the words *WELLCOME BACK FOREVER!*

I'd been bicycling down a steep hill near the river. I was thirteen years old. And a certain neighbor, nineteen years old, was driving his car down the hill behind me. (I won't say his name. Let me call him B——. He was one whom I adored.) And at the foot of the hill, B—— inexplicably turned in front of me so that, hurtling downhill as I was, I would have slammed into the rear of his car if I hadn't swerved desperately to the side. *Doesn't he know I'm here? Why does he want to hurt me?* I screamed, falling in a tangle of metal and spinning bicycle wheels; I cut my knee and leg on gravel, struck my shoulder so hard against the ground that my teeth rattled in my head. I lay stunned, unable for a moment to breathe. But B—— was already turning onto the main road, already B—— was pulling away in a luxuriant expulsion of exhaust. Had he glanced into his rearview mirror in impatience, or derision?—he would have seen only my fallen figure, at the side of the road. But probably he didn't so much as glance back. I limped home crying, bleeding badly from my right knee and leg. My jeans were tattered, soaked with blood.

What have you done! You bad girl, what have you done to yourself!

I never doubted it, wouldn't have needed to be told by my parents that, yearning after B——, I'd deserved the fall. The bleeding and throbbing. The large sickle-shaped scar on my knee and other, fainter scars permanently etched in my flesh. I'd known: B—— had done it deliberately, to show what he thought of a thirteen-year-old's unwanted adulation.

This is what will happen to you. If you love where love is not wanted.

And now, more than thirty years later. Now, amid a throng of well-wishers in the civic center auditorium where, after a protracted ceremony, the mayor of K——, "Carly" Carlson, presented me with the "golden key to the city" (in fact, a heavy eight-inch brass key with an ornamental handle like a paperweight)—there was B——! Pushing forward to shake my hand at the reception, B—— no longer an arrogant nineteen-year-old with eyes that flicked indifferently over me but a solid-bodied, balding man in his late forties with eyes that fixed smilingly upon me. His handshake was firm, enthusiastic. "Would you be kind enough to sign these programs? Thanks!" B—— said. With him were two reluctant teenagers whom he was nudging forward.

I stared at B——, dismayed by the change in him. Did he know me, did he remember *me*?

Inside B——'s middle-aged, jowly face was a boy's lean face, just barely visible. Once, B—— had worn his hair long and shaggy; now his hair was neatly trimmed, a dull graying brown, his hairline sharply receding. Inside his snug sport coat was a prominent paunch. How shocked I was, how disappointed. Staring at the affably smiling man B—— had become, thinking *You? You scarred me for life?* Even as, publicly composed as I always am, meeting the smiles of others with natural-seeming smiles of my own, I was signing B——'s programs, beneath my photograph, in my neat schoolgirl hand. Politely I asked B—— about his life since I'd seen him last: whom had he married? where did he live? what was his occupation? what were his children's names? Aware that such friendly questions would flatter B—— in the presence of his children (who stared at me, having been informed that I was "famous"), yet unable to have predicted how moved B—— would be by the suggestion that, after so many years, I remembered him. So, while others waited with signs of strained patience in the reception line, B—— spoke excitedly and at length of his life, and of the past; I listened to some of this, my mind drifting; thinking *I adored you when you were nineteen, I don't adore you now; you have ruined*

everything I recalled of you, erased the past we'd shared. B——
was saying he remembered how I'd been an honors student in
school, known in the neighborhood for being smart, talented—"It
never surprised any of us, you'd turn out *famous*."

That fatuous word hovered in the air between us like a bad odor.
Famous!

B—— had a camera in hand, asking now, with some of his old
aggressiveness, if I'd pose with Kristie and Teddy, and I said of
course, I'd be happy to, and stood smiling between the silent
teenagers as B——'s camera flashed blindly. My face ached with
smiling, I'd been smiling since arriving in K——. I felt ill, cheated.
There was a black sour taste in my mouth. *You were contemptuous
of me once, you caused me to fall from my bicycle, you made
me bleed, you didn't look back, I adored you, have you forgotten?*
Impulsively, I bent to lift the hem of my black cashmere skirt to
show this middle-aged man in the snug-fitting sport coat the sickle-
shaped scar on my knee. Always I'd thought it a striking scar, mysterious and in its way beautiful, perhaps I was proud of it, vain of it;
but already B—— and his children were gone, they had their auto-
graphed programs, B—— had his photographs, the mayor's aides
were urging them briskly along so that other citizens of K——,
many with smiling, familiar young-old faces, could greet me.

Next, though it didn't seem to be on the itinerary provided by
my agent, I was taken to visit the K—— Senior Citizens Retirement Home. When I hesitated, my smile frozen, I was told by one
of the mayor's aides, "It will mean so much to these people to meet
you. They will treasure the memory for the remainder of their
lives!"

Cameras flashed blinding me as I stumblingly ascended the
steps of an old, badly weathered brick building sporting a slick
limestone facade. The K—— Senior Citizens Retirement Home
appeared to be a crudely renovated warehouse in a desolate urban
area near the river; a chill sulphurous wind blew from the river.
As soon as I was ushered into the building my nostrils pinched at
the odor and moisture flooded my eyes. What a depressing place!

Like a mausoleum, with harshly bright linoleum tile on the floor, relentless rows of fluorescent lighting overhead. I was wearing a black cashmere suit with a gracefully flared skirt to midcalf, and a long-sleeved white silk blouse, and a beautiful, and very expensive, flame-colored silk scarf; I was uneasily conscious of being out of place, perhaps cruelly out of place, in such desolate surroundings. Eyes moved onto me covertly, blinking in awe. *Who? Who is that woman? Why is she here, with us?* The Home supervisor was herding me briskly along a series of corridors even as he spoke importantly of the history of the institution which dated back, he said, to the nineteenth century, though this new location had been constructed in 1989. I tried to express polite interest. I may even have asked questions. For always in such circumstances, despairing of where I'm being led, wishing profoundly to be elsewhere, I manage to exude an air of intelligent interest, curiosity. The supervisor led me through a drafty, deserted dayroom with a dripping ceiling, and along another lengthy corridor, and into an open ward—a vast, dreary dormitory containing rows of beds stretching nearly out of sight; here elderly men and women lay immobile in their beds; a powerful stench of rancid food, aged and unwashed flesh, and stale urine assailed me so that I came close to gagging. The supervisor rang a gong and loudly announced my presence— "Ladies and gentlemen, attention! Here is our visitor, Miss ———, K——'s most celebrated Citizen of the World. Will you welcome her, please?"

Silence. An awkward, painful silence. A spasm of coughing; in the near distance, whimpering and more coughing. I was terrified that I might gag, vomit; I tried not to breathe; breathing as shallowly as possible, digging my fingernails into the palms of my hands.

Virtually shouting, the supervisor repeated his words, and this time a number of the elderly patients stirred, turning their vacant, wizened faces and slow-blinking eyes in my direction. There was a faint, feeble noise of clapping. A collective intake of breath. *Who? Who is it? That woman—who?* I smiled blindly, being led forward by the importunate supervisor; I moved in a haze of confusion and uncertainty between the rows of beds; yellowed eyes moved with me, lurching like small fish in a vast school of fish, fastening on me. A dry rasping urgent voice begged my attention—"Miss! Here! Over *here!*" In the shadowy light that seemed viscous with odor as with dustmotes, I could only just make out an obese, sprawling shape beneath untidy bedclothes; an elderly woman lay there, her large face wrinkled and wizened like something once living abandoned in the rain and sun. I stared in disbelief and dismay—could this be Miss S——, my junior high math teacher, horribly changed?

Often in my dreams of K—— I envisioned Miss S——. Not as I'd envisioned B——, with romantic schoolgirl yearning; but with a thrilling, fainting dread. How I had feared this woman, the most formidable of all my teachers. Yet, how I'd wanted to please her. When I'd been her pupil Miss S—— had been a stolidly built, moonfaced woman in her forties, with a strong-boned, mannish face; severe, yet mocking, eyebrows; though I tried to make myself as inconspicuous as possible in her classroom, Miss S——'s small, deep-set, pitch-colored eyes were continually drawn to me. Now, seeing Miss S—— so altered, a helpless mound of flesh in this public, exposed setting, I felt a stab of embarrassment, shame. I, Miss S——'s former student, here in the Home in my expensive, chic clothes! Announced with the ringing of a gong! Always Miss S——'s cold assessing eyes had lingered on me, as upon two or three other luckless pupils in her class; for some reason she regarded me with disdain and repugnance, even a kind of outrage, as if my very being were an affront to her. Though with my brightly alert, if nervous, classroom manner, my diligence and high grades, I'd managed to please most of my other teachers, I had never, or rarely, been able to please Miss S——. Consequently I believed that Miss S——, of all my teachers, was the one who knew me; not as I wished to be perceived, but as I truly was. When Miss S—— called upon me I invariably stammered, which aroused her scorn; at the blackboard, feeling myself lanky-ugly in her eyes and in the eyes of my classmates, whom Miss S—— encouraged to laugh at me, I fumbled and dropped chalk, and was helpless to replicate the very math problems I'd already completed for homework; if my tests and quizzes were without actual errors, still Miss S—— could deduct, by the rules of her classroom, points for "slovenly penmanship" and "wrinkled paper." (Through junior high school I tried gamely to improve my penmanship; though it seemed to me as good as the penmanship of Miss S——'s favorites, yet it invariably fell short in her eyes—"Slovenly! Unacceptable!" Miss S—— would declare, with a slash of her red pen. And it seemed to me that Miss S—— must have wrinkled my papers herself either by accident or intention, for I was certain I handed them in smooth.) Now I was remembering an episode of shame, agitation. . . . How one day, severely chided by Miss S——, I saw my grade of 98 percent on a math test reduced to 78 percent, and when the bell rang at the end of the class I rushed from the room crying, to the girls' lavatory down the hall; unable to see clearly, propelling myself desperately forward, I pushed the palm of my hand through a pane of frosted glass, shattering the glass and badly cutting my hand. Terrified of the blood, I began to scream; other girls, seeing me, screamed; Miss S—— came storming from her classroom, moving swiftly and deliberately as I'd never seen her, as if she'd known at once who the troublemaker would be. She seized me roughly by the arm and walked me to the school clinic at the far end of the building, scolding me, agitated and excited—"What! What have you done now! Oh you terrible girl! On purpose, wasn't it! Terrible, terrible girl! You'll regret this, I promise!" Behind us, on the floor of the corridor, was a trail of splattered bloodstains like exclamation marks.

I still have those scars, of course. They're faded now, almost invisible. Yet if you look carefully, you can see them—a graceful calligraphy in an unknown language, the longest scar measuring three inches, on the back of my hand; and smaller scars in the palm of my hand. How lucky I'd been, the school nurse informed me, and Miss S—— angrily confirmed, that I hadn't in my clumsiness, which both women suspected to be deliberate and spiteful, severed the arteries in my wrist.

Terrible, terrible girl! I could hear those damning words, still.

Wondering through the years *Why? Why did you torment me, Miss S——? And never any answer.

Now, more than thirty years later. In this strange dim-lit place, amid such odors of melancholy decay. Now, Miss S——, greatly aged, was pleading with me. With *me!* My former math teacher, from out of her tangled, soiled bedclothes like a rat's nest, pleading—with *me! What has happened to you? Why are you not as you were?* Almost I wished that Miss S—— would speak to me in scorn as, surely, in her innermost heart, she would have liked to do. For how piteous it was to see the woman so helpless, so enfeebled; her eyes that had once been so bright with intolerance now faded, frightened, set in hollow sockets, fixed desperately on me. Her tremulous clawlike fingers swiped at my skirt and instinctively I drew back, not wanting to be touched. It was then that I saw, with a thrill of horror, that Miss S——, like a number of the other elderly patients, was shackled to her bed; she strained, and strained to break free, her eyes bulging with the effort, but the leather thongs held her fast; sobbing with frustration, humbled, she fell back helpless as a great rag doll. And her words, too, were slurred, for evidently she hadn't any teeth; her dentures had been removed, and her ashen, flaccid face was partly collapsed; only barely could I make out her plea—"Help me! Tell them! Who I am! Tell them— you know me! Tell them—you—you're my friend!" Now other voices took up Miss S——'s hissing words; I looked, and saw to my shock that some of these individuals, too, looked strangely familiar. Had they been teachers of mine also, or—was it possible?—were they relatives? I stared at the withered faces that seemed to mimic my own, my features repeated, replicated as in a funhouse mirror; these helpless bodies in beds along an entire wall of the ward, stretching out of sight into the shadows. I could barely hear the voices pleading, commanding, a chorus of harsh sibilant sounds— "Help! Help us! You, girl! Please!"

Those adults who'd been cruel or indifferent to me when I was young and powerless, how ironic they should beg for help from me now. Those who'd shown little mercy to me, now they wanted mercy from me. I might have smiled coldly at them and said *But

it's too late, my heart is hardened. I might have laughed at them
straining against their shackles *Help yourselves, why don't you!*
Instead, I hesitated. The supervisor and the mayor's aide were impatient to move me on, but I hesitated. "How—how can I help
you?" I asked. "Any of you?" I saw Miss S——, her talonlike fingers reaching for me; her mouth opened in an anguished O; as if,
even in her enfeeblement, she wished to swallow me up. "What can
I do? It isn't in my power. You're old. . . ." My voice faltered. I did
not mean my remarks to be cruel, only truthful; but they came out
wrong. "You're old. . . ." The stench in the open ward was making
me ill, yet I took a step toward the row of beds, as if helplessly
drawn. It was then that something sticky caught at the heel of my
shoe. I couldn't see at first what it was, then I saw what it was, crying out, "Oh! No," and kicking free of it.

The supervisor of the K—— Senior Citizens Retirement
Home now intervened, saying sternly, "Visiting hours are over,
Miss ———. This way, please."

For a half hour then I walked by the river, in the spongy soil,
stumbling a little in my high heels, desperate to clear my head. To
calm my beating thoughts. I'd insisted upon getting out of the
limousine—"I need to be alone. Please." The car waited up at the
road, its motor running. (Was the mayor's aide speaking about me
on his cellular phone to the mayor, or to another official? Were they
concerned about their guest of honor, did they worry what I might
suddenly do?) I was laughing, out of breath. Perhaps I was crying.
Wiping angrily at my eyes. Across the Susquehanna, at a distance
of about a half mile, were abandoned factories, mills; several of the
old buildings were fire-damaged and covered in lurid graffiti. The
water was leaden-green, subtly iridescent in the pallid light. Perhaps it was contaminated by oil. How many times, how many hundreds of times, I'd walked along the bank of this river as a girl, my
parents' single-storey asphalt-sided house only a mile away, up a
steep incline. My father had worked at one of those factories for his
entire life, he'd been bitter perhaps, he'd never said. At least, he'd
never said in my presence. My mother had died of—I almost said

My mother had died of life, living. I did not remember her so vividly as I remembered Miss S—— seizing me by the shoulder, yanking me from the lavatory door with the smashed pane. I did not remember my father so vividly as I remembered B—— speeding past me, turning sharply in front of me. My parents, like my grandparents, had been dead for years—hadn't they? Yet I could not shake off the terrible realization that I'd seen them in the Home, shackled to their beds. Their harsh sibilant voices. *Help! You, girl! Please! Pleassse!* Yet how unprotestingly I'd allowed myself to be led away.

Of course they're dead! Of course. You're beyond them, you're safe from them forever.

———

There followed then a frenzied blur of activity in K——. Faces, handshakes. In some instances, startling to me, vigorous embraces from strangers. *Welcome home! Why did you stay away so long?* At a luncheon in my honor given by the K—— Arts Council, all the guests, it seemed, wanted their picture taken with me. I became dizzy from continuous smiling; my eyes were seared by the explosive lights. Panicked, I wondered if my eyesight might be permanently damaged. *Is this their plan? Part of their plan?* But the citizens of K—— were so warmly friendly, so genuinely enthusiastic about my visit, of course I was only imagining this. After my unfortunate visit to the retirement home I'd been feeling nauseated; yet I had to eat, and eat, and eat; for to refrain from eating, at such public feasts in my honor, would have been perceived as rude. It was suspicious enough that I'd failed to return home for so many years; I could not risk appearing to imagine myself superior to those I'd left behind. *Yes but I am superior! The proof of it is, I've escaped.*

A visit to K—— High School where, in the airless, low-ceilinged auditorium I'd last seen at graduation, when I'd given a breathless valedictory speech, I confronted several hundred staring adolescents, telling them of my "life and career since leaving K——." A visit to the First Lutheran Church of K—— which my family had attended sporadically, out of a sense of duty, and I a curious but

unbelieving child in their midst, a lifetime ago; a visit to the K——
Public Library, where a white-haired librarian with a bulldog face
insisted she remembered me—"Oh yes, indeed! So very well." And
other stops, leaving me shaken, nauseated. Forced to ask the
limousine driver to pull over to the side where, on a shadowy
street, in a littered gutter, I vomited—a harsh, stinging gruel like
acid. The driver and the mayor's aide must have been embarrassed
for me, but they said nothing. And I said nothing except, when I'd
recovered, wiping my eyes and mouth with a wadded tissue,
"Thank you, driver. Now please drive on."

*Don't you dare. Always looking at us. Even when you aren't
looking at us—you are!* Those girls, those several girls I'd so admired. Following with my eyes. They were two years or more older
than I was, one of them, E——, the most flamboyant, had already
graduated from high school or perhaps she'd dropped out. *Think
we don't see you? We do!* The girls from Sheridan Road, Cayuga
Road. In their snug-fitting jeans and T-shirts, in their bright-
colored swimsuits at the K—— rock quarry, hot August days.
Cicadas screaming out of the trees, heat rising in spirals of dust.
I leapt and dived from the high board into the cool still quarry
water; I was long-legged, tanned, reckless as the older boys. Shivering with anticipation as I climbed to the diving board, imagining
their eyes, the girls' eyes, drawn to my tall lanky figure. Sometimes
they called, whistled. Their boyfriends called, whistled. Or so I
imagined. I didn't look, of course. I never looked. I saw, but I never
looked. *Always looking at us. Think we don't see you? We do!*
Yearning to be their friend, yearning to move with their ease, talk
and laugh among them. L—— with her amazing glossy black
braids hanging down her back, J—— who was a sheriff's deputy's
daughter, M—— who screamed with laughter when the boys tickled her, E—— tanned golden by the sun, freckled, lazy-eyed.
Yearning to be their friend or at least acknowledged by them and
one afternoon I was swimming and by accident collided with an
older boy, E——'s boyfriend, and suddenly he and a friend of his
grabbed hold of my ankles and pulled me under, it was only playful,

not meant to hurt, the boys were laughing and yelling and there came M—— jumping into the pool striking her heels against my lower back, there came J—— like a naughty child to tug at my hair, L——'s nails raked my struggling arms, the boys dragged me along the rocks at the deep end of the quarry cutting my face, bruising my collarbone, my small breasts; within a minute it was over, one of those episodes that erupted from time to time at the quarry, where there wasn't a lifeguard on duty; exhausted and choking and bleeding from the cuts on my face I crawled weakly out of the water and lay panting on the puddled rim never turning my head, never wishing to see. Their murmurous voices, laughter. E——'s voice. In the near distance, the slamming of car doors. *Why? Why do you hate me? I love you.*

And these scars too almost invisible to the eye. On my chin, my cheeks. Each scar a precious memory. How strangely happy I was, at the age of fifteen knowing I would have to flee K—— one day, to save my life.

And now, at my public performance at the Arts Council, before I began there came E—— to squeeze my hand, "Remember? Remember *me*?" smiling almost shyly, an attractive, fleshy woman with bright mascara eyes and rouged cheeks, and close by was L—— with her husband, who was one of the Arts Council administrators, smiling hopefully in my direction, L—— so changed, her hair streaked with gray, cut short, a woman I would not have recognized; and elsewhere in the audience of rapt expectant faces were J—— and M—— or women who resembled them, applauding when I was introduced, such smiles! such claims of recognition! as if we'd been intimate friends after all. And so I performed for them in such a way as to confirm their pride in me, in precisely the way in which, as a professional, I always perform; for we who are professionals show nothing of our truest selves, no more do we expose our souls than we expose our scars for your perusal. Yet I was short of breath, my heart sick as when at the quarry pool I'd lain insensible, panting and sobbing hiding my face where they'd pursued me, in terror, in mimicry of death; and afterward during the applause that was so protracted as to seem subtly mocking I smiled into the audience as into a cauldron of friendly and familiar faces, I did not stare at E—— who appeared delighted with me as with a sister, nor at L—— raising her hands to visibly clap, I did not seek out the faces of J—— or M—— or those women who uncannily resembled them now middle-aged, irrevocably altered. I did not cry out at them fierce with bitterness *Why? Why are you here, so changed? I loved you once, when you were hateful to me. I don't love you now, I feel nothing for you, now.*

And so, my last public appearance in K—— the city of my birth came to an end amid a benign confusion of faces, voices, handshakes. Camera flashes, blinding. It may have been that E—— and I were photographed together; it may have been that L—— and her husband and I were photographed together; so many pictures were taken, my eyes so dazzled I couldn't see; yet I signed my name so many times I lost count, and my cheek was kissed so many times I lost count; my performance continued well past 10 P.M., beyond the time designated on my contract. For "performance" is my life, my public life; whenever I am in public, however unguarded and spontaneous I seem, however "natural," I am performing. After this final, seemingly very successful event in K—— I was allowed at last to escape to the limousine waiting at the rear door to bear me back to the Hotel K—— where in my suite I staggered with exhaustion, the next morning I would be leaving on the 6:40 A.M. train for Philadelphia *escaping with my life! a second time!* so I wanted to sleep immediately so exhausted and disoriented I could barely remove my tight-fitting shoes, my elegant expensive clothes. Lying then in the enormous bed beneath chill sheets. Not quite able to catch my breath, the air seemed thick, viscous. Where was I, what was this evil place?—wind lifted from the invisible river outside my window, flinging icy rain against the glass. My fingers moved over my scarred body—my narrow chest, my small breasts, my knee, my leg, my right hand, my face. Reading like Braille these secret hieroglyphics. I yearned so badly to sleep yet my mind was beating like a frightened heart. Voices murmured out of the shadows of the room, an aged collapsed face with a wide gluttonous O of a mouth, *Welcome to K——! Welcome back to K——! K——'s most celebrated Citizen of the World—welcome!* I realized suddenly that I couldn't breathe, I woke suddenly, desperate to breathe; the air was thick and cloying, like tentacles pulsing around me; I stumbled from the bed and switched on a light and saw on a table close by the enormous, beautiful floral display my K—— hosts had had delivered to my suite, lilies, carnations, asters and giant multifoliate roses now fully budded, my name in ornate black script and the words *WELCOME BACK FOREVER!* The fragrance emanating from the floral display was overwhelming, virulent; the flower petals were sticky, oozing a transparent oily liquid; in panic I carried the container to a window I struggled to open, and in handfuls I threw the flowers out—out, down, into the wind to be borne away into the river.

On my hands and bare forearms were sticky yellow pollen-streaks, harsh as acid. Already my sensitive skin was reddening in streaks, as if scalded, already it was beginning to scar.

An Urban Paradox

For some months there has been a heated public debate in our city, at least among intellectuals and persons of civic responsibility. *Where are these people coming from? This seemingly inexhaustible supply of humanity?* As a scholar and a translator, I have tried to retain a morally neutral perspective, free of all prejudice and bias. Therefore I have taken no sides.

However, it is clear that during the past decade our aging city has become one of the most densely populated cities in North America. Of course, it is a principle that, in the right circumstances, human beings engender human beings; yet that cannot explain the influx of mature men and women into our city, and most visibly onto our already traffic-clogged streets. As I say, I offer no opinion, still less do I offer any remedy. I keep assiduously to myself, spending most of my time in the Institute library, when I am not safely at home a few blocks away. (As a University appointee with tenure, I am privileged to live in the historic district of the city. My life's work, which in no way touches upon these speculations, involves the translation of fifteenth-century Italian theological texts into English, complete with exegeses, footnotes, bibliographies, etc. A challenging task which has required twelve years' intense concentration thus far, begun when I was a graduate student, and nowhere near completion!)

Yet it has happened, and I scarcely understand how, that certain (unmarked) municipal vehicles have begun to seriously distract me from my scholarly routine. These vans are a steely metallic-gray, with dark-tinted windows in front and no windows at all in the rear; they resemble delivery trucks, but there are no visible markings to identify them. Nor are there manufacturers' logos to identify their makers. The vans move unobtrusively about the city, even into the University district, at any hour of the day or night; I assume that they are concentrated in the more populous and crime-ridden urban areas, but they are likely to turn up one of our narrow cobblestone residential streets as well. Rarely do they call attention to themselves by speeding, or making abrupt U-turns in traffic, or driving up onto the sidewalk to bypass traffic, like police vehicles; nor are they equipped with sirens, emergency horns, or flashing light. They are equipped, evidently, with hoses—but they are not fire-fighting vehicles. The windows are so darkly tinted that one cannot even see one's reflection in them—or so it is said. (I mean, so I have overheard. Occasionally I hear University students, or the younger members of the faculty, discussing such matters a bit recklessly.) One certainly cannot, and would not want to, peer inside to see who, or what, is behind the wheel!

When I first began seeing these (unmarked) municipal vehicles, of course I could not have considered them in the plural—*vehicles*; I probably surmised, without giving much thought to the subject, for indeed it had not seemed at the time to warrant much thought, still less concern, that I'd happened by chance, in my absentminded way, to be seeing the same single *vehicle* repeatedly. But then, with the passage of time, I began to realize that there must be more than one of the metallic-gray vans since, by degrees, I had begun to see so many of them.

Of course, I haven't made a count. I would never record, on paper, even in code, actual *notations*.

Several weeks ago, for instance. Shortly after nine o'clock of a weekday evening, hardly a late hour in a city so cosmopolitan as ours. I was returning home from my office at the Institute, taking my usual route past the handsome weathered Gothic stone buildings that have shaped my life, when I saw, or seemed to see, a confused dreamlike scene in the northeast corner of University Memorial Park. A child naked from the waist down, its hair lifting in greenish flames, ran out of the shadows of the plane trees and toward the street, shrieking for help, as if having sighted me (?). (At least, I assume the poor creature was shrieking for help. I could not comprehend a word of its harsh, guttural language, which bore no resemblance to the half-dozen European languages with which I am familiar.) I stood rooted to the spot, not knowing what to do. I am not a man of instinct, still less of impulsive acts. And this was all happening so swiftly! (There were relatively few people on the street, and those who were continued on their way, not glancing left or right.) The child shrieked again, now at the edge of the park—but was suddenly hidden from my view by the appearance of one of the (unmarked) vans which drove up, braked to a jarring halt, and, after no more than fifteen seconds, drove on again, and disappeared around a corner.

The child with the flaming hair had vanished as if it had never been!

Which is why I characterize the episode as confused and dreamlike. One of those myriad episodes, or impressions of episodes, we are apt to experience in the course of a day, especially in public places in which we are not in *control*, still less in *anticipation*, of what is happening.

(Except I saw, I believe—in some sense "saw"—or was left with the optical residue of "seeing"—a glisten of frothy water on the pavement and on the trampled grass where the child had been; I was left with the fleeting, unverifiable impression that a hose (?) had been used—but by whom, I had not seen. Or could not remember seeing.)

After all, such episodes, in public places, are over so quickly!

One no more adjusts one's eyes to seeing what, a moment before, could not possibly have been there, than the vision is gone, irretrievable.

Nor are fellow witnesses helpful. After the child with the flaming hair appeared, and almost immediately disappeared, I hurried to catch up with a fellow pedestrian, a middle-aged man associated with the Institute, his face and name known to me as mine are known to him, and I asked, Excuse me! Did you see—? and my colleague frowned and said, annoyed, Excuse *me*! I'm really in a bit of a hurry.

He walked quickly off, and I followed, somewhat dazedly, and did not look back.

What is wanted, I thought, is a theory—!

In the weeks following, there have been, quite without my seeking them out, similar mysterious sightings. Here in the historic district where one would not expect (would one?) any disruption of the commonweal. Whether these sightings have been by me alone or by me amid others, I am in no position to say. For the mere presence of others does not mean that others *see*. (At the Institute, where privacy is respected at all costs, and where resident scholars can go for weeks, or even years, without speaking to one another beyond courteous hellos, naturally there has been no discussion of the metallic-gray vans and their activities.) I have learned in fact that the presence of others, ostensibly "witnesses," may mean in fact that these others do *not see*.

At the same time, I should say that, since each sighting has been both like and unlike the others, I have no legitimate way of knowing that one sighting is related to the others, or even to one other. I have no legitimate way of knowing that something "seen" by me is in fact "seen" by me and not hallucinated. And since I am not keeping a formal record, not even making a systematic attempt to remember, it is possible (isn't it?) that I am unconsciously exaggerating. Or even inventing.

As I've said, what is wanted, so very badly, is a theory to encompass these mysterious phenomena. Ah, a theory!

This most recent sighting, for instance. It has left me quite dazed. It has left me quite breathless, and suffused with anxiety. *And this is not my nature, but an alien nature.* Very early this morning, at dawn of what would be a hard, bright, windswept March day, a babble of voices—shouts, cries, accusations, pleas, lamentations—woke me from deep, stuporous sleep; and drew me to my bedroom window where I peered cautiously through the slats of my venetian blinds to see what was happening in the street. (I have lived for the past twelve years in this apartment on the sixth floor of an old, venerable building owned by the University. Yes, I have been happy here! I cannot conceive of living elsewhere, any more than I conceive of doing work other than the work I was born to do.) Blinking in amazement, I saw a hellish sight: a gathering of shabby, stunted figures, both male and female, pathetic as animated scarecrows, lurching on diseased legs, or stumps of legs, struggling together over scraps of garbage from an overturned trash can. It was hideous—repugnant! I had never witnessed anything like it, so close to *my* home. Subhuman faces contorted in greed, rapacity, anguish—fury gleaming in a man's eyes—a hunchbacked female scrambling to seize a smashed, rotted melon someone had kicked along the sidewalk—another, younger dark-skinned woman on her knees clawing at something that appeared to be alive, and frantic to escape—a cat? a rat? a small mongrel dog? I was revolted, yet I could not bring myself to turn away. *Who are these creatures, where have they come from?*

Almost at once, as if summoned by my horror, one of the (unmarked) municipal vehicles drew up at the curb below, braked to a stop, and obscured my vision of the struggle. What a relief! And then another van drew up, and still a third. The most I'd ever seen together at one time.

Again, the vans paused only briefly before moving on. Their efficiency, coupled with their eerie silence, was remarkable. There was a confused impression of a flurry of activity—the van's rear doors being opened, uniformed figures rushing out—but it occurred too rapidly for me to see, still less comprehend, like a film run at several times its normal speed. And once the vans were gone, driving off unobtrusively, the street below was empty as one might expect at this hour of the day—except for puddles of water with an odd reddish glisten.

The struggling figures had vanished as if they had never been!

———

All this fierce, bright, windswept March morning I have crouched by my window, tormented by thought.

The street six storeys below is narrow even for the University district, the perspective from my window steep and vertiginous. I do not want to dwell upon it, yet seemingly, being human, and gripped by the human instinct to comprehend, I cannot resist. Leaning weakly against the windowsill and peering through the dusty blind slats down at the vacant pavement where the figures (?) had been, and now nothing (?) is.

Trying to grasp the principle that, having seen what had possibly not been there, can I ever bring myself to see what *is* there—or anywhere.

For once you begin to doubt the evidence of your senses, there is no logical end to your doubting.

At the same time reminding myself that there is no inevitable reason to conclude that the hellish scene that was *not* there after the (unmarked) vans' departure—indeed, *is not* there now—had ever in fact been there. Even in theory. For perhaps I had not been awakened from my sleep, but had merely dreamt the entire episode. What responsibility, then, rests with me?

In certain of the theological tracts I am translating at the present time, it is argued that human beings cannot be held responsible for dreams or dream-visions, no matter how sinful; for some of these may be the work of the Devil, and where we do not consciously choose, direct, and control, we must be absolved of blame. The ancient, primitive world adhered to a different kind of justice, for repeatedly in the old Greek and Roman tales of gods, demigods, and hapless mortals, mortals were held culpable for actions that had in fact been dictated by gods; their "destinies" were not their own, but the fruit of cruel, childlike gods in perpetual feuds with one another. In the enlightened centuries that followed, and into the present time, it is understood that human beings must be judged only if they are free agents. They must be forgiven for that which is no one's fault—whether dreams, hallucinations, or utterly mysterious and unknowable events that resist all classification.

Can what is (unmarked) be (marked)?

And so I have worked out a theory of the (unmarked) municipal vehicles. At least to my personal satisfaction. Others may attack it, but others will know nothing of it; I have not committed it to writing, nor shall I do so. The most pure of intellectual exercises is that which is wholly private.

My theory is, simply: the (unmarked) municipal vehicles do not, in the strictest sense of the term, "exist"; just as the laws they apparently enforce do not "exist." *That which is not imagined as existing cannot exist.*

Which is to say: the (hypothetical) reality beyond the flood of surface impressions we receive by way of the brain's intricate (but necessarily restricted) neurological apparatus is but one factor in the immense field of sensory information available to the brain. No part of it can be deemed *more real* than any other; and when it disappears, if it disappears, the fact of its disappearance—its transience—argues for its *irreality*.

What is not here now, was never here at all. For how to prove it?

What is (unmarked) is (unmarked).

Beyond that, it's a matter of hurrying home well before dark, and shutting one's window and blinds tight against the sky.

Unprintable

"How hideous!—how pitiful. Who *are* they?"

En route to the awards ceremony at the Ethical Arts Center, as the long sleekly black limousine made its way through congested city streets, she saw them. Not clearly, but in glimpses, her vision blurred by the limousine's dark-tinted glass. Strange human figures at the curbside, or wandering out into traffic—to beg? to coerce money from intimidated drivers? Close to the car's rear windows loomed faces that were pale as bread dough, or red-boiled like lobsters, with running sores and lesions and features that seemed malformed, or incomplete; avid, hungrily glistening eyes like rodents' eyes fixed upon her—an impossibility since, in fact, the limousine's windows were so darkly tinted no one could see inside. And even if they could, what had these pathetic strangers to do with *her*? Even if they were capable of recognizing her, they would have no idea who *Celeste Ward* was, nor could they have cared.

She brooded about them: these casualties of a great American city—unwanted creatures, unwanted probably since birth; unwanted as pregnancies in their hapless mothers' wombs. Innocent victims of the Darwinian horror of unthinking, rampaging reproduction—the infliction of male desire upon female acquiescence. What heartrending tragedy, unwanted babies born into the world, lacking the love and nurturing to make them fully human! This was in fact the Cause to which Celeste Ward had devoted her entire adult life—the complex moral issues of planned parenthood, the technology of contraception, abortion rights. The Cause for which she'd sacrificed her own personal, emotional life and for which, tonight, the night of her sixtieth birthday, she was to be publicly honored. Yet: seeing these strange misshapen creatures that rose up, loomed close, fell away from the car as the driver increased his speed, Celeste was stricken with a sense of foreboding. *Why did I accept? Why another public honor? Is it mere vanity?* Celeste Ward, vilified at the start of her crusading career in the mid-fifties, had been, these past few years, so often publicly honored as to have become an American "name" even to those who knew nothing of her actual career and, had they known, would have disapproved; she was accumulating enough awards, citations, honorary doctorates and hefty brass plaques to last her the remainder of her life. Tonight, in a program organized by the Women's Unity Force Foundation, which had funded a number of Celeste Ward's projects, including her most controversial, the promulgation of abortion techniques for the layman, Celeste was to be one of a number of featured feminist speakers and was to be, at the program's culmination, honored for her "selfless contribution to the Cause of promoting women's rights worldwide for nearly four decades." Celeste was flattered of course—yet, wasn't there a posthumous tone to this, suggesting perhaps that her activist years were over? That younger, more energetic women would be taking her place, revising her methods, even her ideas? Her first impulse had been to decline, in a show of modesty that had been in fact a nervous reaction. But the Foundation organizers, and others, had protested. Telephone calls were made, letters sent to her. A special plea from Celeste's publisher, who was reissuing in paperback her much-attacked, much-acclaimed *The Trap of Motherhood: A Sociological Study.* And there was an interviewer from a distinguished women's journal, an intense young woman who idolized Celeste, arguing that a woman of Celeste Ward's achievement owed it to those many women who admired her and whose lives she'd touched to appear in public on the occasion of her sixtieth birthday—"Only think, Celeste, if you hadn't been born! How different things would be for women in America today!" This was an exaggeration, but uttered with such affection, it was impossible for Celeste to say no.

And so, again, another time: yes. The triumph of vanity.

Tonight was a fated night. Celeste, never a superstitious woman, could not shake off a premonition of dread. Since waking that morning she'd been feeling a quickening of her blood, a pressure inside her skull, not pain but on the verge of pain, as if something wanted to burst loose. Birthday cards from old friends, acquaintances, associates in the Cause, strangers—telephone calls, flowers, gifts—raining upon Celeste Ward as if this were, not merely her sixtieth birthday, but her last birthday. She, a solitary woman for whom sentiment was an embarrassment, especially when it pertained to her; exacerbating her aloneness, which had been a fact of her life now for many years. *Happy birthday, Celeste! happy birthday! happy birthday!*—it was a dirge. And how ironic, no one except Celeste knew, for, as she'd been told many times as a child, by her mother, neither her mother nor her father had wanted her to be born.

In that era, 1933, abortion wasn't a possibility, still less a legal right, for most women.

Of Celeste Ward's secrets, this was the most precious because it *was* the most ironic. But she had other secrets, too. Which no biographers would ever discover.

As the limousine turned onto the Boulevard, Celeste saw up the block a group of about thirty demonstrators milling on the sidewalk and in the street, restrained by police cordons, and knew, with a stab of apprehension and excitement, where the Ethical Arts Center was. Her enemies! Enemies of the Cause! These men and women, Christian pro-lifers and fervent foes of abortion, were almost comfortingly familiar. They'd been picketing Celeste Ward's speeches, the Cause, and abortion centers for years; in the South, they could be dangerous, but in this northern city they acquiesced to the law, knowing that local sentiment was strongly against them. Unlike the diseased, deformed street people, who filled Celeste with horror and repugnance, the pro-lifers were almost like kin;

ideological enemies, reliable in their opposition, they had their
roles as she had hers. She'd long since memorized their accusatory
picket signs, their self-righteous prayerful chants—"PRO CHOICE
IS A LIE! NOBODY'S BABY CHOOSES TO DIE!" *They* held no
surprises for her.

And where they demonstrated, there was often news coverage—
which was helpful to the Cause. Celeste saw television camera
crews, reporters in front of the Center, awaiting her arrival. Her!
Already, Celeste was feeling better about the evening.

The stately limousine drew up in front of the building, the uniformed driver opened the door for his distinguished passenger—
"Here we are, ma'am! Careful getting out." Celeste glanced up at
him—then stared. (She would have no time to contemplate the surprise of his blackish-maroon skin, pocked cheeks, blood-veined and
subtly derisive eyes, for events moved too swiftly; no time to consider how the man's face resembled certain of the faces she'd
glimpsed on the street. Unless she was imagining it?) The program
organizers greeted Celeste warmly as several cameras flashed.
There were many well-wishers, most of them women, and very
handsomely dressed women, who had bought tickets for the program; there was a flattering contingent of a half dozen policemen;
the pro-life demonstrators, waving their signs and shouting in her
direction, kept their prescribed distance. With the organizers were
several reporters and television interviewers with questions for
Celeste Ward—such familiar questions by now, Celeste could have
answered them in her sleep. But she rejoiced in these questions,
and in these occasions, because they *were* familiar; even when, like
the present time, she wasn't feeling entirely herself, she could answer such questions clearly and forcefully, confident she was in the
right. Through her adult life Celeste Ward, like other successful
feminist leaders, had appreciated the great value of educating
through the media, even when the media meant to deride; the
great value of manipulating public opinion—"It isn't enough to *be*
right," Celeste would insist, "you must convince others that you
are." Only at the start of her career in the tumultuous, disorga-
nized sixties, when civil rights activism, anti–Vietnam War ac-

tivism, and women's rights activism had frequently clashed, had Celeste betrayed her emotions in public. (And, too many times, in private!) Since then, she'd systematically remade herself as a model of feminist persuasion linked with intelligence, courtesy, and tact. As the last-born in a working-class family of seven brothers and sisters, Celeste had had to scramble for her place in the world—even her place at meals—but, considering her public manner, you would have supposed her of a genteel, well-educated background. Not even her most savage detractors could accuse Celeste Ward of being "shrill" and "unfeminine"—never did she raise her voice, never did she resort to quarreling; never did she allow any camera to catch her attractive features in any sort of grimace. What Celeste Ward might be secretly thinking, what raw emotions coursed through her veins, no one, not even her biographer, would ever know.

Asked, as Celeste was now, by a young woman interviewer for a local television news program, how she felt about being called a "murderess"—as the pro-lifers were chanting—Celeste appeared to think carefully, then said, "I've never taken accusations by ideological opponents as anything but ideological—that is, impersonal. I live with the hope that opponents of the Cause will see that the issue is not 'abortion'—for there will always be abortion—but 'abortion rights.' " This was a reply Celeste had given numerous times, yet she felt the truth and the rightness of the sentiment as if she'd uttered it spontaneously.

She knew she looked, and sounded, convincing. That was all that mattered.

Then, this: as the interviewer asked another, final question, Celeste happened to notice a TV monitor on one of the mobile units and saw, to her astonishment, that there was, on the small screen, in addition to the young woman and herself, a mysterious third party—an upright creature, fleshy, of the hue of raw meat, with a flat, vaguely human face, shallow indentations for eyes and nose, a slack mouth. *What could it be? What horror!* Celeste blinked, and stared, and turned back to the interviewer who was smiling respectfully at her, awaiting a reply, but all Celeste could do was stammer something not very coherent, excuse herself abruptly, and turn away. She did not dare look at the TV monitor again.

Other interviewers would have swooped upon her but the program organizers, officers of the Women's Unity Force Foundation, politely detached her from them and marched her up the stone steps—such dauntingly steep stone steps!—into the lobby of the Ethical Arts Center. She was badly out of breath by this time, her heart pounding. There was a good deal of excited talk aimed at Celeste, only a fraction of which she could absorb. She gathered that the Center's eleven hundred seats had been sold out and the program was to be taped for rebroadcasting over PBS and there were a number of distinguished persons in the audience, including wealthy donors. Someone thrust a bouquet of red roses at her— "Happy birthday, Miss Ward! And many more!" Her hand was vigorously, repeatedly shaken; unfamiliar faces loomed close to hers, their features distorted as if by magnification. Such a crowd! why didn't the Foundation officers see her plight, and protect her! It was all Celeste could do to maintain her composure, as if pulses were not beating, thrumming, in her brain, managing to smile, to exchange greetings—"Yes, thank you, you're very kind, it *is* a happy birthday. The happiest in memory." Many admirers clamored for Celeste's autograph in copies of *The Trap of Motherhood*, which was being sold in the lobby. A fierce-eyed woman with graying-brown hair to her shoulders declared, "This is the book that saved my life, sprang *me* from the trap." She would have squeezed Celeste in a bear hug had not one of the Foundation officers intervened.

Celeste was escorted through the crowd, led into a private lounge backstage. Thank God! The roses were taken from her to be put into a vase. She sat relieved on a sofa, passing her hand over her eyes. Someone offered her a glass of Perrier water, which she gratefully accepted. Someone asked if she minded being photographed. (She murmured yes, in fact she did, but in so low and apologetic a voice, she was misunderstood: cameras flashed.) Her hand shook, nearly spilling her drink. There was something disturbing—something terrifying—she needed to contemplate;

something to do with the TV monitor?—but, in the confusion of the moment, she couldn't remember what it was.

A mistake. Birthday. Should not have accepted. Where?

Another time, the previous week, she'd cancelled an appointment to see her doctor. The thrumming in the brain, the sparks of light in the corners of her eyes—these symptoms, if they were symptoms, had diminished. *Of course, I'm fine. My enemies would despair to know how fine.*

More admirers, more almost-familiar faces loomed near. Members of the Foundation, their friends and family members; other women who were to speak this evening, whom Celeste knew very well—except, damn it, laughingly she forgot their names! She'd been hoping for a few minutes to relax and glance through her speech before the program began at eight o'clock—it was seven-forty now—but evidently that wasn't to be. She heard herself speaking gaily, bubbling with her old famous energy, "Yes, thank you, of course I remember you!—yes it *is* a happy birthday. The happiest in memory—" Though, at the moment, Celeste could barely remember any previous birthday. *Is everything being erased? Is that the plan?* In the midst of a conversation with a woman who claimed to have been a student of Celeste's twenty-five years ago (at Barnard? Vassar? Radcliffe?—it wasn't clear), Celeste happened to glance down at her right wrist, which was smarting, and saw to her astonishment what appeared to be a red bead bracelet—no, it was a thin scratch, oozing blood. What had happened? Had one of her well-wishers accidentally scratched her? More startled than alarmed, Celeste examined both wrists, both hands—there were no more scratches. She dabbed away the blood with a tissue, quickly, so that no one could see. Of course: it must have been the rose thorns.

"Miss Ward? Celeste? You're looking a little pale. Is something—?"

Celeste was about to slip away to a rest room, to hide for a few precious minutes, but here was the interviewer from the women's journal looming above her. A long-limbed coltish girl of about thirty-five with a startled expression, large intense glassy-bright eyes, a nervous habit of smiling too often, especially in Celeste's

presence, and baring her considerable gums. Celeste had not noticed her in the crowded lounge but she did recall, with a sinking
heart, having been informed that the interviewer would be here
this evening; and would in fact be introducing Celeste. "No, not at
all, I'm perfectly fine," Celeste said quickly. There was no avoiding
it, the interviewer sat down beside her on the sofa, spreading
her unwieldy gear—an immense gold-lamé shoulder bag, a tape
recorder, an oversized notebook into which, at inspired moments,
she lunged with a ballpoint pen.

"What an evening! What an occasion! Happy birthday!—I have
a little something for you later, I'll give it to you at the reception,"
the interviewer said breathlessly, yet with an air of apology, as if
this were a matter of great significance. "You *are* well, Miss Ward?
I mean—Celeste. You do remember who I am?"

Celeste had insisted that the interviewer call her by her first
name. Yet, now, to her embarrassment, she could not remember the interviewer's name—though she smiled warmly, and said,
"Yes, of course!" With awkward formality they shook hands; Celeste shivered at the touch of the young woman's cool, bone-thin
fingers. And that damp, gum-bared, toothy rapacious smile. And
those eyes—enormous, dark, avid with curiosity. There was a
certain species of female admirer—earnest students, fervent
disciples—who sorely tried Celeste's patience, though Celeste was
the most patient of women. Just her bad luck, this interviewer was
one of them.

"Do you mind?—I don't want to miss a syllable," the interviewer
said, switching on the tape recorder. "I have just a few quick questions that weren't quite answered, from last time—"

"If you insist," Celeste said, resigned.

It had not been Celeste Ward's wish that there be so extensive a
feature on her. Her heart sank at the prospect. Yet somehow, like
this evening's celebration of her birthday, it had happened. Out of
nowhere the eager young interviewer had appeared, with ample
evidence of her sincerity—published articles on feminist history
since eighteenth-century England and France; lavishly admiring
reviews of Celeste Ward's work. The Cause had given its blessings

to the project; wheels were busily in motion that could not be stopped. *Like a pregnancy, a giant fetus. Taking root. Taking nourishment from any source. Unstoppable.* It was Celeste's belief that the interviewer, for all her professed adulation of Celeste Ward, secretly hoped she wouldn't live too much longer. Or, at any rate, wouldn't continue an active career in the Cause. The interviewer had already accumulated far too much material, including transcribed interviews with people who'd known Celeste Ward from her Minneapolis girlhood onward, and this made Celeste uneasy. Her public life was, as she'd often said, an open book; her private life, of which she never spoke, was something else entirely. *What shame, if my secrets are exposed! I can't bear it.* At the same time, Celeste resigned herself to the fact that, for better or worse, Celeste Ward had had a historical role in twentieth-century American feminism, and that couldn't be denied. Beyond the merely personal was the impersonal, the political. *But no: I can't bear it!*

Like a dog sniffing out a buried bone, the interviewer was asking questions Celeste had managed to elude last time. Childhood memories? relations with her parents, long since deceased? It was hardly the time for such an interrogation, in the midst of others' conversations, and only a few minutes before the program was scheduled to begin. What was wrong with the interviewer? Did she lack common sense, ordinary tact? Her girlish-gawky manner suggested naïveté, like the odd way in which she wore her thick, dry, crackling red-brown hair, parted in the center of her head, brushed severely back and fastened with old-fashioned mother-of-pearl clips; yet Celeste sensed, from time to time, a calculating shrewdness beneath. Like that lover of Celeste's of many years ago who seemed to have wished to triumph over her resistance to him, her virginal fearfulness, and not to have wished to love her, at all. *This one wants my blood. Wants to suck me dry.*

"Miss Ward? Celeste? What is it?"

Shakily, swaying, Celeste had pushed herself to her feet. Why was she wearing shoes with so impractical a heel?—and why this silk-and-wool suit with the long narrow skirt, that made sitting and standing and quick escapes so difficult? Celeste excused herself, saying she wanted to use the women's room before the program began. The interviewer leapt up to assist her as if she were an elderly woman and Celeste all but wrenched herself away. "Please, thank you, I'm capable of walking by myself," she said sharply.

The interviewer stood, teeth and gums bared in a pained grimace, watching Celeste walk away.

The birthday. A mistake? Though she was not, had never been through her life, what you would call a superstitious woman. Nor even, since her early blunders, a woman prone to surrender to weak, wayward emotions. In secret she might have thought that to be a *woman* was in fact to be weak and wayward and generally at the mercy of others—which is to say, *men*—whose primary lust was to propagate the species by seduction, coercion, or both. But though she was a *woman* she was by no means an average woman and in this she took considerable pride.

In this, my escape! My salvation!

Celeste did not think of herself as a fastidious woman, but in private, increasingly with age, she was becoming so. Involuntarily glancing into sinks in public rest rooms—into toilet bowls—steeling herself for the sight of another's filth. Checking out grime on floors, dust in corners. And then her own frowning scrutiny of her appearance in mirrors—not her appearance, which was superficial, but the *self* her appearance suggested. And now that she was so advanced in age the vanity she'd never guessed at in herself, when younger and reasonably attractive, was emerging. Others, her admirers at least, saw a carefully groomed, elegant woman of indeterminate age, with silver-streaked fair hair, a high, virtually unlined forehead, eyes that radiated calm, intelligence, discretion. There was an unmistakable fleshiness to the mouth and the underside of the chin, the sign of incipient collapse—yet, still, Celeste *was* attractive; and made it a point never to appear in public without being perfectly groomed. *I've invented my life, why not my public image?*—she leaned close to the mirror, staring at her eyes which had a sort of bluish shadow beneath. The thin, dry skin of her cheeks, which had borne the brunt of so many years of smiling, was finely creased as a leather glove crumpled in the hand. *What a good, "selfless" woman you are! And nobody to know better!* Celeste heard a scrambling sound, a clicking as of—what?—tiny claws? teeth? She saw a blurred movement in the mirror, beneath one of the toilet stalls, but when she turned, astonished, there was nothing visible. She went to the stall and pushed the door open and screamed—there was something in the toilet bowl, a hunk of raw, bloody flesh, writhing and squirming. What was it! What horror! Aghast, yet even in her shock reacting pragmatically, Celeste flushed the toilet, and flushed, and flushed it.

When the program organizers came to seek her out they found her there, in the stall, her face ashy-pale and her eyes glassily bright, flushing the toilet.

An evening of celebration and applause—"TOWARD THE YEAR 2000." A standing ovation greeted Celeste Ward's appearance on stage and continued for several embarrassing moments before she took her seat, flanked by the executive director of the Foundation, a vigorous iron-jawed woman with whom, years ago, Celeste had had a feud, over issues long since forgotten, and a younger woman, a recently elected Congresswoman actively associated with the Cause. The stage was blindingly lit; there were several immense floral displays, as at a funeral; Celeste Ward displayed unflagging, alert interest as one by one, in a program that seemed to go on interminably, speakers were introduced, gave their prepared speeches, were warmly applauded. From time to time Celeste heard her name and smiled to acknowledge a flurry of quick applause. How safe she was, here among friends! *That thing in the toilet, it had not been hers. Nor had it been alive. Where was the proof?* Her thoughts drifted like froth on the tide. The blinding lights were a kind of comfort. She was thinking of her first lover, so long ago. His name forgotten. And that love—wiped clean, scoured and scrubbed and gone. Yet she could see the boy's face—a boy, not yet a man—though urgent, even anguished in his masculinity—sexual desire rising in his eyes like liquid changing color. *Yes, no, I*

hate you, I can't help myself I love you—I will die if you leave me.
But of course she had not died, she'd survived. And so knew to
counsel other distraught young women, other girls wanting absurdly to die in the bloom of youth. *You don't, you don't die, you
survive. Something else dies, in your place.*

It had been Celeste Ward's life, or—that other's. She'd been the
one to make the choice.

After that first, terrible time. So young. After that, the healing
amnesia. With each subsequent lover, coolly chosen, to prove, yes,
she *was* a woman, she possessed that power. And the "accidents"
seemed somehow part of it—three or four times—or was it, impos-
sibly, five?—as if to prove, yes, she could. Each pregnancy termi-
nated out of conscience and necessity *I have my own life, I own my
own life, no one can trap me* and the proof flushed cleanly away,
gone. The doctors' names—if indeed the men were doctors, in
those days—unknown. Payment in cash: a business deal. The wis-
est course, seeing she had no instinct for motherhood, no wish to be
encumbered; in any case, no father for the baby, nor was likely to
acquire one. The most practical course, considering her career. The
most moral course. *And did I look back?—I did not look back. I do
not recommend looking back. What is gone, is gone.*

Except: her secrets would remain secrets.

Except: she *was* safe, among friends. Listen to the applause!

Her interviewer was introducing her at last, hunched over the
podium like a beaky bird of prey, big teeth and pale gums exposed
in twitchy smiles, heaping her with praise—Celeste Ward rose to a
thunderous ovation, felt a moment's touch of panic as she blinked
into the void beyond the glare, then smiled, stumbled on her way to
the podium but took her place as her interviewer stepped aside
with a rapturous look, and removed her speech from her bag, and
fumbled to put on her reading glasses, and began.

Celeste Ward's much-awaited speech—"Toward the Year 2000."
The words were her own yet unfamiliar. The syllables sounded in
her ears harsh, sibilant; patently insincere; there was a crackling,
derisive undertone—the microphone? someone in the audience?
She could not catch her breath—she, Celeste Ward, who had given

hundreds of speeches! She stopped, began again. Mouthing prepared words in celebration of the Cause to which (since it was so
frequently reiterated, it must be true) she'd given her life. *But
I had no other choice, I had no other life.* The audience was
strangely silent. Her hands shook holding the speech, her unflat-
tering half-moon glasses slid down her nose. She was perspiring,
yet shivering. Through rents in the glare she could see her
audience—rows upon rows of them, stretching to a shadowy horizon—and in the balcony—but there were two balconies!—gazing at
her with flattering intensity. Yet here and there amid the adulatory
crowd of well-dressed women and the occasional man were misshapen, hideous figures, hardly more than upright clots of flesh,
balloonlike hairless heads with eyes set deep and glittering in their
sockets, spindly shoulders and torsos, bloated bellies—Celeste
Ward saw, and looked quickly away. She was terrified of losing her
place in her speech which was like no other speech she'd given in
her career because it had been cynically spliced together out of
previous speeches of hers by a malicious stranger, an enemy who
knew her work intimately, thus could sabotage it with devastating
skill: sudden jumps in logic, incoherent transitions between para-
graphs, repetitive phrases, a number of the words—*eyrrism,
troese, dysphisis*—unknown, unpronounceable to her. This, the final speech of Celeste Ward's career—which cruel fact she was
somehow allowed to know, a chill breeze blowing toward her out of
the future. The audience had begun to grow restless. There were
whispers, coughing spells. Celeste, reading rapidly now, stumbling
and skipping parts of sentences, dared not glance up in terror of
what she would see even as she knew *they can't be here, there is no
trace of them here, only we who deserve to live.* Then words ceased
suddenly. Someone approached her hesitantly asking with hushed
solicitude is something wrong? Miss Ward, is something wrong?
and now there was absolute silence as if a single great breath had
been indrawn as, gripping the podium to keep from falling, her face
chalky-white and eyes wild and mouth trembling, Celeste Ward
cried hoarsely, "—You don't, you don't die! You survive! Something
else dies, in your place!"

She would have slumped to the floor had not someone caught her in thin steely arms.

Then, unexpectedly, this: passing the attack off lightly, backstage. Insisting she was fine, only a momentary dizzy spell caused by those damned lights, she had them occasionally in stressful situations but there was nothing to worry about her doctor assured her and so she who was no hypochondriac did not worry and thank you but no she *would not* consent to be taken to a hospital, what were they, her friends, thinking of?—on the night of her birthday? Her interviewer was holding a glass of water to her lips, tepid city water tasting of rust, but it seemed to help. Of course, Celeste Ward would not miss the reception in her honor and disappoint so many hundreds of well-wishers—"If you think I'd do such a thing," she protested, "you don't know me at all."

So by the genteel forcefulness of her personality managing to convince the organizers against their sounder judgment not to call an ambulance but to show her to a rest room so she could freshen up. This time, a small private lavatory adjacent to a dressing room. Celeste promised to be just a minute, then she'd join them for the reception, infinitely relieved to be alone at last—free of prying eyes, those looks of concern and pity, damned vultures!—and the luxury, thank God, of locking a door. And this lavatory was at least cleaner than the other.

You're safe! nobody knows! it's your secret! don't be weak, ridiculous! Celeste ran cold water into the sink and splashed her fevered face and rubbed her eyes vigorously to restore their vision daring only to glance at herself in the mirror. She was unwell, but *safe! safe!* The thrumming pulses in her brain had begun to leak into one another like spies whispering secrets but she was still on her feet and she was sixty years old and her enemies had not triumphed. Glimpsing one of them then in the mirror, a blurred undersea figure scuttling along the floor behind her, but they could not overcome her, she was alive, she had triumphed, and they had not. Wasn't she superior to them, because of this? That she had life, and they had not? A vast teeming ocean of them, waves threshing with their terrible hunger but it had nothing to do with her. One of them clutched at her ankle with stubbed, mangled fingers, in horror she felt its toothless gums gnawing at her flesh and kicked it away. "No! Leave me alone!" she cried. Another was clawing at her skirt, wanting to tug her to the floor. She screamed, slapped, kicked. But grunting it held tight as another, larger and more robust, with a fully formed hairless head and torso atop a stunted body, seized her right leg at the thigh and began to bite—this one, with powerful teeth! Still another, the size of a spider monkey, leapt to her shoulders, tore open her jacket and blouse and began to suck, bite, gnaw at her breasts. Celeste fought wildly now, blinded, desperate, fighting for her life. Even in the midst of her terror she was incredulous—for had she not, unswervingly, been a good woman? a woman of principle and a woman of character and a woman of exemplary courage and a woman upon whom countless women had modeled themselves? Why, to these hideous creatures, these ravenous mouths, did none of that matter? She, Celeste Ward, of no more significance to them, who were now rising out of the room's dark corners, scuttling rapidly across the floor, than a carcass being devoured by sharks.

She fought, she screamed until they felled her, they had her, all words ceased.

Fatally, the door was locked from the inside. The organizers knocked on it, as minutes passed knocking more urgently, anxiously, calling her name—to no avail. When at last, after about ten minutes, a custodian was summoned to remove the pins from the door's hinges, the first person to enter the lavatory was the interviewer—aghast at what she saw. How the corpse lay on the floor with legs twisted beneath her in a posture of struggle, her jacket and blouse torn open as if, suffocating, she'd torn at her clothing, her eyes open and glassily unfocussed and the thin pale lips drawn back from the teeth in an expression of angry incredulity.

These impressions, Celeste Ward's interviewer would note. Even in the midst of her shock and horror, like any professional.

Intensive

The days are distinct, but
the night has only one name.
—Elias Canetti

Then they are threading a needle slowly and purposefully through you. The pain is registered in sawnotched waves in a TV monitor. You have wakened several times yet each time incompletely. You understand that it was an error to have been born encased in flesh but you can't remember whose error it was. You are lost on B-level looking for Radiation Therapy though following like a dutiful child the color-coded arrows: yellow. You are lost on A-level looking for Oncology. You are lost on Ground Level in a maze of corridors pushing through sets of hefty double doors with oval glass windows like startled wide-opened eyes looking for a telephone or a Women's Room or a red EXIT to take you home though you understand that "home" has now become a concept, an idea like "justice" and "The Good." You open a door marked FIRE STAIRS and enter a stairwell smelling of damp concrete just as, as elevator doors open, a male attendant whistling thinly through his teeth wheels a motionless figure on a gurney out and in your direction.

In Intensive Care the Nurses' Station hums and buzzes with activity. Open cubicles radiate toward the outside from it like spokes from an axle. In each of these cubicles divided from its neighbors by curtained partitions and gleaming palpitating machines is a motionless white-encased figure in a bed. You observe from a safe distance perhaps the ceiling or one of the TV monitors. A clock on the wall of the lounge reads 4:10. There are no windows to determine "day" or "night." Amid the vinyl chairs and Styrofoam coffee cups a man with a blurred face is comforting a woman sobbing in his arms. The Blood Room hums with refrigeration. The Blood Room is a place of sobriety and reflection. Even the Haitian attendant Jean known for his irrepressible high spirits and his gleaming gold tooth is subdued in the Blood Room and in its vicinity. They are threading a needle slowly and purposefully through your ganglia. They are explaining their procedure but their words are muffled as if uttered in a substance dense and suffocating as water. If you listen closely you can hear behind their words not a single beat but numberless beats as of the thrumming of giant motors. The fluorescent lights in the ceiling flicker but do not go out. There is an alarmed beeping on one of the TV monitors in one of the cubicles. Two attendants in white wearing white thin-rubber gloves are swiftly stripping an empty bed tossing defiled linen into a basket with mirthful disdain: a competition, to see who works more swiftly than the other.

They are threading a needle through all the invisible ganglia of your body through which an electric current will flow illuminating you dazzling as a Christmas tree. You must only have faith that the procedure will be effective. That it will not be lethal. You surrendered your name in barter. There is the promise that it will be returned upon your release. Because you have no name there can be no humiliation in the chill white porcelain bedpan except no nurse will carry this object away. Only an attendant will carry such an object away but there are no attendants. The hospital morgue is on C-level taking up the northeast corner of the building. The elevator door opens and a male attendant briskly wheels a motionless white figure on a gurney out into the corridor and away on smooth-thrumming wheels. You realize your mistake: descending an interior stairway smelling of damp concrete and disinfectant and so dimly lit the floor numbers on the walls are unintelligible. And the doors are locked from the outside. A clock on the wall of the lounge reads 12:02. They are threading a narrow straw up into your left nostril slowly and purposefully and down into and through your windpipe and into your collapsed lung. You have faith in the thrumming heartbeat of the invisible giant machines. You are certain you are dreaming this and so there is no terror. It was an error to have been encased in flesh but not your error solely: you are after all but a single "specimen" of a "species." You try to explain this fact but when you begin to scream the respirator tube is dislodged and your oxygen vanishes and the building rises up numberless floors above you and descends numberless floors below you into Earth where instruments of measurement are impotent and all quantifiable distinctions lost.

A clock on the lounge wall reads 7:20. A middle-aged woman with a face like a creased leather purse is hurrying to the Women's Room her hand to her mouth and vomit leaking through her fingers. They are readjusting the IV fluid tube and the pulmonary cavity tube and the heart monitor wire and the brain monitor wire and the catheter and threading you tighter this time. You are pulling at the locked door crying *Help! let me out!* but the doorknob will not turn. You heart begins to palpitate at 255 beats per minutes. A male attendant whistling thinly through his teeth is wheeling a motionless white figure on a gurney into an elevator. The building is a place of mystery composed of concrete, opaque glass brick, Styrofoam and plastic laminated panels the hues of fruit sherbert that when slid open look out upon an emptiness vast and trackless as the night sky if all the stars had become extinct. Where your voice is sucked from you as into a vacuum, with no echo. Where the air tastes of iron dust. The building has no name or no name you can shape with your ulcerated lips. Nor is it located at any point in the Universe relative to any other point you can recall. If it has always existed *here* you were never in your previous life aware of its being *here* because you yourself were never *here* and so had no consciousness of *here* as you have no consciousness of the long-extinct but still glittering star-clusters beyond the Milky Way. *Help me!* as hopeful as a child you follow the black, red, yellow, green coded arrows on the walls long after it is apparent you are lost.

They are threading you slowly and purposefully as you watch untouched from the ceiling or perhaps from the blank glassy-gray screen of the TV monitor overhead. You have explained several times that you are dreaming this and that it is about to end. You are screaming pounding at a locked door in a stairwell deep beneath the ground but there is no one to hear. You are an American and it is difficult to believe that some errors are irreversible and that Time itself is irreversible. The staff is good-natured and kindly though sometimes impatient shaking their heads at how long some of you cling to life. A doctor's name—*Rourke?*—*Rooke?*—is being called over the address system. The percussive beats have become louder and overlap more clumsily. A doll-sized white figure on a gurney is being wheeled along the corridor its head encased in a small plastic tent. Two sinewy attendants with gold earrings gleaming against their rich dark-stained skin are stripping a bed. And then the infected mattress is turned up on its black wire springs. There is a sound of startled pigeons cooing outside the window except there are no pigeons and there is no window. You have several times explained to these strangers who are threading your nerve tissue that you are dreaming this and consequently they should not take it so seriously. A female custodian with a pail and a cheerful yellow squeegee mop is cleaning the floor of the Women's Room. On the floor of the Intensive Care lounge there are stains from spilled coffee. The clock on the wall reads 10:18. The weeping woman and the man who comforted her are gone but are replaced by a weeping older woman and a younger woman who is comforting her. The infinitesimally thin wire connecting your ganglia is prepared for the onslaught of electricity. Someone is crying *Help me! help me to die!* but the words are indistinct and are perhaps other, unknown words. The clock on the wall reads 10:18. You decide that your dream has been completed and slip from the TV monitor overhead and back into your body. Past the Nurses'

Station a blond nurse springy in her rubber-soled shoes walks beside a burly cocoa-skinned attendant grinning at her all teeth and
excited interest, the two of them laughing together on their way to
the elevator out of which a male attendant whistling thinly through
his teeth is wheeling a motionless white figure on a gurney.

IV

Valentine

In upstate New York in those years there were snowstorms so wild and fierce they could change the world, within a few hours, to a place you wouldn't know. First came the heavy black thunderheads over Lake Erie, then the wind hammering overhead like a freight train, then the snowflakes erupting, flying, swirling like crazed atoms. If there'd been a sun it was extinguished, gone. Night and day were reversed, the fallen snow emitted such a radium-glare.

I was fifteen years old living in the Red Rock section of Buffalo with an aunt, an older sister of my mother's, and her husband who was retired from the New York Central Railroad with a disability pension. My own family was what you'd called "dispersed"—we were all alive, seven of us, I believed we were all alive, but we did not live together in the same house any longer. In fact, the house, an old rented farmhouse twenty miles north of Buffalo, was gone. Burned to the ground.

Valentine's Day 1959, the snowstorm began in midafternoon and already by 5 P.M. the power lines were down in Buffalo. Hurriedly we lit kerosene lamps whose wicks smoked and stank as they emitted a begrudging light. We had a flashlight, of course, and candles. In extra layers of clothes we saw our breaths steam as we ate our cold supper on plates like ice. I cleaned up the kitchen as best I could without hot water, for that was always my task, among numerous others, and I said "Goodnight, Aunt Esther" to my aunt who frowned at me seeing someone not-me in my place who filled her heart with sisterly sorrow and I said "Goodnight, Uncle Herman" to the man designated as my uncle, who was no blood-kin of mine, a stranger with damp eyes always drifting onto me and a mouth like a smirking scar burn. "Goodnight" they murmured as if resenting the very breath expelled for my sake. *Goodnight don't run on the stairs don't drop the candle and set the house on fire.*

Upstairs was a partly finished attic narrow as a tunnel with a habitable space at one end—my "room." The ceiling was covered in strips of peeling insulation and so steep-slanted I could stand up only in the center. The floorboards were splintery and bare except for a small shag rug, a discard of my aunt's, laid down by my bed. The bed was another discard of my aunt's, a sofa of some mud-brown prickly fabric that pierced sheets laid upon it like whiskers sprouting through skin. But this was *a bed of my own* and I had not ever had *a bed of my own* before. Nor had I ever had *a room of my own, a door to shut against others* even if, like the attic door, it could not be locked.

By midnight the storm had blown itself out and the alley below had vanished in undulating dunes of snow. Everywhere snow! Glittering like mica in the moonlight! And the moon—a glowing battered-human face in a sky strangely starless, black as a well. The largest snowdrift I'd ever seen, shaped like a right-angled triangle, slanted up from the ground to the roof close outside my window. My aunt and her husband had gone to bed downstairs hours ago and the thought came to me unbidden *I can run away, no one would miss me.*

Along Huron Street, which my aunt's house fronted, came a snowplow, red light flashing atop its cab; otherwise there were few vehicles and these were slow-moving with groping headlights, like wounded beasts. Yet even as I watched there came a curiously shaped small vehicle to park at the mouth of the alley; and the driver, a long-legged man in a hooded jacket, climbed out. To my amazement he stomped through the snow into the alley to stand peering up toward my window, his breath steaming. Who? Who was this? *Mr. Lacey, my algebra teacher?*

For Valentine's Day that morning I had brought eight home-made valentines to school made of stiff red construction paper edged with paper lace, in envelopes decorated with red-ink hearts; the valentine TO MR. LACEY was my masterpiece, the largest and most ingeniously designed, interlocking hearts fashioned with a ruler and compass to resemble geometrical figures in three dimensions. HAPPY VALENTINE'S DAY I had neatly printed in black ink. Of course I had not signed any of the valentines and had secretly slipped them into the lockers of certain girls and boys and Mr. Lacey's onto his desk after class. I had instructed myself not to be disappointed when I received no valentines in return, not a single valentine in return, and I was not disappointed when at the end of the school day I went home without a single one: *I was not.*

Mr. Lacey seemed to have recognized me in the window where I stood staring, my outspread fingers on the glass bracketing my white astonished face, for he'd begun climbing the enormous snow-drift that lifted to the roof! How assured, how matter-of-fact, as if this were the most natural thing in the world. I was too surprised to be alarmed, or even embarrassed—my teacher would see me in a cast-off sweater of my brother's that was many sizes too large for me and splotched with oil stains, he would see my shabby little room that wasn't really a room, just part of an unfinished attic. He would know I was the one who'd left the valentine TO MR. LACEY on his desk in stealth not daring to sign my name. *He would know who I was, how desperate for love.*

Once on the roof, which was steep, Mr. Lacey made his way to my window cautiously. The shingles were covered in snow, icy patches beneath. There was a rumor that Mr. Lacey was a skier, and a skater, though his lanky body did not seem the body of an athlete and in class sometimes he seemed distracted in the midst of speaking or inscribing an equation on the blackboard; as if there were thoughts more crucial to him than tenth-grade algebra at Thomas E. Dewey High School which was one of the poorest schools in the city. But now his footing was sure as a mountain goat's, his movements agile and unerring. He crouched outside my window tugging to lift it—*Erin? Make haste!*

I was helping to open the window which was locked in ice. It had not been opened for weeks. Already it seemed I'd pulled on my wool slacks and wound around my neck the silver muffler threaded with crimson yarn my mother had given me two or three Christmases ago. I had no coat or jacket in my room and dared not risk going downstairs to the front closet. I was very excited, fumbling, biting my lower lip, and when at last the window lurched upward the freezing air rushed in like a slap in the face. Mr. Lacey's words seemed to reverberate in my ears *Make haste, make haste!—not a moment to waste!* It was his teasing-chiding classroom manner that nonetheless meant business. Without hesitating, he grabbed both my hands—I saw that I was wearing the white angora mittens my grandmother had knitted for me long ago, which I'd believed had been lost in the fire—and hauled me through the window.

Mr. Lacey led me to the edge of the roof, to the snowdrift, seeking out his footprints where he knew the snow to be fairly firm, and carefully he pulled me in his wake so that I seemed to be descending a strange kind of staircase. The snow was so fresh-fallen it lifted like powder at the slightest touch or breath, glittering even more fiercely close up, as if the individual snowflakes, of such geometrical beauty and precision, contained minute sparks of flame. *Er-in, Er-in, now your courage must begin* I seemed to hear and suddenly we were on the ground and there was Mr. Lacey's Volkswagen at the mouth of the alley, headlights burning like cat's eyes and tusks of exhaust curling up behind. How many times covertly I'd tracked with my eyes that ugly-funny car shaped like a sardine can, its black chassis speckled with rust, as Mr. Lacey drove into the teachers' parking lot each morning between 8:25 A.M. and 8:35 A.M. How many times I'd turned quickly aside in terror that Mr. Lacey would see *me*. Now I stood confused at the mouth of the alley, for Huron Street and all of the city I could see was so changed, the air so terribly cold like a knifeblade in my lungs; I looked back at the darkened house wondering if my aunt might wake and discover me gone, and what then would happen?—as Mr.

Lacey urged *Come, Erin, hurry! She won't even know you're gone* unless he said *She won't ever know you're gone.* Was it true? Not long ago in algebra class I'd printed in the margin of my textbook

MR.

L.

IS

AL

WA

YS

RI

GH

T!

which I'd showed Linda Bewley across the aisle, one of the popular tenth-grade girls, a B+ student and very pretty and popular, and Linda frowned trying to decipher the words which were meant to evoke Mr. Lacey's pole-lean frame, but she never did get it and turned away from me annoyed.

Yet it was so: Julius Lacey was always always right.

Suddenly I was in the cramped little car and Mr. Lacey was behind the wheel driving north on icy Huron Street. *Where are we going?* I didn't dare ask. When my grades in Mr. Lacey's class were less than 100 percent I was filled with anxiety that turned my fingers and toes to ice for even if I'd answered nearly all the questions on a test correctly *how could I know I could answer the next question? solve the next problem? and the next?* A nervous passion drove me to comprehend not just the immediate problem but the principle behind it, for behind everything there was an elusive and tyrannical principle of which Mr. Lacey was the sole custodian; and I could not know if he liked me or was bemused by me or merely tolerated me or was in fact disappointed in me as a student who should have been earning perfect scores at all times. He was twenty-six or -seven years old, the youngest teacher at the school, whom many students feared and hated, and a small group of us feared and admired. His severe, angular face registered frequent dissatisfaction as if to indicate *Well, I'm waiting! Waiting to be impressed! Give me one good reason to be impressed!*

Never had I seen the city streets so deserted. Mr. Lacey drove
no more than twenty miles an hour passing stores whose fronts
were obliterated by snow like waves frozen at their crests and
through intersections where no traffic lights burned to guide us
and our only light was the Volkswagen's headlights and the glowering moon large in the sky as a fat navel orange held at arm's
length. We passed Carthage Street that hadn't yet been plowed—a
vast river of snow six feet high. We passed Templeau Street where
a city bus had been abandoned in the intersection, humped with
snow like a forlorn creature of the Great Plains. We passed Stur-
geon Street where broken electrical wires writhed and crackled in
the snow like snakes crazed with pain. We passed Childress Street
where a water main had burst and an arc of water had frozen glistening in a graceful curve at least fifteen feet high at its crest. At
Ontario Avenue Mr. Lacey turned right, the Volkswagen went into
a delirious skid, Mr. Lacey put out his arm to keep me from pitch-
ing forward—*Erin, take care!* But I was safe. And on we drove.

Ontario Avenue, usually so crowded with traffic, was deserted as
the surface of the moon. A snowplow had forged a single lane down
the center. On all sides were unfamiliar shapes of familiar objects
engulfed in snow and ice—parking meters? mailboxes? abandoned
cars? Humanoid figures frozen in awkward, surprised postures—
hunched in doorways, frozen in midstride on the sidewalk? *Look!
Look at the frozen people!* I cried in a raw loud girl's voice that so
frequently embarrassed me when Mr. Lacey called upon me unexpectedly in algebra class; but Mr. Lacey shrugged saying *Just
snowmen, Erin—don't give them a second glance.* But I couldn't
help staring at these statue-figures for I had an uneasy sense of being stared at by them in turn, through chinks in the hard-crusted
snow of their heads. And I seemed to hear their faint despairing
cries *Help! help us!*—but Mr. Lacey did not slacken his speed.

(Yet: who could have made so many "snowmen," so quickly after
the storm? Children? Playing so late at night? And where were
these children now?)

Mysteriously Mr. Lacey said *There are many survivors, Erin.
In all epochs, just enough survivors.* I wanted to ask should we

pray for them? pressing my hands in the angora mittens against my mouth to keep them from crying, for I knew how hopeless prayer was in such circumstances, God only helps those who don't require His help.

Were we headed for the lakefront?—we crossed a swaying bridge high above railroad tracks, and almost immediately after that another swaying bridge high above an ice-locked canal. We passed factories shut down by the snowstorm with smokestacks so tall their rims were lost in mist. We were on South Main Street now passing darkened shuttered businesses, warehouses, a slaughterhouse; windowless brick buildings against whose walls snow had been driven as if sandblasted in eerie, almost legible patterns.

These were messages, I was sure!—yet I could not read them.

Out of the corner of my eye I watched Mr. Lacey as he drove. We were close together in the cramped car; yet at the same time I seemed to be watching us from a distance. At school there were boys who were fearful of Mr. Lacey yet, behind his back, sneered at him muttering what they'd like to do with him, slash his car tires, beat him up, and I felt a thrill of satisfaction *If you could see Mr. Lacey now!* for he was navigating the Volkswagen so capably along the treacherous street, past snowy hulks of vehicles abandoned by the wayside. He'd shoved back the hood of his wool jacket—how handsome he looked! Where by day he often squinted behind his glasses, by night he seemed fully at ease. His hair was long and quill-like and of the subdued brown hue of a deer's winter coat; his eyes, so far as I could see, had a luminous coppery sheen. I recalled how at the high school Mr. Lacey was regarded with doubt and unease by the other teachers, many of whom were old enough to be his parents; he was considered arrogant because he didn't have an education degree from a state teachers' college, like the others, but a master's degree in math from the University of Buffalo where he was a part-time Ph.D. student. *Maybe I will reap where I haven't had any luck sowing* he'd once remarked to the class, standing chalk in hand at the blackboard which was covered in calculations. And this remark too had passed over our heads.

Now Mr. Lacey was saying as if bemused *Here, Erin—the edge. We'll go no farther in this direction.* For we were at the shore of Lake Erie—a frozen lake drifted in snow so far as the eye could see. (Yet I seemed to know how beneath the ice the water was agitated as if boiling, sinuous and black as tar.) Strewn along the beach were massive ice-boulders that glinted coldly in the moonlight. Even by day at this edge of the lake you could see only an edge of the Canadian shore, the farther western shore was lost in distance. I was in terror that Mr. Lacey out of some whim would abandon me here, for never could I have made my way back to my aunt's house in such cold.

But already Mr. Lacey was turning the car around, already we were driving inland, a faint tinkling music seemed to draw us, and within minutes we were in a wooded area I knew to be Delaware Park—though I'd never been there before. I had heard my classmates speak of skating parties here and had yearned to be invited to join them as I had yearned to be invited to visit the homes of certain girls, without success. *Hang on! Hang on!* Mr. Lacey said, for the Volkswagen was speeding like a sleigh on curving lanes into the interior of a deep evergreen forest. And suddenly—we were at a large oval skating rink above which strings of starry lights glittered like Christmas bulbs, where dozens, hundreds of elegantly dressed skaters circled the ice as if there had never been any snowstorm, or any snowstorm that mattered to *them.* Clearly these were privileged people, for electric power had been restored for their use and burned brilliantly, wastefully on all sides. *Oh Mr. Lacey I've never seen anything so beautiful* I said, biting my lip to keep from crying. It was a magical, wondrous place—the Delaware Park Skating Rink! Skaters on ice smooth as glass—skating round and round to gay, amplified music like that of a merry-go-round. Many of the skaters were in brightly colored clothes, handsome sweaters, fur hats, fur muffs; beautiful dogs of no breed known to me trotted alongside their masters and mistresses, pink tongues lolling in contentment. There were angel-faced girls in skaters' costumes, snug little pearl-buttoned velvet jackets and flouncy skirts to midthigh, gauzy knit stockings and kidskin boot-skates with blades that flashed like sterling silver—my heart yearned to see such skates for I'd learned to skate on rusted old skates formerly belonging to my older sisters, on a creek near our farmhouse, in truth I had never really learned to skate, not as these skaters were skating, so without visible effort, strife, or anxiety. Entire families were skating—mothers and fathers hand in hand with small children, and older children, and white-haired elders who must have been grandparents!—and the family dog trotting along with that look of dogs laughing. There were attractive young people in groups, and couples with their arms around each other's waist, and solitary men and boys who swiftly threaded their way through the crowd unerring as undersea creatures perfectly adapted to their element. Never would I have dared join these skaters except Mr. Lacey insisted. Even as I feebly protested *Oh but I can't, Mr. Lacey—I don't know how to skate* he was pulling me to the skate rental where he secured a pair of skates for each of us; and suddenly there I was stumbling and swaying in the presence of real skaters, my ankles weak as water and my face blotched with embarrassment, oh what a spectacle—but Mr. Lacey had closed his fingers firmly around mine and held me upright, refused to allow me to fall. *Do as I do! Of course you can skate! Follow me!* So I had no choice but to follow, like an unwieldy lake barge hauled by a tugboat.

How loud the happy tinkling music was out on the ice, far louder than it had seemed on shore, as the lights too were brighter, nearly blinding. *Oh! Oh!* I panted in Mr. Lacey's wake, terrified of slipping and falling; breaking a wrist, an arm, a leg; terrified of falling in the paths of swift skaters whose blades flashed sharp and cruel as butcher knives. Everywhere was a harsh hissing sound of blades slicing the surface of the ice, a sound you couldn't hear on shore. I would be cut to ribbons if I fell! All my effort was required simply to stay out of the skaters' paths as they flew by, with no more awareness of me than if I were a passing shadow; the only skaters who noticed me were children, girls as well as boys, already expert skaters as young as nine or ten who glanced at me with smiles of bemusement, or disdain. *Out! out of our way! you don't belong here on our ice!* But I was stubborn too, I persevered, and after two or three times around the rink I was still upright and able to skate without Mr. Lacey's continuous vigilance, my head high and my arms extended for balance. My heart beat in giddy elation and pride. I was skating! At last! Mr. Lacey dashed off to the center of the ice where more practiced skaters performed, executing rapid circles, figure eights, dancerlike and acrobatic turns, his skate blades flashing, and a number of onlookers applauded, as I applauded, faltering but regaining my balance, skating on. I was not graceful—not by any stretch of the imagination—and I guessed I must have looked a sight, in an old baggy oil-stained sweater and rumpled wool slacks, my kinky-snarly red-brown hair in my eyes— but I wasn't quite so clumsy any longer, my ankles were getting stronger and the strokes of my skate-blades more assured, sweeping. How happy I was! How proud! I was beginning to be warm, almost feverish inside my clothes.

Restless as a wayward comet a blinding spotlight moved about the rink singling out skaters, among them Mr. Lacey as he spun at the very center of the rink, an unlikely, storklike figure to be so graceful on the ice; for some reason then the spotlight abruptly shifted—to me! I was so caught by surprise I nearly tipped, and fell—I heard applause, laughter—saw faces at the edge of the rink grinning at me. Were they teasing, or sincere? Kindly, or cruel? I wanted to believe they were kindly for the rink was such a happy place but I couldn't be sure as I teetered past, arms flailing to keep my balance. I couldn't be certain but I seemed to see some of my high school classmates among the spectators; and some of my teachers; and others, adults, a caseworker from the Erie County family services department, staring at me disapprovingly. The spotlight was tormenting me: rushing at me, then falling away; allowing me to skate desperately onward, then seeking me out again swift and pitiless as a cheetah in pursuit of prey. The harshly tinkling music ended in a burst of static as if a radio had been turned violently up, then off. A sudden vicious wind rushed thin and sharp as a razor across the ice. My hair whipped in the wind, my ears were turning to ice. My fingers in the tight angora mittens were turning to ice, too. Most of the skaters had gone home, I saw to my disappointment, the better-dressed, better-mannered skaters, all the families, and the only dogs that remained were wild-eyed mongrels with bristling hackles and stumpy tails. Mr. Lacey and I skated hastily to a deserted snowswept section of the rink to avoid these dogs, and were pursued by the damned spotlight; here the ice was rippled and striated and difficult to skate on. An arm flashed at the edge of the rink, I saw a jeering white face, and an ice-packed snowball came flying to strike Mr. Lacey between his shoulder blades and shatter in pieces to the ground. Furious, his face reddening, Mr. Lacey whirled in a crouch—*Who did that? Which of you?* He spoke with his classroom authority but he wasn't in his classroom now and the boys only mocked him more insolently. They chanted something that sounded like *Lac-ey! Lac-ey! Ass-y! Assy-Asshole!* Another snowball struck him on the side of the head, sending his glasses flying and skittering along the ice. I shouted for them to *stop! stop!* and a snowball came careening past my head, another struck my arm, hard. Mr. Lacey shook his fist daring to move toward our attackers but this only unleashed a barrage of snowballs; several struck him with such force he was knocked down, a starburst of red at his mouth. Without his glasses Mr. Lacey looked young as a boy himself, dazed and helpless. On my hands and knees I crawled across the ice to retrieve his glasses, thank God there was only a hairline crack on one of the lenses. I was trembling with anger, sobbing. I was sure I recognized some of the boys, boys in my algebra class, but I didn't know their names. I crouched over Mr. Lacey asking was he all right? was he all right? seeing that he was stunned, pressing a handkerchief against his bleeding mouth. It was one of his white cotton handkerchiefs he'd take out of a pocket in class, shake ceremoniously open, and use to polish his glasses. The boys trotted away jeering and laughing. Mr. Lacey and I were alone, the only skaters remaining on the rink. Even the mongrel dogs had departed.

It was very cold now. Earlier that day there'd been a warning—temperatures in the Lake Erie–Lake Ontario region would drop as low that night, counting the windchill factor, as −30 degrees Fahrenheit. The wind stirred snake-skeins of powdery snow as if the blizzard might be returning. Above the rink most of the lightbulbs had burnt out or had been shattered by the rising wind. The fresh-fallen snow that had been so purely white was now trampled and littered; dogs had urinated on it; strewn about were cigarette butts, candy wrappers, lost boots, mittens, a wool knit cap. My pretty handknit muffler lay on the ground stiffened with filth—one of the jeering boys must have taken it from me when I was distracted. I bit my lip to keep from crying, the muffler had been ruined and I refused to pick it up. Subdued, silent, Mr. Lacey and I hunted our boots amid the litter, and left our skates behind in a slovenly mound, and limped back to the Volkswagen that was the only vehicle remaining in the snowswept parking lot. Mr. Lacey swore seeing the front windshield had been cracked like a spider's web, very much as the left lens of his glasses had been cracked. Ironically he said *Now you know, Erin, where the Delaware Park Skating Rink is.*

The bright battered-face moon had sunk nearly to the treeline, about to be sucked into blankest night.

In the Bison City Diner adjacent to the Greyhound bus station on Eighth Street, Mr. Lacey and I sat across a booth from each other, and Mr. Lacey gave our order to a brassy-haired waitress in a terse mutter—*two coffees, please.* Stern and frowning to discourage the woman from inquiring after his reddened face and swollen, still bleeding mouth. And then he excused himself to use the men's room. My bladder was aching, I had to use the rest room too, but would have been too shy to slip out of the booth if Mr. Lacey hadn't gone first.

It was 3:20 A.M. So late! The electricity had been restored in parts of Buffalo, evidently—driving back from the park we saw streetlights burning, traffic lights again operating. Still, most of the streets were deserted; choked with snow. The only other vehicles were snowplows and trucks spewing salt on the streets. Some state maintenance workers were in the Bison Diner, which was a twenty-four-hour diner, seated at the counter, talking and laughing loudly together and flirting with the waitress who knew them. When Mr. Lacey and I came into the brightly lit room, blinking, no doubt somewhat dazed-looking, the men glanced at us curiously but made no remarks. At least, none that we could hear. Mr. Lacey touched my arm and gestured with his head for me to follow him to a booth in the farthest corner of the diner—as if it was the most natural thing in the world, Mr. Lacey and me, sliding into that very booth.

In the clouded mirror in the women's room I saw my face strangely flushed, eyes shining like glass. This was a face not exactly known to me; more like my older sister Janice's, yet not Janice's, either. I cupped cold water into my hands and lowered my face to the sink grateful for the water's coolness for my skin was feverish and prickling. My hair was matted as if someone had used an eggbeater on it and my sweater, my brother's discard, was more soiled than I'd known, unless some of the stains were blood—for maybe I'd gotten Mr. Lacey's blood on me out on the ice. *Er-in Don-egal* I whispered aloud in awe, amazement. In wonder. Yes, in pride! I was fifteen years old.

Inspired, I searched through my pockets for my tube of raspberry lipstick, and eagerly dabbed fresh color on my mouth. The effect was instantaneous. *Barbaric!* I heard Mr. Lacey's droll voice for so he'd once alluded to female "makeup" in our class *painting faces like savages with a belief in magic.* But he'd only been joking.

I did believe in magic, I guess. I had to believe in something!

When I returned to the booth in a glow of self-consciousness there was Mr. Lacey with his face freshly washed too, and his lank hair dampened and combed. His part was on the left side of his head, and wavery. He squinted up at me—his face pinched in a quick frowning smile signaling he'd noticed the lipstick, but certainly wouldn't comment on it. Pushed a menu in my direction—*Order anything you wish, Erin, you must be starving* and I picked up the menu to read it, for in fact I was light-headed with hunger, but the print was blurry as if under water and to my alarm I could not decipher a word. In regret I shook my head no, no thank you. *No, Erin? Nothing?* Mr. Lacey asked, surprised. Elsewhere in the diner a jukebox was playing a sentimental song—"Are You Lonesome Tonight?" At the counter, amid clouds of cigarette smoke, the workmen and the brassy-haired waitress erupted in laughter.

It seemed that Mr. Lacey had left his bloody handkerchief in the car and, annoyed and embarrassed, was dabbing at his mouth with a wadded paper towel from the men's room. His upper lip was swollen as if a bee had stung it and one of his front teeth was loose in its socket and still leaked blood. Almost inaudibly he whispered *Damn. Damn. Damn.* His coppery-brown eye through the cracked left lens of his glasses was just perceptibly magnified and seemed to be staring at me with unusual intensity. I shrank before the man's gaze for I feared he blamed me as the source of his humiliation and pain. In truth, I *was* to blame: these things would never have happened to Julius Lacey except for me.

Yet when Mr. Lacey spoke it was with surprising kindness. Asking *Are you sure you want nothing to eat, Erin? Nothing, nothing—at all?*

I could have devoured a hamburger half raw, and a plate of greasy french fries heaped with ketchup, but there I was shaking my head *no, no thank you Mr. Lacey.*

Why?—I was stricken with self-consciousness, embarrassment. To eat in the presence of this man! The intimacy would have been paralyzing, like stripping myself naked before him.

Indeed it was awkward enough when the waitress brought us our coffee, which was black, hotly steaming in thick mugs. Once or twice in my life I'd tried to drink coffee, for everyone seemed to drink it, and the taste was repulsive to me, so bitter! But now I lifted the mug to my lips and sipped timidly at the steaming hot liquid black as motor oil. Seeing that Mr. Lacey disdained to add dairy cream or sugar to his coffee, I did not add any to my own. I was already nervous and almost at once my heart gave odd erratic beats and my pulse quickened.

One of my lifetime addictions, to this bitterly black steaming-hot liquid, would begin at this hour, in such innocence.

Mr. Lacey was saying with an air of reluctance, finality *In every equation there is always an x-factor, and in every x-factor there is the possibility, if not the probability, of tragic misunderstanding.* Out of his jacket pocket he'd taken, to my horror, a folded sheet of paper—red construction paper!—and was smoothing it out on the tabletop. I stared, I was speechless with chagrin. *You must not offer yourself in such a fashion, not even in secret, anonymously* Mr. Lacey said with a teacher's chiding frown. *The valentine heart is the female genitals, you will be misinterpreted.*

There was a roaring in my ears confused with music from the jukebox. The bitter black coffee scalded my throat and began to race along my veins. Words choked me *I'm sorry. I don't know what that is. Don't know what you're speaking of. Leave me alone, I hate you!* But I could not speak, just sat there shrinking to make myself as small as possible in Mr. Lacey's eyes staring with a pretense of blank dumb ignorance at the elaborate geometrical valentine TO MR. LACEY I had made with such hope the other night in the secrecy of my room, knowing I should not commit such an audacious act yet knowing, with an almost unbearable excitement, like one bringing a lighted match to flammable material, that I was going to do it.

Resentfully I said *I guess you know about me, my family. I guess there aren't any secrets.*

Mr. Lacey said *Yes, Erin. There are no secrets. But it's our prerogative not to speak of them if we choose.* Carefully he was refolding the valentine to return to his pocket, which I interpreted as a gesture of forgiveness. He said *There is nothing to be ashamed of, Erin. In you, or in your family.*

Sarcastically I said *There isn't?*

Mr. Lacey said *The individuals who are your mother and father came together out of all the universe to produce you. That's how you came into being, there was no other way.*

I couldn't speak, I was struck dumb. Wanting to protest, to laugh but could not. Hot tears ran down my cheeks.

Mr. Lacey persisted, gravely *And you love them, Erin. Much more than you love me.*

Mutely I shook my head *no.*

Mr. Lacey said, with his air of completing an algebra problem on the blackboard, in a tone of absolute finality *Yes. And we'll never speak of it again after tonight. In fact, of any of this*—making an airy magician's gesture that encompassed not just the Bison Diner but the city of Buffalo, the very night—*ever again.*

And so it was, we never did speak of it again. Our adventure that night following Valentine's Day 1959, ever again.

Next Monday at school, and all the days, and months, to come, Mr. Lacey and I maintained our secret. My heart burned with a knowledge I could not speak! But I was quieter, less nervous in class than I'd ever been; as if, overnight, I'd matured by years. Mr. Lacey behaved exactly, I think, as he'd always behaved toward me: no one could ever have guessed, in any wild flight of imagination, the bond between us. My grades hovered below 100 percent, for Mr. Lacey was surely one to wish to retain the power of giving tests no student could complete to perfection. With a wink he said *Humility goeth in place of a fall, Erin.* And in September when I returned for eleventh grade, Julius Lacey who might have been expected to teach solid geometry to my class was gone: returned to graduate school, we were told. Vanished forever from our lives.

All this was far in the future! That night, I could not have foreseen any of it. Nor how, over thirty years later, on the eve of Valentine's Day I would remove from its hiding place at the bottom of a bureau drawer a bloodstained man's handkerchief initialed *JNL*, fine white cotton yellowed with time, and smooth its wrinkles with the edge of my hand, and lift it to my face like Veronica her veil.

By the time Mr. Lacey and I left the Bison Diner the light there had become blinding and the jukebox music almost deafening. My head would echo for days *lonely? lonely? lonely?* Mr. Lacey drove us hurriedly south on Huron Street passing close beneath factory smokestacks rimmed at their tops with bluish-orange flame, spewing clouds of gray smoke that, upon impact with the freezing wind off Lake Erie, coalesced into fine gritty particles and fell back to earth like hail. These particles drummed on the roof, windshield, and hood of the Volkswagen, bouncing and ricocheting off, denting the metal. *God damn* Mr. Lacey swore softly *will You never cease!* Abruptly then we were home. At my aunt's shabby woodframe bungalow at 3998 Huron Street, Buffalo, New York, that might have been any one of dozens, hundreds, even thousands of similar woodframe one-and-a-half-storey bungalows in working-class neighborhoods of the city. The moon had vanished as if it had never been and the sky was depthless as a black paper cutout, but a streetlamp illuminated the mouth of the snowed-in alley and the great snowdrift in the shape of a right-angled triangle lifting to the roof below my window. *What did I promise, Erin?—no one knows you were ever gone* Mr. Lacey's words seemed to reverberate in my head without his speaking aloud. With relief I saw that the downstairs windows of the house were all darkened but there was a faint flickering light up in my room—the candle still burning, after all these hours. Gripping my hand tightly, Mr. Lacey led me up the snowdrift as up a treacherous stairs, fitting his boots to the footprints he'd originally made, and I followed suit, desperate not to slip and fall. *Safe at home, safe at home!* Mr. Lacey's words sounded close in my ears, unless it was *Safe alone, safe alone!* I heard. Oh! the window was frozen shut again! so the two of us tugged, tugged, tugged, Mr. Lacey with good-humored patience until finally ice shattered, the window lurched up to a height of perhaps twelve inches. I'd begun to cry, a sorry spectacle, and my eyelashes had frozen within seconds in the bitter cold so Mr. Lacey laughed kissing my left eye, and then my right eye, and the lashes were thawed, and I heard *Goodbye, Erin!* as I climbed back through the window.

Death Astride Bicycle

There he'd come crouched on his flying bicycle. White-glaring crash helmet like a giant insect's head. And the sinewy-muscled legs. Dark-tanned, pedaling like a kid. Mr. Waller our social studies teacher of thirty years ago. Every summer I'd see him, late August home to visit. A week, ten days. Stay with my family and the house isn't far from Mr. Waller's. So it should not have been a surprise, nor even unexpected. Yet it always was. Each time. Stammering Hello, Mr. Waller!—the hot embarrassment rising in my face. Because of course the man was no longer "Mister" now to any of his former students, all of us adults now and presumably equals. Please call me Gordon, eh?—Mr. Waller would say. Laughing, embarrassed too, possibly annoyed, eager to be gone. Lifting his hand in greeting, or farewell. It was never clear if he remembered my name. It seemed he *did* remember my face. Or some face of thirty years ago it resembled.

Say you're a local junior high school teacher. You have two options. Remember all your former students, hundreds of them, and call them by name; forget all your former students, hundreds of them. Grin angrily at them rising like ghosts in your path.

This summer the talk is of Mr. Waller so changed he's not himself.

Who is he, then?—if he's not himself.

It's a way of speaking. Don't be so literal.

Yes, but look! If I am not my*self*, but another *self*, who is this *self* I've become? And where is the absent *self*?

It's a way of speaking! Human communication.

Mr. Waller used to tell us there's nothing more unreliable than human communication. You hear what nobody said not quite exactly that way. You tell it to somebody else who gets it wrong, and repeats it to other people who get it wrong and repeat it, and you all go on believing it till death. That's history.

Waller was teaching that to eighth graders?

It was ninth grade I had him.

Gordon Gregory Waller, how many years you'd never have guessed the man was in his sixties, wiry, trim, tanned, metal-rimmed glasses with a blue tint, a youthful air. Not baggy shorts like older men wear atop their skinny legs but neat-pressed khaki shorts, shorts with an actual crease. And cable-knit sweaters, windbreakers from L.L. Bean. And the bicycle—Italian-made. Four hundred dollars for a *bike*? my father says, incredulous. Come on!

Before the stroke and the fall, or whatever it was, it's said Mr. Waller had been acting different. Not *not himself* exactly (that would come later) but—different. Strange. Hard to explain. He'd grown a goatee, then a beard, he was retired from teaching now and always a bachelor and proud and impatient so there was nobody to check him. Letting his whiskers grow, filmy and flimsy. And stiff hairs sprouting out of his eyebrows and curving like claws. Strange.

The stroke was a fault line that fractured. You see it in the man's face. On one side the old face, sharp-boned and intelligent. On the other side, a melted-wizened look. The squinchy eye, the droopy lid. Downpegged corner of his mouth. For a long time after he returned from the hospital (they said: I wasn't home) it took ten minutes for Mr. Waller to walk, with a cane, to the mailbox across the road from his house, you'd see him and how damned *determined*, didn't matter the weather, even cold rain, wind—that was how he was. You'd run into him at the library, the drugstore, grocery store—slow and crablike in his movements, but not welcoming any help. No thanks!

And after a few months, back on the bicycle again. Shaky, wobbly, falling off, little accidents, but, you know—*determined.*

I tried never to remember Mr. Waller. Ninth grade. The sick hot stab in my belly. Scalding between the legs. I am not that girl now. A smile from Mr. Waller, a slow trailing of his eyes. Yes if he would *see* me, he would know.

Would I have bartered somebody's life for him? My mother's, my father's? I try never to remember.

Mr. Waller's grin is twitchy on one side of his mouth, the other side is unmoving as a scar. He has lost his gingery curls and his head is a dimming bulb, he has lost a third of his body weight, he has become a skeleton crouched over the slow-moving bicycle.

By the mailbox, unexpectedly, he wants to talk. Not talking exactly. Stammering and repeating and clearing phlegm from his throat. This heat! ticks in the high grass! the roof of his house is leaking from last week's rainstorm! Somebody cheated him, a local roofer. You can't trust. What can you do. *His brain is leaking through the roof of his mouth.*

The house will be sold by a distant, younger relative. The roof repaired but strangers will pay the bill. Strangers will inherit the bicycle, carefully pressed clothes out of the closets. Cartons of mildewed books, warped classical records.

That morning Mr. Waller grinned angrily at us. Eyes moist with scorn. Somehow we had displeased him. There were many ways to displease, few ways to please. The subject had been slavery in the Old South. The cruelty humankind inflicts upon humankind in the name of divine sanction or maybe just selfish expediency, Mr. Waller was saying ironically. Always there was fury beneath Mr. Waller's irony and you sat unbreathing and unmoving hands clasping hands on top of your desk hoping the fury would not erupt. Walking up and down the aisles between rows of desks, Mr. Waller asking, Who in this class would wish to be slave-owners? Who would wish, in his innermost heart, to own slaves? Let's see your hands! Come, let's see your hands! There was the silence, and the paralysis. The waiting. Ah hah, very interesting, those of you who might indeed wish to own slaves will not expose yourselves, well I congratulate you, you have learned to camouflage yourself as decent human beings, that is what civilization *is*. I thank you.

The other afternoon, an old man teetering on a bicycle pedaling slowly uphill. No crash helmet now, just the bare bulb of the head. I stood watching, transfixed. I could not turn away. Waiting for Mr. Waller to fall. I was close enough to see but far enough away not to be seen. I think I was hoping for an explosion of blood on the pavement. Blood, brains, leakage. The end.

He didn't fall exactly. Stumbled off the bicycle as the front wheel jackknifed. The bicycle clattered to the street and when I got to Mr. Waller he was muttering to himself, his eyes spilling tears and a trail of spittle down his chin. Did you know how I loved you, I demanded. Did you know I was sick with terror of you, dreamt of you with my eyes open?

No. I said other words, but not these words. I am not a woman to say such words.

There I was lifting and righting the bicycle. Steadying Mr. Waller as we walked. How rail-thin the poor man's arm, bone inside the baggy sleeve. This final encounter. August 1993. Making our way uphill, slow slow somebody breathing like great clumsy wings parting the air.

After a long moment Mr. Waller asked, Which one of them were you?

The Dream-Catcher

A s soon as she saw it, she knew she had to have it.
There amid the finely wrought silver and turquoise jewelry, the handtooled leather goods, glazed earthenware pottery and baskets and coarse-woven fabrics in the Paiute Indian Reservation gift shop at Pyramid Lake, Nevada, the curious item seemed to leap out at Eunice's eye: no more than four inches in diameter, an imperfect circle made of tightly woven dried vines or branches threaded with small filmy feathers. An artifact of some kind, exquisitely fashioned, its colors, like most of the colors of the handmade items in the shop, predominantly brown, beige, black. Eunice found herself staring at it, and there, suddenly, it lay in the palm of her hand—virtually weightless. Remarkable! *Dream-Catcher* the printed label explained. It was so dry Eunice feared it might crack in her fingers. When she lifted it to examine it more closely, noting how the interior of the woven branches was a net, or web, braided with leather thread, in the center of which a tiny agate-like stone dully gleamed, the filmy feathers came alive, stirred by her breath. The feathers too were beautiful, finely marked, streaks and speckles of dark brown like strokes of a watercolorist's brush on a fawn-colored background.

Seeing Eunice's interest in the *dream-catcher*, the Indian proprietor of the store explained to Eunice that it was a gift given only to those who were "much loved"—especially to be hung over a cradle or a crib. "The spiderweb inside catches the good dreams, but the bad dreams—no. Guaranteed!" He called out affably to Eunice, as if speaking to a child. Presumably a Paiute Indian, he was a man of vigorous, muscular middle age who wore a faded black T-shirt, faded jeans, and a handtooled leather belt with a brass eagle buckle; his graying-black thinning hair was caught in a loose, careless ponytail that gave him a disheveled yet playful look. His forehead was veined and knobby—scarred?—as if vexed with thought and the voice of exaggerated good cheer in which he spoke to Eunice, as to other customers, verged on mockery. From an exchange Eunice had overheard between him and a previous customer she gathered he was a Vietnam veteran. Yet he managed to smile at most of his customers as he rang up their purchases; he certainly smiled at Eunice.

"Yes ma'am!—the good dreams are caught for you," the Indian said, handing over Eunice's fragile *dream-catcher* in a paper bag, "—and the bad dreams go away. You hang it over your bed, O.K.?— even if you don't believe, something will happen."

"Thank you," Eunice said. "I'll do that."

Eunice was not so young as she appeared but with her pale, faded-gold hair and her smooth fair skin and large, intelligent gray eyes she was an attractive woman, and she was alone. She smiled at the Indian proprietor though seeing that his smile held no warmth. His lips were drawn back tightly from discolored, uneven teeth, and his eyes, agate-shiny, recessed beneath his blemished forehead, were fixed upon her insolently. As if to say *I know you. Even if you don't know me.* Eunice, who was not accustomed to being treated impolitely, still less rudely, yet maintained her poise, and her forced smile; leaving the store, she felt the man's gaze drop to her ankles and rise rapidly, assessingly up her slender figure. She did not glance back when he called after her, "Come back again soon, lady, eh?" with exaggerated good cheer.

Even if you don't believe. Something will happen.
When Eunice returned to Philadelphia, to her Delancey Street brownstone, she impulsively fastened the *dream-catcher* to the

foot of her bed, and lay down to sleep. Exhausted from the
plane flight, her brain assailed by images, impressions. Her twelve-
day visit to the Southwest, to Nevada and Arizona, was the first
extended vacation she'd taken in years. How vivid, many of its
moments!—the ceramic-blue sky, the extraordinarily complex,
ravaged-looking beauty of the mountains, the dun colors, shimmering salt flats, whitish silence of Death Valley.... Yet, travel itself
fatigued her, and bored her. There was no personal identity to it.
No sense of mission.

Eunice was thirty-seven years old, unmarried, vice-provost at
the Philadelphia Academy of Fine Arts. Her Ph.D. was from Har-
vard; her dissertation, subsequently published as a book, was titled
Aesthetics and Ethics: A Postmodernist Debate. Early on, as a girl,
Eunice had hoped for a life that would be a public life and not a
domestic life, involved in some way with the arts. She had been
the only child of older parents, her father a popular philosophy professor at the University of Pennsylvania, and she had a memory
of herself as a shy, precociously intelligent child, pale hair hanging heavily about her narrow face. The odd mixture of vanity and
insecurity of the "special" child. Yet, disconcertingly mature as a
young girl, Eunice seemed hardly to have grown much older in
adulthood—a common phenomenon among the precocious. Now in
young middle age, she yet retained a slender, lithe girlishness; her
attractive face unlined, her manner cheerful; she possessed an air
of innocent authority that suited her as a professor at Swarthmore,
and subsequently as an administrator there, and elsewhere. Her
reputation among her professional colleagues was for exceptionally
fine, detailed work; she was prized, if perhaps sometimes exploited,
for her generous, uncomplaining good nature. It was said of her,
not unkindly, that Eunice Pemberton lived for her work, through
her work, in her work. If she had a personal life it was kept very
private. If she'd had lovers, she never spoke of them.

Nor was she a religious, certainly not a superstitious woman.
She'd become moderately interested in the culture of the Native
Americans indigenous to the area of the Southwest she'd visited,
but it was no more than a moderate interest, an intellectual's

speculation. Since early adolescence, Eunice had been incapable of believing in anyone or anything "supernatural": she'd inherited from her mild-mannered, skeptical father a distrust of faith, which is to say the objectification of mankind's wish-fantasies into codified religions, institutions. What was skepticism but simple common sense?—sanity? An island of sanity in a seething fathomless ocean of irrationality, and often madness. The contemporary world of militant, fanatic nationalism, fundamentalist religions, intolerance.

Something will happen. Even if you don't believe.

Eunice had affixed the feathered *dream-catcher* to the foot of her bed in the hope that it might stimulate her to dream, for she rarely dreamed; her nights were deep, silent pools of water, featureless, rippleless. Yet, so far as she knew, she did not dream that night, either. Her sleep was unnaturally heavy, like a weight pressing against her chest and threatening her with suffocation. Her breasts ached; she woke several times, her nightgown damp with perspiration. In the early morning, before sunrise, she woke abruptly, eager to get up. Her eyes were sore as if she'd been staring into the desert sun and her mouth was badly parched. And there was an odor in her bedroom as of something humid, overripe, like rotted fruit; a faint odor, not entirely disagreeable. *And so— did I dream? Is this what a dream is?*

Eunice quickly showered, and dressed, and would have forgotten the *dream-catcher* except, as she made her bed, the shimmering feathers drew her attention. How like a bird's nest it looked—she hadn't quite seen that, before. She touched the cobweb of leather twine at its center, and the glass gem which was like an eye. No dream, good or bad, had been caught in it. Still, the *dream-catcher* was an exquisite thing, and Eunice was glad she'd bought it.

In the kitchen, Eunice heard a strange sound, like mewing, or whimpering, from the rear of the house, and went uneasily to investigate. (Eunice had inherited the four-storey Delancey Street brownstone from her widowed mother; it was in an old, prestigious Philadelphia neighborhood within walking distance of the Penn

campus, and only a ten-minute drive to Eunice's office at the Philadelphia Academy of Fine Arts. A handsome property, coveted by
many, though bordering on an area with an ever-increasing crime
rate.) In the winterized porch, on an antiquated sofa-swing, partly
hidden beneath an old blanket, was what appeared to be a living
creature—at first Eunice thought it must be a dog; then, panicked,
she thought it must be a child. "What?—what is it?" Eunice stammered, transfixed in the doorway. The rear porch was shut off from
the house, rarely used. A smell as of decayed leaves, overripe
peaches was so strong here, Eunice gagged.

The creature, neither an animal nor fully human, was about
two feet long, and curled convulsively upon itself. Its head was
overlarge for its spindly body, and covered in long thin damp
black hairs. Its skin was olive-dark, yet pallid, like curdled milk; its
face was wizened, the eyes shut tight, sunken. How hoarsely it
breathed, as if struggling for oxygen!—there was a rattling sound
in its throat, as of loose phlegm. Eunice thought, *It's feverish, it's
dying.* Her breasts ached, the nipples especially, as if she were a
nursing mother in the presence of her infant.

Eunice tried to think: should she run outside, get help from one
of her neighbors? Should she call an ambulance?—the police? There
were friends and colleagues she might call, a married sister in Bryn
Mawr. . . . *But what would I say? What is this—visitation?* She felt
a stab of pity for the creature, struggling so desperately to live; she
understood that it was starving, and that there was no one else in all
the world, except her, to feed it.

Now its eyes opened, and Eunice saw that they were beautiful
eyes, whether animal or human: large, dark, tremulous with tears,
with an agate sheen, recessed beneath the oddly bony forehead.

Aloud Eunice murmured, "Poor thing—!"

Knowing then that she had no choice: she had to nourish the
helpless creature that had fallen into her care, however she could.
She could not allow it to die. So she hurried to bring it water, at
first in a glass, which was impractical; then soaked in a sponge,
which worked fairly well, as if the creature (toothless, with tender,
pink gums) knew by instinct how to suck a sponge. Then she

soaked the sponge in milk, which was even better. "Don't be afraid, you won't die," Eunice murmured, "—I won't let you die." Nursing frantically, the creature mewed and whimpered, its thin hands, very like forepaws, kneading against Eunice's arms. Eunice felt again, with painful sharpness, that sensation in her breasts as if they were swollen with milk.

So an hour passed, swiftly. By the time the creature had drunk its fill and dropped off to sleep, Eunice had soaked the sponge in milk nearly a dozen times. Her breath was coming quickly and her skin was as damp and feverish as the creature's own; she heard herself laugh, excited, frightened. *Yet I've done the right thing: I know it.*

This, then, was Eunice's strategy on that first day: she left the slumbering creature on the porch swing, the door to the back yard ajar and the inner door locked, and drove, as usual, to work at 8:20 A.M. *It will leave, the way it came.* The day was mild for mid-March, snow melting on pavement; an air of reprieve after one of the most severe Philadelphia winters in memory. The poor thing would not suffer from cold, Eunice reasoned. She was certain it would be gone when she came home.

What was wholly unexpected then, as it was to be during the course of subsequent weeks, was how adroitly Eunice shifted her attention to her duties as vice-provost. As if there had not been an astonishing visitation at her home!—an inexplicable intrusion into her life! At the most, during her long, busy day at the Academy of Fine Arts, it might have been observed that Eunice Pemberton was uncharacteristically distracted; several times, during a meeting with the provost and other administrators, she'd had to ask politely, "Yes?—what did you say?" When colleagues inquired after her vacation she said, "It was fine, very—fine. Picturesque." And her voice trailed off, her eyes vague, blinking. Eunice was thinking of the enormous desert sky, of Pyramid Lake and the shabby dwellings of the Paiute Reservation and the handicraft store where she'd bought the *dream-catcher*. She was thinking of the pony-tailed Indian with the insolent eyes. *Come back again soon, eh!*

In fact, Eunice was grateful that the day was so long, and so complicated. At 4:30 P.M. there was a visiting art historian from Yale who lectured on the iconography of Hieronymus Bosch, and following the lecture there was a reception in his honor; that evening, there was a dinner at the home of the president of the Academy, for selected administrators, faculty, and donors, from which Eunice could not slip away until 10:30 P.M. When she returned to Delancey Street it was to hurry trembling to the rear porch, where she saw—now was it with relief, or disappointment?—that the swing was empty, the soiled blanket lay on the floor, the strange creature was gone. As Eunice had anticipated, it had left by the back door, as it had arrived.

Quickly Eunice shut the rear door, and made certain it was firmly locked.

What had the creature been?—a raccoon, perhaps? Suffering some sort of mange, hairless. Prematurely wakened from its winter hibernation. Desperate for food. Lucky for Eunice, it had not been rabid.

And so for the second night Eunice slept with the *dream-catcher* at the foot of her bed. Somehow she'd forgotten it was there, and as she drifted off to sleep, remembering it, with a pang of apprehension, she was incapable of getting up to remove it, her limbs paralyzed in sleep.

Even if you don't believe. Something will happen.

Again her sleep was heavy, ponderous. Her head ached, her heart beat erratically and painfully. Yet this was not dreaming— was it? Someone, or something, was in the bed with her, beneath the bedclothes where no one had ever been. A short, stunted creature, with a veined, knobby forehead, jagged teeth. A bat, clambering upon her. Yes, it had wings, leathery webbed wings, and not arms—it was a bat, yet also a man. Eunice shook her head violently from side to side—*No! no!*—but she could not cast off the loathsome creature. It—he—was pressing his mouth against hers, slick with saliva. And rubbing himself against her breasts, belly, thighs. A rubbery rod, a penis, sprouting from his groin—as soon as Eunice became aware of it, to her horror and revulsion it rapidly hardened, like a plastic hose into which water began to flow. *No!— leave me alone!* In disbelief, her eyes open and blind, Eunice felt the creature prodding between her thighs, forcing her thighs apart; felt the penis like a living thing, blind, groping, seeking an opening into her body. Eunice screamed but it was too late—a sudden sexual sensation rose swift and needlelike in her loins. She grunted, and shuddered, and threw the creature off—except, as she woke, it vanished. It was gone. Alone, panting, Eunice sat up in bed, knuckles pressed against her mouth. Her heart was beating so violently she feared it would burst.

About her, in the handsome old mahogany four-poster bed Eunice had inherited from her parents, the sheets were damp and rumpled. A sharp odor as of decaying peaches lifted from them.

Now you know you've had a dream, now you know what a dream is—yet, early in the morning, waking again before dawn from a thin, wretched sleep, Eunice understood that the hideous bat-creature in her bed had not been a dream.

She heard him, downstairs: an intermittent whining, murmurous singsong. He was in the rear porch, or possibly in the kitchen.

Quietly, slipping on her robe, Eunice made her way downstairs. Her hair was sticky against her forehead and the nape of her neck; her body was covered in an acrid film of perspiration; the tender skin of the insides of her thighs chafed. Yes, he was in the kitchen: the strange sound was coming from there. Eunice hesitated a moment before pushing open the door, boldly entering. *This is my house, my life. He's come to me. Why should I be fearful!*

This time, Eunice saw clearly that the creature was human: batlike about the head, with a monkey's long spindly arms, but obviously human. And male.

Obviously, male.

Eunice had surprised him in the act of pawing open a box of uncooked macaroni. He'd climbed up onto the kitchen counter, and had managed to open one of the cupboard doors.

They stared at each other. The creature was crouched, but Eunice could see he had grown to about the size of a ten- or eleven-year-old boy. He was starkly naked, his ribs showed, his chest rapidly rising and falling as he panted. His head was disproportionately large for his shoulders; his legs were stunted, bowed as if from malnutrition; his skin was olive-dark, with that pallor beneath, and covered in fine, near-invisible black hairs like iron filings. His shrunken genitalia hung shyly between his thighs like skinned fruit. His eyes were fierce, shining, frightened, defiant.

Eunice said, in a voice of surprising calm, "Poor thing!—you're starving."

Never in her life had Eunice felt such a sensation of pity, compassion, urgency. As the naked creature, crouched on her counter, made a bleating, pleading sound, she felt her breasts ache, throbbing with the need to nurse.

But it was solids Eunice fed the creature, for he had teeth now, however rudimentary, set sparely and unevenly in his tender gums. Eunice wrapped him in a quilt, found an old pair of furry slippers for his knobby-toed feet, sat him in the breakfast nook (which alarmed him initially—his instinct was to resist being cornered, trapped) and spoon-fed him three soft-boiled eggs, most of a pint container of cottage cheese, a tangerine. How hungry he was!— and what pleasure in sating that hunger! His eyes brimmed with tears, like Eunice's own, as rapidly he chewed and swallowed, chewed and swallowed. Eunice said, "Don't ever be frightened again! Nothing bad will happen to you. I promise. I promise with my life."

Eunice's voice fairly vibrated with excitement yet she spoke calmly. Her years of authority as professor and administrator stood her well in such an emergency.

As before, Eunice left the creature sleeping on the old sofa-swing in the porch, for he resisted coming farther into the house, even into the living room where it was warm. Groggy after his feeding, he seemed virtually to collapse, to become boneless, very like a human infant as Eunice half carried him out onto the porch and laid him gently on the sofa-swing. How astonished she would have been, as a girl growing up in this house, sitting on this swing years ago and reading one of her innumerable books, to imagine what the future held: what fellow creature would one day lie on this very piece of furniture! Beneath the quilt the creature curled up at once, knees to chest, face pushed against knees, sinking into the deep, pulsating sleep of an infant. For many minutes Eunice crouched beside him, her hand against his bony forehead, which seemed to her over-warm, feverish. Unless it was she who was feverish.

I promise. With my life.

———

Frequently he was gone when Eunice returned from the Academy and forlornly she walked through the empty house calling, "Where are you? Are you hiding?"—her manner stern, to disguise the abject sound of worry. To disguise her helplessness—so female. There was no name for the creature she could utter save *you*; to herself, she thought of him as *he, him.*

In the kitchen, she might find the remains of his feeding, for by degrees he'd become capable of feeding himself, though messily: a gnawed rind of cheddar cheese might be lying on the floor, part of a banana (he had not yet learned to peel bananas, though Eunice had tried to instruct him—he bit into both fruit and peel, and chewed as best he could), an emptied container of raw hamburger. Though Eunice had not yet succeeded in coaxing him into a bathtub, for the sound of running water, perhaps the very smell of water, as well as the confinement of a bathroom, threw him into a panic, it seemed to her that his odor was less defined now. At any rate, she had ceased to notice it.

(Though one day, at the Academy, a colleague who had entered Eunice's office quite visibly glanced around, sniffing, puzzled—did *she* notice the elusive scent? Without breaking their train of conversation, Eunice unobtrusively rose from her desk and opened a window and the offensive odor vanished. Or so Eunice thought.)

By night he might suddenly reappear. One moment the brownstone was empty of all inhabitants save Eunice, the next—the creature was waiting in the shadows on the stairway landing, his eyes

gleaming agate-bright and sly as she ascended into their beam; or
he was gliding noiselessly, barefoot along the carpeted hall outside her bedroom. He'd learned to laugh, somehow—a low, guttural, thrilling chuckle. Thick black hairs now sprouted on his head,
on his chest and beneath his arms; Eunice would never have
looked, but knew that his pubic region bristled with such hairs. He
was growing, maturing rapidly, nourished by her care. His shining eyes glanced level with hers. He could speak, not exactly
but sounds—"Eeee?—eeee? Eeeeeyah?" which Eunice believed
she could interpret.

"Downstairs," Eunice would say. Pointing with her forefinger, so
there could be no misunderstanding. "You're not to be *up here*. But
down there."

Always at such times Eunice spoke sternly to the creature. He
might choose to disobey her but he could not choose to misunder-
stand her, and Eunice knew that that was crucial.

Sometimes, ducking his head, he murmured, "Eeeee?—eeee—"
and turned to rapidly descend the stairs, like a scolded dog. At
other times, a rebellious dog, he threw back his head defiantly,
stared at Eunice from beneath his bristling eyebrows, and drew his
lips taut across his uneven teeth. Maintaining her poise Eunice
said, "You hear me! You know perfectly well what I'm saying—
you!"

With dignity then Eunice would brush past the creature, who
stood long-armed and resistant, in shirt, slacks, sneakers Eunice
had bought for him which he'd already outgrown: brushed past him
coolly, and entered her bedroom, and shut the door firmly against
him. It was a door with an old-fashioned bolt lock.

So long as Eunice was awake, there was no danger.

Often, she sat up in bed, reading, or working on reports and
memos in longhand, for her secretary at the Academy to type out
on a word processor the next morning. She did not think of herself
as an obsessive person, one driven by her work. There was a true
pleasure in such nighttime concentration; the sense, at such times,
of the world radically narrowed, shrunken to the size of the light

that illuminated her bed. *I love and respect my work and that's why I'm good at it*—Eunice's father once surprised her with these words, and so it seemed to Eunice the same might be said of her as well, though she was not one for such pronouncements *I love and respect my work and that's why I'm good at it.* Yet how ironic: a thorn in her heart: that the creature who shared her home with her, whose life she had saved, and continued to save, knew nothing of her outer, public, professional self. *And cares nothing. For why should he?*

At about 1 A.M., and inevitably by 2 A.M., Eunice's eyelids began to grow heavy. The room dissolved to shifting, eerily oscillating planes of light and shadow. There was a muffled *Eeeeee* sound somewhere close by, a faint scratching at the door. Eunice knew she was losing consciousness, and thus control; knew this was dangerous; yet could not forestall the process though she shook her head, slapped her cheeks, forced her eyes open wide. A tarry-dark tide rose about her, and in her.

The *dream-catcher* at the foot of her bed! During the day, she never thought of it—never thought to remove it; at night, it was too late.

So she sank into sleep. Helpless. And *he* took immediate advantage.

Brashly entering her bedroom, pushing the door open as if— there was no door, at all.

The creature was physically mature now. Of that there could be no question. However he presented himself by day, his *Eeeee? eeee? eeeyah?* bleating and pleading, by night he was far different. The size of an adult man, with compact, muscled arms, shoulders, thighs. Covered in coarse black hairs. His eyes glaring, he yanked the bedclothes off Eunice, despite her protests; he gripped her so tightly, she thought he would break her ribs. In the morning, her body would be covered in bruises. In oddly lovely patterns. He mouthed her breasts which had grown abnormally tender, her nipples sensitive to the slightest touch as they had never before been in Eunice's life, her belly which was slick with perspiration, the secret flesh between her legs at which, at the age of thirty-seven,

Eunice never once glanced, and rarely touched except to cleanse, and dry. *No. Stop. I hate this. This is not me!* Yet she found herself desperately embracing the creature, even as he penetrated her body, as a drowning person might embrace anyone, anything— Eunice's arms, her trembling legs, her ankles locked together, gripping his legs between hers. Sometimes, a scream awoke her—a woman's scream, high-pitched, helpless. Horrible to hear.

Eunice pushed at the bedclothes that were suffocating her, forced herself free. The bedside lamp was still burning. It might be only 1:35 A.M., it might be 4 A.M., the dead of night. The liquid silence of night. Utter unspeakable loneliness of night. The door to Eunice's bedroom was shut again, of course—locked.

Yet the bedclothes, and Eunice herself, smelled of *him.* Damp, disgusting. Vile. That overripe peachy odor. Eunice must shower to remove it from her, every pore, every hair follicle.

At the foot of the bed, attached to the rail, was the *dream-catcher.* Delicate as a bird's nest. Filmy feathers stirred by Eunice's agitated breath, it seemed to float upon darkness.

"Oh God. If there is God. Help me."

There came the day in early May, at an Academy luncheon, the conversation paused, like a withheld breath, and, after a moment, Eunice became uneasily aware of everyone at the table, including the provost, looking at her. Had she been asked a question?—if so, by whom? Had she been daydreaming, distractedly stroking the underside of her jaw, which felt sore? The provost, a balding, kindly gentleman known to be grooming Eunice Pemberton to take his place when he retired, thereby to become the first female provost in the one-hundred-seventy-year history of the Philadelphia Academy of Fine Arts, smiled, with pained solicitude, and as if to spare Eunice further embarrassment, turned to another guest, and said, "And what do *you* think—?" and so, in a dreamlike blur and buzz, the moment passed.

Eunice, conscious of a terrible blunder, made a belated effort to listen; to be brightly attentive; to appear to be, in her colleagues' eyes, entirely normal—entirely herself. Yet: *not a one of you can guess what my life is! my secret life!* And in a rest room afterward she saw to her horror that there was an ugly bruise on the underside of her jaw—a lurid purplish-orange, the hue of rotted fruit. How in God's name had she left the house that morning without noticing it?—had she not dared to glance into a mirror? She might have disguised the bruise somehow, might have tied a cheery bright scarf around her neck. Except now it was too late. Of course her colleagues had been staring at her.

They know.

But what is it, they know?

It was in the early evening of that day, a mild, fragrant day in spring, that, on her way home from the Academy, Eunice stopped by a sporting goods store to purchase a hunting knife, with a stainless steel twelve-inch blade.

The shopkeeper smiled, asking Eunice if the knife was for her, if she was a hunter?—expecting her to say no, it's a gift, it's for my nephew, my sister's son, for certainly a woman like Eunice would not want, or need, a hunting knife—would she? But Eunice smiled in return, and said, quietly, "Yes, in fact, it *is* for me. I'm a hunter, too. I've been learning."

When Eunice let herself into the brownstone, it was to an empty house. You would think so. No sound, no murmurous muffled laughter—no creaking floorboards in the rear porch. Or on the stairs. Only the faintest smell of *him*—which might be mistaken for any slightly rotted, rancid kitchen smell.

You would think so.

He had been with her the night before, rudely and selfishly with her. Though she'd told *him* to remain downstairs—she'd been stern, and she'd been forthright. She was not a woman like so many women, even professional women, whose disapproval means approval; whose *no* means *yes*. But he'd paid no attention to her pleas, her words. From the start, he had not.

Yet perhaps the house *was* empty? Eunice no longer turned on the alarm system, for *he* had several times triggered it with his comings and goings. Instead she left lights burning in several rooms, and her radio on continuously. This, police recommended as a way of discouraging break-ins. So far, the simple strategy had worked.

Eunice walked slowly through the first floor of her house. If *he* was anywhere it was likely to be the porch—but, no, the porch was empty this evening. The old sofa-swing, its floral canvas badly faded. The quilt Eunice had given him, now soiled, lying on the floor. And the smell of *him*, unmistakable.

The kitchen, too, was empty. The counters were clean and bare as Eunice had left them; the sink was gleaming, as she'd left it. One of her outlets for nervous energy was cleaning, scouring her kitchen; her mother had always hired a maid for such work, but Eunice preferred to do it herself. Why invite a stranger into her life?—it was enough that a stranger had come into her life unbidden.

The Formica top of the kitchen nook was clean, too. When *he* fed in the kitchen, *he* avoided that corner; only when Eunice was feeding him did he consent to sit there, Eunice close beside him.

Eunice was about to leave the kitchen when she noticed something gleaming on the floor—a small pile of gnawed chicken bones. And, kicked back alongside the refrigerator, part of an orange, which someone had bitten into, peeling and all. It was *his* way of eating, and Eunice shook her head in bemused dismay.

Animal. From the start. Hopeless.

Such shame!—she caressed her bruised jaw, ruefully.

Upstairs, Eunice entered her bedroom, sensing, in the split-moment before the assault, that something was wrong, the very air into which she stepped seemed agitated; yet she wasn't quite prepared for the violence with which she was seized from behind, an unseen man's arms thrown about her torso, shaking her as if in fury—"Don't fight me, bitch!" Eunice dropped her handbag, her briefcase, the bag containing the hunting knife—she was on the floor herself, on her hands and knees, too astonished to be terrified. For it was not like *him* to attack her so roughly, with such evident hatred: it was not like *him* to wish to injure her. Kill her?

Eunice drew breath to scream. She was struck on the side of the head by a man's fist. She fell, half-conscious, lay on the carpet dazed and struggling to breathe and half-seeing a man's figure, a shadowy hulking figure, at her bureau, yanking open drawers, throwing things onto the floor and muttering furiously to himself, an inexplicable violence in his very presence and Eunice understood *He will kill me, he will stomp me to death with no more conscience than he might stomp an insect to death,* she crawled to retrieve the paper bag that lay close by, she had the knife in her hand and pushed herself to her feet and rushed at him, this man she believed she knew yet had never seen before, taller than she by several inches, heavy in the shoulders, dark-skinned, turning to her astonished as with a manic strength she brought the knife blade down hard against the back of his neck. There was an immediate eruption of blood, the man screamed, a high womanish shriek, he tried in his desperation to shield himself with his outspread fingers from the plunging blade, but Eunice did not weaken, Eunice brought the knife down against him again, and again, his throat, his face, his upper torso, as he threw himself from her turning in agony from her she stabbed into the nape of his neck, the top of his spine—sobbing, panting, "You! you! you!" not knowing what she did, still less where the superhuman strength came from welling in her veins and muscles that allowed her to do it, except she must do it, it was time.

Hours later Eunice lifted her head, which throbbed with pain. There was something clotted in her vision. She smelled him, smelled it—Death?—that sweetish-sour, rotted odor—before she saw him. The body. The body he'd become.

She was in her bedroom. A man, a stranger, lay on the floor a few yards away. He was dead: clearly dead: the carpet was soaked with his blood, and there was a trail of blood, like an open artery, on an edge of the hardwood floor beside the wall. The man was a black man in his mid-thirties perhaps. He was wearing a dark nylon jacket, badly stained trousers, scuffed boots. He lay on the carpet on his side, in an attitude of childlike peace, or trust, his head lolling awkwardly on his shoulder, his bloodied mouth slack; he was looking away from Eunice through droopy hooded eyes but she could see the curve of his thick nose, jaw, his wounded cheek—a stranger. It seemed clear that he'd been struck down in the act of yanking a drawer from her bureau; other drawers had been yanked out, and lay in a violent tumble of jewelry, lingerie, sweaters on the floor. The knife with its bloodied blade and handle lay on the carpet close by the body. You would think, seeing it there, that it belonged to the body.

Whose knife?—Eunice did not remember.

Except in a dream how she'd wielded it!—with what desperation, and passion.

There was a stillness here in this room that was the stillness of night. For now it *was* night. A dark tide rising about Eunice and the dead man both, gathering them in it, buoying them aloft. She would telephone the police, she would explain what she knew. *I had to do it, I had no choice.* She would not tell them what she knew also—that her life was over, her deepest life. Hers, and his.

On her feet now, swaying, unsteady, she went to her bed and took into her shaking hands the delicate, finely wrought thing fastened to the railing. The bird's nest, the Indian souvenir, whatever it was, with its woven branches, its intricate interior web, its filmy speckled feathers that stirred with her breath as if stirring with their own mysterious life.

The dream-catcher. Grown so dry and brittle, it broke suddenly in her fingers. And fell in pieces to the floor.

Fever Blisters

"Why am I here?"—on foot, in absurdly high-heeled sandals, in a tight-fitting red polka-dot halter-top dress that showed the tops of her breasts, in Miami. In waves of blinding, brilliant, suffocating heat. Not Miami Beach, which, to a degree, though she had not visited it in years, she knew, but Miami, the city, the inner city, which she did not know at all. And she had no car, she must have parked her car somewhere and forgotten the location, or had someone stolen it?—there were so many scruffy-looking people on the street here, and the majority of them black, Hispanic, Asian, strangers who glanced at her with contemptuous curiosity, or looked through her as if she did not exist. She could not remember where she'd come from, or how she'd gotten here, dazed with the terrifying tropical heat which was like no heat she had ever experienced in North America. Carless, in Miami!—she, who had not been without a car at her disposal since girlhood, and, in the affluent residential suburb of the northerly city in which she lived, a young widow whose children were grown and gone, famous among her friends for driving distances no longer than a block, and often shorter.

It was a nightmare, yet so fiery was the air, so swollen the sun in the sky, like a red-flushed goiter, she understood that she was not asleep but hideously awake—"For the first time in my life." On all sides people were passing her, pointedly making their way around her as she walked nearly staggering in the high-heeled sandals, forced frequently to stop and lean against a building, to catch her breath. The mere touch of the buildings burnt her fingers—the sidewalks, glittering with mica, must have been blisteringly hot. The wide avenue was clotted with slow-moving traffic and flashes of blinding light shot at her from glaring windshields and strips of chrome; she had to shield her eyes with her fingers. How was it possible, she'd come to Miami without her dark glasses?

Had the sun become unmoored?—the temperature was surely above 120 degrees Fahrenheit. The air was thick and stagnant, she had to propel herself through it like a clumsy swimmer. Overhead, a flying pigeon, stricken with the heat, suddenly fell dead to the pavement; she saw, horrified, in the gutter and on the littered sidewalks, the bodies of other birds shoveled in casual heaps. In doorways of buildings derelicts lay unmoving as death, ignored by pedestrians. Everywhere there was a stench as of garbage, raw sewage, an open grave.

Hazy in the distance, luminous with blue, was Miami Beach—causeways, high-rise buildings silhouetted against the fiery sky. She knew the ocean was beyond those buildings but she could not see it. She sobbed with frustration—"So far!" The beautiful city unreachable by her, separated from her by miles of heat, as if the very molecules of the air were ablaze.

She was lost, yet at the same time knew her destination: that dilapidated hotel across a littered, sun-blazing square: *The Paradisio.* This was the hotel, or a derelict version of it, that had once been on the ocean, on Arthur Godfrey Boulevard. Its stucco facade, painted a garish flamingo-pink, with mildewed white awnings, had a foreshortened, stubby look; a limp American flag hung motionless over the portico. How changed *The Paradisio* was, yet unmistakable!—she could have wept, seeing it. For she was to meet her lover there, as they'd done, years ago, in secret.

And she seemed to know, with a thrill of despair, that *The Paradisio* would have no air-conditioning.

"And if he doesn't come?—what will happen to me, then?"

The lobby of *The Paradisio* was so dim-lit, after the dazzling sunshine, she could barely see at first.

Except to note, nervously, lifting her arms so as to hide her over-exposed bosom, that several men, all strangers, were staring at *her*. She looked away, shivering. The lobby was hot, humid, its air impacted as the interior of a greenhouse, yet she felt chill. Was her lover supposed to meet her here in the lobby, or in the cocktail lounge; or was he waiting for her up in the room? And which name, of the numerous names they'd used over the years, would he have used?

She could not recall clearly that first assignation, here in *The Paradisio*. That is—*The Paradisio* that was.

How shabbily romantic the lobby was, and how much smaller than she would have imagined! Frayed crimson velvet draperies, absurdly ornate gilt-framed mirrors, enormous drooping rubber plants with dying leaves; underfoot a grimy fake-marble floor. Her nostrils pinched with the commingled odors of disinfectant, insecticide, and a lilac-scented air freshener. A uniformed bellboy— hardly a boy: an aged black man with a face creased as a prune, and rheumy eyes—walked past her very slowly, carrying luggage in both hands, but taking no notice of her. As if she did not exist. Yet the men elsewhere in the lobby continued to stare rudely at her: one of them was a red-faced white-haired Texas-looking man in a dinner jacket, another was a portly fellow with an embarrassed face, in a wilted sports shirt and Bermuda shorts; another was a stocky silvery-blond gentleman of late middle age in a candy-striped seersucker suit, white shoes with tassels. This man, obviously suffering from the heat, wiped his flushed face with a tissue, yet peered at her shyly, even hopefully—"But I don't know *him*."

The shame of it washed over her, that she, who had prided herself upon the exclusivity of her taste in men, she, who in even the worst years of her marriage had never been so much as mildly promiscuous, should have to have her assignation with a stranger: how sordid, how demeaning!

"Unless that is my punishment, in itself?"

After some awkward minutes, during which time she tried

unsuccessfully to examine her reflection in one of the lobby mirrors, but found her reflection cloudy, like something dissolving in water or radiant waves of heat, the gentleman in the candy-striped seersucker suit disengaged himself from the others at the rear of the lobby, and made his way to her. When their eyes met, he took a quick step forward, smiling—"Ginny, is it *you?*"

She stared in amazement, trying not to show her surprise. She too smiled, shyly—"Douglas, is it *you?*"

They clasped hands. But for the heat, and the envious stares of the others, they would have embraced. She wiped tears from her eyes and saw that her lover was wiping tears from his eyes, too.

On the fifth floor of the hotel they wandered looking for their room, still clasping hands, and whispering together; the hotel was one of those old-fashioned hotels in which corridors lead off in all directions and numerals run both forward and backward. Several maids pushing carts heaped with soiled linen, damp towels, aerosol spray cans of insecticide and room freshener, and supplies of miniature soaps and other toiletries regarded them with barely disguised smiles of contempt. The maids were Puerto Rican, Jamaican, Cuban—Haitian? The youngest was an attractive, busty Hispanic woman who laughed openly at the lovers, took pity on them, and led them to their room at the far end of a corridor rippling with heat. In her torrent of amused Spanish they could recognize only the words, "señor, señora!—this way, eh?" For it seemed that she too was headed for room 555 with her cleaning implements.

The maid's boisterous presence in the room was a distraction and an embarrassment to the lovers, but there was nothing to be done. Out of consideration for their predicament, she began in the bathroom.

Virginia and Douglas clutched hands, whispered.

"*Can* we? Here?"

"We *must.*"

But how unromantic, their room—meagerly furnished, with a sagging double bed covered in a stained, scorch-marked bronze satin spread; an imitation-mahogany bureau with a cloudy mirror; a squat, old-fashioned television set which the maid had switched on mechanically to an afternoon game show. The room's single window had no blind and looked out upon a glaring, smoggy, featureless sky; the ceiling was strangely high, as if set precariously in place, dissolving in an ambiguity of hazy light. And pervading all was the odor of stale cigarette smoke, human perspiration, insecticide and room freshener. Ginny wanted to cry—"It's so cruel, after so many years!" She scanned her lover's face anxiously, even as he scanned hers.

Of course, she recognized him now: Douglas's younger, handsome face was clearly visible in this face: only lined, flushed, a bit jowly, creases beneath the eyes. His hair had gone silver, and thinned, but it was his hair, with its singular wave, and there were his gray-blue eyes, crinkled at the corners, unmistakable.

"Ginny, darling, you *did* love me? Didn't you? Those years—"

"Douglas, of course. Yes—"

Virginia's voice faltered as, in the bathroom, the maid rapped sharply on the partly opened door, and called out to them in Spanish.

Douglas whispered, "I think she wants us to hurry."

"Oh yes. My God."

They embraced, and kissed, tentatively; but their lips were so hot and parched, Virginia flinched away—"Oh!" A tiny fever blister began to form instantaneously on her upper lip.

Douglas stared at her, appalled. "Ginny, I'm *sorry*."

"It wasn't your fault."

It was the heat, and the dazzling light. And no shelter from it.

Yet there was the need to continue, so, stricken with self-consciousness the lovers turned aside to undress, with a hope that the maid would not interrupt further. The game show ended amid rowdy applause, and a sequence of gaily animated commercials followed.

How much longer it took to undress, than ever in the past! Arms bent up awkwardly behind her, Virginia fumbled with the zipper of her tight-fitting dress. She had not worn so low-cut and uncomfortable a dress for a decade, what had possessed her to wear it today? The ribbed bodice, supported from inside, had cut into her tender flesh—"Damn it!" At least, in this heat, she was not wearing a slip;

only a pair of scarlet silk panties, tight too, which she kicked off in relief, along with the high-heeled shoes. Her hair, which she'd thought she had had cut recently, was in fact glamorously long, a thick glossy pageboy that fell heavily on her shoulders; the nape of her neck was slick with sweat. She did not dare sniff at her armpits for fear of what she might detect. And no deodorant! And no makeup! She dreaded to think what the heat had already done to her carefully applied makeup: the pitiless overhead light would expose every flaw in her face.

Fortunately, the bureau mirror was too cloudy to show anything more precise than wavering fleshy forms, like mollusks out of their shells, where she and her lover stood.

She could hear the man murmuring to himself, half a sigh, half a sob—"Hurry, hurry!"

At last, they turned shyly to each other. Virginia saw, with an intake of breath, that her lover had gained perhaps thirty pounds since she'd last seem him in such intimacy: the flesh bracketing his waist was flaccid and raddled, and he had a distinct potbelly. He, of all men, so vain of his body!—"It doesn't seem possible." Among their circle of friends Douglas had been the most competitive tennis player, the most energetic yachtsman; the most generally admired of the men. (Virginia's husband, years older, had been the richest.) Now, though she was making a womanly effort to smile encouragingly, she could not keep a look of dismay out of her face: Douglas's chest and pubic hair were so silvery as to resemble Christmas tinsel, and his legs, even his thighs, once so solid with muscle, were now strangely lank and thin. There was an eerie *disconnectedness* to the parts of his body she had never seen before.

Nor was his penis erect, yet. This too was an anomaly.

In turn, Douglas was staring at her in—amazement? apprehension? dread? *desire?* Self-conscious as a girl, Virginia made a vague effort to hide her breasts, which were still rather full, beautifully shaped, and her belly, where a faint incision showed, curving gently upward like an unbent question mark.

"*You*—you're beautiful!"—the exclamation, passionate as if it were the truth, seemed snatched from him, like a sob.

On the television, an evangelist named Reverend Steel was shouting a sermon about Jesus Christ and alms.

Slowly, Virginia drew the bronze bedspread back, dreading what she might see; and yes, she saw it. So humiliating! demeaning!—"The sheets haven't been changed, since God knows when." Douglas, close beside her, looking, winced. Murmuring, in husbandly fashion, "Well, I don't think, Ginny, we have any choice."

Yes. She knew.

Yet—"If only we could draw a shade!" The room was as bright, she couldn't help thinking, as an operating room. But the window was raw, open, perhaps it did not even have any glass, a great gaping hole in the wall; and outside, a smoggy haze. Where was the city of Miami? Had it been forgotten, or erased? And if Miami was gone, how would she return to her life?—*to where would she return?*

Her lover, reading her thoughts, asked, in a low, worried voice, "*Why* are we here, Ginny, do you know?"

"I don't! I don't know!"

At this, the Hispanic maid leaned out of the bathroom to call out something to them, part Spanish part English; her tone was admonitory and jeering. Douglas winced again, urging Ginny to lie down on the bed. "She says, 'To do it right, this time.'"

"What?"

"'To do it right, this time.'"

Where in the past lying in bed with Douglas had been the extinguishing of consciousness, ecstatic and voluptuous as slipping into warm dark water of sleep, or of oblivion, this afternoon the experience was one of full hideous wakefulness. Shutting her eyes tight did no good, for the harsh sunshine was empowered to penetrate her eyelids; burying her face with erotic abandon in Douglas's neck did no good, for his skin was so slick with sweat it felt clammy. Virginia could have wept—"How are we to make love, in such circumstances!" The fever blister on her lip throbbed like a bee sting.

Douglas, gamely stroking her hair, did not seem to hear. He was speaking with the eager hopefulness of a man intent upon explaining the inexplicable; as a successful corporation attorney, it was his habit to fall back upon words as a means of defense. "—I think when we—

that time—that first time, in Miami Beach?—when we first became
lovers, Ginny?" pausing as if the memory in fact eluded him, so that
Virginia nudged him to continue, gravely, "—we set so much in motion we could not have anticipated. My wife, and my daughter Janey;
your husband and children. We were selfish, unthinking—"

At this, before Virginia could reply, or even collect her thoughts
sufficiently to know whether she agreed, or disagreed, there came
a loud rapping from the bathroom doorway: the Hispanic maid interrupted again, to shout a vehement corrective. Virginia, cringing
in Douglas's arms, the two of them pathetically naked, exposed,
could comprehend only a cluster of words here and there.

Fortunately, Douglas knew a little Spanish. Humbled, he whispered in Virginia's ear, "*She* was the maid for the room, she says.
And we forgot to leave her a tip."

Virginia's eyes flew open, astonished. "What? Is that it? Is that
all?"

In her fever state, she began to laugh. Douglas joined her, in a
helpless spasm. Peals of laughter mingling with ecstatic shrieks
and groans from the television set where Reverend Steel was ex-
horting the faithful in his studio audience to surrender themselves
to Our Savior.

"Is that all? A *tip*?"

How hot, how prickly-hot, their skin!—their skins! In dread
fascination, determined not to wince, or to cry out in pain or distaste, Virginia helped her lover lower himself upon her, and try to
insert his only partly erect member into her; she wished he would
not keep muttering *Sorry! sorry!*—"It isn't romantic at all."
Where they pressed together, the length of her spread-eagled
body, her flesh felt as if it were being assailed by hundreds of tiny
stinging ants.

Now too the maid was running water loudly in the bathroom,
flushing the toilet repeatedly. How inconsiderate!

Virginia could have wept—"It isn't romantic at *all*."

Yet she and Douglas gamely persevered. For, in *The Paradisio*,
there is no turning back.

Lovemaking after so many years is inevitably awkward. Calculation has replaced blind passion. This had an air of the clinical, for Douglas had gained that weight in the torso and stomach, and Virginia, dehydrated from fever, was thinner than she'd been during the five years of their affair. She shut her eyes, trying to recall her fever in that other life. That life out of which she had stepped, into *The Paradisio.* Or had she died? Stricken in the Yucatán, collapsing in a seething pool of sunshine. Luscious bougainvillea flowers reeling overhead. Or was it in the hospital? the glaring lights, and the infection that followed? But, no, for God's sake stop—*"It isn't romantic at all."*

And poor Douglas needed her help, he was whispering to her in desperate appeal, so, sighing, Virginia reached down to caress his poor damply-limp organ, recalling how, once, she'd been so in awe of it, and of him; of how, when *The Paradisio* had been a sumptuous luxury hotel overlooking the Atlantic Ocean, they'd made love passionately, blindly, unthinkingly . . . not once, but several times. And afterward, dazed with love, and with the violence of their erotic experience, they had been reluctant to leave the privacy of the hotel room and return to their spouses: Douglas had gripped Virginia's shoulders hard, declaring, "I will never want anything again!" and Virginia had laughed, it was such an extravagant statement. Yet, hadn't she felt the same way?

"My God."

Virginia opened her eyes, and saw what Douglas meant—several boil-sized blisters had formed on their chests! Virginia pinched one just above Douglas's left nipple, and a watery warm liquid ran out.

"Oh, sorry! Did it hurt?"

Douglas grimaced stoically. His face was a shimmering mask of sweat. "No. Not much."

Impatient with the lovers, the Hispanic maid had begun vacuuming the room, and the roaring pelted them from all sides. "So rude!"—in other circumstances, Virginia would have complained angrily to the front desk; here, at least, the noise drowned out the television evangelist.

Gamely, Virginia resumed massaging Douglas, as provocatively and as sympathetically as she could; for theirs was a bonded plight. She decided not to worry about the fever blisters, but kissed him full on the mouth. "My love! Yes!" Quickly, Douglas became hard, and, like a man rushing with a glass of water filled to the very brim, desperate to spill not a drop, very quickly he pushed himself into her, where she was rather dry, and parched, and feverish, but ready for him—"Oh yes!"

How long then they labored together, like drowning swimmers, the roaring of the vacuum cleaner pervading the room, and the shabby bed nearly collapsing beneath their exertions, neither might have said. Virginia stared open-eyed past her lover's contorted face, where droplets of sweat gathered like tears, seeing that the ceiling seemed to be lifting—floating. *Set so much in motion. Could not anticipate. Selfish, unthinking.* Was it so? Had their attraction for each other blinded them to others? Douglas's unhappy wife, her drinking, dependence upon a succession of therapists; the pretty daughter who dropped out of Bennington to live in a rural commune in Baja California where the principal crop was marijuana. Virginia's husband never knew that she'd been unfaithful to him for years with one of his most trusted friends, yet, shortly before his death (but what a triumphant death: on the golf course, having sunk a diabolically tricky putt, to the envy and admiration of three companions) he had accused her of being a "promiscuous" woman—"So unfairly!" In fact, Virginia had had few lovers in her life and of those Douglas had been the sweetest, the kindest, even as he'd been the first; certainly he'd been the one Virginia had most cared for.

The bed was jiggling so violently, Virginia didn't know if Douglas's accelerating pumping was causing it; or the damned maid, inconsiderately banging the bed with the vacuum cleaner nozzle. Maybe, when all this was over, Virginia *would* complain.

To encourage her lover, she began to moan softly. In pleasure, or in the anticipation of pleasure. Or in a fever-delirium?

Seeing then, vividly as if the girl were sitting at her bedside, her own daughter, a petulant smirky high school girl of some years ago who had astonished Virginia by asking, suddenly, with no warning, one day when Virginia was driving her to a shopping mall, "You and Mr. Mosser—*did* you? When I was in grade school?" and Virginia blushed hotly, and stammered a denial, and her daughter interrupted her carelessly, saying, "Oh hell, Mother!—as if any of that matters *now*."

Virginia wanted to protest, But doesn't everything matter?

She opened her eyes to see her lover's sweaty beet-red face contorted above hers, veins prominent in his forehead, eyes narrowed to slits. His breath was so wheezing and labored, a dread thought came to Virginia: had Douglas died, too?

"No. It isn't possible."

She shut her eyes quickly to dispel the thought, and saw, at once, the most unexpected, and the most beautiful, of visions: Douglas Mosser, aged thirty-five, in white T-shirt, shorts, sandals, leaning to her to extend a hand to her, Virginia, his friend's wife, to help her climb aboard his yacht; smiling so happily at her, his eyes shining; squeezing her fingers with such emphasis, she felt the shock in the pit of her belly. And she cried aloud, now, in room 555 of *The Paradisio*—"I did love you! I still do! It was worth it!"

A fiery sensation immediately welled up in her loins, that part of her body that had felt nothing for so long; and shattered, yet continued to rise; and yet continued. Virginia clutched at her lover's sweat-slick body, weeping and helpless. As he groaned into her neck, "Ginny! Darling! I love you too!"

The bed jiggled, sagged, clanged in a final shuddering spasm.

How embarrassing, their pooled resources came to only $44.67—which they offered to the Hispanic maid, with trembling fingers; and which she contemplated, with suspenseful deliberation, weighing the bills and change in the palm of her hand.

Anxiously the lovers awaited her judgment. Was that bemused contempt in her face, or malice, or a wry grudging sympathy; was it pity; was it, simply, a look of finality—as if she too were eager to leave, after a long gruelling day at *The Paradisio*?

Until at last to their infinite relief she smiled, flashed a true smile, saying, shrugging, "Eh, *gracias!*" and closed her fist around the modest tip, and shoved it into her pocket.

The Crossing

*M*urmuring her name, her name, her name like an incanta-tion. *Stroking and squeezing her cool, limp fingers. Staring at her face that was papery-white and impassive, wimpled like a nun's by tight white bandages that covered most of her head, her shaved and violated skull. It was her bruised eyelids, her injured right eye, at which he stared most intently, leaning as close to her as he could over the bed's high railings. The respirator that breathed for her, the profusion of tubes that sustained her—these he ignored, for they were but temporary, until she recovered con-sciousness and strength enough to sustain herself. Her eyelids quivered almost continuously, had several times since the emer-gency craniectomy fluttered open in his presence, the eyes dilated, bloodshot, and terrible to see—her eyes, yet lacking the glisten of consciousness.*

Yet he spoke her name, he kept his vigil at her bedside, he was fired with hope, untiring. He flew into a fury at the mildest sugges-tion that he should spare himself—the ordeal might be a long one. She was his wife, his wife he loved more than his own life, and cer-tainly beyond his own comfort. He was convinced that, in the next minute, or in the next hour, she would open her eyes of her own vo-lition, she would see him and know him: she would break her si-lence, and speak.

———

A train whistle faint in the distance—that melancholy sound of yearning. Like her own name being murmured, almost inaudibly. *Martha. Martha. Martha.*

It appeared to be early evening. A wan, soft, sepia cast to the light slanting through tall, distinctively narrow windows. She was alone, yet, a bit uneasily, did not feel alone. As if, beyond, or beneath, or through the surfaces of objects, she were somehow being observed; as if what appeared to her to be solid objects were in fact flat and transparent, like a one-way mirror. On all sides in this spacious room, which she knew to be an upstairs guest room in her aunt Alma Buchanan's grand old house on Prospect Avenue, Chautauqua Falls, Martha felt the presence of others; yet, of course, when she looked about, behind a faded Chinese screen, in the empty cedar closet and the adjoining bathroom, there was no one.

Except herself, so unexpected she gave a little cry: her own reflection in a full-length dressmaker's mirror. Tall, willowy and tentative in her movements, younger than she would have judged herself, her face blurred with light as in an overexposed photograph.

Why am I here? How long will I stay?

On the high four-poster bed that smelled of lavender sachet and, to Martha's sensitive nostrils, just a bit of dust, her suitcase lay opened atop an ornamental beige lace spread. Odd she'd brought along this old, handsome, but now rather scratched and inconveniently heavy leather suitcase instead of one of her newer, lightweight suitcases. A relic of the early years of her marriage when she and Roger had traveled frequently to Europe, she'd never been able to bring herself to throw away.

She must call Roger now, she thought. He would be anxious to know whether she'd arrived in Chautauqua Falls safely, for the journey had been a complicated one—in what ways exactly, Martha could not quite remember.

Damn: no telephone in the room?

How like her elderly aunt, to invite Martha to visit her, and to give her a room lacking a telephone.

This annoyance made Martha's head ache—she was not by nature a patient woman, her intelligence pricked and prodded her into action when, sometimes, action was not possible. Pulses throbbed in her head, in her eyes. And how unpleasantly dry her mouth, as if coated with dust.

Aunt Alma was waiting for her downstairs: it was teatime.

Yet she stood indecisive in the center of the room. (*Was* someone observing her? Surely not through the mirror in which her reflection wavered, for the mirror's bland wooden back was visible.) Her attention was drawn to the peculiar creases, sharp, shadowed, in the lace bedspread, where the heavy suitcase lay. Something terrifying in the *depth, darkness* of those fissures she did not want to consider.

Very likely, Aunt Alma herself had crocheted that spread. It was beautiful, amazingly intricate floral and spiral designs; once snowy white, probably, and now faded to the color of weak tea. A relic of that era when young women of "good" families like the Buchanans had nothing more urgent to do with their time than prepare—what was the word? a French word? antiquated, quaint?—nothing more to do with their time than prepare themselves for marriage.

They were virgins in that era, and they were good girls. Dutiful Protestant-Christian daughters. As if marriage, the very wedding ceremony itself, *husband and wife one flesh,* were both the peak of a woman's life and its death-knell.

She would call Roger from downstairs. Too much time had already passed.

Yet the scene outside one of the windows drew her to it, and again she gave a little cry of surprise—the mountains, at the horizon, so vivid! so near! These were peaks of the Chautauqua range, bluish-hazy and crowned with brilliant, if waning sunshine. They were at least fifty miles away, but looked much closer, on the other side of the Chautauqua River that divided the small city into north and south.

The highest peak was Mount Cataract, 2,300 feet above sea level. Shadowed below, illuminated with sunshine above. The shape of a hand lifted in greeting.

How many years since Martha had seen these mountains? She was not one of the more dutiful female members of her family; to her shame, she had not visited her aunt since her uncle Dwight's funeral, at least twelve years ago, when her own parents were still alive. These were the first mountains of Martha's life, the mountains of her girlhood more than thirty years ago, when, with her sister, she'd been brought by their parents for leisurely summer visits to this house. The woman she called "Aunt Alma" was in fact her great-aunt; Martha's mother's aunt.

Trousseau was the word she'd tried to think of. Of course.

Martha struggled to open the window, suddenly she was having difficulty breathing, she was desperate for fresh air—forcing the warped lower window partway up, and leaning out, trembling with relief. How fresh, how pungent the air!—how restorative. It smelled of sun-warmed grasses, and the rich dark loamy soil of Aunt Alma's flower beds, an undercurrent of brackish-bitter air borne on the wind from the Chautauqua River a mile or so away.

Now the train whistle was coming louder, short distinct percussive cries. A train was approaching from the east. Already in brisk systolic puffs a locomotive's curling white smoke appeared above a stretch of trees; in the next moment, the train itself would come into view, crossing the railroad trestle above the marsh, a quarter mile to the rear, and down an incline, from the grand old houses of Prospect Avenue. Martha winced at the sound but shaded her eyes to watch.

As a young girl, how many times she'd awakened in this house to the sound of just such a train whistle, and the rhythmic strokes of a train's powerful piston-driven wheels! How many times awakening in a strange bed, in a strange pattern of light, her heart beating with anticipation, not knowing at first where she was—*What is this place? Who has brought me here?*

As the clattering of the locomotive and its long string of freight cars CHAUTAUQUA & BUFFALO   CHAUTAUQUA & BUFFALO   CHAUTAUQUA & BUFFALO   seemed to rush into the room and upon her.

The impact of the collision was such that her right eyeball had been jolted from its socket. Hanging loose as a jelly on her cheek like a gigantic tear.

———

Teatime with Martha's aunt, in a somewhat airless, overfur-
nished corner of the big front parlor. Close by, a carved mahogany
grandfather clock with dully gleaming numerals and spindly hands
so thin Martha could not see them clearly sonorously chimed the
quarter hour.

"So kind of you to visit your elderly, ailing aunt! Dear Martha,"
Aunt Alma said, speaking with exaggerated care, as if to empha-
size, by the clarity with which she uttered the name *Martha*, that
she had not forgotten her great-niece's name. "I know how busy
you are. Your life! You and your—husband . . ." And now her voice
did drift, for obviously she'd forgotten Roger's name.

Martha spoke quickly to spare her aunt embarrassment. "Oh
no, Aunt Alma, I'm happy to be here. I've missed you. And—this
house."

The elderly woman was smiling somewhat tensely, leaning forward in her wing-backed chair, poor woman how her back was
curved!—such an expression on her face that Martha understood
she had not exactly heard. Martha repeated her words in a louder
voice, like an actress in a play. "I've missed you, Aunt Alma. I can't
think why I haven't visited in so long. I've missed this house, and
Chautauqua Falls—it seems to have changed so little since I was
here last."

Aunt Alma nodded enthusiastically. "Things have changed so
much, haven't they! In all our lives. It *has* been a long time." Her
softly creased face puckered, her eyes shone, in a look of affection-
ate reproach, as if Martha were a child. "I've missed *you*, dear."

Martha laughed, startled and happy. Yes, it was good to be
missed.

How rude it would be of her, at this point, Martha thought, swallowing her tea to relieve the parchedness of her mouth, if she interrupted her aunt to ask to use a telephone. She simply could not.

So Aunt Alma talked, and Martha half-listened. The grandfather
clock, tall and stately, a presence in the parlor like another human
being, chimed the quarter hour. She was thinking how she'd been
so often lonely, in her busy professional life. An educator, married

to an even busier and more publicly involved educator. A childless couple, well known, even renowned, in American academic circles. Countless friends, admiring colleagues. And of course she and Roger loved each other very much—not with the effervescence of first passion, but with the more enduring strength of companionship. Yet, yes, sometimes, Martha had to admit, she was rather lonely—for what, or whom, she had no idea.

How majestic, how thrilling, the train had been, racing across the trestle above the marsh: Martha had squinted trying to see it more clearly, counting the rumbling freight cars whose corrugated rust-red sides had seemed freshly washed, gleaming. CHAUTAUQUA & BUFFALO   CHAUTAUQUA & BUFFALO   CHAUTAUQUA & BUFFALO. So abruptly familiar to her straining eyes, as if it had been only the day before she'd seen them, and not many years.

Martha recalled how, as a girl, though discouraged from exploring certain areas of Chautauqua Falls unaccompanied, she'd been intrigued by the frequently running trains. The tracks of the Chautauqua & Buffalo Line, the Erie & Oriskany Line, and the New York Central Line, converging at the riverfront, had divided the small city into sectors, like the steep hills and gullies, which perhaps only a restless child, investigating on foot, could quite experience.

That trick of perspective as a train rushes away, if you stand on the tracks behind it to watch: a rapid vanishing as if the train is swallowed by its own speed, the very tracks themselves—rails, ties, interstices of gravel—narrowing and disappearing into a mere point on the horizon.

Where do we go when we go—out?

If we disappear at one point, do we reappear at another?

Martha gratefully swallowed her tea, though it had become tepid. She held a fluted, delicately patterned Wedgwood cup that was a cobweb of near-invisible cracks. The china Aunt Alma used for their tea was beautiful, and fragile; must be a century old; like the elegant, fussy furnishings throughout the house. And the house itself, built 1885; solid, almost-ugly; but imposing, like all the Victorian houses of Prospect Avenue. The *frowning house* Martha and her older sister had called it—the juxtaposition of austere dark-brown shingles, steep overhanging roofs, prominent shutters framing oddly narrow, tall windows had inspired them. Martha remembered now, thirty years ago, cascades of English ivy and wisteria vines had shadowed the downstairs rooms; very little seemed to have changed in the interim. The *frowning house* had been old when she'd been a young girl, Martha thought. And now she was no longer a young girl—it was still old. The thought made her smile as if it were an obscure, playful riddle.

These many minutes, Aunt Alma had been chattering warmly; reminiscing, rambling vaguely and happily in the manner of the very old who are grateful for companionship; grown accustomed, not to conversations, but to a simulacrum of conversation, one-sided, wayward, yet invigorating to the speaker, whose fate otherwise would be to sit in silence and solitude, thoughts buzzing round and round in her skull like flies trapped in a glass bulb. At Martha's sudden smile, Aunt Alma smiled too, as if they shared a common memory. For a woman of eighty-six, she did not appear frail so much as tentative; with her watery blue eyes, her finely creased yet still rather beautiful face, her hopeful smile. Her hair, fixed each morning in an elaborate bun, with tendril-like curls on her forehead, was flaxen streaked with silver, resembling the hue of Martha's own hair which had begun to turn a few years ago; her cheekbones were prominent, and her cheeks just slightly sunken, gaunt; the flesh beneath her chin had gone flaccid, partly hidden, for vanity's sake, by a high lace collar and white silk bow. Aunt Alma was a woman of breeding and means—not really educated, but certainly "cultured"—whose inherited household had always been run by servants; the only one who seemed to remain now was a taciturn housekeeper named Betty, who was well into her sixties. Martha felt the difference between herself and her privileged, yet entrapped great-aunt; how suffocated she would have been, in such a life, stuck in this small town in upstate New York forever! She felt a surge of love for Aunt Alma, tinged with pity. But there was no denying how she and the older woman resembled each other: face, hair, eyes. If they were to appear in public together, any neutral observer could identify them as related.

As if reading Martha's thoughts, Aunt Alma said, sighing, "I've been waiting for you, you know, dear. Of course, your sister—" a sudden blank pause, she'd forgotten Martha's sister's name, "—is sweet, to call so often. But I miss *you*, Martha." Her shadowed and slightly sunken eyes blinked rapidly. "But I haven't been impatient—no, not at all. I know how dedicated you are to your life, your teaching career— You and your—husband—"

Martha guessed that Aunt Alma had forgotten what Martha actually did, and where; so quickly she said, "Yes, Aunt Alma, but I'm on sabbatical this spring. I have a grant to finish my new book. So it's a time for research, and contemplation. An ideal time to visit you."

Martha smiled happily. Uttered with such girlish directness, her words had the ring of truth.

The grandfather clock began to chime—not the quarter hour, but the hour. These were strokes of sound pure, melodic, yet somehow piercing, like a blinding ray of light entering one's eye. Martha listened, counting eight chimes—could it be eight o'clock, already?—then nine, ten, eleven—finally, fifteen! Seeing her look of surprise, her aunt laughed, and leaned over to take Martha's hand, gently. She held Martha's hand in her thin, cool, firm fingers, and did not seem to want to let go. Saying, "In Chautauqua Falls, dear girl, you'll find time keeps its own hours."

What *was* the number—?

Martha half-sobbed with frustration. Trying to dial her own telephone number, yet, incredibly, fumbling the digits. She blamed the antique rotary phone: on a Touch-Tone, to which she was accustomed, she would have dialed the ten-digit number swiftly and unerringly, without needing to think.

And damned awkward this was, Martha in an alcove off the downstairs front hall, past which on slippered swollen feet, sighing with arthritic discomfort, the housekeeper Betty plodded, and returned to plod again, and yet again, as if tidying up the parlor after

Aunt Alma's and Martha's modest tea was a great task, involving immense effort of which she wanted the visiting niece to be aware.

The strange thing was, Martha's fingers seemed to recall of their own volition a telephone number of more than twenty years ago!—the number of the first house in which she and Roger had lived. Though Martha instructed herself clearly to dial the correct number, some sort of confusion ensued, as she dialed, between her brain's command and her fingers' execution. She gave up, and tried again; and again. But when she heard the phone ringing at the other end of the line she panicked, and hung up, quickly before a stranger could answer.

As Betty the housekeeper plodded past another time. A dour old woman in bedroom slippers and a black rayon dress that fitted her bulky body tightly. This woman was old when I was a little girl, Martha thought. She is the same age, still. The housekeeper sighed heavily, not so much as glancing at Martha who stood in the telephone alcove rubbing at her right eye, which spilled tears absurdly.

Extensive damage to the brain stem and cerebellum. Trauma to the body—broken ribs, broken collarbone, shattered right knee, countless lacerations. Eight preliminary hours of neurosurgery to reduce pressure in the brain caused by swelling and internal bleeding—12 percent of the cerebellum would be removed in all, after subsequent operations. Surgery to repair damage to the right eye was believed to be successful.

She was yet to regain consciousness but he had faith, he would not give up. At her bedside as soon as visiting hours began in the intensive care unit at 8:30 A.M. Reluctant to leave when visiting hours were over at 7:00 P.M. Stroking her fingers, speaking her name. He knew she was, in her deep coma, aware of him—conscious of his presence. Sometimes her fingers twitched in response to his, her eyelids fluttered on the verge of opening, her pale, bruised lips seemed about to shape words. He knew, he knew! He had not realized how much he loved her, and how powerful the bond was between them.

———

She was standing breathless, trembling with anticipation. A rivulet of sweat like a tear running down her cheek. Just below the steep grassy railroad embankment at the Seneca Street crossing, in a neighborhood of warehouses, vacant lots, the township water tower on its spindly legs.

WARNING   TRAIN CROSSING   STOP LOOK LISTEN

The X-shaped sign was weatherworn but still forbidding. Beyond Seneca Street was one of Chautauqua Falls' several railroad tunnels cut into a massive hill, for this was a steep and riotous landscape, a mysterious rock-strewn earth where once glaciers the size of the Great Lakes had formed. It was the tunnel that had drawn Martha here, for it was a large craterlike hole in the wooded hill, dark as absolute night; for sunlight, on even the brightest days, could penetrate it only to a degree. A complex tunnel, too, with two sets of railroad tracks running side by side, no more than ten feet separating them; emerging from the tunnel and running over a wooden trestle bridge above the street, and above the marsh, westward into town. Martha had made her way to this no-man's-land of reeds high as her head, spongy ground underfoot, a smell of brackish water, by way of a faint path that led parallel to, though hidden from, the generally well-tended, wall- or hedge-protected back lawns of the grand old houses of Prospect Avenue. Except for the isolated cries of birds in the marsh, all was silent here.

There was a profound mystery about this tunnel, at which Martha was staring with such intensity her eyes watered. The mouth of the tunnel was framed by a stone portal, of subtle ornamentation, at its crest CHAUTAUQUA FALLS 1913 carved into the surface. Martha understood that, if she was patient, the mystery would be explained to her, with the ease of a sleeve being turned inside out.

And then, it happened: she heard the train whistle, faint but rapidly approaching; she saw the red signal lights begin to flash. But why were there no crossing gates here?—the railroad tracks were exposed, dangerously open to the street. (Fortunately, there was no traffic. For this was early in the morning, just dawn.) Martha waited, barely able to contain her excitement, clenching and unclenching her fists. She felt the ground vibrate just as the gigantic locomotive came rushing out of the tunnel—there was the speed of it, the size, the deafening whistle and clatter of the great spoked wheels turning and the earth now vibrating beneath her feet like a panicked heartbeat. Billowing vaporish smoke was discharged from the locomotive's smokestack, obscuring the sky. As Martha stood, hands pressed to her ears, she saw in the cab a man lifting his gloved hand to her in greeting, and smiling—the locomotive's engineer?—but in the next instant the locomotive was past her, freight cars were hurtling by, only a few yards away, CHAUTAUQUA & BUFFALO CHAUTAUQUA & BUFFALO CHAUTAUQUA & BUFFALO car after car rattling past, amid a choking odor of tar and creosote. Yet she could neither turn away nor hide her eyes. Standing paralyzed, in awe rather than fear, until at last the caboose went by, and rushed westward across the trestle. Martha climbed the embankment to the tracks so that she could watch the train disappear from this perspective: the tracks, too, radically narrowing, coming to a point to vanish.

The engineer, the man in the cab of the locomotive—who was he?

Martha, shaky and out of breath, wiped her sweaty face on a tissue. Like a brash young girl, smiling into the tissue. She had not seen the man clearly, but her excited impression was that he was red-haired, with a redhead's freckled pallor, and he wore a railway cap at a jaunty angle on his head, and his gesture toward her had been high-spirited, flirtatious. His face strong-boned and manly and his eyes intense, direct, boldly fixed upon *her*.

Does he know me? Did he know I'd be here, waiting?

Keeping his vigil. At her bedside. Speaking her name, stroking her arm, squeezing the fingers that sometimes—he swore, he did not imagine this!—squeezed his in turn. And her eyelids fluttered on the verge of opening, and she writhed, twisted her upper body, a deep yearning groan escaped from her, a groan that was his name—he swore, he did not imagine this! Though the doctors were not encouraging but rather neutral, polite. And so the hours fol-

lowing the accident became days, and incredibly the days became
sequences of days, and finally weeks, and her deep coma was un-
changed, except in those ways that he alone could see.

The respirator had been removed, and she could breathe—in
sometimes erratic surges, sometimes quick shallow infantlike and
rhythmic breaths. Feeding tubes dripped fluids into the veins of her
arms and legs and a catheter bore toxins from her lower body in a
continuous stream like the invisible ceaseless motion of atoms. Ma-
chines monitored her sometimes-erratic, sometimes-normal heart-
beat and the similarly unpredictable activities of her damaged
brain. On all sides this powerful humming and vibrating. Life! life!
life! *the machines promised.*

In Chautauqua Falls, time keeps its own hours.

And so it was, Martha discovered. For though she was visiting
with Aunt Alma for only ten days, each day was endless; and somehow each day was the first day—the first full day, that is, beginning
with her waking at dawn to the faint sound of a train whistle, and
hurrying out, through the surprisingly overgrown, weedy back-
yard of her aunt's house, through the desiccated hedge and into the
untended, marshy area at the foot of the incline. And so along
the derelict footpath a mile or so in the direction of Seneca Street,
the warehouse district, the enormous black crater in the hill into
which twinned railroad tracks disappeared beneath the austere
stone portal CHAUTAUQUA FALLS 1913.

Yet, Martha believed too that this "first day" had its significant
variants, if only she could remember them. For naggingly, as one
senses rather than sees an object in the corner of one's eye, she did
remember—almost.

For instance: exploring the block-long "downtown" of Chautauqua Falls, strolling in and out of familiar stores, she had several
times found herself staring at telephone booths. Wasn't there a call,
an urgent call, she should make? But to whom? And why?

What, Martha wondered, could so desperately *matter?*

And another day, idly following a footpath along the river that
brought her to the underside of the Federal Street bridge, in a

semirural area far from Prospect Avenue, Martha heard a sound of murmurous voices; and knew, even as her intelligence rejected such a possibility, that she was being observed, closely monitored. She cast her eyes upward to the girdered, grimy underside of the bridge, where mourning doves were nesting. Only doves—cooing doves—of course. Yet: *they are following me! watching me! I am never out of their sight!* Shimmering parabolas of light played against the underside of the bridge, reflected water cast upward. There was beauty here, but also deception. She dared not trust the shimmering surfaces of the world.

She rubbed her eyes roughly, in childish vexation. And—when she opened her eyes again, the underside of the bridge had vanished! Nothing remained, at all. Nor any sky, any substance, beyond. The cause lay not in her vision but in the very structure of the world. Calmly she thought *It's gone. It never has been. I am looking into the emptiness of existence.*

He spoke her name, sometimes so sharply, not knowing what he did, a nurse came to admonish him gently, Please sir, not so loud, you'll disturb our other patients. And he blinked in astonishment and outrage. As if he'd believed himself alone, alone with her— how dare any stranger intervene?

Early each morning, as the locomotive rushed out of the tunnel, as the red-haired engineer saluted Martha with his gloved hand, and mouthed a wordless greeting, Martha could make out the man's features more clearly. His smile was broad, yet rather sly; flirtatious, yet also kindly, protective. And his eyes so keenly fixed upon *her*—she carried the impact of their gaze for hours afterward, like an erotic caress, warming the blood of her entire body.

Of course, Martha did not tell Aunt Alma about the railroad engineer, nor where she went early each morning. Nor did she tell her where, through the long day, and well into the evening, she wandered—the streets, alleys, footpaths and trails of the small town; the wide cobbled bridge at the town's center that spanned the Chautauqua River, where people drawn to the water as she was, mainly older men, leaned against the railing and gazed down brooding into the churning, frothy water thirty feet below. Because this part of Chautauqua Falls was on a relatively high elevation, you could see, in the distance, a saw-toothed stretch of mountains, on clear days distinctive as cardboard cutouts. Mount Cataract prominent among them, shimmering, beautiful, crowned with sunshine. The shape of a hand that, teasingly, both beckoned and withdrew in the same gesture.

Strange how, in Chautauqua Falls, Martha never recognized anyone. Nor did anyone recognize her. In fact, they did not seem to see her, or, in any case, with a complacency she might have thought maddening in another context, they looked through her. *As if I am not here. As if I'm invisible.* So long as the red-haired engineer took notice of her, Martha thought, smiling, she really didn't care.

In the eleventh week of her hospitalization, this was noted as a promising sign: her right eye blinked normally as a nurse drew a cotton swab lightly over the cornea.

She was rapidly losing weight of course, weighing now ninety pounds. And with each day in her comatose state the prognosis was less optimistic. Her intellectual abilities, doctors said, were possibly unimpaired but damage to the brain stem and cerebellum was severe. One chance in one hundred of regaining consciousness.

He, her husband, listened; and heard what he chose to hear. For in such situations we must not hear what we cannot bear to hear; God has not made us strong enough.

This he knew, in his stubborn faith: when he spoke her name, when he leaned over to kiss her cool forehead, occasionally she responded with a fluttering of her eyelids; sometimes her limbs twitched, her upper body became agitated. One morning he was greatly excited: he murmured her name and her eyes flew open, the left eye, the eye that was uninjured, focussed upon his face—he was sure! A glisten of recognition that was unmistakable! Her parched lips moved, and a choked, muffled cry issued from her, as from somewhere deep inside her; then she shuddered, and her eyes

shut, as the wave of unconsciousness swept over her again, like
dark water visibly rising.
But he'd seen! He knew.

She had believed herself utterly safe, protected as a baby in the
old-fashioned four-poster bed with the primly hard mattress. But
one night Martha dreamt a terrible dream.

She was not herself exactly. Yet the name—*Martha?*—was
tauntingly murmured. She had been abducted from her home,
trussed up as a specimen in a hellish scientific experiment, like an
infant swaddled in restraining sheets; strawlike tubes pierced
veins in her arms, legs, and even in her groin; tiny electrodes had
been implanted in her skull and chest. She thrashed desperately
from side to side to free herself—tried to scream, but could not—
one of her captors crouched above her, a cruel melted-moon face,
craterous eyes—hideous! *Leave me alone, let me go, don't touch*
me! she screamed in silence.

Saving herself, then, as, as a child, she'd saved herself from
nightmares, with a convulsive wrenching of her body. She broke
free of the constraints holding her, and woke—to her immense,
sobbing relief, in the old-fashioned four-poster bed in her aunt's
house in Chautauqua Falls.

Thank God, only a dream. It could not pursue her this side of
sleep.

Except, next day: in Lyons Pharmacy & Sweet Shoppe where
she went to refill a prescription for her aunt, Martha felt a premonition of—she did not know, had no name to give it; she felt that
trip of the heart that signals an onset of panic.

She had to—do what? Not the task she'd been sent on, which
was perhaps merely a pretext, but—what?

The answer lay somewhere in the store's dingy interior. She had
no choice but to go inside. No one appeared to be on duty.

It was remarkable how little had changed in Lyons, in thirty
years. The high ceiling of hammered-tin squares, long ago painted
a pale sour green; several slow-turning fans that hung from the

ceiling; the rows of predictable not-new merchandise—toiletries, medical supplies, cosmetics, greeting cards, candy bars. Immediately to the left of the front entrance was the old soda fountain with its slightly blemished mirror, and the mauve marble counter that was always stickily damp, and the half dozen frayed leather swivel stools. All empty, and no one behind the counter? There were the old glossy poster-illustrations of hot fudge sundaes, milkshakes, banana splits; advertisements for Coca-Cola, Pepsi-Cola, Royal Crown Cola, 7UP. There, the cigarette vending machine forbidden to minors by New York State law. The air, stirred by the slow fans, was stale, cloying-sweet with the odor of syrup.

Martha stood at the counter, smiling nervously—where was the young man who'd always worked here? Perhaps he was not a young man any longer? But why was he, or someone else, not here, in any case? How badly Martha wanted to order a banana split, just like the one in the picture. Scoops of vanilla, chocolate, and strawberry ice cream, coarsely ground nuts, hot fudge syrup and a dollop of whipped cream and a banana sliced lengthwise—though the banana, Martha recalled, was sometimes too greeny-unripe to have any taste, and sometimes so brown as to be almost rotted.

Martha waited, but no one appeared. "Mr. Lyons?" she called, toward the rear of the store. "Isn't anyone here?"

Even the mirror behind the fountain, laid horizontally to a height of about six feet, was strangely vacant. Where Martha stood, there was blurred light as in an overexposed photograph.

Martha was beginning to be frightened, but Martha was annoyed, too. Boldly she went to the pharmacist's counter at the back of the store, to seek out Mr. Lyons. A sharp medicinal smell, or smells, prevailed here. Behind the first counter was a raised counter, with a frosted-glass partition; behind this partition, the gray-haired pharmacist was usually to be found. *And there he is,* Martha thought, *hiding from me.* She believed she could see the man's head, part of his torso, through the frosted glass. "Mr. Lyons? You have a customer," she said. But there was silence, and the figure behind the glass remained unmoving as a cardboard cutout. "I'm here to refill Mrs. Buchanan's prescription," Martha

said carefully. "She's my aunt. She's an old, old customer of yours."
But still there was no response. The only sound in the store was the
slow, vibrating-creaking sound of the ceiling fans as their dust-
coated propellors barely turned.

Martha's eyes flooded with tears. She was going to scream—a
sudden shaft of pain pierced her head. *No, no,* she thought. *I will
not give in.*

Martha turned to leave the store, but the telephone booth, in a
corner near the front, drew her attention. There was something
about the telephone booth that was crucial, Martha knew. Hadn't
she meant to make a call from it the other day?—she could not
quite remember. She remembered the urgency, the excitement, but
she could not remember whom she'd wanted to call. Who meant so
much to her? She had no living relatives any longer: all were deceased. Except for the elderly aunt whose name too, for just this
moment, she could not quite recall.

Martha stepped into the telephone booth, and eagerly lifted the
receiver—this, too, damn!—an old-fashioned rotary phone. She
dropped a dime into the mechanism and quickly, before her
thoughts could interfere, she dialed the number literally at her fingertips, memorized by her fingertips, a ten-digit number she knew
by instinct was the correct number, the number she needed—ah, it
was life or death, and life must triumph! She was panting, and her
eyes were brimming with tears.

But even as she pressed the receiver so hard against her ear
that her entire body trembled, she understood that the telephone,
like all of Lyons Pharmacy & Sweet Shoppe, was not in business.
There was no dial tone, only dead silence.

Her aunt's name was *Alma,* of course: *Alma Buchanan.*

Though she was not in fact Martha's aunt, but someone else's
aunt. Her great love and need for Martha had drawn Martha to
her, and so long as that love and need endured, Martha would remain in Chautauqua Falls.

———

Feeling sometimes—he swore, he did not imagine this!—her resistance to the kneading, bending, stretching of her muscles he'd learned from the physical therapist, a voiceless tinge of pain.

For pain was sensation, and sensation was consciousness, and consciousness was life.

For he could not allow it that the most random of accidents should disrupt, ruin utterly the course of two such lives. A pelting rain, a stalled truck on a suburban road just beyond a railroad crossing whose warning lights and automatic safety gates had failed to operate as a train approached. And she, his wife, driving alone—

Such a set of singularities! He could not accept it.

Keeping his vigil. Murmuring her name, stroking and squeezing her cool, limp fingers. And now the exercising of her stiffening and atrophying muscles that her wasted body might be deceived into believing itself alive, and normal; and not curl as it seemed to wish to, spine hideously bending, into a fetal position.

Returning home at an unexpectedly early hour of the afternoon. Her first glimpse of the dour housekeeper Betty standing motionless in the kitchen, oddly motionless but Martha would not think of this until later. She came to her Aunt Alma who was seated in a cushioned rocker in the sun porch, simply sitting, upright, her aged, thin hands limp in her lap. "Aunt Alma, I'm back. I'm afraid I couldn't get your medicine," Martha said. The elderly woman seemed not to hear. Was she asleep? But her eyes were open, a sweet blank smile on her lips. "Mr. Lyons wouldn't wait on me! He was there, but he wouldn't so much as—" It was then that Martha saw, to her surprise, that her aunt's gaze was fixed upon her, or upon the place where she stood; but there was no glisten of recognition in the eyes, no more consciousness than in a pair of marbles. "Aunt Alma? Is something wrong?" Martha touched her aunt's arm fearfully. The arm was stiff, ungiving. How still the elderly woman sat, like a dressmaker's dummy arranged in a chair. *It's because I have returned too early. They aren't prepared for me.* The softly creased skin of Martha's aunt's face was an intricate lacy skein of wrinkles laid upon a younger face that might have been Martha's own. The opaque eyes were a pale washed blue, like the sky beyond high motionless cirrus clouds. As Martha stared, in horror, she saw something moving in Aunt Alma's elaborately coiffed silvery-flaxen hair—a small, shiny black beetle? Another beetle emerged briskly from her aunt's left ear and, shy of sunlight, darted into the coil of hair at the nape of her aunt's neck, appearing, and disappearing, in virtually the same instant.

Martha lurched backward out of the sunporch, screaming.

She knew: she must leave Chautauqua Falls. Before she became one of the dead.

But she could no longer remember clearly any region that was *not* Chautauqua Falls. Nor any time not eerily distended, watery and concave, as if seen through a prism. In this slow protracted seemingly endless and cyclical time of Chautauqua Falls, how could there be any time *other*?

In the sixteenth week another craniectomy was performed, and tiny blood vessels cauterized, to reduce swelling. Again, to his dismay, she had to be put on a respirator, her left nostril cruelly distended. An aspirator too was hooked into her mouth, making a continuous sucking noise and preventing saliva from accumulating in the back of her mouth and drowning her. To all eyes save his her sleep was deep and profound as an inky sea into which one might fall, and fall, and fall, and never touch bottom. Yet he was stubborn. The long ordeal had, in a way, strengthened his faith. He knew what he knew. And he knew that she knew. Gripping her skeletal fingers in his and occasionally feeling—he swore, he did not imagine this!—their spasmodic pressure against his; that resistance, however fleeting, that signals life, life, life!

Rushing out of the tunnel beneath the stony portal CHAUTAUQUA FALLS 1913, shortly after dawn, was the train. One moment the tunnel was absolute blackness as of a hole gouged violently in the fabric of light itself, the next moment the train blurred with speed.

The whistle was deafening, and the clattering iron wheels in their harsh percussive rhythm like some ancient shifting and cracking of the earth's layered rock. Out of the smokestack poured boiling white smoke and vapor, ascending skyward, obscuring the very sun.

She was waiting at the crossing. The locomotive bore down upon her like a great devouring beast but she stood bravely, stubbornly, her head uplifted. She steeled herself for the onrushing clatter to overwhelm her—she was standing only a few feet from the tracks—but instead the train began to slow—in a series of shrieking hisses, the locomotive was braking. The red-haired engineer swung out of the cab to stare at Martha in anger—no, he was smiling—the cap at a jaunty angle on his head, and his eyes shadowed but kindly. Through hissing exhalations of steam he called to her, "Come up, miss! And take care." As Martha trotted breathless alongside the slow-moving locomotive he reached out a gloved hand to her, to grasp; she gave her hand to him, and in a single motion, his other arm securing her, he swung her up into the cab.

And at once the locomotive began to accelerate, gathering speed as it rushed westward across the trestle bridge.

The call came for him at 7:35 A.M., at home. She'd died within the hour, they'd been unable to resuscitate her. He wept, bitter and aggrieved. He would always so weep, thinking of her, and of this. How, at the end, he'd been nowhere near.

Shadows of the Evening

1.

In the late winter of 1928, when she was sixteen years old, my mother's mother Magdalena Schön journeyed alone by train from the Black Rock district of Buffalo, New York, five hundred miles eastward to the seaport of Edmundston, Massachusetts. Never before had the shy, inexperienced girl traveled anywhere by herself; rarely had she ventured out of the German-Hungarian neighborhood in which she'd been born, to immigrant parents from southern Germany; she spoke accented English which felt to her, in the presence of strangers, like a speech impediment or a physical deformity. She was terrified of leaving home but had no choice: there were seven children in the family, too many to feed and clothe and care for, and an eighth soon to be born, so her parents had decided to send her to live with an elderly aunt of her father's, a widow with no children who was bedridden after a stroke and terribly homesick for someone from the family, who lived by herself in Massachusetts. *But why must I go, why must I be the one?* Magdalena protested, and her mother said, smiling, as if this were an answer, *Your aunt Kistenmacher married a rich man, she will leave us money.*

In a state of shock mistaken for acquiescence Magdalena was put on a crowded New York Central coach car with a single battered suitcase and a satchel containing sandwiches and drinking water and a prayer book and a rosary; she'd been cautioned *Don't speak to anybody, not even the train men. Just give your tickets.* Stiff and upright in her seat beside a sooty window Magdalena gritted her teeth against the train's lumbering and lurching and ceaseless vibrating; she dared not look at anyone, least of all the brusque, uniformed conductor who took her ticket; for most of the first day she stared sightlessly out the window or shut her eyes, her lips moving in silent prayers to the Virgin Mary she came to know, less than one hundred miles into her journey, were useless. She did not cry though from time to time bright tears glistened on her cheeks like raindrops. For crying, too, was useless.

She was thinking *My mother doesn't want me! My mother sent me away.*

For of the myriad facts that might be said of Magdalena Schön, this was the cruel, inescapable fact, the fact she would recall for the remainder of her life which would be a long life *My mother didn't love me but sent me away.*

The coach car was uncomfortable, overheated, jammed with travellers, most of them men who gazed upon Magdalena with interest. Some stared at her without knowing what they did, like men dreaming with their eyes open; others were more deliberate. Magdalena gave no sign, of course. She had long learned, since the age of twelve, never to meet the eyes of strangers even by chance. She was an attractive girl of moderate height who looked as if she'd grown swiftly in the past year. Her skin was fair, healthy, lightly freckled; her eyes were wide-set and thickly lashed, a deep, placid blue; her wavy wheat-colored hair was dense as a horse's mane and had been neatly plaited and wound in two coils around the sides of her head, like a telephone operator's earphones. On her lap was the satchel into which she looked repeatedly, as if checking to see what might be lost. She hadn't any appetite for the food her mother had packed for her which had begun to smell rancid but could only sip from a jar of lukewarm water, to ease her parched mouth, and then she burst into a spasm of coughing, with a sound like hoarse weeping. She wore rust-colored clothes that might have been handed down from an adult woman, and old-fashioned leather shoes, or boots, with complicated laces. She looked, not like 1928, but like 1918. In school she'd been one of those children of immigrant parents so shy and uncertain of themselves they were considered "slow"; at home, she'd been made to feel there was something wrong with her that justly provoked impatience in others. She wore a perpetual expression of chagrin and vague embarrassment. When someone, usually a sister, came to her defense saying *Leave Magdalena alone, she can't help it* Magdalena was stricken with emotions of gratitude and shame as if she'd swallowed something delicious the wrong way.

A man seated across from Magdalena did speak to her, as the train came clattering and shrieking into the Albany station that evening, asking if she'd like to join him for dinner in the dining car; but Magdalena, staring out the window with dolorous eyes, her rosary twined through her fingers and her lips silently moving, seemed not to hear. The clumsy satchel was on her lap. She had ceased thinking and in a haze of oblivion sat prepared to be hurtled eastward into the deepening night to a fate so vast and incomprehensible she had ceased trying to consider it as she'd given up considering the geometry problems certain of her boy classmates at school solved so readily. Thinking, as the train wheels rolled, *She sent me away. Sent me away. My mother didn't love me but sent me away.*

And then at dawn to her surprise Magdalena woke stiff-necked and dry-mouthed from a night of patchy, disturbing dreams to see a slow explosion of light at the horizon; an unknown river creased and sparkling in the darkness and broad as the Niagara. The train was rushing over this river on an elevated bridge Magdalena could see curving dizzily ahead, a skeleton bridge on stilts. In the distance was a city built on a peninsula that must have been Edmundston, her destination. Overhead the sky was still partly darkened, rippled and ridged with cloud. Wind made the train rock. Magdalena bit her lower lip in panic, or was it excitement?—never had she been so far from home, never could she have found her way back. Far to her right the hilly, rocky land fell away and there emerged a vast body of water, choppy and glittering with light. Magdalena rubbed her eyes, she'd never seen anything so beautiful. It seemed to her suddenly that the world was luminous before her; the future lay ahead, welcoming; the world behind, of dismal Black Rock, the airless crowded tenement flats, the endless winter of icy, snow-locked streets, the stink of factories and the soot-blackened walls and air singed with smoke that caused people to cough and choke until tears ran down their cheeks—all that was behind her, diminished and narrowed and rapidly retreating like a tunnel that has the power to terrify while you are in it but is forgotten as soon as you merge into daylight.

The sun lifted from the horizon and broke through a dense bank of cloud. Shafts of light fell obliquely earthward. To Magdalena's right, the vast stretch of water shifted suddenly to dark greeny-blue, near its surface transparent as cut glass. Magdalena exclaimed in childlike wonder, "Oh, what is *that*?" and a man seated across from her said, proud as if it were his own possession, "That, miss, is the Atlantic Ocean."

The Atlantic Ocean! Magdalena's parents hadn't told her that Edmundston was on the ocean. All Magdalena knew of the Atlantic Ocean were horror tales of her parents' terrible stormy crossing years before her birth, a crossing her pregnant mother had barely survived. Magdalena's brothers and sisters had been imbued all their lives with a sense of the ocean's terror, not its beauty. But the Atlantic Ocean at which Magdalena stared was beautiful—and immense!—like nothing she had ever seen before. She hoped that her great-aunt's house was near the water so that she could stare and stare at it forever.

2.

Now came the time of surprises. Now Magdalena was continually surprised, like a child wandering in a hall of marvels.

Her first surprise was at the Edmundston train station. It had been arranged that she would be met there by her great-aunt's driver and so, stepping down uncertainly from the coach car, struggling with her suitcase and satchel, she glanced quickly about. The confusion and commotion of so many disembarking passengers, so many strangers, threw her into a panic. *What if no one is here? What if this is a mistake, a dream? They have sent me away to be rid of me.* Then she saw a dark-uniformed man with a visored cap standing on the platform calmly holding a sign— KISTENMACHER. It took Magdalena a moment to realize that KISTENMACHER, a stranger's name, now referred in some crucial way to her.

At her approach, the uniformed man greeted her, "Miss Schön?" and took her suitcase and satchel from her as if they weighed nothing and walked briskly through the crowded, noisy station to a long black car shiny as a hearse parked outside. In a daze of relief and excitement Magdalena hurried in his wake. *Miss Schön!* A man had called her *Miss Schön!* She saw how others watched her with curiosity and respect as the driver opened a rear door of the car and helped her climb inside. Never had Magdalena seen a car so luxurious as this except in photographs; the rear was cushioned in soft gray plush, the windows were so clean and clear, just perceptibly tinted, you would hardly know there were windows at all. Through the traffic-crowded streets of downtown Edmundston they seemed to glide soundlessly as in a dream, and along a wide, windy avenue, and through a park where the grass was stubbled with slow-melting snow, and then they were ascending into a high, hilly residential district of cobblestone streets, clean-swept brick sidewalks, and large, beautiful old houses behind wrought-iron fences and stone walls. Magdalena stared, enchanted. She'd become breathless as if she'd been running. She would have liked to ask the driver many questions but was too shy to speak. For his part, the driver was utterly remote, formal. He'd spoken with her only once as they'd started out, to ask if she was comfortable, and Magdalena had stammered yes, thank you. Never in her life had anyone asked her such a question! The driver sat on the other side of a glass partition and she could see only the back of his head, and the back of his visored cap; there was a rearview mirror above his windshield, but Magdalena could see no face in it.

As the train had entered Edmundston, Magdalena had lost sight of the beautiful glittering ocean; she'd been propelled, as through a tunnel, past a confused succession of factories, warehouses, the rears of run-down houses and tenement buildings disconcertingly similar to those of Black Rock; its speed ever slowing, like a great beast run to earth, the train had passed over a canal of the color of rust. Everywhere was hazy, sepia-tinged smoke or mist she knew would smell and taste like something burnt. But in the residential district in which her aunt Kistenmacher lived, the air was clear and sparkling as if rain-washed. Even the clouded sky opened to piercing blue as the driver brought them steeply uphill on a cobblestone street named Charter, to their destination.

Magdalena continued to stare as the long shiny black car glided soundlessly into the driveway, past ten-foot stone pillars, one of them marked 1792. The Kistenmacher house was not the largest of the houses Magdalena had been seeing, nor the most impressive; it was a three-storey narrow house of aged brick of the hue of pinkish flesh, softened by time; moldering with time; in the facade were crude blocks of granite that had darkened with rain. The roof of the house was unusually steep, with rotted shingles and a prominent chimney listing to one side at its peak. Several of the black-lacquered shutters needed repair, repainting. Winter-damaged ivy clung to the brick like scraggly claws, and lichen grew in the cracked bricks of the elegant front stoop with its tall columns and graceful, if partly rotted portico. But Magdalena felt tears sting her eyes, for she'd never seen, up close, any house so beautiful.

Will I be living here?

I, Magdalena Schön?

The girl whose mother had not loved her; had sent her away.

Magdalena's next surprise was Erica Kistenmacher.

Within minutes of being shown to her room on the third floor, by a woman in a dark dress and a stiff-starched white apron, Magdalena was taken to see her great-aunt. "Mrs. Kistenmacher has been waiting for you since dawn, Miss Schön," the woman said quietly. There was an air in this remark of the most subtle reproach but when Magdalena murmured anxiously that she was sorry, the woman seemed not to hear, nor did she even look at Magdalena. She was of no age that Magdalena could have guessed, older than her own mother; with thin gray hair neatly contained by a hairnet and a solid, stocky though not plump body, deftly defined motions as she led Magdalena along a corridor without a backward glance. Magdalena had been told that her great-aunt was lonely and required a "companion" and so she had come to imagine the Kistenmacher house as empty except for her great-aunt and now she saw how erroneous such a notion was. Rich people require servants, she was to be a servant here as well. The woman rapped lightly on a door, and after some delay the door was opened not by Magdalena's great-aunt as she'd naively expected, but by another somber, unsmiling middle-aged woman; a nurse; stockily built too, with a flushed face, in a white uniform and starched white cap over leaden-gray hair. Not greeting the anxious girl but rather scolding Magdalena at once, she said, "Miss Schön, at last, come in, hurry!—so we don't get a draft. And don't tire Mrs. Kistenmacher, she's in a state of nerves as it is." Magdalena stepped into a room so airless and overheated it took her breath away, and the nurse quickly shut the door behind her. It was a spacious, high-ceilinged bedroom so crowded with furniture and fabrics, vases and glassware, glittering figurines, candlestick holders, scattered books, mirrors with old glass that subtly distorted the reflections they framed, that Magdalena had difficulty seeing her great-aunt until the woman whispered, "My dear! Come!" On a divan in a patch of wan sunlight, covered by a satin quilt, there lay a white-skinned, doll-like old woman with one of her arms tremulously lifted, her fingers stretched in Magdalena's direction and her face creased in joyous expectation.

Many times, Magdalena's father and mother had spoken of the young woman Erica Schön who'd traveled to Boston from her home in southern Germany to work as a nanny for a rich family; who, at the age of nineteen, had married a much older man, a widower; they'd moved to Edmundston, Massachusetts. For years, Erica Schön was out of contact with her family; she'd married defiantly, outside the Roman Catholic Church. A photograph of

Magdalena's father as a boy, taken with his youthful aunt, many years ago, was all Magdalena had had to help form her image of her great-aunt Kistenmacher; but the young woman in the photograph with her crimped hair, almost-pretty face, long nose and intelligent, squinting eyes bore no resemblance at all to the woman on the divan. Somehow, Magdalena was not prepared for her great-aunt to be so old. Stammering a greeting, Magdalena took the woman's lifted hand—what thin, icy fingers!—thinking *She's a stranger. It's a mistake. She will send me away, like my mother.*

But the old woman was delighted with Magdalena, saying in her hoarse, hissing voice that she recognized her at once, for Magdalena had the "Schön face"—a heart-shaped face—"But so much prettier than most of us!" Though the frowning nurse hovered near, Magdalena was urged to sit on a stool close beside the old woman, who gazed at her hungrily, and continued to squeeze her hand. With dismay Magdalena saw that her great-aunt's clouded left eye was fixed upon something over Magdalena's shoulder; the entire left side of her face was frozen, in an attitude of pained exactitude; her left arm lay limp beside her, the childlike fingers curled, useless. *Your aunt Kistenmacher has had a stroke, she must be fearful of her death. If you are good to her, she may be generous to us.* Yet Magdalena hadn't much idea of what a stroke was, nor had her parents explained. Magdalena surmised within a few minutes that the poor woman was nearly blind in her "good" eye; and very hard of hearing; it seemed unlikely that she could walk unassisted, or perhaps at all; her voice was gone, or she hadn't the strength to project it beyond a rasping whisper. Most disconcerting was the way in which, not knowing what she did, she occasionally interjected a word or a nonsensical syllable ("eh," "yi") into her speech. She smelled of sweet talcum and something harshly acidic, like medicine. How pale her skin, papery white and so thin Magdalena could see the delicate blue veins quivering beneath like nerves; her face was finely creased, as if it had been many times crumpled and released, like silk. Yet she trembled with excitement, thrilled with Magdalena as a child with a new playmate. Magdalena couldn't understand her completely but she seemed to be asking

Magdalena to speak of her home, her family, most of all her father, but when Magdalena began speaking she interrupted her repeatedly, smiling with half her face, her bright eye fixed upon Magdalena's face. With her groping right hand she touched Magdalena's hair, stroked the thick braided coils at the sides of Magdalena's head; she'd once worn her hair like that, she seemed to be saying. She touched Magdalena's face—the "Schön face"— and drew her fingertips across Magdalena's lips. Magdalena had to suppress the impulse to shiver, though the room was very warm. "Do you know me, dear? I am your Aunt Erica," she said, "please call me 'Aunt Erica,' dear," and Magdalena said, uncertainly, "—'Aunt Erica.' " The words sounded false in her mouth, as if the syllables were wrongly accented. Eagerly Aunt Erica cupped her right hand to her ear whispering, "Eh? Eh? What?" so Magdalena repeated in a louder voice, her face burning, " 'Aunt Erica.' " The frowning nurse in white had positioned herself behind the divan and was staring at Magdalena with open hostility. But Aunt Erica was squeezing Magdalena's fingers in hers, and smiling with half her mouth, so pleadingly that Magdalena felt her heart ache with love; unless it was pity; that raw, exhausting emotion she felt for the crippled people, usually men, she saw on the streets of Black Rock, victims of accidents in the great iron foundry in which her own father and older brothers worked. The elderly invalid was whispering hoarsely what sounded like, "I knew you would come to me one day, dear child, I had faith you hadn't abandoned me like the rest of the Schöns," and in the midst of these words a nonsensical outcry *Yi!* like a cry of pain, and Magdalena, frightened, mutely nodded, for how else to respond; her aunt's frail fingers gripped her own much stronger fingers tight; the stale, sweetish-sour odor was overpowering; and when Aunt Erica began to cry, sobs racking her limp body, Magdalena began to cry, too; for she was so tender-hearted, the sight of another's tears always provoked her own.

"—I'm so h-happy to be here, Aunt Erica—th-thank you for inviting me—"

But at this point the nurse stepped brusquely forward as if she'd been waiting for just such a development. Adjusting the quilt higher on the invalid's shoulders, and scolding, "Now you see, Mrs. Kistenmacher, didn't I warn you?—a night of bad nerves, and now you've made yourself feverish over this girl you don't even know."

What a surprise to Magdalena Schön, for the first time in her sixteen years she had a room to herself.

On the third floor of the beautiful old Federal-style house on Charter Street, Edmundston, with a view of the river approximately a mile away, to the south; and, if she leaned out her window, craning her neck, of the ocean several miles to the east, a vaporous strip of light alternately silver, blue-green, plum-colored, black. She knew this was the fabled "Atlantic Ocean" though she hadn't truly seen it since the morning the train had brought her into Edmundston; a dreamlike morning itself now rapidly retreating into the past.

There were hours when Magdalena was lonely in her neat, clean, attractive room at the top of the Kistenmacher house; but she was not homesick. She did not believe she would ever be homesick for the crowded rooms of Black Rock.

Though sometimes in the night by lamplight she read her prayer book, which had been a gift for her confirmation in the Roman Catholic faith from her parents, her lips silently and urgently moving. Sometimes she fell asleep with her rosary entwined in her fingers and woke in the morning startled to discover the crystal beads stretched snakelike across her throat.

Her Aunt Erica did not attend church of any kind, having the excuse of being an invalid. "If God wants to seek me out, He knows where I am," the elderly woman one day whispered to Magdalena, with a wink of her good eye. Magdalena laughed at such witty boldness though she was inwardly shocked—a little.

Perhaps, sending her off to Edmundston, so far away, Magdalena's parents had tacitly assumed she would drift away from the faith of the Schöns. Not once, she realized, had they cautioned her about seeking out a church where she could attend mass. *Neither one of them loved me, they sent me away.* But why was Magdalena dry-eyed? Her heart beat rapidly with another kind of excitement.

The tall, narrow, lattice-paned windows of Magdalena's room were the most wonderful thing about the room, emitting light in the early morning from the direction of the river. Even as she slept this warm light entered her sleep, beckoning to her. *Wake! Wake! Hurry! Come!* She seemed to hear a voice lifted in song, unknown to her; neither male nor female; clear as struck glass, unspeakably beautiful. *Magdalena, come!* In the white lace-trimmed cotton nightgown her aunt had provided for her, barefoot, her waist-long hair in loose dense wavy coils down her back, Magdalena tiptoed to a window to gaze out in wonder. These spring days, the sky was likely to be brilliantly blue, or layered in fine-etched clouds of subtle gradations of silver; the sun shone warmly, or a light rain fell, or a heavy rain buffeted by winds and laced with lightning. How new, how fresh, every morning, how Magdalena's eyes stared! Not wishing to recall how for all of her life until just recently, five hundred miles westward in Black Rock she'd shared sleeping quarters with others, often a bed with a sister, or two sisters; the windows of the ground-floor tenement flat in which the Schöns lived, impossible to keep clean, looked out grudgingly upon a weather-stained ruin of a wall next door, or upon a potholed, muddy street, or a trash-filled vacant lot; there had been nothing to see, and so she had trained herself to see nothing. Here in the Kistenmacher house she was obliged to share her room with no one, a pretty girl's room of filmy white curtains, white walls and white satin fabrics; she was obliged to share her thoughts with no one. She would not be judged, she would not be found wanting, she would not be scolded, she would not be slapped, she would not be the object of family pity—*Leave Magdalena alone, she can't help it.*

From every angle at her window in the early morning light she saw a beautiful sight, or a curious sight, or an intriguing sight. Gazing out upon cobblestone streets steeply falling away from view like streets in a child's storybook, the cobblestones often glistening with rain fallen during the night; one morning in early April she saw flocks of robins bathing themselves in puddles in the street, and heard the high, sweet, many-times-repeated cries of other birds she could not recognize, with crested heads and olive-grey

feathers; she heard the curious clawlike cries of seagulls; she studied the roofs of neighboring houses, all of them as old as the
Kistenmacher house, and most of them considerably larger and in
better repair, and she wondered at the lives within; her eyes moved
upon tall handsome chimneys of brick and stone; and tall, graceful,
green-budding trees she believed to be elms; and in the near distance, downhill from Charter Street, there were several church
spires that gleamed fiercely in the sun and even on overcast days
were luminous as if lit from within by their own secret light. And
there was the river, and the bridge that spanned the river, partly
obscured from Magdalena's view by buildings; the bridge that
drew Magdalena's eye again, and again. The river, she'd learned,
was the Merrimack River, and the bridge was the Merrimack
Bridge; beyond the bridge was a part of the city known as "lower
Edmundston" or simply "lower town"—the waterfront area of tenement buildings, aged buildings (like the Old Custom House) dating
to colonial times, warehouses and fisheries, docks, boats of all sizes
and types from small fishing boats to ocean freighters. All of the
female occupants of the house on Charter Street, including even
the invalid mistress of the house, were prone to speak of "lower
town" with an air of unease, as if "lower town" might be inhabited
by dangerous persons. Magdalena had the idea none of them had
ever visited it.

(Yet hadn't Aunt Erica's husband Mr. Kistenmacher, deceased
now for eighteen years, had dealings as a broker with shipping
lines that operated out of Edmundston harbor? Of the meager
facts about the man that Magdalena had gathered, this was one
that intrigued her.)

In this time of surprises the most remarkable and in some ways
the most disconcerting was Magdalena's immediate discovery that,
in her great-aunt's house, as niece and "companion," she had so little to do.

"Aunt Erica, *I* can do that," Magdalena said eagerly, at their first
meal in a small formal dining room, when the maid Hannah
appeared out of the pantry to clear away plates; but Aunt Erica

patted Magdalena's wrist as one might subdue a headstrong child, shaping with her lips the admonishment "No."

"But, Aunt Erica, at home—"

The older woman squeezed Magdalena's wrist to silence her, so that somber, sturdy Hannah in her dark dress and stiff-starched white apron wouldn't hear. Her hoarse, cracked voice was almost fierce—"*This* is your home, dear child, and there are new rules here."

It stunned Magdalena to realize she wasn't to be a servant after all.

Of course she'd assumed, as her parents had assumed, that she would be "helping out" her aunt. Of all her sisters and brothers, Magdalena was the most cooperative, good-natured and uncomplaining about household chores; her happiest memories of home were preparing meals with her mother, rolling and cutting noodle dough, baking brown bread; even laundry day which involved hours of tedious back-aching labor, including hanging wet, heavy men's coveralls, denim jackets and work-shirts, sheets, quilts, blankets on a straining rope in the back yard, had not fazed her. Magdalena had been a strong, capable worker even as a child; she'd liked to take orders from her mother and older sisters because it was a way of pleasing them. A way of being loved.

Now in the house on Charter Street she was "Miss Schön" to the real servants. Apart from cleaning her own room and washing out her clothes, which she insisted upon doing, she had no tasks other than being a companion to her aunt, and this involved only a few hours of the day, depending upon Aunt Erica's health and disposition. Magdalena sat with her and talked, or listened to the older woman speak in her rambling, disconnected way; sometimes Magdalena read poetry, mainly verse by women poets of whom she'd never heard, or the Bible; though gazing at her intently with her good eye, Aunt Erica would soon fall asleep, her face slack and mouth wetly agape in an expression of childlike surrender. Magdalena didn't know whether to continue reading, or tiptoe quietly away; she guessed that her aunt took comfort from her mere presence and could hear her words even while asleep. *If I have the power to make Aunt Erica happy* she thought. Once, while Magdalena was reading poetry, her aunt fell into a doze and began to hum in a singsong rhythm, the right side of her pale, wrinkled, doll-like face suffused with tenderness. Without opening her eyes, Aunt Erica murmured, "The music of your voice, child. My own childhood in it."

Magdalena doubted this: she was an American-born girl. Except by an accident of family, she was not "German."

At such times the dour-faced nurse, whose name sounded like "Helge," remained close by in an adjoining room, knitting; the rapid click of her needles sounded, to Magdalena's sensitive ear, censorious. Except for a few hours a week, Helge seemed always to be on duty; she was devoted to her patient, if often exasperated with her, as if Mrs. Kistenmacher was a willful child who needed constant watching. Helge had taken up residence in the Kistenmacher house after Mrs. Kistenmacher's stroke nearly two years before. Clearly she was jealous of Magdalena and resented her presence in the household, her place in the invalid's affections, and Magdalena supposed she could not blame her. Not once had Helge smiled at Magdalena, nor would she call her "Magdalena" as the girl had asked. Aunt Erica would embarrass them both by addressing Helge in her rasping, urgent voice, "Isn't she pretty, Helge? She's come to *me*—I knew she would. Do you like her hair? I wore my hair like this, too—when I was a girl." The nurse's slitted eyes moved onto Magdalena for the briefest fraction of a second; her nostrils pinched; she could not be induced to reply to such ridiculous remarks but said, with dignity, "Well. It's time for your nap, Mrs. Kistenmacher. You've made yourself feverish, Dr. Meinke will have to be told." Between the nurse and her invalid patient was the figure of the formidable Dr. Meinke, who came to the house on Charter Street to examine Mrs. Kistenmacher every ten or twelve days.

Sometimes Magdalena had breakfast with her aunt, and sometimes a midday meal called "dinner" at 2 P.M.; these meals were served in the smaller of the two dining rooms downstairs, or, if she was feeling unwell, in Aunt Erica's airless overheated bedroom on the second floor. Walking with a cane and assisted by Helge and Magdalena, Aunt Erica insisted upon being "up"—"up and dressed"—as often as her strength allowed; she could not manage stairs, of course, but the house was equipped with an elevator. This was an alarmingly creaky cagelike structure that could hold no more than two people comfortably. Required to ride with her aunt in the elevator, while Helge grimly trod the stairs, Magdalena felt suffocated, panicked. *What if we're trapped in here together? What if we fall?* It was the first elevator in which Magdalena had ever ridden and she'd heard that terrible accidents happened sometimes, elevators stuck between floors or falling down shafts, crushing their occupants. By the time the little cage creaked to a stop, and Magdalena fumbled for the latticework door to unlatch it and swing it open, and help her aunt shuffle out, she was breathless and trembling.

Aunt Erica whispered, "Thank you, dear! You're so kind." Gripping Magdalena's wrist with her claw-fingers.

Meals shared with her aunt were awkward for Magdalena because the older woman ate so slowly. Dinner, invariably a hot, heavy meal in the German style, might last more than an hour, at the end of which Aunt Erica would have eaten only a few morsels. At these times Magdalena was acutely conscious of the nurse Helge hovering just outside the door, and of Hannah in the pantry, waiting for her mistress to ring a little silver bell to summon her. (Hannah also prepared meals, a duty she took very seriously. Magdalena had several times offered to help her but had always been rejected: "Miss Schön, *I* am Mrs. Kistenmacher's cook.") On Mondays there came to the house on Charter street a husky red-haired woman of about forty named Mavis who did laundry and heavy cleaning, and this woman was friendly with Hannah, who hired her, and often Magdalena could hear the two whispering and laughing together, in Magdalena's very presence. One day at dinner, Magdalena was miserable hearing Hannah and Mavis in the pantry, peeking through the swinging door at her, and under the pretext of seeking out a glass of fresh ice water for her aunt, before the older woman could ring her little bell, Magdalena stormed out into the pantry and confronted her startled tormentors—"Why don't you like me? What have I ever done to you?" Tears brimmed in the girl's eyes but the women turned away embarrassed and sullen.

Following that, relations between Magdalena and the household staff would be more strained than ever.

Aunt Erica, aware of far more that happened under her roof than one might imagine of one with sight and hearing deficiencies, scolded Magdalena for such behavior—"Child, it isn't *fitting.*" Her admonishments were playful but accompanied by light slaps on Magdalena's wrist clearly meant to evoke more solid blows.

On the second Sunday of Magdalena's residence at the house on Charter Street, her aunt invited a number of people for "afternoon tea." Magdalena was surprised to learn that Erica Kistenmacher knew so many people. What a flurry of faces, names, handshakes! The majority of the visitors were women of her aunt's age, widows like her, and neighbors; but there were gentlemen as well, former business associates of the late Mr. Kistenmacher, and legal and financial advisors of Mrs. Kistenmacher; and the formidable Dr. Meinke, white-haired and garrulous. Among the guests was a youngish man of about twenty-seven, a junior associate of Mrs. Kistenmacher's accountant, whom eventually Magdalena Schön would marry; but, at the time of their first meeting, Magdalena scarcely heard his name in her confusion, and scarcely saw his face, and forgot him, as she forgot most of the others, almost immediately afterward.

3.

Now the day is over
Night is drawing nigh
Shadows of the evening . . .

From her room at the top of the brick house on Charter Street Magdalena Schön looked out restlessly upon the mysterious city of Edmundston. Repeatedly her attention was drawn to the

Merrimack River glittering like a snake's scales, and the Merrimack Bridge that seemed almost to beckon to her. Now the weather had turned warmer, now the evenings were longer, she dared to open her windows wide, and leaned out, breathing in an intoxicating fragrance of lilac laced with fresh, chill gusts of air from the ocean. Her eyes were widened, sharpened. It seemed to her that she could see vividly a long distance, as in hazy-gloomy Black Rock where the air was singed with smoke and fumes from the iron foundry, she'd hardly been able to see a quarter mile. And how acutely she could hear!—sounds from miles away.

Crystal-like chimes of a church's bell. And another bell deeper, more solemnly tolling like a great, ponderous heart.

A rougher, more rhythmic music—an accordion?

A beautiful voice, lifted in song. Difficult to determine at this distance if it was male or female. *Now the day is over, night is drawing nigh* . . . The voice was blown on the wind, now distinct, now fading. She leaned out her window dangerously far, cupping a hand to her ear like her deaf Aunt Erica. How exquisite, how beautiful this music, how it called to her: *Magdalena, come! Hurry!*

These sounds were wafted to her from the direction of the Merrimack Bridge, and beyond: "lower Edmundston," "lower town."

"Just for a walk. Just for an hour."

So Magdalena told herself, late one afternoon when the commingled smells of lilac and the sea made her blood rush so she felt almost faint with longing. And her pretty shimmering-white room at the top of the house on Charter Street seemed to her a box, a cage, suffocating.

"I won't go far, I promise. I won't get lost. . . ."

It would be Magdalena's first venture outside of the house on Charter Street since her arrival weeks before. Out of the high, hilly residential district of dignified old houses and elegant tree-lined cobblestone streets. Out of the fair, blossom-fragrant air of upper Edmundston and into the denser, more brackish air of lower Edmundston. Magdalena had spent more time than usual with Aunt Erica that day, both in the morning and in the early afternoon following dinner; now she was free for what remained of the day, and eager to have her adventure. Draping a russet-red silk shawl around her shoulders, one of her aunt's numerous gifts; leaving her head bare, despite the wind and the uncertain spring sky, alternately bright with sun and roiling with thunder-bearing clouds. She should have waited for a calmer day, she knew, but her pulse raced, she was filled with longing, yearning, for—what?

"Just for a walk, really. I promise not to get lost."

Like a guilty child she was explaining herself to Aunt Erica, who, if she knew, would have disapproved. *Not fitting, child! Not fit for a lady, to walk on foot into lower town!*

But Aunt Erica had retired for the day, even now Aunt Erica was napping in her room that smelled of talcum, medicine and mildew, blinds drawn tight against the afternoon sun. Even as Magdalena had been reading to her from the Bible, the Book of Psalms, the old woman lapsed by degrees into a light, snoring doze, her papery-white doll's face empty of expression. Magdalena had gazed upon her aunt with sympathy, yet horror. She'd calculated that Erica Kistenmacher wasn't so very old—in her late sixties. And you could see that once, not so long ago, she'd been a youthful attractive woman with eyes, a sweet mouth. Magdalena shivered despite the overheated room thinking *I will never be so old! I will never be you, Aunt Erica!*

A grandfather clock in the hall was quietly chiming the hour of five o'clock as, stealthy as a cat, Magdalena descended the stairs from the third floor to the second, and from the second floor to the first. Except, in the foyer, at the front door, she had difficulty working the lock. Glimpsing Magdalena as she passed in the hall, Hannah called out, startled, "Miss Schön! Where are you going?" Magdalena said, guiltily, "Just for a walk, Hannah. In the neighborhood." Hannah approached, her hands folded in her stiff-starched white apron; she was frowning as if she had more to say, but did not speak at first. Magdalena's cheeks burned pleasurably—it was the first time Hannah had spoken so directly to her, and looked her full in the face. Magdalena said, "I won't get lost, I promise. I won't go far." Hannah hesitated, biting her thin lower lip; then murmured,

"Here, miss. I'll get the lock. You'll have to ring to be let back in, you know. This door is always double-bolted."

So Magdalena escaped the house on Charter Street, walking downhill in the fresh warm lilac-intoxicated air, trusting to instinct to make her way toward the Merrimack Bridge. Noting how, before long, the houses she passed were smaller, less "historic"; there were woodframe bungalows, row houses, shops and stores and a wide, traffic-heavy street called Fayette, upon which streetcars clattered. This street led to the Merrimack Bridge which Magdalena crossed with some hesitation, for she had to walk on a narrow, mesh-floored pedestrian walk of a kind she'd never seen before, beneath which, all too visibly, the river rushed, not luminous or glittering in sunlight but slate-colored, oily-looking. How harsh the river smelled, close up—there was no fragrance of lilacs here. And how noisy the waves, not rhythmic, slapping at the stained foundations of the bridge. Magdalena crossed with a rapidly beating heart, wondering if she should be doing this; so far from the beautiful old house on Charter Street, and from the safety of her window on the third floor; there, she'd had no idea of how broad, how windswept, how formidable a presence the river was; across the distance, the Merrimack Bridge had looked almost delicate, its vertical girders like lacework; up close of course they were heavy, coarse, and badly rusted; and traffic rumbled past noisily, in a continuous stream of enormous trucks, delivery vans, automobiles out of which the eyes of strangers moved upon Magdalena bareheaded in the wind, wrapped in a russet-red silk shawl, hurrying on foot in a place where few pedestrians walked. *Hey! Girl! Want a ride, girl?* Magdalena didn't hear, staring down transfixed at the mesh walkway before her and the river rushing beneath like destiny.

Noises on the bridge were so distracting that Magdalena no longer heard any music; by the time she reached the other side of the river, panting, wiping grit from her eyes, adjusting her windblown hair and clothing, she'd forgotten the music; and, beginning to hear it again as she turned onto a street of row houses and small commercial shops, she was surprised and gladdened. Not a single music but numerous musics, predominantly now the rollicking rhythmic sound of an organ grinder, which made her smile, and led her into a neighborhood of crowded brownstone buildings in which tenants leaned out of upstairs windows shouting gaily to one another in the street, and rough, dark-haired but beautiful children played boisterously in the street, and men in shirtsleeves sat smoking in front of their shops, and gathered at corners where there were taverns. How like Havass Street in Black Rock—Magdalena smiled to see a greengrocer's shop, and a baker's, and a tailor's, and a butcher's; she shut her eyes as she passed the butcher's, smelling familiar odors of raw meat, blood, sawdust. Often she'd been sent on errands to the butcher's and had had to endure the butcher's rough teasing, and the sights of things in his shop, shiny, squirmy, glistening, oozing blood, her eyes refused to see. But the language or languages Magdalena was hearing spoken here were not familiar to her, not English, not German, not Hungarian though similar to these languages. Nor were most of the people fair-skinned like her but darker in complexion, or olive-pale, with black hair, gleaming black eyes. And how they looked at her, the men's eyes cast like nets at her. At an outdoor café men sat at tables playing cards, smoking and drinking and talking loudly among themselves and as Magdalena passed by on the sidewalk she was aware of their voices dropping to murmurs, or silence; and, in her wake, resuming again, with an intensity she didn't want to consider. She noted how couples walked openly here, arms around each other's waists—a sight you would never see in Black Rock.

The source of the rollicking organ music was in a side street narrow as an alley, where an elderly white-haired man sat on a stoop playing a hand organ for a small gathering of appreciative listeners, mostly children. How happy, how thrilling, the organ grinder's music—there was nothing like it in Black Rock!

Yet Magdalena walked restlessly on, drawn by the smell of water, and found herself in a riverfront area of warehouses, docks, fishing boats; for some fascinated minutes she watched men gutting fish on the dock, and wondered that she wasn't repelled; everywhere was a strong garbagey odor of fish. Yet she thought, standing at the end of a dock, shading her eyes staring into the infinite distance, *I can breathe here.*

Still Magdalena walked on, hearing the mysterious words *Now the day is over, night is drawing nigh* . . . borne on a gust of wind. Soon she found herself in a neighborhood of very old, mostly abandoned buildings with part-collapsed roofs, and thistles and young trees growing everywhere in profusion; no one appeared to be living here now. Over the street was a curious carved archway across which monkeylike figures scuttled daringly, giggling; seeing Magdalena, they whistled and hooted at her, and vanished. Children?

As Magdalena stared upward, a handful of pebbles fell at her feet. She hoped they hadn't been meant for her.

Quickly Magdalena walked on, climbing a steep hill at the top of which was a very old church made of crude, weatherworn stone; the singing seemed to be issuing from the rear of this church, so Magdalena hiked into the churchyard, a tangle of wild rose and briars amid which grave markers tilted at crazy angles. On the markers were chiseled words too faint to be discerned but the numerals were clearer—1712, 1723, 1693. Magdalena stared. So long ago! She had been born in 1912. It made her feel dizzy to contemplate the emptiness before she'd come into being, like a geometry problem of incalculable complexity.

The singer was close by, voice lifting in pure, heartrending sound. A tenor voice. Singing a church hymn, obviously a Protestant hymn, not known to Magdalena. *Now the day is over, night is drawing nigh* . . . There was a shadowy recess where the church walls formed a three-sided rectangle with the crumbling stone wall of the churchyard; or perhaps it was an actual entrance into the interior of the church; the singer stood just inside, oddly in the dark, practicing, rehearsing. A young man, Magdalena thought. She strained to see him without drawing too close, her heart beating quickly. *Shadows of the evening . . . steal across the sky.* There was a pause, and a sound of hoarse breathing, and again the song resumed, at the same pitch and in the same tempo. *Now the day* . . . This time there seemed to be a just-perceptible strain to the singer's voice, an undercurrent of agitation, though it was no less beautiful than before, and perhaps even more beautiful. Magdalena listened, transfixed. She seemed to know that the young tenor would be handsome, dark-haired like the men she'd been seeing in lower Edmundston, with bright dark eyes, thick-lashed eyes. Yet she was fearful of revealing herself to him, even to walk casually across the churchyard so that she could, by glancing sideways, peer into the church. He might abruptly cease his singing if he knew he was being heard. And Magdalena had no business in the churchyard of a Protestant church, after all.

But she listened for a daringly long time, taking care to keep herself hidden, until at last she crept stealthily away, for it was nearing dusk.

Thinking, as she made her way back to Charter Street, to the high, hilly residential neighborhood above Edmundston and to the massive front door of her aunt's house at which she had to ring the bell to be admitted, *Who is he? What does he look like? Why didn't I try to see him, at least?*

4.

So it happened that Magdalena Schön fell in love. Though she was never to acknowledge the fact.

Hearing the singer's seductive voice not only as she stood leaning out her window lifting her face to the fresh, gusty air, but as she slept in her bed of white linens, white satin and wool; and during the day, at odd, unpredictable moments elsewhere in her aunt's house; sometimes even in Aunt Erica's presence as the old woman hoarsely, excitedly chattered. So faint as to be almost inaudible, yet unmistakable. *Now the day is over . . . Shadows of the evening . . .* She who had not once felt homesick for Black Rock, for the crowded rooms of her childhood, nor even for her parents, sisters and brothers she believed she had loved, now felt a heart-longing for lower Edmundston; for the Merrimack River and the Merrimack Bridge and the waterfront docks and the ancient weather-stained church with its crazily tilting grave markers and the faceless singer in the church whose surpassingly beautiful voice haunted her like the very beat, beat, beat of her blood. Again and again he sang his utterly simple verse. *Now the day is over . . . Now the day is over . . .*

One afternoon Aunt Erica broke off her rambling, not very coherent chatter to smile at Magdalena puckishly with half her mouth, and exclaimed, "Dear child, are you thinking about your family? Are you lonely for your family?" And Magdalena roused herself, with a vague smile, as if not knowing where she was exactly, and said, "Oh, Aunt Erica, he has such a high, clear, strong voice. It's a man's voice, but not like one you would ever hear."

> *Now the day is over, night is drawing nigh . . .*
> *Magdalena, come!*

Another afternoon of gusty clouds, distant music. Magdalena slipped away from the house on Charter Street, and retraced her steps to lower Edmundston; to the ancient church where again the mysterious singer was practicing his hymn. This time Magdalena saw that there was no sign on the front of the church; no indication of its denomination; the stone cross on its roof, crude and weather-stained, yet possessing its own primitive beauty, had partly collapsed, forming hardly more than a T. Moss grew in rakish patches on the roof of rotted shingles. There was but a single window in the building, deep set in the stained stone wall. The church must have been very poor, in such need of repair. Yet the tenor was singing as before, more deliberately perhaps, as if determined to perfect his song. *Now the day is over, night is drawing nigh . . . Shadows of the evening steal across the sky.* Magdalena heard the agitation, the passion in the voice not discernible at a distance; when the singer paused, she could hear him panting for breath. She dared to approach the alcove, her heart beating very hard, and saw at last the shadowy figure within. It was indeed a young man; a handsome young man, or so he appeared in the indistinct light; he was standing at the front of the little church near the altar, his body tense; his hands gripped into fists; tendons standing out in his neck. She felt a sensation of profound yearning pass over her, a swooning sensation of a kind she'd never before felt, as if the very earth beneath her feet were shifting; as if all volition had been drained from her. She thought *I must help him!*

As the young man sang he moved his head restlessly from side to side, and ran his fingers through his hair, which was, as Magdalena had envisioned, black hair; thick, lustrous black hair. His skin was olive-pale, rather waxy; despite his beautiful voice, there was something unhealthy about him; he blinked his eyes repeatedly, as if trying to clear his vision. Magdalena came closer, waiting for him to see her. Her heart was pounding so violently she believed she might faint, yet she couldn't turn back. *I must, I must help him. That's why I have come.* There was a rich, ripe smell of decay inside the church, an earthy, stale smell that contrasted sharply with the smell of the outdoors and the fresh gusty air blown from the east. When the young man paused in his singing, licking his lips, Magdalena said hesitantly, "Excuse me, but—what a beautiful song. I've never heard such a beautiful song."

The young man turned to stare at Magdalena, or in her direction. Clearly he was distracted, confused; he'd believed himself alone, and she had intruded. For a moment Magdalena feared he would ask her to leave, or turn away in anger himself; but finally he smiled, a faint, hurried smile, and returned to his singing. He was standing alone at the altar, his chin somewhat raised and his head slightly back, the tendons in his slender neck prominent as before, and his hands shut into fists. Magdalena saw his body tremble as he sang. *Now the day is over, night is drawing nigh* . . . Magdalena came closer, seeing that the young man gazed at her as he sang, through his dark, thick lashes; she thought, perhaps, he was singing to her now, as if speaking to her through these mysterious, exquisite words. For some minutes he continued to sing, and Magdalena stood transfixed listening. For now the song was yet more beautiful and seductive. Magdalena, too, stood with her hands shut into fists; a pulse beat hard in her left temple, as in the singer's; and another pulse, an artery, beat in her throat, as in the singer's. Magdalena had draped her aunt's russet-red silk shawl around her shoulders before setting off to lower Edmundston, but the wind had blown it loose; she had a vague awareness that her meticulously plaited hair was coming undone. So, too, the singer shook hair out of his eyes, and when he finished his verse Magdalena saw that his pale, intense face was damp with perspiration; his skin appeared almost translucent. Without needing to be summoned, Magdalena boldly hurried to him, a stranger, and standing on tiptoe wiped his heated face with a handkerchief; a freshly laundered white linen handkerchief her aunt had given her, which she then carefully folded and returned to her pocket. "Thank you," the singer murmured almost inaudibly; without smiling; and began to sing again, and again completed his verse, though on a somewhat strained note; or so it seemed to Magdalena, who watched his face anxiously and saw his expression of dissatisfaction. In a vague, impatient gesture, as of self-loathing, the singer indicated his throat as if meaning he was thirsty; his throat was dry, parched. Magdalena understood at once, saying, "Wait!" and hurried out of the church to find drinking water . . . for hadn't she noticed, on her way into the churchyard, an old stone well amid the tall grasses, with a crank handle and a wooden pitcher? She located the well, and leaned over it to sniff the water within, which was so deep inside the earth she couldn't see even a glimmer of a reflection. How icy-cold, how pure and good the water smelled; and how eagerly Magdalena drew a pitcher of it up, with her strong, capable arms, to bring to the singer awaiting her inside the church.

He drank from the pitcher thirsty as an animal, his eyes nearly shut in a kind of ecstasy. Handing it then back to Magdalena, and indicating that she, too, should drink, since water remained; and so she did; and never had she tasted water so delicious, feeling as before her very soul swoon as if all volition had been sucked from her. How happy she was! The happiest she'd been since leaving Black Rock, since leaving her mother's kitchen where her joy had been in doing as she was instructed, and doing it well. She saw the singer gaze upon her with gratitude and interest as he murmured, again almost inaudibly, "Thank you." Magdalena smiled, blushing; she could think of nothing to say to him except, "Will you be singing here—on Sunday? Are you practicing for Sunday?" The young man smiled sadly at her, with a shrug of his shoulders; he was tall, with a proud, erect posture, yet thin; his shoulders were thin; he spoke in a lowered, hoarse voice, as if he half feared being overheard by someone other than Magdalena, and half invited it, "I must sing, I have no choice." Magdalena wasn't sure she'd heard correctly, and so could think of no reply. Turning from her, the singer began again, now pacing about in front of the altar, with more vigor, self-assurance. *Now the day is over, night is drawing nigh . . . Shadows of the evening steal across the sky.* Surely this time he'd sung it perfectly? Surely now he could go on to the next verse? But no, the singer shrugged again irritably, and brushed his hair out of his eyes with a violent gesture. He said, in his speaking voice which was so curiously flat, hoarse, hushed, as if his throat hurt him, "I am happy only when I am singing, and singing exhausts me."

Magdalena found herself sitting in a pew at the front of the church, not noticing that the pew was broken, filthy with cobwebs. In a state of ecstasy she listened as the singer continued his painstaking practicing, grim and determined yet singing with passion; his eyes were very black as if all pupil, fixed and glassy, turned inward. At last he broke off again, a gleaming film of perspiration on his pale face, and Magdalena hurried to wipe it away. He caught hold of her wrist and held her, and said, "How kind you are! What is your name?" and Magdalena told him, and he said, "A beautiful name. My name is—" speaking a sibilant word that Magdalena didn't catch, and was too shy to ask him to repeat. Magdalena said, "Where do you live?" and the young man said, with a twitch of his lips, "I live here," and it wasn't clear to her what he meant—for surely he didn't live in the church. Or possibly he'd spoken ironically. He asked where she lived, and Magdalena bit her lower lip, and said, "I don't have any home really. My mother sent me away, she didn't love me." Unexpectedly she confided in this stranger, for he was gazing at her with such compassion; tears filled her eyes; she heard herself saying, "There were too many mouths to feed, I think. It would not have been possible for any of us to die." What a strange thing to say! Yet the young man was not

surprised, frowning, saying, "Yes, it is the way of all nature—too
many mouths. Which is why I sing, Magdalena." Again, Magdalena
didn't understand; but dared not reveal her ignorance. The young
man said, "Will you stay with me awhile? Will you help me, Magdalena?" and Magdalena said eagerly, "Help you? How?" and he
said, "Stay with me! I have only a little way to go, to get it right."
And so he sang again, more passionately than ever; and Magdalena
listened enchanted. For now, surely, he'd perfected the verse? She
could not imagine anything more beautiful. But he broke off, and
shook his head sadly; Magdalena offered him the pitcher of water,
in which some remained, forgetting that she'd drunk from it; he
waved it aside without seeming to see. He said, "I began to sing because I wanted to sing, and now I sing because I am made to sing."
Magdalena said, naively, "But who makes you?"—for she could see
no one else anywhere near. The church was empty except for the
singer and herself; the churchyard was empty, with a look of aban-
donment and desolation; beyond the part-collapsed stone wall of
the churchyard there was a steep drop, and rocky land below
obscured by mist, and the sound of restless, choppy waves—
the ocean, so close? But no human figures, no human inhabitants.
Only gulls circling above, emitting cries of hunger. The singer was
pacing about before the altar, though scarcely aware of his surroundings; repeatedly he found his way blocked by a pew, or the
communion rail or the minister's pulpit, and so moved blindly
around it, frowning, his mouth twitching. As much to himself as to
Magdalena he said, "My father sang, and his father; it was their
fate, too. They died young—it's said. I never knew them of course.
They died of burst arteries. In their throats." He stroked his slender, pale throat; gently he stroked the sinewy blue artery that
Magdalena had noticed swelling as he'd sung. "It's said to be a
curse. But I don't believe in curses." Magdalena shivered, for there
was a rising wind; by quick degrees it was growing dusk; though
now the season was well into spring, and the evenings were longer.
She said, "How can I help you?" and the young man said, with a
sudden boyish, hopeful smile, "Sing with me, Magdalena!"
    Magdalena was astonished. Sing? With such a gifted singer?

"But—"

"Yes, you must! Then my strength will be doubled."

So, shyly, reluctantly, Magdalena tried to sing. She, who had never sung before in her life except privately to herself, or in the company of sisters, singing with this commanding young man as he clasped her hand in his and gazed into her eyes. *Now the day is over . . . Night is drawing nigh . . .* But Magdalena's voice was too weak; the young man broke off so that they could begin again. *Now the day is over . . . Night is drawing . . .* But again something was wrong, Magdalena's cheeks burned with shame of her breathy, thin, girl's voice; though she tried to sing with as much accuracy and strength as she could summon, hers was a wholly untrained voice, lacking pitch, solidity, beauty. Oh, most of all beauty! The young man winced as if he felt actual pain at the sound of her voice and abruptly broke off, pushing her hand from his. Bitterly he said, "You're not trying, Magdalena!" and Magdalena stammered, in childlike protest, "But—I am. I am." But the young man had turned away, sullenly, saying, "Go away and leave me, you mock me."

So Magdalena was sent away, hurt and mortified.

So Magdalena fled the little church, and the churchyard, and lower Edmundston, tears streaking her cheeks.

Hearing, behind her, a pounding, reverberating silence like the waves of an invisible sea; a silence that beat against her eardrums like a great heartbeat, threatening to drown her. And beneath this silence the voice of the singer, not so strong as before, but as exquisite as ever. *Now the day is over, night is drawing nigh. Shadows of the evening . . .* And at the house on Charter Street, in the gathering dusk, she had to ring the bell (which was erratic, defective) for some minutes before grumbling Hannah came to unlock it, to let her, weeping, inside.

5.

"What—what is this *thing*! This encumbrance that is always with me!"

Suddenly in the midst of Magdalena reading the Ninety-sixth Psalm to her, Aunt Erica began slapping and pushing at her limp left arm with the clawlike fingers of her right hand. A fury seemed to seize her, like a flame passing over her frail, doll-like body; she began to cry in high-pitched angry sobs. Helge who had been knitting close by threw down her needles and hurried to her, as Magdalena, sitting on a stool by her aunt's divan, stared at the stricken woman in astonishment. Helge said, chiding, "Now, Mrs. Kistenmacher! Now you know what that is," and Aunt Erica cried, "I don't! I don't *know!*" and Helge said, "Yes, you do, Mrs. Kistenmacher. Say it: 'my arm,' " and Aunt Erica shrieked, *"No."* Using the strength of her right arm and legs, the elderly woman was trying desperately to push herself up the back of the divan, like a wounded, blindly flailing creature; her eyes bulged in their sockets. Magdalena watched in horror. What could she do? How could she help? Helge had seized Aunt Erica's right hand to calm it, and her; she placed the hand firmly on the left hand which hung useless at the invalid's side, in a way that suggested she'd done in the past. She said, "You see? This is your hand, too, Mrs. Kistenmacher. This is your arm, too. *It is all you,*" and Aunt Erica whispered, "No! *It is not,*" though ceasing her futile struggle, and Helge said, "You mustn't turn against yourself, Mrs. Kistenmacher. Dr. Meinke has told you."

For a moment it seemed that the elderly invalid had returned to her senses. She was panting, and staring at her left arm in its crocheted pink woolen sleeve; experimentally she released the left hand from her right hand, and leaned as far away on the divan as possible without losing her balance. Then her moist little rosebud mouth opened like a bird's beak and her good, right eye narrowed to a squint and as Magdalena and Helge looked on, helpless, she began to scream, and scream.

6.

Magdalena thought *He has sent me away, I must never approach him again.*

Magdalena thought *I failed him: he detests me.*

Magdalena thought, sifting her shiny black rosary beads through her fingers *God, give me strength not to approach him again. God, give me pride.*

And so for days Magdalena obsessively barricaded the windows of her room against the gusty sunshine and tumult of spring. She made certain that the windows were shut tight, and locked; and the blinds drawn flush to the sills. During the day she avoided windows elsewhere in the house whenever possible and didn't dare go outside, even to walk about the grounds. At night she slept poorly, pillows pressed against her ears; though she could hear little beyond the anxious pulsing of her own blood, she imagined the singer's voice with unnerving clarity as if he were standing, not miles away in a deserted church, but just outside her bedroom door. *Now the day is over . . . Night is drawing . . .*

Fiercely Magdalena whispered to herself, "No!"

The wind off the river was damp, chill, smelling of something brackish and metallic. Invisible grit was driven into Magdalena's face, stinging her eyes. How ugly the river looked, the color of molten lead, reflecting a heavy leaden sky. And the riverfront structures and boats, how shabby, derelict. Magdalena was hurrying across Merrimack Bridge, breathless and shivering. Despite the bridge traffic and the harsh lapping sounds of the river she could hear distinctly the young man singing, calling to her. It seemed he was singing with a renewed passion, or desperation. And had he not pleaded with her, *Will you help me, Magdalena?*

This time, Magdalena was determined not to fail him.

Where are you going, child? Aunt Erica had asked, playfully tapping Magdalena's arm. *Your thoughts are flying away from here, and where?* Magdalena had murmured, embarrassed, that she was going for a walk; just in the neighborhood; it was such a beautiful May afternoon (for so the weather had been beautiful, in the hilly district above Edmundston); she promised she wouldn't go far. And Aunt Erica had laughed, her good eye cold twinkling, saying *I don't go far, there's two of us.*

And so Magdalena made her way along the rough riverfront streets, and into the older, deserted neighborhood, and to the old church at the top of a hill. She saw to her surprise that the church-yard was more overgrown and desolate than she recalled, as if a storm had swept violently through it. Dead tree limbs lay scattered amid the graves, smashed urns, numerous gravestones overturned, severely cracked. Beyond the stone wall where there should have been land, Magdalena saw, as before, an opaque wall of undulating mist, more oppressive than before as it seemed to be quivering with its own malevolent life. And beyond the mist was—the open sea? The great Atlantic Ocean that had so broken her parents, and others who'd made the crossing, they never wished to see or speak of it again? Magdalena could see no water but believed she could hear, beyond the tenor's strained, hopeful voice, its forceful ar-rhythmic sound. Always, beyond the human voice, the sound of the great ocean.

And the shrill, cruel shrieks of the gulls overhead, always cir-cling, lunging for their prey.

Another surprise awaited Magdalena at the rear of the church, for she saw that it was hardly a church at all any longer, but rather a ruin; mound of rubble; most of the roof had collapsed inward, and was covered in patches of moss. Yet there remained a narrow en-tranceway like the opening to a cave, hardly more than the size of a man of ordinary height, into the cobwebbed, shadowy interior. Still the singing continued. A pause, and coughing; quick panting; and again the singing. *Now the day is over . . . Night is drawing . . .* Magdalena trembled with excitement and dread—for what if the young man should banish her, again? At once? As soon as he saw her? *Shadows of the evening . . .* These notes were, to Magdalena's eager ear, as flawless as ever, of surpassing beauty.

She drew nearer to the entrance, and could make out the singer's figure, in approximately the same place as before, pacing about before a ruined altar, in and out of crevices of shadow black as pitch. His fists were clenched, his shoulders hunched with ten-sion. Yet—there was something wrong with him. He was not so young now, nor so handsome. When he whirled at the sound of her footstep, scowling in Magdalena's direction while not seeming to see her, Magdalena realized to her horror that he'd grown skeletal; his face was wizened and sickly pale, as aged as her Aunt Erica's; his neck was emaciated, the ropy tendons and artery prominent. His eyes were narrowed to slits like those of a frightened, ferocious animal. *He doesn't know me!* Magdalena thought. *He doesn't see me.*

Yet, and this was a truth Magdalena would recall for the remainder of her life, and would entrust to no one except, one day, many decades later, her granddaughter who loved her, she would have cast aside all her pride and fear, and gone to the singer, to present herself to him in any way he would accept her, if there hadn't suddenly stepped out of the shadows another figure—a queer stunted old-young woman, with a wizened monkeyish face, deft and solicitous, clearly compelled by adoration; this person came quickly to the singer as he leaned weakly against a broken pew, and wiped his oily-damp forehead with a cloth; and lifted a pitcher to his mouth, steadying his shaky hands so that he could drink. Ah, how thirsty he was! His emaciated chest rising and sinking with the effort of swallowing! And blind, empty, blank as an idiot's fixed stare, his beautiful eyes turned in Magdalena's direction.

The haglike woman was stroking the singer's thin hands, whispering words of praise and encouragement; he seemed to be listening, and his bloodless lips twitched in a sort of smile; at last he threw his head back proudly, his gray hair thin and straggly on his death's-head of a skull, and began another time to sing. *Now the day is over . . .* At first his voice quavered, for it was no longer a young man's voice; the ghastly tendons and artery in his throat grew taut; then by degrees his voice grew stronger, richer, as if drawing strength from the man's physical being, sucking life from his very soul. Magdalena recalled his mysterious words uttered not in pride nor certainly in protest but in simple resignation *I must sing, I have no choice.*

So singing now, as always: *Now the day is over, night is drawing nigh. Shadows of the evening . . . steal across the sky.*

So for the second and final time Magdalena knew herself

banished from this place, and fled too stricken with grief even to weep. A rising sea-wind snatched at her like crude, jeering fingers.

7.

"Please let me in! It's Magdalena!"

Desperately she rang the doorbell but there seemed to be no sound inside—was the doorbell broken? The afternoon had rapidly darkened to night and the house on Charter Street was darkened upstairs and down; Magdalena had been frantic trying to locate it in this neighborhood that, by night, she didn't recognize. She was exhausted from miles of walking, most of it uphill, on slippery wet cobblestones, beset by the wind. She pounded on the heavy oak door with her bare fists, frantic, sobbing like a terrified child. "Please! Let me in! It's Magdalena!" When at last the outdoor light was switched on she could saw a woman's stern face at a vestibule window; it was Hannah staring at her without recognition. Magdalena's thick long hair had come undone from its neat coils on both sides of her head and was snarled and windblown; she was to discover afterward to her amazement that most of its fair, wheat-brown color had drained from it, as color drains from the world at the hour of a solar eclipse; her young face was lined and haggard, her clothes were disheveled, with a look of being torn. "Hannah, Hannah, please! Have mercy!" Magdalena begged.

At last, as if reluctantly, Hannah seemed to recognize Magdalena's voice, if not her face; she relented, and swung open the heavy oak door. "Miss Schön! I wouldn't have known you," she said, staring at the girl with wonder and sympathy.

The Temple

There, again, the vexing, mysterious sound!—a faint mewing cry followed by a muffled scratching, as of something being raked by nails, or claws. At first the woman believed the sound must be coming from somewhere inside the house, a small animal, perhaps a squirrel, trapped in the attic beneath the eaves, or in a remote corner of the earthen-floored cellar; after she searched the house thoroughly, she had to conclude that it emanated from somewhere outside, at the bottom of the old garden, perhaps. It was far more distinct at certain times than at others, depending upon the direction and velocity of the wind.

How like a baby's cry, terribly distressing to hear! And the scratching, which came in spasmodic, desperate flurries, was yet more distressing, evoking an obscure horror.

The woman believed she'd first begun hearing the sound at the time of the spring thaw in late March, when melting ice dripped in a continuous arrhythmic delirium from chimneys, roofs, eaves, trees. With the coming of warm weather, her bedroom window open to the night, her sleep was increasingly disturbed.

She had no choice, then, did she?—she must trace the sound of its origin. She set about the task calmly enough one morning, stepping out into unexpectedly bright, warm sunshine, and making her way into the lush tangle of vegetation that had been her mother's garden of thirty years before. The mewing sound, the scratching—

it seemed to be issuing from the very bottom of the garden, close by a stained concrete drainage ditch that marked the end of the property. As soon as she listened for it, however, it ceased.

How steady the woman's heartbeat, amid the quickening pulse of a May morning.

Out of the old garage, that had once been a stable, the woman got a shovel, a spade, a rake, these implements festooned in cob-webs and dust, and began to dig. It was awkward work and her soft hands ached after only minutes, so she returned to the garage to fetch gardening gloves—these too covered in cobwebs and dust, and stiffened with dirt. The midmorning sun was ablaze so she located an old straw hat of her mother's: it fitted her head oddly, as if its band had been sweated through and dried, stiffened asymmetrically.

So she set again to work. First, she dug away sinewy weeds and vines, chicory, wild mustard, tall grasses, in the area out of which the cry had emanated; she managed to uncover the earth, which was rich with compost, very dark, moist. Almost beneath her feet, the plaintive mewing sounded! "Yes. Yes. I'm here," she whispered. She paused, very excited; she heard a brief flurry of scratch-ing, then silence. "I'm here, now." She grunted as she pushed the shovel into the earth, urging it downward with her weight, her foot; it was a pity she'd so rarely used gardening implements, in all of her fifty years. She was a naturally graceful woman so out of her element here she felt ludicrous to herself, like a beast on its hind legs.

She dug. She spaded, and raked. She dug again, deepening and broadening the hole which was like a wound in the junglelike vege-tation. Chips and shards of aged brick, glass, stones were un-covered, striking the shovel. Beetles scurried away, their shells glinting darkly in the sunshine. Earthworms squirmed, some of them cut cruelly in two. For some time the woman worked in silence, hearing only her quickened heartbeat and a roaring pulse in her ears; then, distinctly, with the impact of a shout, there came the pleading cry again, so close she nearly dropped the shovel.

At last, covered in sweat, her hands shaking, the woman struck something solid. She dropped to her knees and groped in the moist dark earth and lifted something round and hollow—a human skull? But it was small, hardly half the size of an adult's skull.

"My God!" the woman whispered.

Squatting then above the jagged hole, turning the skull in her fingers. How light it was! The color of parchment, badly stained from the soil. She brushed bits of damp earth away, marveling at the subtle contours of the cranium. Not a hair remained. The delicate bone was cracked in several places and its texture minutely scarified, like a ceramic glaze. A few of the teeth were missing, but most appeared to be intact, though caked with dirt. The perfectly formed jaws, the slope of the cheekbones! The empty eye sockets, so round ... The woman lifted the skull to stare into the sockets as if staring into mirror-eyes, eyes of an eerie transparency. A kind of knowledge passed between her and these eyes yet she did not know: was this a child's skull? had a child been buried here, it must have been decades ago, on her family's property? Unnamed, unmarked? Unacknowledged? Unknown?

For several fevered hours the woman dug deeper into the earth. She was panting in the overhead sun, which seemed to penetrate the straw hat as if it were made of gauze; her sturdy body was clammy with sweat. She discovered a number of scattered bones— a slender forearm, curving ribs, part of a hand, fingers—these too parchment-colored, child-sized. What small, graceful fingers! How they had scratched, clawed, for release! Following this morning, forever, the finger bones would be at peace.

By early afternoon, the woman gave up her digging. She could find no more of the skeleton than a dozen or so random bones.

She went up to the house, and returned quickly, eagerly, with a five-foot runner of antique velvet cloth, a deep wine color, in which to carry the skull and bones up to the house. For no one must see. No one must know. "*I* am here, *I* will always be here," the woman promised. "*I* will never abandon you." She climbed to the second floor of the house, and in her bedroom at the rear she lay the velvet runner on a table beside her bed and beneath a bay window through whose diamond-shaped, leaded panes a reverent light would fall. Tenderly, meticulously, the woman arranged the skull and bones into the shape of a human being. Though most of the skeleton was missing, it would never seem to the woman's loving eye that this was so.

In this way the woman's bedroom became a secret temple. On the velvet cloth the skull and bones, unnamed, would be discovered after the woman's death, but that was a long way off.

V

The Journey

How slowly the journey begins. Traversing the lush green landscape by inches. Weeks are required to cover mere miles. Each blade of grass, each sticky moist bud, blossom, tendril, exposed root distinct. You learn not to suck them in your mouth though your instinct is to do so. You smell them, you touch them with wondering fingers. So dense is the snarled foliage overhead you rarely see the *sun* and have no word for sun but you feel its humid heat that seems not only to descend upon you but to rise up out of the rich dark fecund earth. Soft as flesh. The earth *is* flesh. And these fleshy-pulpy fruits, so delicious. High overhead, almost invisible in the foliage, are curious flying shapes—birds? squirrels? monkeys?—creatures for which you have no names. Their cries penetrate the silence, filling you with astonishment. All things fill you with astonishment. Even these brightly black hard-shelled beetles with glittering eyes crawling over your outstretched fingers like a single caress.

And everything pulsing with a low murmurous *thrum*. The grainy marrow of your bones vibrates with that *thrum*.

By degrees the swampy soil rises. You won't have noticed, the ascent is so gradual. And the drier land. Into which your feet don't sink. What relief you feel, now that maddening slowness is behind you. Here, in the sun-splotched plain, passage is much easier. And objects are clearly defined. Six-foot grasses undulating in the wind, isolated stands of stark white birches, outcroppings of pale striated rock. What a healthy windswept terrain, where miles can be covered within mere hours, hundreds of miles within days, thousands of miles within weeks. There are serrated mountains at the horizon, etched with a galaxy of faces, and not a face replicated. The sky is a vivid burning blue in which the sun dominates like an eye opening wider, and wider, and wider. You begin to see the contours of the earth. A powerful tide draws you forward. You are not the first to mistake it for a personal destiny.

Now spiky trees with leaves that glare like metal move swiftly by. The air is so brightly brittle it crackles with electricity. The colors of the salt flats are sere, autumnal. As your speed increases you begin to recall the earliest stage of your journey when you did not understand it was a journey. Nor even that you were following a plotted course. How happy you were, in that innocence!—though even as you remember it, you are forgetting it. *The journey* is itself an invention of the present time. With nostalgia you recall a past time that did not exist for, at the time you inhabited it, you had no consciousness of it. Now, traveling at hundreds of miles an hour, you are impatient to travel yet faster. You are obsessed with the horizon beyond which a mysterious and unimaginable landscape beckons.

In this high plateau, tilting toward—what? The sea? Unless it is an immense crater, thousands of miles in diameter? At the speed at which you now move it is virtually impossible to discern the shapes of objects. They have become nameless, indefinable, a continuous stream. And the sun flying overhead, and the moon. Horizon to horizon. You are intoxicated with speed, your lungs expanding in joy. You wonder whether, passing as you are, swift and fleeting as a shadow on the barren earth, you are, in any true sense of the word, *here* at all.

Yet you rush forward, impatient. Electricity coursing through your veins. Faster and faster the terrain passes beneath you but still you feel a terrible, an insatiable hunger to overcome the present moment, to break the ties of memory, to leap into the future. It is only memory that links you with previous stages of your journey and memory has begun to bleach out, like bones, in the desert sun. You come to see that *memory* too is an invention. The very *past* is an invention. And as you approach the speed of light you become aware of a curiosity of the landscape: what had appeared, at slower speeds, to be dense, heavy, textured, durable earth is in fact thin as a playing card! The rock outcroppings skimming beneath your feet, the melancholy eroded mountains, the wan curve of the horizon— sliding panels set carelessly in place and beginning, like cheap stage scenery, to warp and buckle, curl at the edges. And the sun so immense it contains the entire sky, and the moon swallowed up in it. Unless it is the sky that contains the sun and the moon and all the planets, indistinguishable as grains of sand.

The journey ends. Rolled up swiftly and efficiently behind you like a carpet, or a giant sheet of paper.

The stories included in this volume have appeared in the following publications, often in variant forms. To the editors of these publications, all acknowledgments and thanks are due.

"The Sky Blue Ball" in *Ellery Queen* (1995)
"Death Mother" in *Kenyon Review* (1995)
"The Hand-puppet" in *Tales of the Impossible*, editor David Copperfield (1995)
"Schroeder's Stepfather" in *Ellery Queen* (1991)
"The Sepulchre" in *Doubletake* (1994)
"The Hands" in *Epoch* (1995)
████████ in *Fear Itself* (1995) and reprinted in *The Year's Best Fantasy and Horror 1996*
"Labor Day" in *Western Humanities Review* (1995), reprinted in *Demon and Other Tales*
"The Collector of Hearts" in *Seventeen* (May 1998)
"Demon" in *Demon and Other Tales* (Necronomicon Press, 1996)
"Elvis Is Dead: Why Are *You* Alive?" in *The King Is Dead: Tales of Elvis Postmortem* (1994)
"Posthumous" in *Ellery Queen* (1994)
"The Omen" in *Pequod* (1993), reprinted in *Demon and Other Tales*
"The Sons of Angus MacElster" in *Conjunction* (May 1998)

"The Affliction" in *Bomb* (1995)

"Scars" in *Artes* (1997)

"An Urban Paradox" in *Witness* (1994), reprinted in *Demon and Other Tales*

"Unprintable" in *Mother* (1996)

"Intensive" in *Gettysburg Review* (1996)

"Valentine" in *Michigan Quarterly Review* (1996)

"Death Astride Bicycle" in *Western Humanities Review* (1995)

"The Dream-Catcher" in *Off-Limits: Tales of Alien Sex* (1996)

"Fever Blisters" in *Little Deaths* (1994)

"The Crossing" in *Ruby Slippers, Golden Tears* (1995)

"Shadows of the Evening" in *Century Magazine* (Summer 1998)

"The Temple" in *Demon and Other Tales*

"The Journey" in *SoHo Journal*, reprinted in *Demon and Other Tales*

"The Sky Blue Ball" is included in *The Year's Best Fantasy and Horror 1998*.

· A NOTE ON THE TYPE ·

The typeface used in this book is a version of Century (Expanded), originally designed by Theodore L. De Vinne (1828–1914) and Linn Boyd Benton for De Vinne's *Century* magazine; it was probably the first type developed for such a specific purpose. De Vinne, an innovative though practical printer and a scholar of typography, thought the type then used in periodicals feeble and proposed that the thin strokes of the "modern" typefaces be thickened while keeping the economical narrow letter forms so characteristic of late-nineteenth-century fonts (one of the "ungenerous" aspects of contemporary type that made William Morris look to the past). Century was later developed for wider use by Benton's son, Morris Fuller Benton (1872–1948), who did more than anyone else to advance the concept of a type "family"—several "weights" of a typeface with uniform design.